KT-199-791

Lyn Andrews was born in Liverpool in September 1943. Her father was killed on D-Day when Lyn was just nine months old. When Lyn was three her mother Monica married Frank Moore, who became 'Dad' to the little girl. Lyn was brought up in Liverpool and became a secretary before marrying policeman Bob Andrews. In 1970 Lyn gave birth to triplets – two sons and a daughter – who kept her busy for the next few years. Once they'd gone to school Lyn began writing, and her first novel was quickly accepted for publication.

Lyn lived for eleven years in Ireland and is now resident on the Isle of Man, but spends as much time as possible back on Merseyside, seeing her children and four grandchildren.

Praise for Lyn Andrews' dramatic Merseyside novels:

'The Catherine Cookson of Liverpool' *Northern Echo*

'An epic story told with Andrews' innate compassion, keen eye and warm heart' *Lancashire Evening Post*

'Gutsy . . . A vivid picture of a hard-up, hard-working community . . . will keep the pages turning' *Daily Express*

'A compelling read' *Woman's Own*

'A vivid portrayal of life' *Best*

'She has a realism that is almost palpable' *Liverpool Echo*

'An enjoyable, well-rounded novel' *Historical Novels Review*

'Plenty of realism and if you enjoy wartime sagas this one will please' *Nottingham Evening Post*

Lyn Andrews

Where The
Mersey Flows

HEADLINE

Copyright © 1997 Lyn Andrews

The right of Lyn Andrews to be identified as the Author of
the Work has been asserted by her in accordance with the
Copyright, Designs and Patents Act 1988.

First published in Great Britain in 1997 by
HEADLINE PUBLISHING GROUP

This edition published in 2020 by
HEADLINE PUBLISHING GROUP

3

Apart from any use permitted under UK copyright law, this publication may
only be reproduced, stored, or transmitted, in any form, or by any means,
with prior permission in writing of the publishers or, in the case
of reprographic production, in accordance with the terms of licences
issued by the Copyright Licensing Agency.

All characters in this publication are fictitious and any resemblance
to real persons, living or dead, is purely coincidental.

Cataloguing in Publication Data is available from the British Library

ISBN 9780747251767

Typeset in Palimpsest Book Production Limited,
Polmont, Stirlingshire

Printed and bound in Great Britain by Clays Ltd, Elcograf S.p.A.

Headline's policy is to use papers that are natural, renewable and recyclable
products and made from wood grown in well-managed forests and other
controlled sources. The logging and manufacturing processes are expected
to conform to the environmental regulations of the country of origin.

HEADLINE PUBLISHING GROUP
An Hachette UK Company
Carmelite House
50 Victoria Embankment
London EC4Y 0DZ

www.headline.co.uk
www.hachette.co.uk

For Sally Mimnagh, winner of the 1996 O'Brien Book-seller Award, (Eason & Son, Dublin), who has become more than a business associate – *Do Mo Anamchara*. And for my future daughter-in-law Karen Hudson, one of the loveliest girls I know.

Acknowledgements

My grateful thanks go to Eric Taplin who has so generously allowed me to use his books, *Near to Revolution: Liverpool Dockers and Seaman 1870–1890* and *The Docker's Union: a Study of the National Union of Dock Labourers 1889–1922*. Without such detailed accounts of the situation, conditions and events that led to the Liverpool Transport Strike of 1911, this book would not achieve the authenticity of background that I try so hard to create. Mr Taplin's works are excellent and I would recommend them to all students of Liverpool's history.

Lyn Andrews
Southport, 1996

Chapter One

May 1910

'Yer look great! Yer look really great an' I'm not just sayin' it.' Nora O'Brian's blue eyes sparkled with enthusiasm and a smile lit up her small oval face.

Nora was nearly twenty, a slim, pretty girl with a mane of chestnut hair that this morning she'd taken great care in sweeping up in a loose knot on the top of her head, and that hadn't been easy. Not when all you had was a small brown-speckled mirror on the wall, which to use to full advantage meant wedging yourself between the wall and the bed she shared with her sister. Or used to share, she corrected herself. She was ready, wearing a cotton dress covered in a pattern of pale blue and white flowers and a straw boater with a blue ribbon.

She *was* happy that her sister was getting married, she'd told herself time and again. After all, they were both getting dangerously close to the age when people started giving you pitying looks and mentioned the fact, carelessly in conversation, that all the girls you went to school with were married and were starting families. A few more years and you got the title of 'old maid' bestowed on you. What didn't make her happy was that her sister had chosen to marry Edward Neely, a man almost twice her age. A man Da had met in the public library in William Brown Street. They'd struck up an acquaintance, both were trying to better themselves,

1

although Edward Neely was a good way ahead of Da. Apart from the fact that personally she didn't like him, it looked like an act of outright desperation on Ethna's part – she was well turned twenty-three.

It wasn't as though she'd never been out with any lads, had what people called 'hopes' of them. There was the time when she'd had 'hopes' of Tommy McNally but he'd up and married a girl from the slums in the south of the city and no one had seen him again.

A shadow crossed Ethna's face, and the blue eyes, so like those of her sister, lost some of their excitement.

'I wish we had a long mirror so I could see myself.' She bit her lip, nervous and unsure of Nora's verdict of approval.

'Holy God, Ethna. Yer look great. Their eyes will be standin' out on stalks when yer walk up Oil Street an' up the aisle.'

Ethna smoothed down the skirt of the new cream muslin dress that she'd saved so hard for. She'd walked to and from work for months even though it was a fair stretch and she was worn out by the end of the day. She'd brought home leftovers from work to save a few pence of the housekeeping money. The dress had been bought at Frisby Dyke's in Lord Street and had a high frilled neck and the fashionable leg-o'-mutton sleeves. The bodice and cuffs of the sleeves were pin-tucked and it was nipped in at the waist by a sash of peach-coloured ribbon. The ankle-length skirt showed off the neat, cream, high-buttoned boots that she knew Da had worked many hard hours to get the money together for. She'd seen them in the window of Miller's shoe shop and had sighed wistfully when she'd spoken of them. There were times, though, when she wished she'd never opened her mouth about them. Poor Da. After half killing himself at the docks he'd gone out chopping wood, picking rags and anything else to earn extra pennies, tuppences and threepenny bits to add to his little hoard. She kept on lifting up her skirt to admire them, she'd never had anything like them before. The wedding finery disguised a thin, undernourished body. The unaccustomed new cream cotton gloves, Nora's contribution, covered the red, work-roughened hands. Nora had done her hair and then placed the large brimmed hat, trimmed with a big peach flower, over the carefully arranged curls. She'd never had a hat in her life before. Like the rest of the girls and women in the dirty, narrow, overcrowded street that ran down to Waterloo Road and the Trafalgar Dock, she had always worn a shawl.

Life was grim at the best of times in this neighbourhood. Men, desperate for work, often gave up in despair and spent what money they got in the pubs. There was a pub on every corner and the dockers were paid what money was due to them in the pubs and if they wanted more work they stood the foreman a drink. That made it all the easier for them to squander what little they got. Women, too, often gave up the battle against dirt, disease and hunger and took solace in drink. Children then were guaranteed to go cold, hungry and barefoot. There was a wide gap between the 'haves' and the 'have nots' and the residents of Oil Street fell into the latter group.

It had been Nora who had insisted Ethna should save up for a really special outfit for the one day in her life when she'd be the centre of attention, even if it was only for a few hours. The neighbours *would* gape in amazement, admiration and envy.

Ethna smiled at her sister. 'You look great too, Nora.'

'Well, the pair of us might look like the high an' mighty today, but most of this lot will all end up in Dan Fogarty's pawnshop on Monday morning. When are yer ever going ter wear it again? An' when am I ever going ter wear this straw "gussie" again an' the gloves? For Mass on Sunday? No, Mr Fogarty will give us a good price an' we need the money. They'll have served their purpose.'

The smile had vanished from Ethna's face and apprehension filled her eyes. 'I wish yer hadn't said that about the high an' mighty. Yer know what 'er at number five said, it's a bad omen getting wed today.'

Nora sat down on the edge of the bed, heedless of crushing the skirt of her dress which she'd pressed so carefully. 'Oh, take no flamin' notice of that old bag of bones. We've all been plannin', scrimpin' an' savin' for today for months an' months. It's not our fault the flaming owld King has to go an' die and then they decide to have the funeral today. Anyway, you know what Father Hegarty said when we mentioned it. "Go on ahead with the nuptials, girl. There won't be many around here – meself included – who'll shed a genuine tear for that lecherous old glutton. The meals he put away were disgraceful, they would have fed half of Liverpool."'

Ethna felt that the curate was wrong to speak like that of the dead. He was known to hold very radical views, a fact the parish priest often took him to task about although he, too, was an Irishman. Ethna had heard him one evening, long after devotions were over and the church almost empty. She'd lit a candle and had been saying a prayer for her mam.

'Do you not fully realise that we're part of a great empire, Francis? Taking Christianity, education, organisation and medicine to so many poor heathens in places the likes of you and I have hardly heard of?'

'Aren't there enough poor heathens in this country and our own?'

'Not heathens, Francis,' Father Finnegan chided.

'Well, they march their grand armies in and take other people's land and rights away from them. They rob them

4

of their culture and their gold, silver, copper and coal while they're at it and all. Haven't there been Irishmen from time immemorial who didn't want to be a part of any empire?'

'Old rebellions, long over, Francis, and there's many Irishmen who do want to belong and it's not the place of the Catholic Church to be preaching sedition. It's souls we care for, Francis, not politics. There'll be no more of this or the Archbishop will be down on us both. He could see fit to have us both removed to other parishes.' Father Finbar Conor Finnegan, named for the patron saint of his native city of Cork, had raised his voice and spoken very firmly. Ethna remembered those words now.

'Yer know what Father Finnegan said, I told yer. We've to take no notice of Father Hegarty's views about all that,' Ethna told her sister with some spirit.

'He said the King was misguided and sinful like most of us are, but God is forgiving. And anyway, what was he supposed to *do* with his life when that old misery guts wouldn't step down and let him *be* King? God, I bet she was a real tartar of a mam. I remember seeing pictures of her in the paper. He wasn't a bad man, Nora.'

'Oh, no! He just stuffed himself full of food and drink and smoked big fat cigars and had the flaming cheek to parade those women around the place, shaming the poor Queen. I heard that one of those high-class tarts was even allowed into his bedroom before he died! He was supposed to be head of their Church, defender of their faith. He was a great example, wasn't he? Anyway, stop worrying about him. All that's going on down in London. This is your day, Ethna, an' to hell with the lot of them.'

The older girl's smile returned. 'Well, the new one looks better. Younger, more serious, more sober—'

'Ethna O'Brian – soon to be Mrs Neely – shurrup

5

about kings an' all that! It's yer wedding day an' Da an' Declan will be waitin' for us downstairs.' Impulsively Nora hugged her sister. 'It's what yer want? Really an' truly?'

'Of course it is!' Ethna's voice was firm but there was a small nagging doubt in her heart. In the arguments both Da and Nora had put up there was a lot of truth. Edward Neely *was* old enough to be her Da. He was reputed to be 'careful' with his money and he was, but he was also a decent man with a good, steady job as a foreman with Cavendish's Haulage and Porterage. He had a small but well-kept house on Kirkdale Road and she was fed up with filling her mam's place. Mam had died just after Declan was born, ten years ago, and at the age of thirteen she'd been left to see to the young baby, Nora, Da, and the housework, which wasn't an easy task in Oil Street.

When Declan was six she'd had to go back to work with Nora in Williams' Clothing Factory – sweatshop, more like – in Paradise Street. They'd both had a variety of jobs since then but she was sick and tired of it all. The worries, the constant battle against dirt and trying to make ends meet when none of them knew for certain they'd have work to go to the next day. These were the reasons why she'd accepted Edward's proposal. It was an escape.

Negotiating the narrow stairs was not easy with the wide brim of the hat and the unaccustomed high-heeled boots, but when Ethna and Nora entered the dismal, poky kitchen, her da's careworn, weatherbeaten face broke into a smile and the tiredness left his eyes.

'Eh, Da, doesn't she look great! Like one of them real ladies that gerrof the trains at Lime Street with 'undreds of cases an' all the porters near kill themselves rushin' ter 'elp, or them at Riverside Station gettin' on the big

6

ships!' Declan, scrubbed clean, his usually unruly hair plastered down and wearing his Sunday clothes, looked in awe at the total transformation of his sister. This wasn't the Ethna who nagged about climbing walls, hanging on to the back of moving trams and carts that did serious damage to the toecaps of his already battered boots. Ethna who was always making sarcastic remarks about all his mates being hooligans of the first order and all bound to end up in Walton Jail.

'Da, will yer tell her to stop worrying about getting married on the day they're burying King Edward. She's mithered to death with her at number five saying it's a bad omen,' Nora pleaded.

'She's cracked, is that one. Everyone says she is. 'Arry's mam says she's a witch an' can put curses on people.'

'I wish someone would put a curse on you to shut you up, Declan O'Brian! If I hear one more word about Ma Brennan an' omens, I'll belt yer,' Nora threatened.

Joe took his elder daughter's hand and tears pricked his eyes. 'Don't mind that one. Oh, yer mam would 'ave been so proud of yer, luv. Mighty Mouth there's right. Yer look like a real lady, forget what Ma Brennan has ter say. No one takes much notice of the likes of us or cares what we do, we don't matter. It's not going to be in the *Daily Post* that Ethna O'Brian got married on the day they buried the old King. God rest him.'

Ethna risked the damage to the correct angle of her hat and threw her arms round him. 'Oh, Da, I wish she could have still been here, I really do, but you'll be all right. I'll still see yer.'

'She's not goin' ter live on the moon,' Declan muttered, poking his finger between his neck and the Eton collar starched rigid by Ethna. It was scratchy and chafing.

He'd never been so clean and tidy since he'd made his first Communion.

Nora clipped him sharply across the ear and glared at him. 'Put yer cap on an' behave yerself for once! An' if we don't get up to church soon, Father Finnegan an' yer future 'usband will think you've changed yer mind.'

Out in the street women stood on their doorsteps or in small groups, enjoying the sunshine. Young or old, they all wore the uniform drab clothes of the slums – long coarse black skirts, faded blouses, grey calico or sacking aprons. Some of the older ones had hairstyles fashionable before the turn of the century. Kids with dirty, bare feet, ragged trousers and dresses and thin grey faces sat on the broken steps of the houses or squatted in the gutter, playing with the only toys they had, bits of wood and refuse. Further up the street a few lads played football with a ball made of rags. It didn't bounce of course, but it was better than nothing.

Nora's heart turned over. How well she remembered the times when she, Ethna and Declan had gone barefoot, in patched and mended hand-me-downs. Of days in winter when the house was freezing cold because Da had been unable to get work and there was no coal. Only by pawning everything, then resorting to begging, had they been able to pay the rent of three and sixpence. He'd got nothing for months one summer after he'd had a petty argument with a foreman. He had tramped the hot streets and docks day in and day out, coming back exhausted and despairing and with nothing. Somehow they'd managed. He hadn't admitted destitution and given up. He hadn't made the heartbreaking journey to the Brownlow Hill Workhouse, the greatest shame of all to any man's pride.

Ethna, in her stylish gown and hat and carrying a small

8

posy of flowers, looked totally out of place in Oil Street where poverty and squalor held sway.

'Ah, God, doesn't she look like a real toff, Maggie,' Eileen Molloy called across to her neighbour.

Ethna smiled and held her head higher. The sun was warm and her doubts were receding as she basked in the admiration.

'Yer do, queen, God luv yer. Yer poor mam would 'ave been proud of yer, girl,' Maggie Cullen said.

'Wouldn't yer think they'd 'ave put if off, like, with His Majesty being buried today?' Maura 'Ma' Brennan, the neighbourhood troublemaker from number five, commented in a loud voice to her neighbour as they passed.

Nora spun round, her eyes hard. 'Yer wasn't sayin' that two weeks ago when he died, was yer? I seem to remember something like "Well, he'll be no loss, the bloody owld lecher!" Gerrin and mind yer own business!'

The woman glared at her but went indoors muttering, 'Ard-faced little get.'

'Good on yer, Nora! The bloody owld hypocrite, God stiffen 'er,' Eileen Molloy called after the wedding party as it turned the corner.

They were all perspiring and Joe was having trouble with his breathing when they finally reached the church. The parish priest stood in the doorway to welcome them, his white and gold vestments a glorious contrast to the drabness and dirt that surrounded the church.

It was cool inside and as Ethna Mary O'Brian became Mrs Edward John Neely, Nora bent her head and covered her face with her hands and prayed that her sister would be happy. She prayed that Ethna was doing the right thing, for it was as Father Finnegan had said and Ethna had repeated, 'until death do us part'.

Edward Neely looked very dignified, she had to give

9

him that. His suit was of good quality and well made, his high winged collar stiff and white, his necktie a sober grey. His bowler hat, the symbolic headwear of foremen everywhere, was held in his right hand as he escorted his young and bright-eyed bride down the aisle after the Nuptial Mass was over.

'Will there be any cakes or jelly?' Declan tugged at Nora's sleeve while outside the church the new Mrs Neely posed for the traditional photo with Mr Neely and the parish priest. There wasn't going to be the usual wedding breakfast, followed by a party to which half the neighbourhood usually invited themselves. Joe had no money to spare and Edward had said that would be taking things too far, some decency and dignity must be preserved. Instead, a bit of a cold meal would be set out in his front parlour in the house on Kirkdale Road.

'Oh, don't you start already. God, it's all you think about, stuffing your face.'

Declan was affronted. 'I 'aven't had me breakfast. I 'aven't 'ad nothin'. I 'ad ter go ter Communion.'

'We all did!' Nora snapped. She was starving hungry herself.

'Well, it's supposed to be a party,' he replied, annoyed that a perfectly normal question had led to Nora biting his head off. It was supposed to be a day when everyone was nice to each other. He'd been bragging to his mates about the great spread a man like Neely would put on.

As the wedding party made its way to Kirkdale Road, by tram, a form of transport that had disappointed and peeved everyone except the bridegroom, Nora relented. 'I think there'll be some sandwiches and pies and a wedding cake. A small one.'

'That's not much, is it? I 'eard he was an owld miser.'

'Shurrup! They'll hear you. Anyway, who told you that?'

'Arry Moore. His mam does a birrof cleanin' for 'im, like. Not regular, she says he's too tight-fisted fer that.'

Nora sighed. She'd suspected as much from the odd things she'd gleaned from her da's conversations and the occasional unguarded comment from her sister. The fact that Ethna was to carry on working added to her unease. Neely's wage and position surely meant there was no need for Ethna to continue to go out to work. People would say it demeaned him. Wasn't he able to afford to keep a wife? Only women whose husbands were unable to get steady work or who had large families to feed and clothe were forced to work outside the home.

This had occurred to Ethna too, after she'd accepted Edward's proposal. She had assumed she would give up her job. After all, working in the kitchens of Heilbron's Emigrant House in Great Georges Square wasn't much of a job for the wife of a foreman at Cavendish's. The large barracks-like building housed refugees from Europe who were due to emigrate to America and Canada as steerage passengers on the Cunard ships. Mr Heilbron had a written contract with Cunard. It was hard work and didn't pay much. The wages at Williams' sweatshop were higher. That was piecework and if you were good you could earn twelve shillings a week, although not many did and you had to buy your own thread.

She glanced across the room to where her husband was standing talking to her father. They would go home soon, back to Oil Street. Her few things had been brought here to Kirkdale Road last night by her da and when her family had gone she would take off her finery and prepare the evening meal. Then later on . . . She didn't want to dwell on what faced her that night. It wasn't very pleasant the first time, from what she'd gathered. Some of the older women said it was purgatory and the only way to get through it was to think hard about something else, or say

11

the rosary in your mind and pray that the result wouldn't be yet another mouth to feed. She supposed it might have been different had she really been passionately in love with him, but she wasn't. She'd never been passionately in love with anyone. Even Tommy McNally's defection hadn't really upset her. But she should be thankful she had escaped to a decent house with nice things and a bed with clean white sheets and pillowcases, a luxury she'd never experienced in her life before.

'Da, I think it's time we went now,' Nora interrupted quietly. 'Before meladdo here makes himself sick. He's had four pieces of cake on top of pies and sandwiches and ginger pop.'

Joe nodded his agreement and extended his hand to his new son-in-law, who was only eight years younger than himself. 'Well, Eddy, it's been a great day, one ter remember. And you've got a good girl, we'll miss her.'

'Da, I'm just a couple of tram stops away from yer,' Ethna reminded him.

'Now don't you worry, Joe, she'll be down to see you each Sunday afternoon. I like to have time then to read the newspapers and the *Journal of Commerce*. Keep up with events, like.'

Joe O'Brian nodded. He liked an hour's peace to read too, although the *Journal of Commerce* was way beyond his means. His one Sunday paper was a luxury. During the week he was sometimes lucky and found a discarded *Echo* which he'd read from cover to cover, for he was that unusual being, a quiet, teetotal docker who after his wife had died had educated himself entirely by reading. He was glad Ethna was settled, he hoped she'd be happy. Neely was a steady man who'd not lead her a dance with his antics like many a young lad would.

Ethna was gathering the leftovers and putting them in a piece of greaseproof paper.

'Ethna, put them out back in the larder,' Edward instructed her. 'They'll do for our supper and maybe stretch to my carry-out for Monday.'

Ethna looked at him, confusion in her eyes, embarrassment flushing her cheeks. 'I . . . I thought Nora could take them home, like, for their tea. I . . . I could make you something else.'

Nora intervened. 'No. Do like he says, Ethna. Our Declan's already stuffed himself like a pig and Da and me aren't too fond of tongue, yer know that.' There was no way she was going to give Neely the satisfaction of seeing the disappointment she knew they all felt. Ham and tongue were luxuries they seldom had. 'Right, then, we'll gerroff now. We'll see yer next Sunday.' She kissed her sister on the cheek and inwardly breathed a sigh of relief as she took the hand Edward Neely extended. She couldn't have brought herself to give the man a sisterly kiss on the cheek.

She was annoyed and hurt. Edward Neely knew their circumstances; what were a few leftovers to a man like him? 'Oh, Lord, look after her,' she prayed as they walked towards the tram stop. Da was silent too. Nora was about to throw the wilting posy into a rubbish bin but her father stopped her.

'They'll liven up in a jamjar of water. Keep them, luv, they'll brighten the place up and she paid good money for them – her own money too.'

The glance that passed between them made her realise that Da, too, was disappointed and humiliated.

Moonlight pierced the chink in the bedroom curtains and threw a single faint beam across the bed. Ethna lay stiffly listening to her husband's snores. The tears rolled slowly and silently down her cheeks. It had been awful, far worse than she had imagined, and it had hurt. He'd been rough with her, showing no concern or tenderness at all. Thinking only of his own pleasure, his own need. Some of the things he'd said in the height of his passion had shocked her deeply. She'd never suspected that there was such a foul, disgusting side to him. She'd thought he was a quiet, rather stuffy man.

When it was over, without a word he'd rolled off her and gone straight to sleep. The older women were right. In fact it was worse than purgatory, far worse. But no matter how she felt, she was his wife now and she must look to the future. She was away from Oil Street and all its squalor, she had to be thankful for that. He had a good steady job, a clean comfortable home and maybe . . . maybe it would be better next time.

Chapter Two

Across the city in a large, elegant house on the wide, tree-lined thoroughfare that was Prince's Avenue, preparations for another wedding took place that day and the bride-to-be was also disturbed and annoyed about the government's decision to hold the state funeral of King Edward VII that day, Saturday, 21 May.

'Rhian, will you keep still!' Leah Cavendish was losing patience with her elder sister. Leah's auburn hair, inherited from her dead mother, was already dressed. Her large-brimmed, lavishly trimmed hat lay on the silk bedspread with her gloves, but her green eyes were full of irritation. 'How on earth am I going to get this hat pin in properly without sticking it right into your head if you keep moving? I know you hate the hat but that's not *my* fault.'

Sitting at the walnut dressing table with its inlaid mother-of-pearl top, Rhian looked at her sister in the mirror. She wished she'd inherited Mother's hair, eyes and skin as Leah had done. After all, she was the daughter who had been given a Welsh name, her mother's choice. Edwina Cavendish, née Lloyd-Thomas, came from an old, well-connected Welsh family who had held their lands and property for centuries.

'I wish I didn't look so much like Father,' Rhian grumbled, tweaking a few wisps of light brown hair further down on to her forehead. Her eyes were pale

15

blue, like his, and a stranger seeing herself and Leah together would never have taken them for sisters, she thought.

'Don't say things like that, Rhian. Not today.' Pain filled Leah's eyes. It was three years since John and Edwina Cavendish had been killed in a collision between their car and a traction engine that had suddenly lumbered out from a farm gateway into their path. They'd been on their way home after visiting friends in Bath. Leah had been seventeen then and had only recently come to terms with the fact that she would never see her beloved parents again. Rhian had been twenty and they'd clung together sobbing when Aunt Poppy, accompanied by a police inspector, had broken the terrible news.

After the funeral, Rhian suddenly seemed to grow up and capably took on the responsibilities of running the household, although there had been a few bad decisions. Ernest, her fiancé, had probably instigated most of those decisions, exerting his future power, flexing his muscles. He had much to gain, after all.

Leah's gaze flitted over the bedroom. The long sash windows let in the bright sunlight which caught the crystal drops of the lamps, making them throw out prisms of light like tiny rainbows. Deep rose-pink velvet curtains were looped back from the windows with heavy gold cords. The carpet was cream with a design of roses of all shades from deep red to palest pink strewn across it. Cream Regency strip silk wallpaper covered the walls and the ornate plaster ceiling and cornices were picked out in pink and gold. The chaise longue beneath the window was covered in gold brocade. The bedspread was the same colour. Against the pale walls, the walnut and bird's eye maple wardrobes, chests and tallboys glowed richly. Her own room was similarly furnished but in white and Wedgwood blue.

It was a beautiful house; Mother had had such good taste.

Rhian's voice broke her reverie.

'I'm sorry. I'm trying to sit still but I'm just . . . nervous.'

Leah was surprised. 'But you've been engaged to Ernest for ages.'

'I know. It was what Mother and Father would have wanted. He came calling long before . . .' She didn't want to think about her parents' death. Not today when there was another, far grander funeral taking place in London with all the crowned heads of Europe attending.

Leah raised her eyes to the ceiling. Rhian used that phrase so often these days that it grated on her nerves. She didn't like Ernest Armstrong. She thought him smarmy and arrogant, and that arrogance had grown over the two and a half years he had been engaged to Rhian. Her sister seemed to adore him and wouldn't have a word said against him.

'It's just that all my life I always dreamed of a big society wedding. We *are* people of note in this city, and I can't now.'

Leah sighed. All the arrangements had been made months ago. It *was* to have been a big society wedding and she'd never seen Rhian so happy or excited since the accident. Then the King had died and everything had had to be cancelled, except the ceremony itself.

'You could have changed the date, Rhian. You could have got married later in the year, September maybe, it's a lovely month. Mellow sunlight, golden leaves.' She thought about what Miss Winthrop, the housekeeper, had said about May weddings. That they were unlucky. Just why this was so or on what grounds the information was based she'd never found out, but there was no way she was going to repeat the prediction to her sister.

17

'No, Ernest said it must be kept as today but have it very, very quiet. He said people would understand and I think they do.'

Oh, yes, it *had* to be today. Ernest couldn't wait any longer to get his hands on the money and the business and take up residence in this house as lord and master, Leah thought as she tilted the hat more to one side.

'He assured me it was what Mother and Father would have wanted.' Rhian's tone was sanctimonious.

Leah's quick temper flared up. 'Rhian Cavendish! I swear if you say that once more I'll drag this ruinously expensive hat and its hat pins off your head and stamp all over it! Then you'll *really* hate it! You've no idea how infuriating it is to hear you keep saying that. You sound like a cuckoo clock! Anyway, Aunt Poppy doesn't understand. She thinks you should have postponed it for a year. That it's in very bad taste to go ahead when the whole country is in mourning.'

Rhian was shocked at Leah's outburst and exasperated by her aunt's views.

'Oh, she's just old fashioned. Things have changed since Queen Victoria died but she won't believe it.' Tears threatened to overcome her and if she cried then her eyes would look all swollen and her skin would go blotchy.

'Not that much, they haven't.' Leah had finally accomplished her task and stood back to admire the effect. 'Well, get up and look at yourself in the mirror. You look lovely, you really do,' she added in a gentler tone.

Rhian stood before the long cheval mirror in its gilt frame and was disappointed in her reflection. She was wearing the dress that had been made for her by Miss Gladys Drinkwater, one of Liverpool's most sought-after and exclusive seamstresses with premises in Bold Street. It was of white satin covered with white silk organza. The bodice was decorated with hundreds of seed pearls and drop pearls which extended right down the front panel of the skirt and edged the long train. She was wearing her mother's pearl and diamond earrings but oh, how much better she would have looked with the matching diamond and pearl diadem and the long floating veil instead of this hated hat. It was of finest sugar-spun white straw, decorated with white satin roses and ribbons, but it just wasn't the same. Nothing was.

There wouldn't be huge banks of flowers in the church. Nor would the joyous notes of the Bridal March from Lohengrin burst thunderously from the organ to announce her arrival. The full choir would not now sing 'Sheep May Safely Graze' and 'Jesu, Joy of Man's Desiring' followed by 'Jerusalem'. The pews would not be filled with guests vying to outdo each other in their finery as they usually did on these occasions. She was beginning to feel that Leah was right and Ernest was wrong; they should have postponed the wedding.

The door opened and their Aunt Penelope came into the room. She had been nicknamed Poppy as a child by her brothers who were all younger and had had difficulty in pronouncing her baptismal name.

Although seventy years old, Poppy's back was as straight as a ramrod and she never used a cane to lean on even though arthritis plagued her. She wore a pale grey chiffon dress, edged at the neck and cuffs with black velvet ribbon. Her gloves, hat and handbag were black too. She had told the girls she would not be swayed by tearful requests or hysterical remonstrances to wear something other than grey, black, purple or mauve, the official and acceptable colours of mourning. In fact she considered herself very lenient; one usually wore black, particularly when mourning a King

Emperor, however much one had disapproved of his way of life.

Leah smiled and removed a pile of clothes from the chaise longue, ignoring her aunt's pursed lips as she glanced around the untidy room. Miss Winthrop had urged Rhian to dismiss their maid, Tilly, who had been inclined to be cheeky and lazy. Since then there had been a succession of girls, sent by an agency Ernest recommended as the 'very latest way to obtain staff'. None of them had been suitable, the last the most dreadful of them all. She had been caught smoking, actually *smoking* a cigarette outside the kitchen door. Miss Winthrop had almost fainted in shock and horror.

'Oh, tell her she looks lovely, Aunt, please,' Leah begged. 'She doesn't believe me.'

Poppy nodded but looked at her niece without much pleasure. 'You do but I still say you should have postponed it, Rhian. It's not seemly at all. The Reverend Hunter will start the ceremony with prayers for the repose of the soul of King Edward and for the health and happiness of King George and Queen Mary. It's not exactly the best way to start a wedding ceremony, is it?'

Rhian bit her lip but Leah frowned at her aunt. She was not in awe of Poppy as Rhian was and in fact was very fond of her. 'You can't blame her entirely, Aunt,' she said. 'Ernest wanted it to go ahead. It's his decision, Rhian is only being . . . dutiful.'

Rhian gave her a grateful look but Poppy tutted. 'Don't be impertinent, Leah, although I can understand your speaking up to defend her.'

Their eyes met and understanding flashed between them. Leah knew her aunt didn't like Ernest Armstrong either.

'I've instructed Blackett to bring the car round to the front door. We will *not* be so totally insensitive as to drive to church in an open carriage for everyone to see and remark upon.'

Leah nodded. It was a measure of her aunt's deep feelings for propriety, for Poppy hated and mistrusted cars, especially after the tragic death of her brother and his wife. Poppy insisted on keeping the carriage, the open landau, and the two matched greys stabled in the mews at the rear of the house. In summer she liked to be driven through the large and beautiful park at the end of the avenue to take the air. The car was a fairly new addition, suggested by Ernest, of course, but paid for with Rhian's money.

'Well, are we ready?' Poppy asked briskly.

'Yes, Aunt,' Rhian answered in a small, nervous voice.

'Good, your cousin Richard is "steadying his nerves", as he calls it, with the contents of the whisky decanter in your father's old study. If left any longer to his own devices, he'll get inebriated and will turn this wedding into a complete and utter fiasco.' Leah, dressed in lemon georgette, handed Rhian the bouquet of white lilies and yellow roses. She picked up her posy of white and lemon carnations and then gathered up Rhian's train with her free hand.

Poppy was glancing around the room and Leah looked uncertainly at her aunt.

'Are you ready, Aunt?'

Poppy nodded, the grey and white ostrich plumes that adorned her hat wafting with the movement. 'When you get back from Italy, Rhian, for God's sake get a decent girl in. This room is disgusting. I'll speak to Winthrop and if she can't get someone, she'll just have to do it herself. That other little chit, Tilly, was better than any of the specimens we've been sent so far. Employment agencies for domestics, indeed. They always came on personal recommendation before.'

21

Leah raised her eyes to the ceiling, while Rhian, in a last childish gesture, stuck out her tongue at her aunt's back.

Prayers for the deceased King Emperor and for his son, George V, and his Queen, formerly Princess Mary of Teck, were indeed a gloomy way to start a wedding service, Leah thought as she listened to her sister's low and often stumbling responses as she promised to love, honour and obey her husband. Oh, Rhian would certainly obey Ernest, she was sure of that. But life ahead didn't look very promising for herself.

Ernest would be totally unbearable once that ring was firmly on Rhian's finger. Their father's business, his money and the property he owned would effectively come under his control. Half of the entire estate belonged to herself of course and she was glad Aunt Poppy would at least continue to be her legal guardian until she was of age or got married, but her responsibilities towards Rhian had now ceased. Nevertheless, Aunt Poppy would make sure that Ernest didn't get too big for his boots and that when she did reach twenty-one she would have a say in how the business was run – should she want to. She didn't in fact care or understand much of the business but she wouldn't let Ernest know and she would, if necessary, learn. Her father had left a will. It was lodged with Mr Rankin, the family solicitor. Oh, Ernest wasn't going to lord it over *her* for ever.

The wedding photographs were taken at home in the wide hall with its thick Persian carpeting, fine paintings, and marble jardinières containing huge floral arrangements. Great care was taken to arrange Rhian's train so it fell gracefully, like a waterfall, down the last steps of the sweeping staircase. Then there was a five-course lunch for the wedding party in the green and gold dining room with its Oriental theme and collection of jade ornaments.

After the meal Rhian, with Leah to assist her, went up to take off her bridal finery and change into the pale lilac crêpe dress and short jacket which was her 'going away' outfit. At least the colour didn't offend Aunt Poppy, they giggled. A honeymoon first beside Lake Garda and then in a villa in Tuscany lay ahead of Rhian.

She became serious. 'Oh, Leah, did I sound awful? I was just so nervous and Cousin Richard smelled like a distillery.'

Richard was standing in for his father who was out in Rhodesia visiting one of his brothers. All his uncles and their offspring were scattered around the Empire, so some old uncle from Rhian's father's side was to have done the honour but had been stricken with gout last week. Richard was the only male relative they could find to give Rhian away.

Leah hugged her. 'No, you were fine, Mrs Ernest Seymour Armstrong. I never knew that Seymour was his middle name. And as for Richard, I saw Reverend Hunter actually back away from him, his lips all tight and drawn in as if he was sucking a lemon. You can bet Aunt Poppy will have something to say to Richard about that!' She stepped back and took her sister's gloved hands in her own. 'Oh, I'll miss you!'

'No you won't. You're always saying how I irritate you.'

'Only when you say "It's what Mother and Father would have wanted,"' she laughed before giving Rhian a kiss on the cheek.

'We'd better go down, Ernest will be getting impatient.'

Leah nodded. 'Your trunk and bags are already in the car.' She'd heard her new brother-in-law inform Blackett

23

to bring them down and she hadn't liked the tone of voice he'd used. Ernest Seymour Armstrong had become what he'd set out to be, master of this household and a rich and respected businessman and property owner, but it didn't give him the right to treat people like dirt. Neither she nor Rhian had been brought up like that. She'd never heard either of her parents deliberately humiliate anyone. 'Firm but fair' was what her father always said.

Leah suddenly felt a stab of sadness as she glanced around the room Rhian would never again use. It was a mess. She'd take Aunt Poppy's advice about getting a replacement while the newlyweds were away. She'd ask Reverend Hunter if he knew anyone suitable. Maybe someone they'd have to train but who would be eager to learn and pleasant. Then Aunt Poppy couldn't complain and neither could Ernest. His efforts so far had been dismal with that agency.

Ernest, Aunt Poppy and Richard stood in the hall waiting for them. Further back, at a respectful distance, stood Miss Winthrop and Mrs Knowles, always referred to as just 'Cook'. With them was the boy who did the boots and sharpened the kitchen knives and a hundred other small tasks besides, and Mrs Thomas who came in three times a week to do the heavy cleaning.

The happy couple departed with kisses, handshakes and wishes of happiness and then the small number of staff went back behind the green baize door to the kitchens and servants' quarters built at a time when a staff of six or seven people worked there. These days numbers were more modest.

'I don't know what she sees in him, puffed up, poe-faced oily prig,' Richard whispered loudly to Leah as they waved after the car. He was a little unsteady on his feet.

'Neither do I but it's her choice and it's all signed and sealed. I suppose you'll be off to your club now.'

24

Poppy heard her. 'Not before I've had a short conversation with him, he won't!'

'Oh, Lord, now you're for it,' Leah hissed.

Richard shrugged. 'Anything the old bat says will go in one ear and out the other,' he answered, grinning foolishly.

His remark, attitude and tone of voice annoyed Leah. 'Really? That's probably because there's nothing in between to stop it!' she replied waspishly before turning away abruptly and going back upstairs.

With her hand on the brass knob of the drawing-room door, Poppy's mouth twisted into a grim smile. She could never see Leah bowing and scraping to any man the way Rhian did and in a way she was glad.

Chapter Three

The euphoria of the wedding had worn off and as Nora trudged home from work she felt miserable and depressed. She missed Ethna. She missed her to talk to, laugh with and argue with. Da was always very tired after work, or after tramping around looking for a day's work, and she kept forgetting he was no longer a young man. After his meal he often fell asleep in the battered old armchair. And as for Declan, well, even when he was there you'd not get a sensible conversation out of him.

The sun was still warm on her back as she walked along King Edward Street. She'd saved most of the money she'd got from Dan Fogarty for the wedding outfits. She considered it a luxury to ride home on the tram every day and besides, it was healthier to walk in the summer. You could smell the salty, tangy breath of the river.

She'd done so many jobs since she'd left school, all of them menial, all of them in a factory of some sort. She'd really like a change but she wasn't well dressed or well spoken enough for shop work, or not in one of the big shops in town where there were plenty of other girls to talk to. Working in a small local shop wasn't very interesting and the pay was buttons. That just left domestic service. The pay there was very poor too. There was very little time off, the work was often hard and the hours very long and yet it would be great to see how the rich lived, how they dressed, what they ate and drank. She'd be surrounded by beautiful things. Furniture, ornaments, pictures. The rooms would be light and airy, not poky, damp and gloomy. She could perhaps pick up tips that would enable her to get a job in one of the really posh shops – one day.

She frowned as she turned the corner and saw Declan and his cronies sitting on their doorstep.

'What have you been up to?'

'Nothin'! I was just waiting for you to get home. I'm hungry.'

'Well, there won't be anything to eat until Da gets in. Why don't you go and sit on Jimmy Murphy's doorstep and annoy his mam for a change?' She glared at the lad in question. 'I'm sick of fighting me way through gangs of scruffy little hooligans to get into me own house.'

'Me mam's took bad. We can't go round our house,' Jimmy cried, alarm written all over his thin, grubby face.

'Another one of her headaches? Been at the gin again?' Agnes Murphy often had bouts of despair and took to sitting in the snug in the nearest pub until the money and the drink ran out and someone dragged her home yelling and cursing. Nora sighed heavily. She didn't really blame Agnes. Ten kids and a consumptive husband who could only work now and then, all packed into that two-up, two-down kip of a place. No wonder she despaired.

After the meal of herrings and bread and margarine and tea, Nora made some dripping butties for her da's carry-out tomorrow. She washed the few dishes and tidied up. Joe had been lucky, he'd found a discarded newspaper and was looking forward to a good read. He'd had two full days' work so far this week, that was ten shillings, and maybe he'd be lucky and get perhaps a couple of half days as well.

28

'Da, do you miss our Ethna?' Nora asked.

Joe lowered the paper. 'Of course I do, luv, but we'll get used to not having her here all the time and she'll be around on Sunday.'

'I know.' Nora bit her lip, wondering how to word the next question. Joe had disappeared behind the paper again.

'Da, I'm sorry to keep mitherin' you, but can I ask you something?'

With a sigh Joe lowered the newspaper. 'What?'

'Would you . . . would you mind if I . . . I went too?'

He looked at her, startled. 'Who are you going to marry? You've never mentioned this, girl! Who's the feller?' His brow darkened. 'You've not gone an' got yerself in trouble?'

'No! No, I didn't mean anything like that. There's no feller, no "trouble". Oh, I'm so fed up with working in a factory, Da. I've worked in Ogden's since I was fourteen. I want to work somewhere *different*. Somewhere where I'm surrounded by nice things and nice smells. No dirt and stink and mess. I'd like to go into service.'

Joe dropped his paper and the sheets slipped out of order as it fell to the floor. 'Into *service*? You're nearly twenty and you've no training at all for any kind of service. Besides, it's long hours, bad pay, no time off. It's sheer exploitation.'

'I know all that, Da.'

'Well, I won't stop you, Nora, if it's really what you want, and there's always a home to come back to here. I'm well able to look after meself. I had to when your mam died and Ethna had to see to you and our Declan. We can get a meal at any number of places that would cost less than buying stuff in and having to cook it.' He smiled at her. 'And Mrs Molloy over the road would be

29

more than willing to do the washing and ironing, such as it is.'

Nora nodded. It was a well-known fact and cause of much gossip and speculation in Oil Street that Mrs Molloy had designs on Joe O'Brian, she being a widow and always finding some excuse to pop in.

'But what about mellado out there kicking that ball of rags up the street with his mates?'

She felt awful. Guilty, selfish, mean and heartless. Leaving her da to come home to an empty house. Having to keep Declan under control and fend off the not very subtle advances of the really awful Mrs Molloy. 'I don't know. Maybe . . . maybe he could just play in the street until you got home.'

Joe raised his eyes to the ceiling. 'God Almighty, that doesn't bear thinking about! But apart from that, have you anywhere in mind?'

'No, I thought I'd ask Father Finnegan if he knew anyone. He knows me. He knows I'm honest, I'm not hard-faced, I'm willing to work and I'll be eager to learn.'

He could see the look of determination in her eyes. He thought she was mad. The only difference between domestic service and factory work was that in service you could be sure of a decent roof over your head and food in your belly. They worked you to death for a pittance.

'Well then, why don't you go up and see him and then if he's got any suggestions or ideas, we'll discuss it all with Ethna when she comes on Sunday.'

Nora smiled. 'I'll go up there now. Thanks, Da.'

He grinned wrily. 'It's not often a man manages to get rid of all his daughters so quickly. If I could only get shut of Declan too, just think of the peace and quiet I'd have.' He gathered up the newspaper and began, intently, to put the pages back in order. He didn't want her to see his regret and pity. She wasn't at all likely to get into any kind of domestic service. She was too old and hadn't a notion of the way of going on in a big house.

Father Finnegan said he would try but didn't hold out much hope. Then he asked her about her father and brother – who would care for them? He wasn't very happy with the answers to his questions. Joe O'Brian was a man he had great respect for. He was a member of the Men's Confraternity, a good worker, sober, and making an effort to educate himself; he deserved better than to come home to an empty house after a day's work, a house without light and heat and then having to eat in one of the many canteens, or 'cannie houses' as they were known, where a bowl of scouse or a plate of hash could be had for a couple of pence. Declan basically was a good lad, but he'd need watching, he was easily led. Father Finnegan suggested that the boy go straight from school to Ethna's house and remain there until he knew his father would be home from work. Although Edward and Ethna Neely would be at work too, he knew the lad wouldn't dare get up to mischief in Edward Neely's house.

When Ethna arrived on Sunday after lunch, she hugged all of them very tightly.

'You nearly squeezed the breath out of me, girl,' Joe laughed, holding his ribs.

'And yer nearly suffocated me,' Declan cried indignantly. Ethna must have gone mad, carrying on like that. He hoped she wasn't going to make a habit of it. Suppose she did it when one of his mates was here? God, it didn't bear thinking about. He'd never hear the end of it and she'd only been gone a week, not a flaming year.

'I missed you.' She meant it very sincerely.

'Well, sit down now and tell us all about it,' Nora said.

31

'I'll put the kettle on. Later you and me can sit in the yard, it's a lovely day.'

'Sit in the *yard*?' Ethna's voice rose to a screech of disbelief. The yard was dreadful. The privy was at the end, as was the ash pit, and both smelled far from pleasant – they were shared by the Cullens who lived next door. It was also dark and dank, it never got any sun.

'Well, you know Da likes to read his paper. It's your one bit of pleasure, isn't it, Da? You won't want us nattering away ten to the dozen like a pair of parrots, will you?'

Ethna sensed Nora wanted to speak to her about something privately and there were things she herself wanted to tell her sister and preferred to do out of the hearing of her da and brother. If you wanted the whole neighbourhood to know something, all you had to do was tell Declan it was a big secret. Da didn't call him 'Mighty Mouth' for nothing.

Ethna told them all about the comfort of her new home. How easy it was to keep clean. How great it was to have a decent dolly tub, scrubbing board, mangle and clothes line and, best of all, how much of a relief it was to know that there was a good steady wage coming in to pay the bills. She dutifully passed over her wages to Edward and he gave her back the housekeeping money and money for her fares. He was always stressing how important it was to save for a rainy day – not that she could ever foresee a 'rainy day', she thought to herself. And she was annoyed that there was to be no little allowance for herself. No, he would give her the money for her clothes and such like as and when she needed it. She only had to ask.

There had been hardly enough to survive on in the past but she'd never had to *ask* for money. Da and then Nora had turned over their wages to her. She'd always set aside as much as she could for Da's expenses, and

32

Nora and Declan had asked *her* for things. She'd been keeping house since she was thirteen.

She had asked Edward timidly whether she could keep her wedding outfit. There might be another occasion when she could wear it. The request had been met with a firm refusal. The day was over. It had served its purpose. She was now the wife of a working-class man; where did she expect to go in all that finery? So it had gone to Dan Fogarty's and the money was handed over, even though she'd bought the dress and hat, Da had bought the boots and Nora had paid for the gloves.

When they'd settled themselves in the yard on two old crates that were the beginnings of the winter firewood collection, Nora looked closely at her sister.

'You *are* happy, Ethna?'

'Oh, yes, everything's great.'

'But?'

'Well, he's not much of a one for chatting, like. He comes home from work, gets washed and changed, has his tea, reads the paper and then a chapter or two of a book and then it's . . . bed.'

'You knew he wasn't exactly the chatty type. Doesn't he talk to you at all?'

'Yes, but it's just that he was more talkative before, interested, and he took me on the occasional outing before we were married.' She couldn't hide the note of discontent in her voice.

'And what about the . . . the bed bit?'

Ethna chewed her lip and shrugged. 'Mrs Cullen and Mrs Dodd were right. It's awful, it really is. I always feel . . . used and somehow dirty.'

Nora looked at her sister with concern. She'd paid no attention to all the old biddies in the street and their dire tales. They were old, no one would really want to do it with them. But young people, that was supposed to be

33

so different. It was supposed to be so . . . so wonderful. Then she realised that although Ethna was young, Edward Neely certainly was not and that her sister wasn't head over heels in love with him.

Ethna sighed heavily. 'I suppose I'll just have to put up with that side of it.'

Nora nodded, thinking about her next words. 'Ethna, I went to see Father Finnegan the other day.'

'What for?'

'Well, I want to change my job.'

'So what did you go to him for? Do you want to be a priest's housekeeper?' A thought occurred to Ethna. 'Oh, Holy Mother of God! You don't want to be a nun, do you?'

'No. I want to go into service in a big house.'

Ethna was aghast. 'Jesus, Mary and Joseph! What for?'

'Because I'm sick of factories. Sick of living here, sick of only having potatoes, bread, dripping, and cups of tea to live on, with maybe a bit of salt fish on Sunday morning after Mass and Communion. I want to see what a big posh house is like. Get good food, have people to talk to.'

Ethna's eyes were wide with amazement. 'You're mad. No one will ever take you on, except as maybe a scullery maid and all you'll see then are dirty pots and dirty floors you'll have to scrub. They'll kill you with work.'

'I know and I know the pay is terrible and they only let you come home now and then.'

'Or sometimes not at all.'

'If it's a decent family they give you time off.'

'What's Da going to do? What about our Declan?'

'Da says he won't mind. He can get a pie or a bowl of scouse anywhere along the Dock Road and Mrs Molloy will see to the washing and the house—'

'Too flaming right she will,' Ethna interrupted. 'And

34

she'll have him up the aisle of Our Lady's before you can turn round.'

'No, Da's quite capable of keeping her in her place.'

'Well, what about that young hooligan? Holy Mother of God! Nora, just think what he'll get up to running the streets until Da gets home.'

'Well, that's what I want to ask you. Father Finnegan suggested it. He said Declan's not a bad kid, but he's easily led, so if he went to your house and stayed there until you or Edward come in—'

'*Our* house?' Ethna looked at her with horror. 'You mean let him loose in *Edward's* house? By himself? On his own?'

Nora nodded. 'Oh, please, Ethna. He'd behave there, I know he would. He might even get down to his homework like Da is always telling him to.'

'I'll wait and see how things go. I'm not promising anything, Nora. It might be ages before you get a place anyway.' Mentally Ethna prayed that her sister would *never* be accepted anywhere.

On warm summer Sunday afternoons, after his lunch but before benediction or devotions, Father Finnegan liked to take a walk into the city. Sometimes he went as far as the Pierhead to watch the ships on the river for it was as crowded as any road. Usually, though, his meanderings took him to St John's Gardens at the back of St George's Hall. For over ten years now he'd been making the journey, ever since he'd become parish priest. The tranquillity, the beauty of the flowerbeds, the neat pathways, the roses and shrubs were a delight. It was an oasis of beauty in the heart of a city that was rich in fine public buildings but so very poor in its dirty, sprawling, overcrowded slums.

He stood with his hands clasped behind his back,

looking up at a statue. Behind him the buildings of the waterfront were etched against a clear blue sky: the great dome of the offices of the Mersey Docks and Harbour Board, the squat roof of the Cunard Building and the slowly rising tower of concrete and steel, the first of its kind in the country, that would eventually become the Royal Liver Building. He'd seen sketches, architects' impressions of the finished thing. Its two towers would each be crowned with the figure of the mythical Liver bird. One would look out across the city, the other across the river to the ocean beyond. It would also be the first sight the Irish emigrants would see.

'A good man. A brave man, Father.'

The priest turned from the statue and smiled at the speaker, a good friend who also wore a clerical collar but a black suit instead of the long soutane.

'And your man over there wasn't without courage.'

Reverend Hunter nodded his agreement. Theirs was an unlikely friendship which had been forged here in these gardens – the Catholic priest whose parish was one huge slum and the High Anglican priest whose parishioners were among the most wealthy people in the city.

First had come polite nods, then comments on the weather and then a sort of unsure, stilted form of conversation that had eventually relaxed and blossomed into a close friendship.

'Both of them courageous and compassionate, Finbar.'

Reverend Hunter inspected the recently erected statues, one of Canon Major Lester, the Protestant clergyman, the other of Father James Nugent, the Catholic priest, depicted with his arm round a ragged urchin. In their time, often on the same platform in a city divided by religious bigotry and violence, they had spoken out and tried to tackle the plight of the slum urchins.

'Ah, but has it done any good, James?'

36

'This city had the very first society for the prevention of cruelty to children. A whole year before the national one was formed. We had the first medical officer of health. Some people have tried and have gone on trying. Now there are more jobs than ever before. The port is thriving.'

'Aye, for some it is. But there's unrest all around. The seamen are about to strike for a decent wage, better conditions and for a job that's secure, and the dockers and carters have said they'll come out in support. You know as well as I do, James, the humiliating way the dockers must go twice a day to the stands, hoping to be picked for work.'

Reverend Hunter shook his head sadly. 'Like beasts herded into pens waiting to be auctioned off.'

'After all these years wouldn't you think I'd be used to it by now? They use the same system in Dublin and there was the same dirt, poverty and hopelessness of it all in my parish there. They want to work. They want the dignity and security, to be able to afford to live decently, improve themselves and maybe see a better world for their children. At least, most of them do.'

'If they strike, they'll bring the port to a standstill.'

'Isn't that just what they've done in London? Oh, these are troubled days all right, my friend. Troubled days and I've the added burden of a curate who preaches sedition at the drop of a hat. He wants Ireland out of the Empire altogether. I've asked him, what's the use of resurrecting memories of old and failed rebellions? Or to go planting the seeds of political discontent in young and innocent hearts and minds? It's now that matters. It's nineteen hundred and ten and we should be putting all our efforts into fighting poverty, violence and disease here in this city.'

He fell silent and they both stood looking towards

the river. There was enough sectarian violence in this city as it was without encouraging the political kind as well. There were full-scale riots on St Patrick's Day and on 12 July when the Orangemen commemorated King William's victory over King James at the Battle of the Boyne. Why add home rule or republicanism to it all?

Father Finnegan decided to change the subject. 'How did the wedding go on then? The one you had last week?'

'Quiet. The old lady, Miss Cavendish, didn't approve and to be honest neither did I. It would have been better if they'd changed the day. And the young person who gave the bride away was a disgrace. He was drunk, intoxicated, swaying to and fro, slurring his words. I was disgusted to say the least.'

'Ah, now that's something I view with abhorrence and anger, and I tell them so too and in no polite way. To be drunk in the house of God is tantamount to sacrilege. I celebrated a wedding myself last week. The bride's mother is dead these ten years and the poor family had made any number of small sacrifices to pay for it, so it went ahead – at the urging of my curate, I might add. He's young, he's not had much experience yet; I try to forgive him and guide him but when he vilifies King Edward, God rest his soul, with ugly accusations I can't stay silent. God is forgiving and your man had a lot to put up with from the old Queen.'

Reverend Hunter had a good idea of just what Father Hegarty had called the dead King. He himself disapproved and was embarrassed by the lifestyle and the sins that had been committed by the head of his Church. But, as his friend had said, God is forgiving and the man had had his own crosses to bear.

'Now that reminds me, James, I have been asked a favour and maybe you're just the man I need to speak to it about it, you having so many of the wealthier personages in this city in your parish.'

'What is it?'

'The sister of the girl I married last week, young Nora O'Brian, came to me and begged me to help her get a place as a domestic.'

Reverend Hunter's brow creased in a frown. 'How old is she? Has she done any work in service before? What kind of a family are they?'

'She's nearly twenty and has always worked in a factory. But she hates factories, she's sick to death of them, so she told me. She'd be willing to learn, she swore she would, and I know she would too. She's a good girl, I hear her confession. I can vouch for it. Her father is a good, sober man who works hard when he can get work and has a powerful interest in literature. Books, newspapers, journals – he reads anything he can get his hands on. And in his own quiet way, he's becoming an educated man. He has a huge thirst for knowledge.'

Reverend Hunter nodded slowly. Only yesterday young Leah Cavendish had asked him if there was anyone he could recommend and now Father Finnegan was putting in a plea for this Nora O'Brian. A factory girl, untrained, from a decent but poor home. She was bound to be ignorant of the habits and ways of the upper classes. Still, his friend's judgement of her would be sound.

'I do know of someone who is in need of a maid, but I don't know if this Nora O'Brian would be at all suitable.'

Father Finnegan looked at his friend hopefully. If their positions had been reversed he'd not have a second thought, he'd try to get the child fixed up in a good house.

Slowly Reverend Hunter nodded. 'I'll ask. I'll explain and I'll let you know.'

'How?'

'I'll send a note down to you with the messenger boy.'

Wasn't it a great thing to have a boy just to run the errands? Father Finnegan thought. He smiled at Reverend Hunter. Their views and interests and aims were close in many things and yet their lives were poles apart.

They took a turn round the gardens to admire the roses before shaking hands, wishing the blessings of God on each other and parting.

Chapter Four

Nora smiled as she handed over her pawn ticket to redeem the dress and straw boater she'd worn at Ethna's wedding. She liked Dan Fogarty the pawnbroker, he was always pleasant to her.

'What's this you've come for?' he asked, glad that this morning he might be receiving money instead of lending it out on the things that came to him.

'The straw gussie and the cotton frock. I'm going after a new job.'

As he moved towards the back of the dark, cluttered shop where bundles were stacked high, he called back to her, 'And I'll be after going at that brother of yours with a cleaver if he comes in here once more singing "Moses, ri toora li, toora li aye".'

Nora pursed her lips; if news of Declan's persistent cheek got back to Ethna she'd refuse to allow him over her doorstep. As it was, Edward wasn't at all happy with the idea – always assuming she got the job, which was far from certain. She'd been elated when Declan had come home from school with a note for her from Father Finnegan telling her she was to present herself at number sixteen Prince's Avenue tomorrow at nine thirty and ask for Miss Cavendish. Cavendish's was one of the biggest carters in Liverpool, and Prince's Avenue, well, that was really posh.

'I'm dead sorry, Mr Fogarty, honest I am. He's a holy

terror. He has the whole lot of us worried as to what's going to happen to him. Our Ethna says he'll end up in Walton Jail and sometimes I think she's right.'

'To you, Nora, I'll say boys will be boys, but I'll belt him one if I catch him hanging around here.'

'And me da will thank you for it, too. When Declan and those mates of his caught those lads from up Netherfield Road chalking "The Pope is a bastard" on the wall of Our Lady Immaculate's Church at the bottom of St Domingo Road, they half killed them, and then me da belted hell out of our Declan.'

'Your da is a tolerant man, Nora. He's ahead of his time with his thinking. It'll be a long time before attitudes change, especially around here.'

'I'll tell me da he was mocking your religion an' he'll get a belt,' Nora replied firmly, wondering what they would do without pawnbrokers. The money lenders charged exorbitant rates. People around here owed a lot to Dan Fogarty who was that rare being in Liverpool, an Irish Jew.

Next morning Nora was up at six. She'd been restless and unable to sleep. It was already very warm as she walked slowly along Prince's Avenue in her freshly ironed dress and smart hat, her hair tucked tidily beneath it. She was wearing Ethna's cream buttoned boots; her da had given her the money to redeem them too, just for the day. Nervously she looked about her at the houses; they were very big and very grand. They were set back from the wide pavement with stone steps leading up to the front doors, their high-gloss paintwork and glistening brass knockers and knobs shining in the early sunlight.

Outside number sixteen she paused and looked up. It seemed to tower above her. She counted the storeys. There were four, and that was without the cellar. Iron railings surrounded the meticulously kept garden and two huge stone pillars supported the gates. There was a small notice attached to the railing: 'Hawkers and tradesmen – rear entrance.'

Did she come into those groups? Nora looked down at the piece of paper in her hand and decided she did. She turned and saw a small gate set into the railings and a path that led down the side of the house. To her surprise there were more buildings here. Outhouses of some sort and stables. They must keep horses but you'd need hundreds of horses to pull all the Cavendish wagons you saw on the streets. She wondered where they were, the rest of the teams; probably out and about in the city.

'Are yer going to stand there all morning or what?'

Nora jumped, startled. She'd been looking around, nervous and preoccupied, and hadn't noticed the young lad in the doorway. He was about fourteen, probably just left school, she thought.

'I'm to see a Miss Cavendish at half past nine.'

He looked like an older, tidier version of Declan. 'No one told me yer was comin'.'

'I've got a note, a proper appointment, so clear off and tell someone that I've arrived.'

Muttering to himself, he went inside. Seeing as she was young she must have come to see Miss Leah.

Leah looked up as Percy imparted Nora's instructions. She smiled and told him to bring the girl through into the breakfast room.

Cook and Miss Winthrop were in the pantry discussing the day's menu and Mrs Thomas was dragging the beds around upstairs, laying the dust with a damp mop. No one saw Nora being led into the breakfast room.

Leah stood up from the table where she'd been making a list of all the people who had sent wedding gifts to Rhian. Despite the fact that the elaborate wedding breakfast and festivities had been cancelled, thank you notes would still have to be written when her sister arrived back.

'Miss Cavendish?' Nora asked timidly. The slim girl with the fiery halo of hair and wide green eyes was looking at her in a bemused way. Nora's gaze flitted over her clothes: pale pink-and-white-striped blouse with a cameo broach fastened to the high neck, a deeper pink skirt, the waist pulled tightly in by a broad belt of white leather decorated with pink flowers.

Leah nodded, she in turn noting the cheap cotton frock that had been carefully ironed, the straw boater hat with its blue ribbon trim, the thick chestnut hair beneath it and the wide blue eyes that were regarding her with uncertainty.

'I . . . I have this.' Nora thrust the piece of paper from Father Finnegan into Leah's hands. She didn't dare look around her although she was longing to do so.

'You're Nora? Nora O'Brian?'

Nora nodded. 'I've never ever done . . . been in service before, miss, but I got so sick of that dirty, smelly factory. I'm willing to take anything, miss, I really am. I'll scrub floors and pots, polish, do anything.'

'We already have a scullery maid for that.'

Nora's face fell but Leah had warmed to her. It would be nice to have someone her own age to talk to now that Rhian was a grown-up matron.

'I can do housework, tidy things away. I can do a bit of sewing and I'm quite good with hairstyles and . . . and things like that.' She gazed at Leah pleadingly.

'I'm sure you can do all those things and I'm sure we can find a place for you, Nora.'

Nora's face split into a huge grin. 'Oh, miss, I'd be made up . . . er . . . very glad if you could. I'd work until I dropped in a lovely house like this.'

44

The girl was obviously completely overcome by her surroundings but her naivety, her pleasure, wonder and enthusiasm drew Leah to her.

'I'll have to discuss it with my aunt first, before I can offer you anything. Would you like to sit down?'

'Oh, no, miss. I'm fine truly I am.' Nora swallowed hard, with disappointment. She should have realised that no one would let a young girl like that interview and take on domestic staff. It was a huge responsibility. She clenched her hands together tightly as she waited.

When Leah entered her father's study, where all domestic staff were interviewed, she found her aunt dressed in a rather old-fashioned gown of heavy black bombazine. She wore jet earrings, a single strand of jet beads and the gold locket that never left her possession. She was writing slowly in her journal, something she did from time to time, when the mood took her.

'Well, what is it, Leah?' Poppy asked irritably, laying down her pen.

'The girl I asked Reverend Hunter about, the new maid. She's here, Aunt. And she was on time.'

'Then why didn't Winthrop bring her to me in here?'

'Young Percy brought her straight to me. I don't think Miss Winthrop knows she's here.'

'What kind of staff do we have here, in heaven's name! Ever since your poor mother passed away things have gone from bad to worse, but we won't dwell on that.'

'She's nice, Aunt Poppy,' Leah said, hoping to calm her aunt. 'She's clean and neatly dressed. It's only a cheap cotton dress but you can tell she's taken great care in pressing it. Her hair is tidy, she's wearing cotton gloves and she has a nice boater and button boots.' Leah had taken an instant liking to Nora O'Brian.

'Indeed?'

'But there's a bit of a problem. She's never done any

45

kind of domestic work before, except at home of course. Just work in factories.'

The old lady's eyes widened in amazement. '*Factories*? He has sent us a *factory* girl?'

'She hates it, Aunt Poppy, and she's not rough or loud and she's *so* eager. She says she'll do anything and everything. Can't we give her a chance, please? I know Reverend Hunter wouldn't have sent us someone dreadful. We've had a succession of that type already. The last one smoked cigarettes, for heaven's sake! Miss Winthrop and Cook could train her, I could help her too, she said she's good with hairstyles. Then when Rhian and Ernest come back she would be installed and nicely trained.'

She saw her aunt's mouth relax from its tight, hard line of disapproval. She had hoped that her words about Nora being installed and trained by the time Ernest got back would at least persuade her aunt to see the girl.

'Oh, very well. Seeing as she's here, bring her in.' Poppy settled herself in Leah's father's chair facing the wide desk whose top was covered with embossed leather. She picked up a pen from the silver inkstand and began to tap it on the desk. A factory girl indeed!

Nora was shaking as she followed Leah into the dark and rather gloomy study. This Miss Cavendish, dressed entirely in black, looked very formidable and absolutely terrifying.

Poppy didn't beat about the bush. 'My niece informs me you have always worked in factories.'

'That's right, Ma'am, but I just couldn't stand the dirt and the smell and the noise and,' she dropped her voice and her eyes, 'some of the language, Ma'am. Like I told Miss Cavendish here, I'll do anything, really I will.' She took another deep breath and looked Poppy Cavendish in the eyes. 'My mam died ten years ago. My da works hard when he can get work on the docks, but we've never had much, Ma'am. My sister was thirteen and she brung . . . brought us up. Factory work or street trading was all that was open to me. But I'm a quick learner and Father Finnegan spoke for me, like, to the Reverend gentleman.'

There was so much honesty and pleading in Nora's voice that Leah's heart went out to her. She knew what it was like to lose your mother; she had had all the luxuries money could provide to help ease that grief but poor Nora had had nothing. Her eyes pleaded with those of her aunt.

Poppy was undecided. It was a gamble, but as Leah had said, the girl couldn't be any worse than the creatures they'd had to endure from that agency. At least this chit had been recommended by the Reverend Hunter, via her own parish priest, although it crossed her mind that it was odd the two men should be friends. She replaced the pen and made her decision.

'Very well, you are engaged. You'll be provided with two uniforms, one for morning, one for afternoon and evening. As you are not trained or experienced, you will have one half day a month off, Wednesday, and you will be paid six pounds ten shillings a month. You will of course live in – there are rooms on the top floor. You will take your meals below stairs. When can you start?'

Nora was so shocked she couldn't speak, but Leah nudged her gently.

'Oh, right now, this minute, Ma'am! Oh, thank you! Thank you, Ma'am.' She dipped a curtsy.

'Well, I don't think there's any need to be curtsying. I'm not a grand duchess, a princess or Queen Mary.' Poppy inclined her head but her tone was brusque. 'Go with my niece and wait until Miss Winthrop, the housekeeper, comes to take charge of you.'

47

Both girls' eyes were shining as they left the study. Nora placed her hands on her burning cheeks. 'Oh, miss! Oh, miss! I . . . I just don't know what to say. It was you that got me it. If you hadn't spoken up for me, like, she'd have shown me the door!'

Leah laughed. 'Aunt Poppy can be quite fierce, I grant you, but she's fair-minded.'

Nora became bashful. 'I'll never be able to thank you, miss. Is that what I'm to call you?'

'Yes, or Miss Leah. My sister Rhian, now Mrs Ernest Seymour Armstrong, must be addressed as Ma'am. She's on her honeymoon in Italy. Our parents were killed, in a car accident, three years ago.'

'I'm sorry, Miss Leah.'

'I know you mean that. You said your own mother had died ten years ago.'

Nora nodded. 'And is Miss Poppy in charge, like? I mean head of the family?'

'My esteemed brother-in-law thinks he will be, but Aunt Poppy can get the better of him any day she feels like it, though I have to admit she's getting old. But then Ernest is not really *that* bright.' Leah was leading Nora to the back of the house towards the servants' quarters.

'I don't like my new brother-in-law either,' Nora confided. 'A right misery guts and he's years older than our Ethna. They got married on the day of the King's funeral. That set some tongues wagging all right.'

'Did they? Rhian was married that day too.'

'A woman down our street, Ma . . . Mrs Brennan, said it was a bad omen and no good will come of it. It drove our Ethna into hysterics. I just hope it doesn't turn out to be true. I think Ethna was just getting married to escape.' They spoke easily, as though they'd known each other all their lives.

'From what?'

48

'From being poor and having people pity you, saying a couple of years older and she'll be an old maid.'

Leah pealed with laughter. 'Do people really say that? How old is Ethna?'

'Twenty-three.'

'The same age as Rhian. I'll be twenty in November. How old are you?'

'I'll be twenty in October, Miss Leah.'

Leah's green eyes danced. She felt happier than she had done for a long time. 'I just know we're going to get on, Nora, I really do!'

'So do I.'

They had reached Miss Winthrop's quarters behind the green baize door.

'This is Nora O'Brian, Miss Winthrop. Aunt Poppy has told her she can start immediately, although she'll need a lot of help, she's no experience in service, I'm afraid.'

With trepidation Nora watched Leah close the door behind her. She didn't like the look of the thin, sour-featured Miss Winthrop. She felt she'd already done something wrong by just being here. By being employed.

Over the next two weeks there were many silent tears, many hours of backbreaking work, so much to remember, what to do and what not to do, what to say and when.

Leah tried to help her in any way she could and to her surprise Miss Poppy Cavendish told her she was making good progress. She must stick with it and master everything. That had amazed Nora until Leah told her that there was only one more week left before the honeymooners would return and both she and Aunt Poppy were determined to present her as the perfect tweeny-cum-ladies' maid.

Nora hadn't been home. Not after the first day when she'd gone back to Oil Street to break the news and pick up what bits she would need. She had hugged her da and Declan, promising if he behaved she'd give him a whole shilling pocket money a month.

'I won't need much for myself, Da. I'll get clothes and good food so I want you to have the six pounds a month.'

'Don't be daft, Nora. What with his tanner pocket money, you'll only have nine shillings a month for yourself.'

'It's plenty, Da. I've got my dress and hat. I'll save a bit and buy a winter coat later on, when I'll need one. Now you won't have to worry about being out on strike, having no work or money for the rent or food. I want you to get yourself lots of blankets and a good thick quilt, aye, and one for Declan too. I want you to have a fire roaring up the chimney every day in winter without worrying about coal. I want you to get good boots, warm socks, a heavy overcoat, a new muffler and cap and gloves. All the things you've had to do without most of your life. If you don't feel well in winter, if your back starts playing up, I don't want you to have to go dragging yourself down to the docks, looking for work in the damp and cold. Stay in bed, Da, you've earned it.'

There were tears in Joe's eyes. 'I couldn't do that, luv. I couldn't break the habits of a lifetime and it would be idle to be lying in bed just because I've a few twinges.'

'But you'll get all the rest, bit by bit, promise me?'

'I promise. I'll save three pounds a month, more if there's no strike and I can get jobbed.'

'Then you'll have nine pounds by October and you'll know that every month after that there will be six pounds coming in.'

'We'll see, Nora, luv. We'll see.'

She hugged him tightly. Over the years he'd worked so hard and suffered so much for them, it was the least she could do. Declan had already disappeared, no doubt to boast of his forthcoming wealth. But he'd only get it if he behaved. She was going to be very firm about that.

Nora was ready, as were Miss Winthrop, Cook, Blackett, Mrs Thomas and Percy, all standing in a line in the hall awaiting the imminent arrival of the new master and mistress. Leah and then Miss Winthrop had inspected Nora and pronounced her 'perfect' and 'tidy' respectively. She wore her black uniform dress, with the starched white cuffs and collar and the stiff white apron; her hair was confined under a starched and pleated white cap. Her face glowed with health, her eyes with excitement. Imagine having spent a whole month in Italy for a honeymoon. Ethna hadn't gone anywhere.

She dipped a curtsy to both Mr Armstrong and his wife, who looked a very pale, washed-out sort of person beside Miss Leah. And it was obvious who had the upper hand in this marriage, she thought. Mr Armstrong didn't seem particularly pleased to see her when the housekeeper introduced her as the new tweeny.

'How long have you been here, girl?'

'Nearly three weeks, sir.'

Ernest did not answer but the colour in his cheeks deepened.

'O'Brian, follow Mrs Armstrong and Miss Leah up. Help with the unpacking and—'

'The unpacking can wait a while, Miss Winthrop. I'm dying for a decent cup of tea. You wouldn't believe the muck they serve as tea in Italy.' Rhian was tired, she felt hot and sticky and had a headache coming on. As the cab had driven them home, Ernest had been totally engrossed in the newspaper he'd bought. It appeared that there were more strikes – the seamen, the dockers and, worst of all from Ernest's point of view, the carters.

51

'Well, that's a nice homecoming, I must say!' he'd exclaimed.

'What is?' Rhian had asked him wearily.

'It would appear that my entire workforce are out on strike – again! By God, the Shipping Federation have got something to answer for. It's the damned seamen who started it again.'

Rhian had said nothing, she didn't really care about business matters.

When Nora arrived with the tea tray, Rhian was sitting at her dressing table, her hat and gloves thrown carelessly on the bed.

'Oh, thank you, Nora. I'll pour.' Leah smiled at Nora who left, closing the door softly behind her. Later she would have all the unpacking to do, before she served dinner.

'Since when did we call servants by their Christian names?' Rhian snapped.

'Since Nora arrived. Oh, come down off your high horse! Ernest's obviously been busy teaching you airs and graces. Nora's nice. She's pleasant and she's efficient, she works very hard indeed. A house this size should have more servants.'

'Well, I suppose that's all that matters. Did she come from the agency?'

'No, Reverend Hunter recommended her, via her parish priest.'

'Oh, a Catholic.' Rhian sniffed.

Leah didn't like her sister's tone at all. She sounded just like Ernest. 'And from a very poor home, by all accounts, but she's a good worker, polite, self-effacing and unobtrusive. Totally unlike that lot that did come from the agency. And she doesn't smoke either.'

Rhian shot her an annoyed glance but she was too tired to argue.

'What was it like? Was it beautiful? Did you go to Verona and Venice and Florence?'

Rhian relaxed a little. 'It was very, very beautiful. Of course some buildings are so old they need constant repair and look a bit unkempt and the canals in Venice do smell rather and there is a lot of poverty, but it's so . . . so . . . cultural.'

'And did Ernest enjoy it?'

'He enjoyed some things.'

Leah waited for her to elaborate but she didn't. Obviously Ernest hadn't enjoyed himself much. Rhian would tell her it all in due course. She could wait. 'Well, he doesn't seem very happy to be home.'

'That's because there are more strikes and the carters are involved.'

'Oh.' Leah frowned slightly. She'd heard bits and pieces from Blackett and Miss Winthrop, and Nora had said her father couldn't work because all the dockers were out in sympathy with the seamen and no matter how hard up he was, he was no strike-breaker. Strike-breakers were 'scabs', as Nora had explained to her.

The conversation ceased as Blackett, assisted by Percy, brought up the trunks and bags. After they'd gone, Leah sat on the bed.

'Did you buy anything?'

Rhian seemed to become more like her old self again. 'Oh, lots of things and Ernest bought me the most gorgeous gold necklace and earrings worked in a Florentine design.'

They were young sisters again, chatting excitedly.

Ernest ate only a very light lunch and then went straight to the company offices and yard that were adjacent to the Collingood Dock.

There were men standing at the gates with placards

that read 'SUPPORT THE SEAMEN'. They booed and jeered as Ernest drove through the gates. The yard was silent. Enormous mounds of coal were piled everywhere. There was no sign of the young lads who shovelled it into sacks or loaded up the freight trucks of the dock railway that ran beneath the overhead railway. The trucks were loaded with all kinds of things – pig iron, steel, scrap metal, rocks used for ballast – but mainly it was coal. Coal to feed the furnaces of the liners. The Cunard liners alone used a thousand tons of it a day. The carts were lined up, the horses all stabled, but there was not a single carter or coalheaver in sight.

Ernest took the steps up to his office two at a time. His four foremen stood in the outer office talking.

'What the hell's going on here, Neely, and just how long has it been going on?'

Edward Neely took a deep breath. 'They walked out in support of the seamen, as have the dockers. We tried to reason with them, Mr Armstrong, but it was no use. The seamen's strike is unofficial. Sexton and their own union leaders have condemned them. No one can reason with them.'

'Didn't it enter your head to hire other men? Half the city is out of work, living in poverty in the slums!'

Charlie Tiptree shook his head slowly. 'We did consider it, sir, but for one thing they'd have no experience hitching up and loading up and for another it might well have caused more trouble.'

'What do you mean, more trouble? What's going on out there *is* trouble. It's more than trouble, it's anarchy!'

'Our own men might well have tried to stop them coming in. There would have been fights, the police would have been called,' Tiptree said grimly.

'So? Isn't that what they're paid for? To deal with fights and affrays?'

Jim Billington spoke up. 'Sir, it might be best if we leave it for a day or so. I've heard a rumour that Mr Alfred Booth, chairman of Cunard, is trying to talk the seamen into going back. If he succeeds, everyone else will go back too, without causing bad feeling and more trouble.'

Ernest could see the sense in this, angry though he was. Just who the hell did these men think they were? What did they want this time? A pension from the company as well as the government? They got that pension by causing uproar in Parliament, tearing the government apart and causing an election. And now they were at it again. Ernest ground his teeth. 'Well, what are you standing there for?' he snapped.

The four men looked at him, puzzled.

'Get your jackets off, roll your sleeves up and start to get at least one of those trucks loaded. The contract with Cunard is our life blood, our bread and butter. If we lose it then you could well lose your jobs. I know their damned ships are laid up like everyone else's, but at least when the strike is over the stuff should be available for them to start coaling.'

With faces like thunder, all four stripped off their jackets and rolled up their sleeves, leaving their bowler hats beside their jackets. It wasn't their place to do manual work. It was bloody humiliating. When the men and lads who worked under them got to hear of this – and they would, the pickets on the gate would make sure of it – they'd probably come down to gloat and jeer. The foremen were all furious but they had no option, unless they wanted to join the ranks of the unemployed. A foreman who walked out like his underlings would be a marked man. He'd never work again.

When Edward Neely reached home he was exhausted,

red-faced, sweating and filthy dirty. His journey on the tram had been a nightmare, so much so that had he not been so tired he would have got off and walked the rest of the way. The remarks from the passengers had been too much to bear. He hadn't answered them. He'd stared straight ahead but he'd removed his bowler and hidden it under his jacket.

'Edward! What happened?' Ethna cried, her hand going to her throat, thinking he had been in some kind of accident.

'Never mind what bloody happened, Ethna. Get some hot water on. I want a bath, a meal and a drink, in that order, and I don't want to hear any of your yammering about what your da's doing or what her next door said today. I just want some peace and quiet. Now get that water on to heat!'

Declan had seen him come up the path and with a quick word of farewell to his sister had slipped out the back. Old misery guts looked as though he'd been in a fight although there was no sign of any blood.

As Ethna lifted down the metal tub from the yard wall, she sighed heavily. She'd been dying for him to come home. She'd been so excited all afternoon when she'd realised she'd missed her period. She was as regular as clockwork and always had been, she could almost time it to the hour, so she *knew* she was pregnant. All those awful nights had been worth it. She was going to have a baby and she was delighted – or she had been. She knew that she couldn't tell him tonight and tears of disappointment welled up in her eyes. She had to tell someone. Nora! She'd go up and see Nora for a few minutes, he couldn't object to that. She'd say it was to let him relax, in peace and quiet.

It wasn't as easy to go out as she'd anticipated. He was in a foul temper. Nothing was right. The water in the

56

bath was too hot, there was a draught coming in under the door. His meal was not cooked to his liking and the jug of ale that she'd run down to the pub on the corner to get was too warm. When she finally got out, she was in tears. At least she had her tram fare and it was a lovely summer evening.

As she walked up Prince's Avenue she looked about her in awe, just as Nora had done. Imagine living in a house like this!

Her knock on the back door was opened by a plump, red-faced, middle-aged woman.

'Can I see my sister, please? I won't keep her long.'

'Who are you?' the woman demanded.

'Ethna Neely, Nora's sister.'

'Wait there.'

The woman disappeared and Ethna stood looking across the small piece of land not occupied by buildings. There were trees and shrubs, but there were also flowers.

Nora was alarmed to hear her sister was standing on the back step and ran to the door.

'Ethna! What's the matter? Is it Da? Is it our Declan?'

'No. No, there's nothing wrong. I . . . I just came to see you. Visit you.'

'Well, come in. They're all great here really, even though they look a bit stern.'

Ethna looked down the small corridor that opened into the big kitchen and was intimidated. She shook her head. 'I . . . there's something I want to say and . . .'

'All right. We'll sit out here on those upturned buckets. It's a warm night. So, what is it that's brought you all the way out here then?'

'I just had to tell someone and Edward has been in such a terrible mood since he got home. Mr Armstrong made the foremen shovel coal into the railway trucks.'

'Never!'

'Well, they don't want to lose any contracts and the men are on strike.'

'How can they lose contracts when the ships are tied up? I can see why Edward had such a cob on though. It mustn't half have dented his dignity.'

'It did. He took his hat off on the tram and hid it under his coat and you know how proudly he wears it.'

Nora burst into laughter.

Ethna looked at her sister. She'd filled out, the neat black dress suited her and she had lost some of the very broad Liverpudlian twang.

'Mind you, Mr Armstrong only got home from his honeymoon today and then went scarpering off down to the yard. He came home in a foul temper too. Miss Leah says her sister said she feels as if she's walking on broken glass, Mr Ernest's that touchy. Let's hope it all gets sorted out soon.'

'You've settled in well here, haven't you?' There was a trace of envy in Ethna's voice that Nora didn't miss.

'I have and I haven't. I mean I don't know what the mistress or the master are like to work for, although I've a good idea that he doesn't like me. So I suppose I'll have to wait and see how it goes. But it's so lovely, Ethna. Oh, the furniture, the curtains, the linen, the carpets, the crystal and china. It's a real joy to have everything so clean and sparkling. Miss Leah laughs at me when I say I love cleaning. Oh, Ethna, you should see Miss Leah's clothes. She's got hundreds of dresses! She's really nice. I think she's a bit lonely, she doesn't seem to have any friends. She once told me that every single girl she knew had a screw loose. They spent all their time dressing themselves up, hoping to catch a man's eye, and when they did they just giggled and acted as though they'd been let out of the asylum for the day. She said she's not carrying on like that for the benefit of any man and she's not running after anyone. With her looks I don't think she'll have to make much of an effort. I think she's had an offer already but turned him down. I heard Cook and Mrs Thomas talking one day. But she's lovely to work for and she's given me two dresses and a hat. I've unpicked all the trimming off the dresses and some of the ribbons on the hat, they were too fancy for a servant to wear.'

'I . . . I . . . came to tell you something, Nora.'

Nora looked at her closely, praying it wasn't the fact that she had discovered that being married to misery guts was terrible and now she wanted to leave him and go back to Oil Street. 'What?'

'I've missed the curse.'

'For how long?'

'Just the month, but you know me, as regular as clockwork and I've been feeling a bit off, but I put it down to the heat.'

'If *you've* missed one, you must be expecting. Have you told him?'

'I was going to tonight, but every time I opened my mouth I got my head bitten off!'

'Wait a while. I bet he'll be made up, really made up. Are you?'

'I think so.'

'You only think so? Da will be over the moon!'

'I can't tell Da yet, not before I've told my husband.'

'Well, whenever you tell him, he'll be delighted. And me an aunty!' Nora hugged Ethna close and felt the bones of her rib cage. She certainly hadn't put on any weight. She didn't seem to be faring much better despite her step up in life. Neely obviously didn't give her enough money to keep a good table.

'You'll have to take care of yourself now. Eat more, for a start.'

They both looked up as Leah came round the corner from the garden where she'd been reading. She'd left Rhian recovering, a hand towel soaked in eau de cologne across her forehead, the curtains closed. Ernest had taken a very light supper and then closeted himself in the study. Anyone foolish enough to speak to him got a look that would kill for their trouble.

'Hello, who's your visitor, Nora? Why are you sitting on buckets? You should have taken her in the house.'

Nora and Ethna got up.

'It's my sister, Ethna, Miss Leah. She wanted to tell me something, well,' she struggled to find the word.

'Confidential?' Leah suggested.

'That's it.'

Leah smiled and held out her hand to Ethna. 'I'm Leah Cavendish, it's nice to meet you.'

Ethna took the hand with the soft white skin. 'I'm Ethna Neely, miss. My husband Edward is a foreman at Cavendish's.'

'Ethna came to see me because he's like a bear with a sore head over the strike,' Nora explained.

Leah raised her eyes to the misty and slowly darkening sky. 'Oh, don't remind me. Rhian's gone to bed claiming travel fatigue and no one dare look sideways let alone open their mouth to Ernest.'

Ethna felt awkward. 'Well, I'd best get back home.'

'You must come and see Nora as often as you like,' Leah said firmly.

Ethna smiled her thanks, hugged Nora and then made her way towards the path.

'She looks about as happy as Rhian does. They were married on the same day, weren't they?'

Nora nodded. 'He's old enough to be her da and now she's, well, she's expecting. That's what she came to tell me.'

'After a month? How does she know?'

'We always used to say we could set the time and day of the month by our Ethna's . . . curse. I'm just wondering how he'll take it.'

Leah looked at her quizzically. 'And I'm just wondering if Rhian's travel fatigue is really something else.'

'God, wouldn't that be a coincidence! Married on the same day and – oh, I'm sorry, miss. I forgot I shouldn't speak like that to you.'

Leah laughed. 'Don't be, Nora. I look on you as a friend not as a servant. Do you really think Rhian could be in the same condition?'

Nora smiled. 'It's been known.' She felt happy for Ethna but even happier that Leah Cavendish had said she considered her to be more than a servant.

Chapter Five

Two weeks before Christmas, Ernest, looking like the cat that had got the cream, announced pompously to the staff that his wife was pregnant. Everyone was delighted.

'I'll be an aunt, just like you'll be,' Leah laughed. They were dressing the huge Christmas tree that stood in the hall.

Nora handled each ornament, each bauble, very carefully. The gold and red and silver decorations caught the light from the chandelier; she'd never seen anything so lovely, she told Leah.

'Did you never have a tree at home?'

Nora shook her head. 'Sometimes we would go and see the one in Church Street but we were lucky if we got an orange, a new penny and a penny toy in our stockings. Sometimes Da could only manage the shiny new penny. Ethna always knew. She'd say, "There's no point in hanging up stockings, it's not our turn this year."' Nora sat back on her heels as she remembered all those other Christmases. Well, this year things would be different.

'Poor Da, he'd try so hard to get jobbed, specially near Christmas. He'd fight and shout and jostle on the stands for night work. It paid twelve shillings and you knew it was for a whole week, not just a half day here and there. But he was getting older and they usually picked the young fellers.'

Leah looked at her with compassion in her eyes. How little she knew of the world, the *real* world outside these walls. She only ever went into town to shop and that was by car and confined to Bold Street, which people said compared favourably with Bond Street in London. She had been showered with every luxury all her life. Nora and Ethna had had to scratch enough money to live from day to day all their lives and she was sure that often they'd gone to bed cold and hungry. The word 'hungry' broke her train of thought.

'Oh, Nora, I nearly forgot. Will you take Aunt Poppy's tea tray up?'

Nora got to her feet and stood for a minute looking at the tree. This would be the first *real* Christmas she'd ever had.

She knocked but there was no reply, so she knocked again and opened the door. Her mouth dropped open at the scene before her.

Poppy Cavendish was sitting in a chair facing her writing desk which had been turned round to face the picture of Queen Victoria that hung on the wall. On the top of the desk lay a pile of letters and a sepia photograph of a young man in uniform, but it was not a uniform Nora recognised. What startled her most was the fact that Poppy Cavendish was dressed in a crinoline gown of blue organza, looped up and decorated with bows of white ribbon. The crinoline had gone out of fashion years and years ago and the dress was so girlish and frivolous it looked preposterous on a woman of seventy. Miss Cavendish also wore a diamond and sapphire necklace with matching earrings and bracelet. The bracelet was worn over long white gloves. The old woman looked bizarre.

Nora put down the tray but Miss Cavendish didn't

seem to have noticed her. Nora touched her gently on the arm.

Poppy looked up; she was perfectly calm and rational but her eyes were full of tears. 'You think I'm mad, don't you, girl?'

'I would never think of you like that, Miss Cavendish. Never. You've been so good to me.'

Poppy took Nora's hand. 'I wear this dress when the mood takes me. When I think back and feel cast-down,' she paused. 'He was handsome, dashing, filled with a zest for life and I loved him so much.' Her tone changed. 'And I'll never forgive that bitter old harridan! She had a lot to answer for. She led him and so many others to believe that we were going to help, to join in their war! Even the *Alabama* was built by Cammel Laird for the Confederate navy.'

Nora was mystified, her eyes fixed on the old lady's face. It was twisted with hatred mingled with sorrow. 'You mean the old Queen?'

Poppy nodded.

'But . . . but which war?'

'A war over long before you were born, although your father would remember. The war between the Confederate and Union States, in America. North against South. A civil war, the worst kind there is, brother against brother, father against son.' She picked up the photograph. 'I begged him to wait. To see if plans were really going ahead, but no, this was the big adventure, this was what life was really about, he said. There was something in his nature that was restless. So very restless.'

Nora was now kneeling beside the chair, her hand held tightly in that of Poppy's.

'And what happened?' she asked timidly.

'He was lucky at first.' The fingers of Poppy's other

65

hand rested lightly on the envelopes and letters discoloured by age. 'But then there was a huge battle at a place called Gettysburg and he was killed. They buried him there and it wasn't even his country or his war. These are all I have left.' She fingered the locket but didn't open it. 'Memories, letters, a photograph. This dress was his favourite. My Alice Blue Gown he called it.' Her expression had softened while she had been speaking but it became hard as she looked again at the picture on the wall.

'And she let them go, knowing there would be no help coming from this country or its Empire. Some say she was ready to sign the Declaration of War but Prince Albert stopped her. What kind of a Queen was she? *She* was the ruler of this Empire, not *him*. Callousness and arrogance are the characteristics of the House of Saxe-Coburg-Gotha. They let the poor people who worked in the cotton mills starve to death because there was no raw cotton coming into Liverpool. She let the Irish starve and die in their hundreds of thousands when the potato crop failed and yet they and everyone in the Empire reveres her memory! There's hardly a town in the country that doesn't have a statue of her but I hate her! Does that shock you, child?'

Nora shook her head. 'I . . . I . . . never knew, Ma'am. The likes of us were too busy trying to stay alive. So you never . . .'

'I never married, child. There wasn't a man who could fill his place in my heart.' She smiled sadly. 'When you fall in love, Nora, and you will, you'll know what I mean.' She suddenly shook off the mood of melancholy. 'Now, will you help me take off this ridiculous dress? How we ever managed to breathe, let alone dance, in these things I don't know.'

When Nora left, she paused for a minute on the landing.

It was so sad. So very sad. How beautiful Miss Poppy must have looked all those years ago, running lightly down this very staircase, the organza dress fresh and unfaded floating around her, the light from the chandelier catching her jewels and making them sparkle. She must be so lonely. She'd ask Da about that war. She'd never heard anyone mention it before. She remembered the Boer War, it ended nine years ago, and people talked about the Crimean War, but not that one in America.

'Put that tray down and go and supervise that useless lad who has brought the coal,' Cook snapped at Nora as she entered the kitchen.

'Where's Blackett and Percy?' she asked.

'Blackett's on an errand for the master and it's Percy's afternoon off. It's yours tomorrow, so make yourself useful today. You've been upstairs for hours.'

Nora didn't answer. The coal, the best anthracite, was delivered once a fortnight. It was stored in one of the disused outhouses in the stable yard. Without much grace, she snatched up a shawl that belonged to Mrs Thomas and let herself out of the back door.

A strong blustery wind shook the skeletal branches of the trees and shrubs, and a few dry, brittle leaves that had escaped Percy's attentions with the broom twisted and turned like tiny dervishes. She walked over to the outhouse but there was no sign of the carter. She waited, pulling the shawl closer, until at last through the back gate he came, shoulders and head bent beneath his burden. With a quick, expert twist he upended the sack and shook out the coal.

'That's the second,' he informed her with a grin.

She couldn't help but grin back. He was only young, and his eyes were hazel but because his cap was pulled well down she couldn't see what colour his hair was. His face was covered with coal dust and his clothes were impregnated with it.

'How many are there to come?'

'Another twelve.'

'*Twelve*?'

'This isn't much. Usually it's thirty-five tons a week a coal carter shifts, up and down stairs, too, most of the time.'

He disappeared down the path again. Thirty-five tons a week! She wondered how much he was paid for that. Out in all weathers, too, with only sacking pinned round his shoulders to keep out the weather.

'I haven't seen you before,' he said, tipping the next sack.

'And I haven't seen you, but then it's usually Blackett who does this job.'

'Where is the lazy old geezer?'

'Gone on a message for Mr Armstrong.'

His expression changed. 'It must be dead nice to be waited on hand and foot.'

'I wouldn't know. I do the waiting on bit, amongst other things.'

He smiled at her and she smiled back.

'What's your name?'

'Nora. Nora O'Brian. What's yours?'

'Pat Ryan. How old are you?'

'Mind your own flaming business!'

'I only asked. There's no need to go off the deep end. I'm twenty-four.'

She liked him. There was something about him, about the way he made her feel, that she couldn't really describe, yet she felt comfortable with him.

'If you must know I'm twenty and I've been here since summer. Before that I worked in factories and lived in Oil Street with me da, who's a docker, our Declan, who's a holy terror, and until May our Ethna. She's married to a foreman at Cavendish's. Edward Neely's his name. Mam died when I was ten. There, that's my life history. Are you satisfied?'

'Is your da's name Joe? Joe O'Brian?'

She nodded.

'I know him – well, I know of him. The only docker in the 'Pool who never takes a drink and who has read the works of all the famous writers. He's much respected for that, I can tell you. Fellers often go to him for advice. He's better educated than bloody Neely, Tiptree, Billington and Masterson put together. It's your da who should be up in the office, not those four fools. That Masterson hardly opens his mouth at all. When I first started I thought he was dumb.'

During the unloading they held a rather fractured, stilted conversation, for it was cold and getting dark. Nora went in and made a quick pot of tea. She poured out two mugs and handed him one. He was nearly finished now.

'I'll have to make sure old Tom's rheumatics don't have him back at work too soon,' he laughed good-naturedly as he took the tea.

'Oh, don't you usually bring the coal then?' There was a note of disappointment in her voice that he didn't fail to notice.

'No. Tom's off bad, he's getting too old now to be up and down stairs, so they give him the easy runs. I'll say that about Billington, he's got a bit of sympathy in him, unlike the others. I don't envy your sister.'

Nora pulled a face. 'Neither do I. Old misery guts we call him – not when she's there, like.'

He handed her the mug, his dirty fingerprints showing clearly against the white glaze. 'Ta, that was great.'

They looked at each other in silence then he spoke.

'Will you think me very forward if I ask you to come out with me, next time you're off, like?'

Nora's cheeks blushed prettily. 'No, and I'm off tomorrow, but only for the afternoon.'

'What about Saturday night then or even Sunday night?'

'Wednesday afternoon is all the time I get off. And it's only once a month.'

He was incredulous. 'Once a *month*? You've got to be kidding me.'

'I'm not. I told you, when I came here I'd only worked in factories, so I'm not trained, properly, like.'

'I thought they did away with slavery a couple of hundred years ago.'

'I don't mind, really I don't.' She hadn't, until now.

'I'll see if I can get someone to swap shifts or maybe just an hour or so. Will I call for you? We could walk in the park if it's not too cold.'

She nodded. Darkness had descended and all she could see of him now were the whites of his eyes and his teeth as he smiled at her.

'I might be late.'

'I won't mind. I'll wait.' She returned his wave as he walked away.

'I didn't intend you to stay out gabbing to him, taking him tea!' Cook was flustered.

'It was so cold and he had to make fourteen trips.'

'He's young and fit and lucky to have a job at all. Miss Leah's been looking for you. I swear if she comes in one more time and pokes her finger into this cake mixture I'll give in me notice. She used to do it as a little girl and I didn't mind, but now she's more of a hindrance than a help, under me feet all the time,' she grumbled.

'She told me that you taught her and the mistress how to cook.'

Cook paused in her task and smiled, a faraway look in her eyes. 'I did. Nothing fancy, but the mistress wanted them to be able to run a household, to fend for themselves, should they ever need to. God rest her soul, she was a wonderful woman.'

Nora left her to her memories and went in search of Leah. She found her sitting staring out of her bedroom window into the vast dark sky which looked as though someone had thrown a handful of glitter across it. The stars were very bright.

'You wanted me, miss.'

Leah turned, her eyes dancing, her expression eager. 'He asked you out, didn't he?'

'How do you know?'

'I was watching you. I was sitting here on the window seat. Anyone could see he liked you, Nora, right from the first minute he set eyes on you.'

Nora became bashful. 'Do you really think he does? I did like him even though I don't really know what he looks like under all that muck.'

'Handsome, I'd say.'

'He's wiry but very fit. He told me this was an easy house, the usual man's off. He humps over thirty-five tons of coal a week! Can you imagine it, Miss Leah, and up and down stairs too.'

'What's his name?'

'Pat, Patrick I suppose, Ryan.'

'And did you accept his invitation?' Leah was eager.

'I did, sort of.'

'How, sort of?'

'Well, he'll have to change his shift or get someone to swap a few hours with him.'

Leah saw the situation plainly. How on earth was Nora

71

going to go on seeing this Pat Ryan, if she wanted to, if she only had one afternoon a month off? She thought it was awful but Rhian refused to discuss it.

'He can't keep doing that.'

'I know, miss.' Nora's voice was forlorn.

Leah drew her knees up to her chin, an expression of deep thoughtfulness on her face. 'You could say your father or your sister's not well and that you'd like to see them for a couple of hours a night.'

'How could I tell lies like that? It's tempting fate.'

'Don't be superstitious. How else are you going to get out? I'll cover for you, afternoon or evening. They won't suspect me. It's getting near Christmas, too, so you're entitled to see more of your family.'

Nora bit her lip, unconvinced. Miss Leah made it all sound so easy.

'I'll see how it goes tomorrow, miss. If he can't get away then . . .'

'Then I'll tell my dear sister that you'd like to visit your sister, with her being due in February. Surely she can't refuse that, being in the same state herself.'

She waited nearly all afternoon for him. She had dressed with care, wearing the russet-coloured coat she'd bought in Blacklers over a brown skirt and soft cream wool blouse Leah had given her. Her boots were of shiny black leather and she wore a brown felt hat with a black velvet ribbon round it.

The winter afternoon was already drawing to a close, she thought miserably. It would be too late to walk in the park. He can't have been able to find anyone to swap even a few hours with him. She turned away from the scullery window and was about to take off her coat when she heard the side gate squeak and her heart leapt. She opened the door to the corridor and then she was out in the yard.

She hardly recognised him. He was tall and quite handsome with a fresh complexion, hazel eyes and light brown curly hair. He was wearing a tweed jacket over dark trousers and his cap was pushed back, but he had no warm overcoat. Just a muffler round his neck.

'I'm sorry, Nora, I really am. I couldn't get away. Devlin was going to come in for a few hours and take my place, but then they gave me a load to take right across the city.'

'It doesn't matter. Did you take your clothes to work?' she asked as he held the gate open for her.

'No, I went back to change and get a good scrub down first.'

'Where's home?'

He shrugged. 'I don't have one. Not like most people have anyway. I live in a boarding house in Lightbody Street with a couple of Irish lads over here for work. My mother died having me and my da drank himself to death eventually. I sort of fended for myself after that. I was twelve then but I said I was fourteen. I did all kinds of bits of jobs until I got taken on by Cavendish's. Casual at first but steady now. Own horse and cart.'

'What's its name?'

'The horse?'

She laughed up at him, her face glowing, her eyes sparkling. 'Well, I didn't mean the flaming cart!'

'Aley.'

'Aley?'

'Aye, because it won't flaming well pass an alehouse. She was old Fred Watkins' horse before he took bad an' died, God rest him, and I have a terrible time with her. Stubborn as a mule and you know how many pubs there are in this city.'

Nora laughed with delight.

'I admit it has its funny side but it's not half maddening

73

when you've loads to deliver on time. Mind you, she knows when the last load's gone. I have a hard job to hold her then. It's her oats and her stable she's thinking of then. I have a horror that one day she's going to get it into her head that she's running in the Grand National. God help us all if she does.'

Nora couldn't restrain her laughter at the picture his words conjured up in her mind.

The park keeper was just fastening the gates and Nora's face fell.

'Sorry, miss, we close them up at half past four in winter.'

'Never mind, there's a bench over there.' Pat pointed out a wooden bench of the type usually found in gardens. It bore a brass plaque but it was too murky to read the inscription.

'Probably in memory of someone's wife or husband,' Nora said, running a finger over it which left a mark on its damp surface.

'I might be luckier next time. If I give the lads plenty of notice, they'll swap. No one really cares, as long as the deliveries are made on time.'

'Miss Leah suggested I should say I want to go and visit my sister or my da. Our Ethna's expecting and it *is* getting nearer Christmas and I would like to see Da. She said she'd cover for me. She said they wouldn't suspect her of lying. And I did tell them at home, that there might be the odd time I might have to stay on.'

'Then she's a rare one all right,' Pat said. He longed to reach out and touch Nora's hand. She looked so pretty, so neat and tidy. So small, too; it made him feel protective of her.

'She is. From the first day she's been so good, so kind to me. We have the same date, the twenty-fourth, for our birthdays. Mine's October, hers is November. We're more like friends than servant and mistress.'

Pat frowned. 'I wouldn't put too much faith in that. If you upset her or do anything she doesn't like, she'll turn on you, like the rest of them. She's a Cavendish which means she's always going to have the upper hand. When it boils down to it, Nora, she is the mistress and you are the servant.'

'Mr Armstrong isn't a Cavendish. I didn't know the old master and mistress, they were killed in a car accident, but Miss Leah and Miss Poppy Cavendish have treated me well.'

'Is she still alive then, the old one? I thought she'd kicked the bucket years ago.'

'She hasn't and I don't think she will for a long time yet either. Miss Leah says Ernest, Mr Armstrong, thinks he's in charge, but really it's Miss Poppy.'

She told him how she'd found Poppy Cavendish dressed in the old-fashioned crinoline.

'She's cracked.'

Nora turned on him. 'No, she's not. She was just remembering him. She said when I found my one true love I'd wait for ever for him. It's so sad. She must have been beautiful when she was young and she never got married.'

'They're all lovely, those who have the money. With nice clothes and jewels and no worries, even the plainest would look good.'

Nora gave a little sigh. 'I suppose you're right. Do you know, Miss Poppy has a picture of Queen Victoria in her room.'

'Oh aye, she would.'

'No. She hates her. She has it there to curse at. I've heard her. Can you believe that? She blames her for the death of her young man. For making people think we were going to send help and fight alongside American soldiers. Con . . . Con . . .' she struggled to remember the word. 'Confederate soldiers,' she said triumphantly.

'You shouldn't interfere in other people's wars.' He sounded stern and forbidding.

'She let the mill workers starve because there was no cotton coming in and Miss Poppy said she let the Irish die too in the famine.'

'In that case Miss Poppy Cavendish would get on well with a lad I board with, Sean Maguire. He's always on about the poor and the downtrodden.'

Nora looked up at him thoughtfully. 'But he's right though, isn't he, Pat? We *are* downtrodden. Sometimes Da could only just manage to scrape the three and six rent and we lived on bread and cups of tea. We went barefoot and ragged and often there was no money for coal or wood for a fire. That's how Mam died, of pneumonia. Now at least our Ethna's settled and I give Da most of my wages. I don't need much. I get plenty of good food. I have a nice, clean room up in the attic with plenty of blankets and a quilt on the bed. It's like paradise.'

He couldn't help himself, he reached across and took her hand. 'You're a loving, thoughtful girl, Nora O'Brian. There's many who would think themselves well out of a slum house and hang on to the money to spend on themselves.'

She was glad it was dark for her cheeks were burning and the sensation that she was feeling as his fingers twined in hers was making her a little light-headed.

'I think . . . I'd best get back.'

They both stood and walked slowly back down the avenue. At the side gate they paused.

'When will I see you again, Nora?'

She thought hard. 'Sunday afternoon? It's always quiet

on Sundays and after a big lunch, they only have a light tea at about six o'clock.'

He smiled down at her. 'Then I'll wait for you on the corner of Mulgrove Street and Prince's Avenue and we'll have the whole afternoon together.'

Ducking her head to hide her flushed cheeks and sparkling eyes, she nodded. 'The corner of Mulgrove Street at half past two?'

He smiled at her. 'At half past two.'

Chapter Six

A February gale was sweeping upriver from the sea, bearing on it white flecks of snow. Everyone on the tram was muffled up to the eyes against it, but none were of such a broad girth as Ethna. She had only weeks to go now and she had begged and pleaded with Edward to accompany her to Prince's Avenue. She'd received firm, unequivocal replies.

'He's your brother. It's your father's duty to see he attends school. And if Declan skives off school then it's your da who will go to jail. You know that and so does Declan.'

In vain she'd pleaded that Da had to work.

'He gets money from your Nora, you told me that yourself.'

Oh, how she wished she'd never opened her mouth about Nora's contributions to either Da or Declan.

'And you can see how stupid an act it was to give that young thug a shilling a month pocket money.'

'He's *not* a thug! He's *not*! He's easily led,' she'd cried, but it had been no use and so she had put on her heavy coat, then a shawl, tied a large headscarf round her head and walked ponderously to the tram stop.

''Ere, missus, yer shouldn't be out on a night like this in your state. Give us yer hand, luv.' The conductor got off the tram and signalled for the driver to wait while he assisted her.

When she reached her stop she hauled herself up.

''Ave yer got far ter go now?' the conductor asked.

She shook her head. 'No, not far. Just to see me sister, she's in service up there.'

He peered into the blustery darkness. Large flakes of snow swirled round the street lamps like moths did in summer. He got back on the platform.

'Just 'ang on 'ere a mo, will yer, till I see 'er up the street.'

There were no dissenting remarks or shouts.

'God luv 'er. She shouldn't be out on 'er own on a night like this,' one woman commented to her neighbour.

'What kind of a feller is it that would let 'er come out in the first bloody place?' a man asked grimly.

When Ethna had reached the back door, she leaned against it heavily while the conductor hammered loudly on it.

'What the 'ell do yer think yer playin' at?' Blackett yelled, then his voice changed as he saw Ethna. 'Oh, God Almighty. Nora! Nora, come 'ere quick!'

Nora appeared in the corridor behind him and when she saw her sister she screamed.

'On the tram she was, miss, on 'er own. It's treacherous on foot so I brung 'er along meself.'

'Ethna! Ethna, what's wrong? Is it the baby?'

'No.' Ethna was almost on the verge of collapse.

'Blackett, have you any money on you?' Nora asked. He nodded.

'Then give this man some for his trouble.' She now had her sister's arm round her neck to support her.

'No need fer that, luv. I've left a tram full of people, they'll skin me alive if I don't get back soon. Either that or they'll have gone off with the bloody tram themselves!'

Both Cook and Miss Winthrop had come to Nora's aid. They got Ethna into an armchair, after taking off her coat and scarf. Cook was already heating some milk. 'Hot milk with a bit of cinnamon, it always works a treat.'

Nora held Ethna to her. 'In the name of God and His Holy Mother, what's wrong, Ethna? Has he belted you? Has he thrown you out? Is it Da?'

Ethna was shaking her head.

'Give her a chance to recover, Nora,' Miss Winthrop said sharply, glancing at Cook who nodded her understanding. She went off to find Percy to instruct him to be ready to run to Prince's Nursing Home for help if needed.

'It's Declan,' Ethna at last managed to get out, her breathing more even. The warm spiced milk and the heat of the fire were taking effect.

'What's he done? Is he hurt?'

'He's not hurt – yet. But Da's going to murder him!'

'What for?' Nora couldn't think of anything so bad that it would make Ethna drag herself all the way up here.

'He's been skiving off school. Him and Jimmy Murphy and Jackie Price. Da had the man from the School Board round and you know the law, Nora!' Ethna burst into floods of tears, the whole ordeal just too much for her.

Nora's eyes widened in horror. 'Oh, Holy Mother of God! The law's been! That means Da will have to go to jail! Da in jail! How many days did he skive off, Ethna?'

'Five. A week. Oh, God, Nora, I'm so mortified and Edward—'

'Oh, to hell with flaming Edward! It's me da! Me da will have to go to Walton for five days.' She looked around her. Percy looked stunned, as did Blackett, but Cook and Miss Winthrop were shaking their heads and making soft sympathetic noises.

'I should never have given him pocket money.'

'I don't know how long it would have gone on, Nora,

if Billy Stanton hadn't seen them down a back jigger and you know what a nosy interfering old sod he is. It must have been him who reported them. Declan always came in at the same time, as if he'd been to school. I . . . I . . . didn't know!'

'Hush, it's not your fault. Where's Da now and where's that flaming little monster?'

'Da dragged him off to see Father Finnegan, but it won't change anything. Da will have to go to jail. It's the law. He'll go before the magistrates next week and so will Mr Murphy and Mr Price.'

Nora nodded grimly. She was right. The law made parents responsible for their children's attendance at school. It was assumed that there would be someone at home to see the miscreants attended school. But mostly both parents had to work.

Rage was boiling up in Nora. How dare he! How *dare* he humiliate them all like this! She shrugged on her coat.

'Where are you going?' Cook asked.

'I'm going to give that little sod the hiding of his life! And there will be no pocket money ever again. Not a single farthing does he get out of me in future and what's more I'll ask Mrs Price to see him right into school with their Jackie, to show him up in front of his classmates. And then if the mistress and Miss Leah don't mind, I'll collect him and take him to your house, Ethna.'

Ethna nodded weakly, she didn't feel at all well.

'You've gone a terrible colour, luv,' Cook addressed Ethna who did look awful.

'It was all such an effort and I've got a pain in my back.' Her face contorted with agony.

Miss Winthrop took charge. 'Nora, get that coat off, you're staying here. Percy, get yourself along to the

82

nursing home as fast as you can, we need help, a midwife. Nora, you'd better go and tell the mistress what's going on. No, on second thoughts, not the mistress, tell Miss Leah.'

'But Da—'

'Will he thank you for leaving your sister at a time like this? Just to vent your anger on your brother who by now is probably wishing he'd never been born.'

Nora told Leah of the situation and they agreed that Ernest should be informed and advised that his own pregnant and nervous wife should be coaxed into going upstairs, as far away from the kitchen as possible. The heavy curtains were drawn over the doors. They were there to keep out the draughts but tonight it was hoped they would muffle the sound of Ethna's labour. Blackett was dispatched in the car to inform Mr Neely. When the midwife arrived with Percy, she ordered the big wooden kitchen table scrubbed with carbolic soap.

Cook was aghast. 'The table? My kitchen table?' she cried.

'It's the best possible thing. It will be scrubbed down with bleach afterwards and I have brought rubber sheets to cover it. We'll need plenty of old towels, linen and newspaper. Oh, and some cushions to prop her up.' She was icily calm amidst the confusion and Ethna's agonised screams.

Nora stayed at her sister's side, her hand crushed in her grip. She was fuming inside. She swore that after this Da would retire. He had had enough to put up with all his life. He'd done the best he could for all of them and that little fiend wasn't going to cause him another moment's worry. Edward bloody Neely could cough up ten shillings to add to the six pounds she gave him. Da hadn't been well lately and a week in prison could well break him, in mind and in body.

No, Da's working days were over. He could sit in his home, with a good fire in winter and read. He'd earned that much.

At three minutes past midnight, with Leah and Edward Neely sitting silently in the morning room, Blackett and Percy dispatched to bed, and surrounded by Nora, Cook, Miss Winthrop and the midwife, Ethna's agony was over. She had a son. A son with a healthy pair of lungs, as the midwife proclaimed. It was Miss Winthrop who cleaned the baby with olive oil and cotton wool. She did it so gently and so competently that Nora wondered if she had ever had one of her own but had had to part with it.

Nora brushed out Ethna's tangled hair while Cook and the midwife cleaned up.

'Oh, Ethna, he's gorgeous! He's dead gorgeous!' Nora felt elated.

Leah, hearing the thin protesting wail, was unable to contain herself and came in, followed by the new father.

'Oh, look at his tiny little fingers and toes,' she exclaimed, before remembering that she was blocking the father's view of his son. She moved aside.

Edward made no attempt to touch the baby until Ethna held him out and there was no other course but to take him from her. He did it awkwardly.

'What will you call him?' Leah asked smiling. So this was what Rhian's baby would look like, her nephew, if it was a boy.

'Alexander Joseph after Edward's father and Da.' The fear immediately came into Ethna's eyes. 'Da!'

'Hush now,' said the midwife. 'You can't possibly be moved until the morning.'

'There's a small spare bedroom on the first floor. We

could light a fire and put a hot water bottle in the bed,' Leah offered.

Miss Winthrop nodded and after the midwife departed, it was also agreed that Edward would sleep on the sofa in the study.

After all the commotion had died down, Ernest came downstairs. Rhian was sleeping peacefully. He shook hands and congratulated Edward, but there was no offer of the customary drink to 'wet the baby's head', Nora noticed. They were all exhausted and she wished Ernest had stayed upstairs with his wife.

He peered intently at the baby which was swaddled in a sheet and a thick towel.

'Must be a grand feeling, Neely, to have a son. An heir to carry on the name, if nothing else. Yes, very proud you must feel. I'm hoping that Rhian, Mrs Armstrong, will produce an heir too. Someone to run Cavendish's when I'm long gone.'

'But it won't be Cavendish's, will it, Ernest? It will be Armstrong's. That being the case, I hope and pray you have a daughter because she in turn will marry and then it won't be Armstrong's either.'

Everyone in the room turned and looked in amazement towards the door. Poppy Cavendish's gaze swept over them all, before she turned and closed the door behind her.

Nora shuddered. There had been real hatred in Miss Poppy's eyes. Sometimes she was so strange.

A week later, as Nora saw her da come through the small door set into the massive iron studded doors of Walton Jail, her heart sank. She could see in his face that the five days of incarceration had taken a harsh toll. She rushed to meet him, her arms open wide and he clasped her to him.

'Oh, Da. You don't at all look well.'

Joe managed a grin. 'Would you, luv, after a week in that place?'

'Look, Miss Leah has come with Blackett to take you home.'

Joe looked in astonishment at the car and shook his head. 'Nora, luv, I can't arrive in Oil Street in that.'

'Why not?'

'It's too grand for the likes of me.'

'Da, it wasn't you who did anything wrong! It was Declan, everyone knows that. They all sympathise with you and Mr Price and Mr Murphy.'

Again Joe shook his head.

'Well, at least let me drop you on the corner of Great Howard Street,' Leah said. The car had been her suggestion and it had caused a huge argument between her and Ernest.

'You want to take the car to meet a common jailbird?' he had asked incredulously.

'He did nothing wrong except work for a pittance to keep a roof over their heads! How could he make sure Declan went to school?' she said frostily.

'Well, you're not having it. I won't have my car being used as some sort of—'

'*Your* car?' Leah interrupted, her temper rising. 'Just whose money paid for it? Yours? Like hell it was, it was Rhian's money and mine, so don't go telling me what I can and can't do.'

He wagged a warning finger at her. 'Don't you ever speak to me like that again, do you hear me? You insolent chit!'

Leah's green eyes blazed and the slap could be heard echoing round the hall. Ernest staggered, his hand to his face where the red marks of her fingers were livid against his pale skin. Then his face turned puce and his mouth twisted into an ugly grimace. He raised his arm. Leah stood her ground defiantly, still shaking with anger, but before he could hit her Poppy's voice stopped him.

'Lay one hand on her and I'll call the police and have you arrested for common assault. You may think, Ernest Armstrong, if indeed you have enough brain cells for such a process, that you alone own this house and the business, but you don't and you never will. Half of it belongs to Leah, which means that since your excuse for buying that damned car in the first place was that it would be needed for company business, she is entitled to use it too.'

How long Poppy had been standing on the stairs neither of them knew. Ernest stormed off into the study and slammed the door so hard that the glass in the fanlight above the front door shook.

'I hit him.' Leah was still shaking.

'I saw you and although I cannot stand the man, I will not tolerate such brawls in this house. We still have standards, Leah, remember that. Do what you like with the car.' She had then turned and gone back upstairs.

Joe was eventually coaxed into the car. He sat twisting his gnarled, workworn hands together.

'I've been and lit the fire and Mrs Molloy has got bread and butter and sausage and other things, so you won't have to go out. Our Declan's at school and I can tell you, Da, he'll never skive off again.'

Reluctantly they dropped him off on the corner of Oil Street and Great Howard Street. Nora's heart ached for him. He seemed to have shrunk, his back and shoulders were bent, his head down. She'd railed against the system to Ethna each time she saw her. Ethna was concerned but she was totally occupied with the baby, much to Edward's annoyance.

Leah touched her on the arm. 'You shouldn't let this opportunity go to waste,' she whispered.

'What opportunity?' Nora whispered back.

'Well, they think you'll be with your father all afternoon. Can you get word to Pat? Could he arrange a few hours off?'

She and Pat had been 'courting' in secret for two months now and she loved him. She often thought about Miss Poppy's words about true love and she knew Pat Ryan was her true love.

'I don't know. Anyway, how am I going to get word to him?'

Leah leaned forward to speak to Blackett. 'Will you take us to the yard, Blackett, please?'

Nora's eyes widened. 'No! I can't speak to him there.'

'But I can.' Leah was enjoying herself.

Blackett looked just as anxious as Nora but they both remained silent until they pulled into the yard.

'Don't get out, miss, the air is full of coal dust. You'll be covered in it and your clothes will be ruined.'

'Then will you go and find someone for me, Blackett, please?'

He was wary, thinking of his own clothes and the car's upholstery. 'Who, miss?'

'Pat Ryan, and if he's not here then find out where he is.'

With great reluctance Blackett got out to ask the nearest man whose fully loaded cart was on the big weighing scales that were set into the floor of the yard. He pointed and then motioned to Pat.

'He's here!' Leah cried as Pat came over.

'Nora!' he exclaimed, gaping at her sitting in Ernest Armstrong's car.

'Miss Leah insisted we go and pick Da up and take him home. Can you . . . can you get any time off, do a swap even for an hour?' Her eyes pleaded with him. They saw so little of each other and she loved him so much.

88

'I can't, luv. I just can't.'

'Yes you can. I own half of this business and I want you to pick up a large box from the general post office in Victoria Street,' Leah announced.

'Can't Blackett go, miss? I'm filthy dirty.'

'Blackett is going to drive me home. He will also go up and see Ethna's husband and tell him I'm borrowing you for a couple of hours and that he will have to rearrange his schedules or dockets or tickets or whatever he calls them.'

Ernest had come out of his office. It was built on a gantry above where the carts were kept overnight. Only Neely and Tiptree were in the outer office. The other two foremen were in the yard.

'What the hell is my car doing here? Blackett is not supposed to be here for me until six.'

'I think we are about to find out, sir,' Tiptree said quietly as Blackett ascended the stairs. It was clear that he was very uneasy.

'Well?' Ernest barked at him.

'Miss Leah wants to borrow one of your men, sir. She's got a big parcel or box or something she wants collecting from the GPO in town.'

'Why can't you go?'

'She wants me to drive her home, now.'

Ernest felt the anger rising in him. How dare she come here, flaunting herself in the car that he knew the men looked on as his sole property. And laying down the law too. She could have sent word to the GPO and they'd have delivered it. In fact it would have been delivered as a matter of course, so what was she playing at?

'Which man?' he snapped.

Blackett looked out of the window, as did Neely. Pat was still standing by the car.

'Pat Ryan, sir.'

'Is he permanent or casual?'

'Permanent. A good worker, too, sir,' Tiptree put in.

'Even more reason why I shouldn't release him.'

Blackett cleared his throat and looked very pale and apprehensive. 'Miss Leah said she particularly wanted him as he will be quick. He won't dawdle and waste your time.'

'Did she indeed?' Ernest replied through gritted teeth. 'How very considerate of her.' That little madam was going to have to be taken down a peg or two, she was getting far too big for her boots. 'All right, Blackett, tell Miss Leah he can go, but he's to come straight back here and make up the time.'

They all looked at him questioningly. The whole thing was a tissue of lies, surely he could see that? Miss Leah Cavendish was up to something.

Ernest watched Pat Ryan cross the yard and get his jacket and cap. The car drove slowly through the gate. He looked at his watch, then at Ryan. He'd give the man ten minutes to get out of the gates, then he'd follow him.

Nora insisted on being dropped off at the bottom of King Edward Street.

'I'll get the tram home, miss. I can't thank you enough.'

'Go on, he'll not have much time, not if I know Ernest, he's not that stupid. It'll dawn on him that the imaginary parcel would be delivered anyway.' Leah smiled as the car drew away.

Nora walked briskly down Bath Street and it wasn't long before she saw him running up towards her. She ran to meet him.

'Is she mad?' Pat gasped.

'No. She's just kind and thoughtful. Come up this back jigger where we won't look so odd.'

'You brazen hussy, Nora O'Brian.' He laughed and let

90

her take his hand and pull him into a narrow passageway between the warehouses.

'You're going to get your coat covered in coal dust and your face and hands too. A nice cut you'll look on the tram going home.'

'I don't care.'

'Take your coat off.'

'What for?'

His eyes were dancing. 'Turn it inside out and put it back on again. Then any dirt will be on the inside. Of course your dress will get all mucky.'

'It'll wash.'

After she'd reversed her coat she slid her arms round his neck. It was a darkish passageway, no one would see them. 'Oh, Pat, I wish I could get more time off without having to tell lies all the time. Miss Leah's so good but I hate lying to Mrs Armstrong and Miss Poppy.'

He kissed her gently on the forehead. He had nothing to offer her. Nothing. Not even a decent roof over her head. A glorified dosshouse, that's where he lived. And it was 'men only', not that he would have taken her there.

'You could leave.'

She looked up at him. 'And do what? I couldn't go back into a factory now, not now, Pat.'

He sighed. 'I've nothing to offer you, Nora, but I do love you.'

'You've a steady job, that's more than my da ever had to offer my mam, God rest her.' She shivered as a cold blast found its way down the passageway and he drew her closer.

'I love you too, Pat, and one day, well, one day something good might happen.' Love and trust and longing shone from her eyes and he held her and kissed her, fighting back all the frustrations that crowded in on him – his longing for her, a place of their own with

91

good furniture and, in time, children and a better future for them.

Darkness was falling and the lamplighter had passed on down the road, whistling as he went about his task. Ernest Armstrong stood just outside the circle of feeble yellow light thrown out by the gas lamp. It was cold and a mist was creeping in from the sea, covering the river and the docks like a pall of smoke. Soon it would thicken into dense yellow fog and the mournful sound of the foghorns would be heard all night long, but there was still light enough to see and recognise the couple locked in an embrace. Nora O'Brian and Pat Ryan. Leah, bloody Leah, had set this up. She'd planned it and would lie to them all about it. Oh, she could act the innocent very well when it suited her. She was devious, a trait his own wife was, thankfully, devoid of. He touched his cheek, a gesture that reminded him of Leah's insolence, the slap and the way she had stood her ground, almost daring him to strike her. Had she known her aunt was on the landing? Very probably. Well, he'd put a stop to all this, once and for all, and he'd teach Miss Leah Cavendish a lesson into the bargain.

Chapter Seven

As soon as he returned, Ernest spoke to Neely who was sorting out the dockets to give to the men for the next day's work.

'How long has Pat Ryan been working here?'

Neely thought hard, rubbing his chin. 'About six years steady and two casual.'

The other three foremen exchanged glances. Ernest Armstrong's mouth was set in a tight, thin line and that always meant trouble.

'He's a good worker, sir. Not a day late or taken off sick while he's been here,' Billington said.

'Has he a family?'

'No, sir. He lives in a lodging house.'

'He's a union man. I saw the button in his jacket.'

'Aye, but they won that right from the deep-sea shipping lines last August. The right to wear them without being penalised.'

'And I seem to remember that the unions promised not to interfere with working practices, so there can be no comeback, no strike over this. Make up any money due to him and tell him to be off these premises in half an hour and never to come back!'

They were all flabbergasted, even though they knew what kind of a man their boss was, particularly Neely. He'd learned a lot from Ethna's bits of chat. Information passed on by Nora. Instant dismissal just for going on an errand for Mr Armstrong's sister-in-law was pushing it a bit.

Billington spoke up. 'It could have serious consequences, sir.'

'If you're threatening me with a bloody strike, you can follow him! You all can! I'll close the place down. You'll all be locked out!'

'There won't be any need for that, sir. Oh, the men will blow off for a day or so but it won't be bad. There'll be no strike, no need for a lock-out,' Neely said firmly. The other three glared at him before dropping their gaze and wondering what young Pat Ryan had really done. They'd probably never find out. The men certainly wouldn't tell them.

Neely was uneasy as he approached Pat who was heaving sacks of coal on to his cart. None of the foremen had wanted this task, but Neely had drawn the short straw.

He tapped Pat on the shoulder. 'Ryan, you're to leave the loading up. Get your jacket, cap and anything else that belongs to you and leave – now. Here's what's owing.' He held out the small brown envelope.

Pat looked at him blankly. 'What the hell have I done?'

Neely shrugged. 'How should I know? They're Mr Armstrong's orders. He also said if there's any trouble over it he'll lock everyone out.'

Pat took the envelope and turned away so Neely couldn't see the shock and anger in his eyes. He picked up his things and without a word to anyone walked out of the gate of Cavendish's for the last time.

When Ernest arrived home, much earlier than usual, Leah and Rhian were taking afternoon tea in the drawing room.

'Ernest! You're home early.' Rhian's eyes lit up and

she bent forward awkwardly towards the silver teapot on the low table before them.

'Leave it. I'll pour,' Leah instructed.

'You received your parcel then?' Ernest's tone was sarcastic.

Leah gazed at him steadily and nodded curtly.

'What parcel?' Rhian inquired.

'It's a secret. It's for you, dear, but not to be opened until the baby is born.' He smiled.

He was a damned good liar, Leah thought.

'Leah, I wonder if you would be so kind as to find Nora and ask her to remove the tray? I know I can ring for her, but I'd like a little time alone with Rhian.'

Leah felt uneasy but she went to look for Nora.

As soon as the door had closed, the pleasant, concerned look disappeared from Ernest's face.

'Rhian, my dear, we are going to have to get rid of Nora O'Brian.'

'Nora? Why?' Rhian was feeling tired, she usually had a rest in the afternoon and she didn't want to discuss Nora's behaviour now.

'Because she has been lying to us about visiting her father. She's not been home at all. She has been carrying on with one of my carters. A man by the name of Patrick Ryan. I saw them myself this very afternoon, up a narrow passageway between two warehouses, arms round each other's necks. No shame at all. And I'm sure Leah knows and has encouraged it.

'She came into the yard in the car this afternoon and I watched Blackett approach one of my men, who then called Ryan over to the car. Nora must have been in the car with Leah. Then she had the temerity to send Neely up to me to say she wanted to borrow Ryan to pick up an imaginary parcel, while Blackett drove her home. Rhian, we *cannot* keep people like that in this house. She must go. I don't want to upset you, dear, not now, but it is so unpleasant. You do understand? Before we know it there'll be illegitimate children.' He shook his head, his face full of mock sorrow.

Rhian didn't answer, she was trying to take it all in. Leah. Leah and Nora and this Ryan person. The baby kicked and she had a horrible thought. What if Nora was already pregnant by this man Ryan? Nora was so trusting. But Ernest was right. Nora would have to go. They had been more than generous to the girl by taking her on in the first place and her manners, speech and appearance had greatly improved. What had made her do this? Sneaking off to see men and heaven knows what else. They didn't really know the girl at all. Leah and Aunt Poppy had engaged her and she'd been horrified to learn that Nora had always worked in a factory.

Nora was a little nervous as she came in to collect the tray. Leah had been uneasy when she'd relayed the master's message.

'Did you meet your father then, Nora?' Ernest asked innocently.

'Yes, sir, and thank you for the use of the car.'

'I suppose you stayed to see him settled down? Cook something for him, do a bit of shopping?'

'I did, sir. I told him, too, that he's got to retire. He's too old now to be heaving stuff around at the docks. He's not too well. He's always been a porter, never a stevedore although he's got more brains than most of them.' The stevedores were in charge of the loading and unloading of ships and had a better rate of pay and more responsibility than porters.

Ernest's expression changed. 'Then you'll have to find another job to keep him and yourself.'

Nora looked at him blankly. 'I . . . I . . . don't understand, sir.'

'I will *not* employ staff who lie and cheat. You've been seeing Pat Ryan on the sly, using excuses and alibis, aided and abetted by my dear sister-in-law. Well, this afternoon I saw you both with my own eyes in an embrace in a public place. You've deceived us and after all we've done for you. I am most disappointed in you and my poor wife is distraught.' He took Rhian's hand and looked down at her with a concerned expression.

'Pack your things then collect your wages from the study and go back to the slum you came from. I'm sure you'll have no trouble getting work in a factory. I knew you were unsuitable the minute I saw you. I would never have engaged you in the first place. Now leave us.'

Nora's face was ashen with shock. She'd been sacked. Sacked! There would be no references, she'd never get another job like this and there'd be no money for Da's retirement.

She got to the top landing and sank down on the stair, sobbing. Everything had gone wrong, except her love for Pat. They wanted to get married. Surely Mr and Mrs Armstrong could understand why she wanted to spend more time with Pat.

It was Leah who found her. She'd heard the door to the drawing room close, then open as Ernest helped his wife to her room for a rest before dinner.

'Nora! What's wrong?'

Nora raised a tear-stained face. 'He saw us, Miss Leah. This afternoon. Pat and me and he's . . . he's sacked me! I'm to pack now and then collect my wages. Oh, God, what will I do? I won't have a reference, I'll never get another job like this and what about Da? I swore he would retire in comfort!' The sobs overtook her again and she covered her face with her hands.

Leah gathered Nora into her arms. Part of this was her fault. Nora had lied, but it was Ernest and Rhian's fault that she had to do it and she herself was a party to the deception. But that was no reason to throw Nora out on her ear and on the very day her father had been released from jail for something he hadn't done and had no control over. Slowly the rage began to burn inside Leah.

'Go up to your room and lie down. You will *not* be sacked!'

Nora raised her head, her eyes swimming with tears. 'Will . . . will you speak for me?'

'You know I will, Nora. Most of it is my fault anyway.'

They both stood up and Leah watched as Nora went slowly up the stairs to her attic room. Then Leah turned and went in search of Ernest. He was in the study and the sight of him sitting in her father's chair fuelled her anger. She left the door open. This was one argument she intended the whole household to hear.

'So, you've finally come to inform me of your part in this fiasco,' he said smugly, leaning back in his chair. 'Well, you've done her no favours, and Ryan neither, for that matter. I sacked him this afternoon when he returned from collecting your mythical parcel.'

Her eyes glinted dangerously. She never knew it was possible to hate someone so much. 'How dare you! How *dare* you sack Nora O'Brian! Aunt Poppy took her on. If there was any dismissing to be done then it should have be done by her, not you. Oh, I blame myself, I should have gone to Aunt Poppy about giving Nora more time off. She's such a godsend and all we give her is a few hours a month. We'd not get another girl so willing to work so hard for such a pittance! And she is her father's only support, he's not old enough for the government pension.'

'It's done. She deserved it, no matter whose task it was to dismiss her. Now, I've work to do.' He drew a sheaf of papers towards him.

Leah leaned across and snatched them out of his hands, tore them into pieces and flung them in his face.

'You don't own this house or the business. As Aunt Poppy reminded you, half is mine.'

His eyes were dark with anger and his lips set in a grim line. 'But not until you are twenty-one, Leah, and a lot can happen in a year! That girl goes!'

Leah was shaking with fury. He was right. Everything was held in trust until she was twenty-one and there were a million and one things he could do in a year.

'Then if she goes, I go!'

He was taken aback but fought hard not to show it. It was probably only a bluff anyway. 'Don't be so damned naive!' He met her defiant gaze. 'Very well. Go and live with her. Go and live in that slum. I give you two weeks and you'll be begging to be allowed back home.'

'I'll never beg for anything, Ernest Armstrong, and I'll come back to *my* home when I feel like it.' She knew if she stayed she would hit him, probably with the heavy alabaster ashtray which would cause a great deal more damage than the palm of her hand, so she turned and walked out into the hall.

She began to climb the stairs then stopped. She had no money to speak of. Not real coinage, pounds shillings and pence. She had an allowance paid by Aunt Poppy as executor of her father's will, but she only had five pounds in cash left from the last time she had gone to the bank.

He'd been right about one thing. From what she'd heard, Nora's home was a slum house. If she was going to live there, she'd need more money than her allowance to help make the place decent. She raised her chin defiantly and carried on up the stairs to her aunt's drawing room.

Poppy was reading, a lorgnette held in front of her. She didn't raise her eyes from the page but her eyebrows lifted a fraction. 'You've been rowing with Ernest again.'

99

'He's sacked Nora and he had no right to do that.'

Poppy snapped the book shut and lowered the lorgnette. 'Why did he?' Her eyes were cold, her expression grim.

'Because she has been seeing a young man who works for us. I should have asked you or Rhian about giving Nora more time off but we'd become so accustomed to her being here. It . . . it was as though we *owned* her. So she had to lie to get out to see him. Today Ernest saw them together and I'm afraid I arranged that meeting.'

The old lady tutted and shook her head.

'You, miss, should keep your nose out of other people's affairs! You have always been inclined to meddle, even when you were a child.'

'Oh, Aunt Poppy, don't let him do it, please.'

Poppy looked irritable. 'Leah, your sister is the mistress of this household.'

'No, she's not! You are! You are older. Rhian does whatever he tells her to do. Please don't let him send Nora away, she's more to me than just a servant. She's my friend.'

But instead of her irritability disappearing Poppy's expression turned grim.

'I know, child, and that in itself goes against the grain. You should choose your friends with care and from the same class as yourself.'

'But they're all awful! They're so stupid! Always prinking and preening and making idiotic remarks. Laughing and giggling at the drop of a hat. They're fools and I don't want them as friends.'

Poppy sighed, wondering what could be done.

'I reminded him that he didn't own everything and he reminded me that until I come of age I have to rely on him and that he could do a lot in a year. Sell off my shares, have me examined and pronounced unfit to cope, things like that, I suppose.'

Poppy's eyes narrowed. 'Oh, did he? Leave all that to me, Leah. I'm a match for him any day.'

'I told him that if Nora went, I'd go with her and I *will*!'

'Leah, you can't be serious. It's one thing to stand up to him and have the girl reinstated but to go and live with her – it's out of the question!'

Leah's eyes became hard. 'I still intend to go. I won't let him get the better of me. I *won't*!'

'You'll be doing the girl no favours by imposing on her. You'll embarrass the whole family.'

Leah refused to acknowledge her aunt's words. 'I'll need some money.'

Poppy gazed at her intently. How like her mother she was. She never doubted for a second that Leah meant what she said. She was a very loyal girl and by far the more stubborn of the two. In her condition, Rhian could not be brought into this argument, but as Leah had said, she'd only support Ernest anyway. Why not let Leah go? It would be a test of her character to see how long she could stick it out and, what was infinitely more gratifying, it would annoy Ernest intensely.

'Very well, you'll have four hundred pounds paid into your bank as well as your allowance which you can draw on at your discretion, but I warn you, Leah, don't draw too much out at a time. You are going to live with people who will only earn a quarter of that in a year at best.'

'And my things? My furniture from my bedroom?'

Poppy nodded.

Leah could hardly believe that her aunt had relented so quickly; she'd expected a hard and long fight. She knew her aunt had more idea than she did of what sort of life she was rushing headlong into and wondered why Poppy had not tried harder to dissuade her. Leah felt a moment's unease. This was a decision that shouldn't have been made in such a hurry, but it was too late now to go back on it. She threw her arms round her aunt's neck.

Poppy stroked the thick auburn hair. 'Remember, Leah, this is still your home. The door will never be closed against you and I'll be seeing Mr Rankin to make contingency plans for your inheritance, which as that jumped-up, patronising, pompous little clerk downstairs reminded us is really only nine months away.'

Leah went to see Nora and found her lying on her bed, her face towards the wall.

'Nora. Nora, it's all sorted out. You're going home but I'm coming with you.'

Nora sat up and wiped her tear-streaked face with her cuff. 'To live?'

Leah nodded.

'But why, Miss?'

'Because I *won't* stay under the same roof as flaming Ernest. I *won't* take orders from him. I *won't* be humiliated or treated like a child.'

'But you *can't* live with us, Miss! Not in Oil Street. I'm used to it but you've always lived in luxury. This place is like a palace. Our house is a . . . dump. There's only one cold water tap, the kitchen floor is flagged, the . . . the . . . privy is at the bottom of the yard and we have to share it with the people next door. Oh, miss, you *can't* come and live with us! I'll manage, I always used to.'

'I could help out, financially. And what about your father, Nora? You promised him . . .'

The tears welled up again in Nora's eyes. 'If you and Miss Poppy give me references I'll get a job and if our Ethna's husband coughs up a few shillings . . . I know Pat will be glad to help out, and we'll manage.'

Leah swallowed hard. 'Oh, Nora, I'm so sorry but that toad down there has had Pat sacked too. So you see you will need some help with money, Until things are settled.'

102

'Oh, no! It was such a steady job, six years permanent, and he worked so hard.' The tears flowed freely again and again Leah put her arms round her. Nothing was going to stop her now. She didn't care how dirty, how small, how unhygienic the house in Oil Street was, she was going to go with her friend and support her, and what's more she'd damn well stay. In time she'd buy a house of her own. For the foreseeable future her life was going to change drastically but she didn't care. Nora was the only real friend she had, and she was going to be by her side when she needed her.

Blackett and Percy were bringing down the cases. The trunks were already on the floor near the vestibule. The rest of her belongings, including her furniture, would follow tomorrow. Ernest, coming out of the study, nearly tripped over a case.

'What the hell is going on? What's all this stuff doing down here?'

Neither the man, nor the boy answered but Leah appeared, dressed for the winter evening. Behind her came Nora, also with her coat and hat and gloves on.

'Are you deaf as well as stupid, Ernest?' she said calmly and slowly as though she was explaining something to a halfwit. 'I told you that if Nora goes, so do I. We're off now, don't disturb Rhian. Just give her my love. And we're going with Aunt Poppy's blessing.' Her eyes narrowed. 'She has advanced me a sum and she will be seeing Mr Rankin very soon to have some safeguards drawn up. She is, after all, executor of Papa's will.'

Ernest spluttered but at last managed to get himself under control. 'You can't do this, Leah! Think of Rhian. What am I going to tell her?'

'Whatever you like, Ernest, but I'll write to her, care of Aunt Poppy, and explain my reasons.'

'You're mad! You need certifying!' His laughter was bordering on hysteria. He knew full well that it was Poppy Cavendish who ran things. She was a shrewd woman which was very probably why she was a spinster. Men didn't want intelligent, outspoken wives.

'You're going to leave all this to live in filth and squalor?'

'I'd live in a mud hut rather than here with you, Ernest Armstrong! You remind me of something slimy that crawled out from under a stone.' Leah took Nora's arm. 'I'm going to savour every minute of the drive. It will probably be the last time I'll ever ride in a car again,' she said laughingly.

Ernest stared at her across the width of the hall. God Almighty, what a hornet's nest he'd stirred up!

When they were outside, Leah gave Percy ten shillings. 'You're a good lad, Percy.'

'Thanks, miss. I'll miss yer.'

She slipped three pounds into Blackett's hand and thought she saw the hint of a tear in his eye as he thanked her. She and Nora got into the car.

'Oil Street, Blackett, please,' Leah instructed firmly.

Nora tried again. 'Miss Leah, you shouldn't be doing this, you shouldn't! What will people think?'

'I don't care what people think.'

'I mean people in our street.'

Leah didn't answer for a while then she said, 'They must take me as they find me but I'll not antagonise them. This is a journey home for you, Nora. For me it's a journey to a new life.'

Chapter Eight

Leah's resolve and determination were turning to growing trepidation as the car drove slowly along the cobbles of the Dock Road.

On her left lay the docks and beyond them the dark waters of the Mersey. The lights along the rigging and masts of cargo ships in dock and the illuminated funnels of passenger liners were bright and gave some feeling of hope. But on her right, warehouses, grain silos and factories crowded together like huge, black, misshapen creatures and, between them, as if cowering together beneath the gigantic buildings, were the mean streets of back-to-back terraced houses.

The lights in some of their curtainless windows were feeble and flickering. Candles and oil lamps, Leah surmised. Above the street lamps a corona glistened as gaslight mingled with the misty rain. The car turned into Oil Street which was little more than a narrow, cobbled roadway. Blackett unloaded the cases and left them on the pavement by the door. He wished them good night and good luck and then they were left alone in the dark drizzle. It was too dark to see the condition of the paintwork on the door, but Leah noticed it was brown. Everything around her seemed to be brown. At least Nora's house had curtains.

Nora hammered on the door and it was Declan who opened it to them.

'Nora! What do yer want? Da, it's our Nora!' Declan bawled down the lobby.

Nora ignored him and walked in, indicating that Leah should follow her. There was no light so Nora led Leah by the hand.

Joe had risen from his battered armchair, the late edition of the *Echo* laid aside. There was a good fire and the room was tidy, but the heat seemed only to enhance the odours in the room. Damp, rotten wood, stale cooking and another smell Leah could only describe as decay.

'Nora, you didn't need to come all the way down 'ere again. I'm comfortable, you can see that. You shouldn't have gone wasting tram fares.'

'I didn't. I came by car. We both did.'

Joe looked confused.

'I got the sack, Da.'

He gazed at her in silence for a few seconds. 'What for?' he demanded. 'That was a good place, they were good to you, Nora.'

'I know but . . . but, well, I've been walking out with a nice lad – Pat Ryan – and to get out to see him I had to . . . to make excuses and today we got caught. I got the sack and he's been chucked out of Cavendish's. But I love him, Da.' She spread her hands expressively in front of her.

'Oh, Nora, you flaming little fool! I suppose this means you've come home?'

'No, Da, not me – us.'

Nora stepped aside and Declan's mouth dropped open. Joe was staggered.

'Miss Cavendish! Jesus, Mary and Joseph! Miss Cavendish, you can't . . . I mean this place . . .' Joe was lost for words.

'Only a while, a few weeks, Mr O'Brian, if you don't mind. Tomorrow I'll start to look for a place of my own.'

Declan suddenly found his voice. 'There's an 'ouse goin' empty in Vandries Street.'

'Is that far away?' Leah asked, trying hard not to gag as the waves of stuffy, foul odours washed over her.

'Just the next street, miss.' Declan wished he could go and tell his mates about this. A *real* posh lady, Miss Cavendish, staying at their house. But for one thing it was too late and for another Jimmy Murphy and Jackie Price were being kept in. Their fathers had been released from jail that day too. Jimmy Murphy said his mam had belted him every single day that his da had spent in Walton. Every step of the way to school that she'd dragged him had been accompanied by a clout. There wasn't even enough gin to drown her sorrows, which didn't improve her temper.

'Good, I'll take a look first thing. Declan, would you go and bring the cases and trunk in from the step, please? I've only brought my clothes – for now. Some furniture, bedroom furniture will come tomorrow, if you don't mind, that is?'

Joe was nearly in tears with the utter humiliation of it all. 'Miss Cavendish, you can't stay here, it's not fit, you're not used to . . . Compared to your house, this . . . this . . .'

'Is your home and Nora's home and as the song says, there's no place like it. Very few people in this city have houses like my sister's. I'm very grateful for your hospitality.'

Joe looked beaten. Why in the name of God had Nora let her come here?

'Da, I told her not to come. I begged her.' Nora turned again to Leah. 'Miss Leah, it's not fitting. A hotel would be best.'

Leah pulled herself together. This was what she'd

107

chosen, no matter how rashly, so she'd better get some things sorted out.

'Nora, I came with you because you were always more than a servant to me. I look upon you as a friend so will you stop calling me Miss Leah. Call me just plain Leah from now on and that includes you, Mr O'Brian.'

Joe shook his head. 'I couldn't and meladdo there certainly can't. I'll box his ears if he does.'

'How many bedrooms are there, Nora?'

'Two. Da and Declan can share and I can sleep down here,' Nora offered, cringing at the thought of the bedroom.

Leah looked around at the sparsely furnished, uncarpeted floor 'Where? No, we'll share.'

Nora's cheeks flamed red with embarrassment. How could she share that old iron bedstead with its lumpy flock mattress, no sheets or pillows even, with Leah Cavendish? Leah was used to big airy rooms, warm rooms with carpeted floors, velvet curtains, beautiful furniture, vases of flowers and so much more. Nora twisted her hands together nervously.

'Right, we'll go up then and get sorted out.' Leah forced a smile and a note of enthusiasm into her voice.

Neither of them had ever experienced such a night in their lives before. Nora lay rigidly on the edge of the bed, ashamed and upset. The furniture consisted of no more than the bed and an orange box and, because it was the back bedroom, the windows were curtainless. When the clouds drifted away, bright moonlight illuminated the damp patches on the walls, the greenish-grey fungus that mottled the window frame. The floor was bare, there wasn't even a rug, and it wasn't very clean. Surely Ethna could have come down once a week and given the place the once-over.

Nora had had the men in to 'stove' the house while her father had been in Walton, but she knew the bugs would be back soon. She prayed for the night to be over. For the first fingers of the spring dawn to creep across the sky.

Leah had lain just as still and stiffly on the other side of the bed, trying not to think about what might be crawling on the bare floor or up the damp walls or – worst of all – in the bed with her. The urge to scratch herself was so great that she fought with it nearly all night.

She had seen the ragged, barefoot urchins – there were so many of them – usually at the railway stations, begging to be allowed to carry bags. She had seen women with thin, pinched faces peering from the folds of their shawls, many of them barefoot too. She'd felt pity for them, but it had been a detached pity, she had no idea that this was how they lived. No idea that poverty such as this existed. Their carriage horses were better housed, fed and shod.

She must have eventually dozed off; the sunlight coming in through the curtainless window woke her. Now that March was nearing its end, the sun was stronger and brighter. For a few seconds she couldn't remember where she was, then as her gaze swept round the room, she remembered.

'Nora. Nora, are you awake?' she asked softly.

'I am, Miss Leah.' Nora sat up. 'Oh, God, this place looks even worse in the daylight. Please, won't you go back?'

Leah got up. The boards were cold and rough beneath her bare feet. 'No. Today I'm going to see that house in Vandries Street and if it's for rent I'll have it and then I can get started on it.'

'I'll scrub it out from top to bottom for you.' Nora was eager, she didn't want to have to spend another night like the last one. It wasn't right. It just wasn't right.

*   *   *

109

The whole area was appalling, Leah thought as she and Nora walked along Waterloo Road, always referred to as the Dock Road. Even the spring sunlight made no difference. In fact it made it worse. The houses and warehouses were blackened by layers of soot. Decaying rubbish clogged the pavement and gutters. She was trying not to remember Prince's Avenue and its gardens and the beautiful park. She concentrated instead on avoiding as much of the filth that covered the cobbles as she could.

Breakfast had been awful. Coarse-grained, stale bread spread with margarine and a cup of tea and Nora saying over and over that she must get some shopping in. All the cups were badly cracked and none of them matched; hers was the only one with a saucer. The table had been spread with newspaper. The range needed cleaning and blackleading. Ash had fallen on to the flagged floor. There were no curtains on the window that overlooked the back yard. There were no pictures, no ornaments, no touch of colour or brightness. On one wall was a simple wooden cross, around which had been draped cheap glass beads.

'Mam's rosary. No matter how bad things were, we never pawned it.' Nora's voice was quiet and filled with longing and grief.

Tears started in Leah's eyes. She knew she was embarrassing them all, humiliating them even, and it wasn't at all what she had intended. Aunt Poppy had tried to warn her but she'd refused to listen. She tried to adopt an optimistic attitude.

'Nora, I'm sorry.'

'I'm sorry, too. We haven't much of anything.'

'No, I didn't mean that. I mean I'm sorry that I've embarrassed you all. I had no right, no idea. I just didn't think. I assumed . . .' She fell silent, biting her lip.

'That's all right.' Nora found it easier not to address Leah by any name.

As they turned into Vandries Street, which was a replica of Oil Street, Leah became aware that her appearance and clothes were attracting the attention of the housewives who were either vigorously brushing the strip of pavement outside their home or scrubbing and whitening the worn and broken steps.

'Come to see 'ow the other 'alf live?' one said, a note of sarcasm in her voice, as she sat back on her heels, scrubbing brush in hand.

'Don't say nothing,' Nora hissed but Leah smiled at the woman.

'I hope I'm going to be your neighbour,' she said, pointing to the obviously vacant house. 'Will you tell me your name?'

'Florence, Florrie Burrows.'

Leah stretched out her hand. 'Then I'm very pleased to meet you, Mrs Burrows.'

The woman gaped and was so flabbergasted that she took the soft white hand in her own red, work-roughened one. 'An' what's yer name?' she finally got out.

'Leah. Miss Leah Cavendish.'

'Holy God! It's the gentry come to rough it with us slummies,' a woman across the street shouted raucously. Nora looked around uneasily. How was Leah going to cope with this lot?

'Let's go and have a look at the house,' she suggested. 'It might not be suitable anyway.'

'Oh, none of them is *suitable*, Nora O'Brian, but we 'aven't got the money. Yer should know that! I seen youse in rags an' with bare feet many's the time.'

Nora turned on her. 'I know that, Lizzie Madden, and I'm proud that I've managed to come up a bit in the world, but you should know I'm no snob. You were one of me mam's friends. You all want better things for your kids, don't you?'

111

Lizzie Madden came over to them and Florrie Burrows also got to her feet.

'We 'eard yer was in service in some posh 'ouse,' Florrie said conversationally.

'I worked for Miss Leah but I got the sack. I've been walking out on the sly with a feller who worked at Cavendish's because I hardly got any time off.'

'I thought I'd not seen much of yer,' Lizzie commented, leaning on the wall of Florrie's house.

Nora knew she was doing the right thing, telling them the truth. It would help Leah.

'So, I had to make excuses. Miss Cavendish helped me and when I was caught yesterday and given me marching orders, she stood by me. She said if I went, she went.'

The two women exchanged glances. A few more had come to join the group, all glad of a diversion from their daily grind. They were introduced by Lizzie who had taken it on herself to become adviser to Miss Cavendish, seeing as she herself had been Nora's mam's friend. 'Well, they say there's nowt so queer as folk an' yer must 'ave guts, Miss. Where exactly did yer live, like?'

Leah smiled wrily. 'In a house you'd think was a palace, on Prince's Avenue.' Her expression changed. 'It was partly my fault Nora was dismissed and she was more than just a servant to me, she's a friend. But in nine months' time, my pompous brother-in-law is in for a nasty shock.'

''Ow, like?'

'I'll be twenty-one.'

It meant nothing to them and they were losing interest.

Nora smiled at Leah. The ice had been broken. Leah would still be looked on with some suspicion but at least she would be treated with some respect, outwardly at least. What they said about her in their own homes was a different matter entirely and she would have to watch that they didn't rob her blind or come begging and borrowing with the most outrageous cons. They wouldn't view it as theft or fraud. They had nothing. Leah had everything.

'There's nothin' in the house, yer know. They done a moonlight flit,' Lizzie informed them.

Leah looked questioningly at Nora.

'They packed up and left at night, probably owing God knows how much rent to the landlord.'

'Who actually owns the houses?' Leah asked.

'Your guess is as good as mine, miss. The rent feller calls on a Friday night an' if he can't get yer then 'e's back on Saturday. Yer can ask for repairs to get done till yer blue in the face, but it doesn't make no difference. It's a flamin' disgrace, it is.' Florrie folded her arms and sniffed. 'Maybe when yer get settled, like, yer could get them to gerra move on. You bein' a lady an' all.'

'I'll certainly try,' Leah promised. 'Does anyone know where we can get a key from?'

'It's attached,' Lizzie Madden said.

Nora slid her hand through the letter box and withdrew the key that was attached to a long piece of string. Leah was fascinated. 'Doesn't anyone break in?'

Lizzie laughed. 'What for? There's nowt ter pinch. Well, I'd better gerron, but iffen yer need any 'elp, just shout, queen.'

Leah thanked them all politely as Nora opened the door.

As she viewed the interior of the house, Leah's heart sank still further. It was almost uninhabitable. It should be condemned, in fact the whole street should be. Cracked and leaking guttering had let water seep in and drip down the walls. Most of the floorboards were missing.

'It's going to take a lot of time and work, Nora, and not just scrubbing either. Most of the woodwork is rotten.

113

There's plaster falling off the ceilings, and damp running down the walls.'

Tears started to prick Nora's eyes. 'Oh, go home, Leah! Please go home! You don't have to do this for me.'

Leah's chin jerked up and she took Nora's hands in her own. 'Yes I *do*, Nora. I ruined your future, your life. I owe you my loyalty.'

'Then where do we start?'

'I'd say brick by brick. Pull the whole damned place down and start again.'

Nora uttered a cry of delight, Pat was standing in the lobby.

'Oh, Pat! I'm so sorry! You lost your job because of me.'

He took her hand. 'And you lost yours too.'

'The whole mess was started by me,' Leah said. 'That's why when the sainted Ernest sacked her I came too.'

'Percy told me Nora had been sacked but he never mentioned you at all, Miss Leah.'

'He's probably been threatened with the sack himself if he does.'

'What will you do, Pat?' Nora's eyes were fixed on his face.

'Try the docks. Sean Maguire, one of my mates from the boarding house, says he'll have a word with the blockerman. Sorry, the foreman,' he added seeing the puzzled look in Leah's eyes.

'What about you, Nora?' he asked.

'Back to factory work, I suppose. I'll try Tillotson's. I'll try them all if I have to.'

'You could go back into service, Nora. You know Aunt Poppy and I would give you references.'

Nora shook her head. 'No, I'll earn more in a factory and I'd have more time here, to be with Da and Pat.'

It was on the tip of Leah's tongue to say that Nora

would not need to work, she had enough money for both of them but she bit back the words. Nora and Pat were both unemployed but they had their pride.

'Pat, do you know anyone who could replace all the window frames here, put new doors on and new floorboards and stair treads? Is there anything that can be done about the damp and the flagged floor?'

'Lino is what most people cover the flags with. There's nothing much can be done about the damp except to replace or mend the broken gutters and keep on whitewashing over it. My mate Andy will do all your carpentry jobs, he's just been laid off and he'd be glad of the cash. I heard it was stoved after the last lot left, but I'd have it done again.'

Leah felt faint. Oh, not bugs again! Crawling things that brought disease, contaminated food.

Pat noticed her pallor. 'There's nothing that can be done except stoving. It's because the houses are so old and the walls are coated with God knows what, but whatever it is the bugs love it. I'd get a cat, too; that'll keep some of the vermin down.' As soon as he'd said it he regretted it, seeing her eyes widen with new horror. 'I'm sorry. There's not much that can be done about them either, you're too near the docks and warehouses. The rat-catcher does come round sometimes though.'

Leah managed a weak smile.

'I'll have it stoved every week if necessary and we'll get two cats.' She touched the damp wall and anger flooded her face. 'It's a disgrace! An outrageous disgrace to allow people to live in places like this and charge them rent too! There's no proper water supply, no proper drainage or sewage. Not even the most basic privacy, a toilet. They have to share.'

'Aye, and three and six makes a big hole in a wage

115

of less than three pound, especially if you've got kids.' Pat's voice was bitter.

Leah looked stricken. She'd given Blackett three pounds just as a tip and now Pat was telling her men worked twelve and fourteen hours a day, six days a week, for less than that. She had a lot to learn.

'Pat, could you see your friend Andy? And then why don't you two make the most of your freedom? Have a day out, go to New Brighton or Southport – my treat and I insist.'

'What will you do?' Nora asked.

'I'm going to wander around my new neighbourhood and try to find where this rent collector lives, so I can inform him I'm taking up residency. I'll find out where things are, talk to my new neighbours, and then I'll buy some groceries and a couple of newspapers and journals and take them round to your father. I *can* cook simple things. Cook taught me years ago. Tomorrow we can go and see Ethna, if you'd like that. I presume her husband will be at work and if your friend comes to start on this place we don't want to be under his feet, do we? I'll need a plumber or coppersmith too. I refuse to share a toilet. I'll have a bedroom made into a bathroom.'

Nora and Pat both stared at her in admiration. She really did intend to stay, it wasn't just a fad. She had more backbone, more guts than either of them had ever believed possible. She was coping so well but then she also had money and that made a big difference. She had lived in the lap of luxury for all her twenty years but she was a fighter. She also had great confidence; she would ask for a thing to be done and it would get done – quickly. People around here would respect that. With that head of thick auburn hair and those green eyes, Pat knew she would have a temper. She'd have all the tradesmen in the neighbourhood terrified of her before long. With her colouring she must have Irish blood in her somewhere, he mused, yet Nora had said no, her father had been a true English gentleman. Her mother had been Welsh. The Celtic blood obviously came from that side of the family.

Leah smiled and waved enthusiastically as they walked down the street. When they'd turned the corner and there was no possibility of their returning, Leah sat down on the bottom stair, dropped her head in her hands and began to sob. This was a nightmare of a world she'd moved to. She'd brought it on herself but she wouldn't go back. She wouldn't give Ernest the bloody satisfaction. She'd collect her things and occasionally visit Aunt Poppy, but even with no knowledge of how to cope with this kind of life and the conditions her neighbours had to endure, from now on this bug-infested, decrepit house would be her home and Nora's too, if she wanted to share it. She thanked her mother for the wisdom and foresight she'd shown in ensuring her daughters weren't completely ignorant of how to look after themselves.

Leah wiped away her tears and glanced around, a new light in her eyes, a new determination flowing through her.

Chapter Nine

As March turned into April there were some doubts about the renovations to number four Vandries Street. Inquiries were made of a master builder to ensure that the other houses suffered no damage or were not likely to collapse like a pack of cards.

Leah had apologised to half the street for the noise and inconvenience, as new windows and doors and floor-boards were fitted, new guttering and a downspout put up both at the front and back of the house. In fact she had paid for new guttering for the entire side of the street on which her new home was situated. This had resulted in some heated arguments with the neighbours on the opposite side and she often felt she was treading on eggshells.

She had asked Mr Turner, the 'rent feller', as everyone seemed to call him, just exactly who did own the houses. Sensing hostility and demands for a meeting with the landlords, he had shrugged his shoulders and said, 'Oh, some firm of lawyers in town,' and that was as far as she'd been able to get.

Because of all the mess inside Vandries Street, Leah had moved in with Nora and, little by little, things began to improve in Oil Street. Lino for the kitchen floor, the end of the roll, Leah had said, so the assistant let her have it cheap. A sofa and a rocking chair and dresser that a pawnbroker had almost begged her to take off his

119

hands as he'd had them for months. A Lewis's van had delivered a huge parcel containing sheets, pillowcases, blankets, towels and some brightly coloured tablecloths and tea towels.

Nora and Eileen Molloy scrubbed the place from top to bottom and cleaned all the paintwork and windows. Two pairs of heavy curtains appeared, allegedly bought from a second-hand shop, but Nora could see they were brand new, as was the crockery bought from Ray's, and all the little bits of bric-a-brac.

One Saturday afternoon two lads about Declan's age arrived carrying a rolled-up rug.

'From the feller in de market, missus. 'E paid us sixpence to bring it.'

When it was unrolled, Nora could see it was virtually new and would cover the entire floor of the tiny front room.

'Leah, you'll have to stop it. I really mean it. You'll run out of money, what with buying all this and having to pay for what's being done at your house round the corner.' Nora felt far easier now with Leah. There were times when she slipped up and started to say 'Miss'. Leah would glare at her and then laugh.

'No, I won't. Before I left, Aunt Poppy arranged with the bank to give me some extra. Quite a lot extra, really.'

'She'd have fallen down in a faint if she'd seen what the house was like.'

'She still would!'

They both laughed and Nora was happier than she'd been for a long time. Now she was at home, it was easier for Pat to come and see her. Da liked him and found him good company. Pat had been lucky. As promised, Sean Maguire had had a 'word' and Pat was almost fully employed every week. Sometimes he felt so guilty and ashamed when he was picked out and older men, haggard with worry and despair, were left on the wooden platforms, passed over.

They all sat down one night to 'sort things out', as Leah put it.

'You know, Miss Leah, you are a very bossy young woman,' Pat said to her.

Leah laughed. 'I know. My mother was the same and my aunt calls me a meddler. Well, shilly-shallying about isn't going to solve anything. So, this is what Nora and I thought. When Vandries Street is habitable, which shouldn't be long now, Nora will move in with me.'

'Ah, great! I can have me room back,' Declan exclaimed enthusiastically.

'No you can't,' Nora said firmly.

'Why not?' he demanded.

'Because Pat will have it – if he wants it, that is,' Leah told him.

'That will be great! I'll be able to see you as often as I like, you'll be just round the corner.' Pat grinned across the table at Nora.

Joe, too, was smiling. He liked the lad and Declan appeared to too. Then a shadow crossed his face. 'What about 'er over the road?'

Nora was brisk and businesslike. 'I know she's got designs on you, Da, the whole street knows, but Mrs Molloy's been very good. She'll come over to cook your dinners, that's all. I'll do all the washing and cleaning and shopping.'

'And when will you find the time to do all that?' Joe asked.

'Well, we haven't quite sorted that out yet,' Leah said evasively.

'I'll pay you my lodging money, Joe,' Pat said. 'Same

121

as I do to her in Lightbody Street, but it's more comfortable here and, well, it's been a long time since I had what you could call a family life.' He smiled at Nora who felt tears of pity prick her eyes.

Joe nodded.

Declan frowned. 'She'll be living round the corner, he'll be here and they'll both be in and out all the time. It seems daft ter me. I don't know why the two of youse don't get married and get yer own 'ouse.' Declan was thinking only of having his room to himself again, and it was quite posh now too.

'Well, we might just do that.' Again Pat smiled at Nora.

Joe was thoughtful. 'I'd be glad in one way, Pat, but I know what life's like on the docks. When times get bad, men are laid off with half a day here, half a day there. I don't want our Nora to have to live like her mam, from hand to mouth, day to day. It's no life. And these days there's so many strikes. The railwaymen are out now.'

'We'll be fine, I promise.' Pat looked across at Nora; her face was radiant with happiness. 'I've been learning, being shown the ropes, like, from Sean. He's a stevedore.'

'He's young for a stevedore. That job takes years to learn, lad.'

'He's a fast learner. He's clever, really sharp. I reckon he'd do better than many bosses, but he has no time for the bosses. He's a great admirer of Tom Mann and Jim Larkin.'

'Larkin was born in Ireland, even though the family come from Liverpool.'

'Sean's Irish, a Dubliner,' Pat explained. 'They have even worse working practices over there, so he tells me.'

'Oh, don't start on about Ireland, Larkin and the unions,' Nora said with mock annoyance.

122

Leah got up. 'I'm going back to Prince's Avenue.' She wouldn't call it home any more. 'I want to arrange for some extra things Aunt Poppy promised me to be ready on Friday. I've ordered a cart to bring it all down. I'll buy the rest of the things I'll need. I'm going to give my aunt a list and ask her to check that everything that is supposed to go on the cart does go on it. I don't trust Ernest Armstrong.'

'Will everything be done for you to move in?' Pat asked.

'Nearly everything. The kitchen floor isn't finished. The furniture that belongs to me should be down tomorrow.'

Nora looked up at Leah. 'You miss her, don't you? Your Aunt Poppy.'

'Yes, I do, and Rhian.'

'Will this be the first time you've been back?' Pat asked.

'Yes, though I write to Aunt Poppy.'

'Shall I come with you?' Nora offered.

'No, I'll be fine on my own.' Her tone was bitter. 'I told Ernest I'd come and go as I pleased.'

Leah hardened her heart and bit back the tears as the tram moved up the avenue.

Percy opened the door to her.

'Miss Leah! Come in.'

'Hello, Percy, I see they haven't got a maid yet.'

He rolled his eyes. 'We've 'ad two, but Cook's always comparin' them to Nora and so is Miss Winthrop. Then they tell the mistress, then there's a row between the mistress and 'im. The maid gets sacked an' the mistress sulks. Dead 'appy 'ouse this is now, I tell yer.'

'I'll go up and see Aunt Poppy and then Rhian. Is your lord and master home yet?'

The lad nodded but pulled a face.

Poppy was as imperious as ever but Leah knew she was happy she'd come.

'I was wondering when you were going to get round to paying me a visit, miss, instead of scrawling a few lines on a piece of paper. I had given you until the end of the month and then I was going to come and see you.'

Leah paled. She couldn't let Poppy see where she lived now. At all costs, she must keep her away from the house in Vandries Street.

'I've been so busy, I'm sorry.'

'Busy doing what?'

'I found a house to rent but it's needed so much work doing on it. It should be habitable by Friday. It's only got two bedrooms and one I've had made into a bathroom. Oh, it's awful for them, they all have to share toilets which are at the bottom of the yard and wash in the kitchen sink and bathe in a sort of tub in front of the kitchen fire, if they can afford the coal. They keep the tubs in the yard.'

'No wonder they're so dirty.'

'They can't help it. Doing the weekly wash is a nightmare for them. Every bit of water has to be boiled in a pot or kettle. There are no facilities unless they carry it down to the public wash house and carry it all back again. And they have pride, they don't like their neighbours seeing the state of what they've got or mainly what they haven't got. Nora and her neighbour Mrs Molloy have a mangle and half the street uses it. They take turns. Then all the clothes are hung over something called a maiden, which is like three wooden gates all loosely attached. The clothes are draped over them and the whole thing is put in front of the fire to dry. In summer it's hung on a line in the back yard.' She didn't say it was also hung on a line that stretched from house to house across the street.

124

'Doesn't it ruin the carpets?'

'Aunt Poppy, there *are* no carpets. The kitchen floors are flagged, and freezing cold in winter.'

Poppy shook her head. 'God help them.' She had been brought up in a wealthy Victorian household where standards of cleanliness and manners were rigid, but the general consensus of her parents and their friends was that the poor were idle and wasteful and it was their own fault they were poverty-stricken. As she'd grown older she'd read the newspapers, even the ones her father had forbidden in the house. She would read them in the park and she had begun to form her own opinions, none of which she had revealed to her parents or brothers. Her opinion was that the poor, and especially the women, got a raw deal from life. She had never been tempted to join the Women's Suffrage Movement, however; that would have been going too far.

'I've made out a list, as you asked in your letter and I've ordered the removal men, but I don't trust Ernest. Could you make sure everything on the list is put on the cart for me, please?'

'I'll give the list to Blackett and he can report to me. You surely don't expect me to stand in the hall like some kind of clerk?'

'No, of course not.'

'How is Nora? We've had two more highly undesirable and inefficient maids since she left.'

'She didn't leave, she was sacked,' Leah reminded her.

Poppy nodded, and went on, 'Ernest insists Rhian interviews the candidates and she is hopeless, to say the least, apart from being only a month away from her confinement.'

'Nora's quite happy. Her young man, Pat Ryan, has been taken on at the docks. It's never steady work but a

125

friend of his spoke up for him. I think they'll get married soon.' Leah's face softened as she thought about it. She envied Nora a little. Whenever she saw Pat, her whole face would light up as though he was the centre of her entire world.

Poppy, too, was thinking of a young man, in a grave in a foreign land. She sighed heavily.

'What's that on your knee?' Leah asked, to change the subject.

'My knitting.'

'Your *knitting*?'

'Yes. I decided I should learn to do something useful before I die, so I'm knitting. It amuses me.' She picked up a ball of wool and two needles on which hung a very misshapen square.

'What is it?'

'I have no idea. I'll just wait and see what it looks like when it's finished.'

Leah pealed with laughter. 'You're supposed to have a pattern to work from, even I know that. Didn't Miss Winthrop, er, advise you?'

'Don't mock, child, or I'll give you whatever it ends up as and I'll make you wear it.' The old lady sighed. 'Oh, life gets so tedious. So very tedious. Sometimes I feel I've lived too long, and a useless life at that, too.'

'No! Don't think like that, please. I couldn't stand it if you . . .' She couldn't say the word. 'Not . . . not after Mother.'

Poppy laid a hand on her arm. 'I'm sorry, I shouldn't have said that to you. I'm just a cantankerous old woman feeling sorry for herself. A thing I have no right to do at all, not after what you've just told me. Now leave me to my knitting and go and see Rhian. She misses you terribly.'

Leah got up and kissed her aunt on the cheek. 'I will

and I'll come and see you at least once a week in future, I promise.'

Poppy nodded firmly and commenced work energetically, but when Leah had gone she let the needles and wool fall into her lap. Oh, how she wished she was young again.

Rhian looked enormous but her eyes lit up when she saw her sister. She was lying on a chaise longue, propped up with cushions. She had been reading.

'You look the size of a house but radiant just the same. You're sure it's only one?' Leah kissed her and sat on a low stool beside the chaise.

'I hope so, but it's so tedious and tiring and I feel and look a mess!'

'It won't be long now and you'll be back to your slim self with your son or daughter and Ernest as proud as punch with the two of you.'

A shadow crossed Rhian's face. 'Yes, he will.' Her voice lacked enthusiasm but Leah thought it best not to pursue this line of conversation.

'Aunt Poppy has taken up knitting, of all things.'

'I know. I just hope she doesn't expect me to dress the baby in anything she's made!'

'Have you seen the state of it? It looks like a woolly dishcloth.'

They both dissolved in laughter. Laughter that died when Ernest entered the room.

'Is this a visit or have you come to your senses and decided to come home?'

'A visit. I told you I would come and go as I pleased and I haven't changed my mind.' Leah stood up. 'I'll go now, Rhian, but don't worry, I've promised Aunt Poppy I'll come and visit.' She turned to Ernest, her green eyes full of contempt. 'When you're at work so as not to annoy you.'

The sisters embraced and Leah went into the hall to collect her jacket which Percy had hung in the cloakroom. When she emerged, Ernest was in the hall. He'd followed her.

'Don't tell me you've come to escort me off the premises.' Her tone was cutting.

'No, but you're to stay away from Rhian, she tires easily.'

Leah laughed. 'Do you think I'm such a fool as to believe that? What you really mean is stay away so I don't encourage her to form her own opinions. Then she'll stay the docile, obedient little wife and mother.'

He flushed.

'Oh, and by the way, Pat Ryan has found alternative employment and I have found a small but decent house. So the removal people are coming on Friday for my belongings. I've left a list with Aunt Poppy who will get Blackett to check the items off.'

His colour deepened at the implied insult. He caught her by the shoulders and shook her. 'You are a spoilt, stubborn, troublemaking, bad-minded little bitch!'

She was about to laugh and free herself from his grasp when quite suddenly he pulled her roughly to him and kissed her full on the lips. A harsh, bruising kiss.

Shocked, she pulled away and twisted out of his grip.

'How *dare* you! And with my sister lying in there expecting your baby! Is that how you think of me? As a tart? A trollop? You're scum, Ernest Armstrong! If Father were here he'd have you horse-whipped. But then if he had been here, you would never have married Rhian. She's too good for you because for all your pride and posturing you're nothing but a jumped-up clerk! You're worse even than the drunks who fall out of the pubs and go looking for prostitutes. They have the excuse that it's the drink and they don't pretend to be gentlemen!

If you lay a hand on me again, I'll tell Rhian, Aunt Poppy, the Reverend Hunter, the servants, your business associates and anyone else I consider important. By God, I'll humiliate you, Ernest Armstrong!'

As she slammed the door behind her, she stood on the top step shaking. He was disgusting! She felt degraded, dirty. She rubbed at her lips with her handkerchief and shuddered. It had been a horrible feeling.

The following morning Ernest called Edward Neely into his office. He'd lain awake all night thinking about Leah and what she had called him. He hadn't been able to help himself. He'd been filled with a burning lust for her. A lust that tormented him and which he realised wouldn't easily be quashed. He wanted her. He'd never felt like this about Rhian. Their love-making had no spark of fire, let alone a burning passion. He'd married her for money and power. But Leah had scorned his advances and had humiliated him and she wouldn't hesitate to carry out her threats if he ever lost control of his emotions again. And that was something he had to put a stop to because she would then hold his entire future in her grasp. She could ruin him.

'Neely, I want you to do me a favour. You'll be well paid, if you're discreet.'

Edward Neely looked suspicious but waited for his boss to carry on.

'I have been insulted and humiliated and I want the person responsible silenced for good. Don't worry, who ever you find to do it will be well paid too. Do you know anyone who would do the job?'

Neely appeared to give the matter some thought but there was no need. He knew a man who would murder his own mother for money for ale. 'There's someone I know of, name of Macardle. He lives in Blackstock Street.'

'I don't care where he bloody well lives! I'll pay him ten guineas and I'll pay you five if the matter is carried out to my satisfaction.'

'Right, sir, consider it done. I'll go round and see the man after I've finished here. Who is the culprit. What is the address?'

Ernest wrote something on a small piece of paper and handed it to Neely. 'I've no exact address.'

The colour drained from Edward Neely's face as he read the name. God Almighty! Leah Cavendish! A young girl of twenty and Nora's friend.

'Sir, I—'

'You do want to keep your job here, Neely, don't you? Especially as there's so much unrest. There may even come a time when I'll have to lay off my foremen.' Ernest's voice was menacing.

There was nothing he could do. It was blackmail. He'd never get another job like this, he'd lose everything. Neely nodded, stuffed the paper in the inside pocket of his jacket and left. He would go and see Macardle tonight, get it over with, and then try and dismiss it from his mind. Ethna was taking the baby down to her da's. Leah would be there too, but it would be easy to lure her away. Some fault on the repairs to the house. Anything.

Macardle lived with his wife Annie and four kids in an upstairs room in an old house in Blackstock Street off Scotland Road. There were God knows how many occupants of the house. A family in each room, at least. Neely shuddered as he looked at it but he was lucky, he didn't have to enter the malodorous hall or climb the bare, rickety stairs, Macardle was on his way out.

'Macardle. I've a job for you.'

The man already smelled of ale and his dark matted hair

130

hung over his forehead, almost meeting his eyebrows. His eyes narrowed with suspicion.

''Ow much does it pay?'

'A guinea, when it's been done.'

''Ave yer gorrit on yer now?'

Edward Neely was no fool. 'No. When the job's done I'll come round.'

'How do I know yer will?'

He turned away. 'Oh, all right, if you don't want it.'

'I never said that. What is it?'

'Doling out a few clouts to a woman. Just up your street, I'd say.' He glanced towards the staircase. Annie Macardle had been in hospital many times and Macardle himself had been in jail as many times for putting her there.

'What woman?'

'Follow me. I've arranged for someone to go and get her out of the house where she's staying while repairs are being done on her own house round the corner. When she gets to the jigger, it's up to you but don't bloody kill her or you'll swing for it. She's got family with money and position.'

Macardle nodded and followed Neely with a shambling gait.

Everyone was fussing over the baby so Neely could sit and listen for the knock. When it came he offered to go. He was back in seconds.

'Leah, they want you to go round to the house. Something about cementing the kitchen floor.'

'How will she see the damned floor at this time of night?' Joe asked.

'They rig up arc lights.'

'I asked to have the flags cemented over. To keep the

dirt out of the cracks, keep out the damp and to give a smooth surface for the lino. I'd better go.'

'Take a torch,' Nora advised, pouring Ethna a cup of tea.

'I'll come with you,' Pat offered.

'Oh, there's no need for that. You've only just finished your tea. I'll be back in a few minutes.' She took her jacket from the row of coat pegs attached to the back of the door.

A man she'd never seen before, dressed in the rough clothes of a builder, said Mr Romford, who was in charge of the job, had hit a bit of a problem with the floor and would she come and tell him what she wanted him to do about it so he could get the lads going first thing. They were all working late to finish it by Friday.

Leah nodded and followed him down to the bottom of the street. The communal back entry of Oil Street and Vandries Street opened on to the main road just round the corner, but when Leah turned it, the man had disappeared. She stood staring around for a few seconds, puzzled. Then a figure loomed out of the entry, caught her by her hair and dragged her into the entry itself.

She began to scream and lash out, despite the pain of having her hair pulled out by the roots. The first blow caught her on the side of her face and sent her reeling against the wall, then a pain exploded in her ribs and she began to slide down. Dimly she realised that if she fell she'd never get up, so with every ounce of strength she possessed she began to scream, over and over again. A hand smelling of stale tobacco was clamped over her mouth, and another burst of pain exploded in her midriff. She bit hard into the flesh covering her mouth and the man swore but let his hand drop. Again she screamed and began to kick out wildly but she was exhausted, terrified and in terrible pain.

She didn't hear the running feet, but she heard another man's voice and she heard the heavy blows and her attacker's groans. She heard him fall and then groan twice, as a steel-capped boot came into contact with rib bones.

Through rapidly swelling lips, a face that felt as though it was on fire and eyes half blinded by tears, she dimly made out the tall figure of her rescuer.

'Jaysus! What the hell has he done to you?'

She couldn't speak but she could see him more clearly now. He was tall and well built with very dark hair and astonishingly deep blue eyes.

'Can you lean on me at all, do you think?'

She bent towards him but groaned in agony.

He examined her face as closely as he could in the darkness. 'Ah, what's the use of all this. There's not a beam of light to see by.'

Before she could protest, Leah was lifted gently off her feet and carried back on to the main road where he made for the nearest street lamp.

'My God. You look as though it's the infirmary you'll be needing.'

She shook her head, although it caused a knife-like pain to shoot through it. 'No. No, just take me to Oil Street.'

'Tell me where it hurts the most.'

She leaned against his broad shoulder. 'Ribs, face,' she replied weakly.

'What did he do it for? What class of a man was he anyway?'

The strong arms round her, the broad chest she leaned against gave such a feeling of safety. 'I don't know who he was or why . . .'

'Am I right in thinking you don't belong round here?'

She nodded, and again the pain racked her.

'You're a lady. I can tell by the way you speak.'

She was in too much pain to try to hold a conversation and suddenly he gently brushed her hair away from her bruised and swollen cheek.

'Holy Mother of God, you're Leah Cavendish. You're the one staying above with the O'Brians until your house is finished.'

She looked up at him quizzically, her green eyes filled with pain and tears.

'I work with Pat Ryan. He said to come down tonight and we'd go for a jar. Meself, Pat and old Joe because the house would be full of women an' the noise would give you a headache worse than if you'd drunk a bottle of Paddy and a crate of porter.'

'You're Sean . . . Sean Maguire,' she whispered, her eyes closing with relief.

The kitchen was bedlam after he'd carried her in. Nora and Ethna both screamed and Ethna kept on screaming until Neely slapped her across the face and told her to shut up.

Sean glared at him. He'd never liked Neely and he thanked God he didn't have to work with him.

'Leah! Oh my God!' Nora was distraught.

'Who did it? Who did it, Leah? We'll belt the livin' daylights out of him!' Pat's voice was full of fury.

'Sure, she doesn't know. I've already asked her and she's in no state for a bloody inquisition, but whoever the hell he was he'll be wishing he'd never laid a finger on her. I left him laid out and he'll be nursin' more than a few broken ribs too.'

Neely sat down suddenly, unnoticed by everyone except Sean. Macardle, when he'd recovered, would come looking for his money no doubt, even though he hadn't finished the job. Neely was unaware that Sean was watching him.

Sean's eyes narrowed – Neely had gone pale. The man had a hand in this somewhere, Sean was sure of it. Who did Neely work for? Ernest Armstrong, Leah's brother-in-law. And wasn't Leah living here because that bastard had sacked Nora and got rid of Pat?

Joe, although shaken, took charge. 'Edward, take our Ethna and the baby home, she's calmed down now. Nora, get some water and try and bathe Leah's face. Declan, get yourself round to the dispensary and ask them the name and address of the nearest doctor and then go and get him, fast.' They'd never had money for a doctor before, so they didn't know one. 'And you two get off to the pub, out of the way.'

'Now isn't that a nice way to be treated and me doing my shining knight on a white horse bit? Himself there is flinging us out to the pub.' Sean bent over Leah whom he'd laid gently on the sofa. 'I suppose I'll have to go, but are you all right?'

Again she attempted a smile. 'I . . . I . . . will be.'

He picked up her hand gently. The nails were broken and bleeding. 'You clattered him yourself, I see.'

Again she tried to smile. 'Thank you.'

'You can give me the medal when you've recovered,' he quipped but there was something in those blue eyes that made her feel more than just gratitude.

Chapter Ten

It was Pat, Sean, Joe and Declan who moved all the furniture into Leah's house in Vandries Street. They laid lino, even in the tiny scullery, and put down carpets in every room and up the stairs, all of them marvelling at it.

'Carpet down the stairs!' Declan spoke for them all.

'How the hell do you clean it?' Pat asked.

'She's got one of them things that you push up an' down and it takes up all the muck. I've seen them advertised.' Joe looked at the brass stair rods in his hands and shook his head. They were a puzzle to him.

'What class of an object would you say it was, Pat?'

'A carpet sweeper called a Ewbank, I think.'

Sean was working on the carpet in the lobby. Why couldn't she just have a bit of a runner like everyone else who could afford carpet? But the ways of the rich were different, he thought bitterly, and she was one of them. She'd spent as much on this house as would have fed and clothed the entire street for a year, and without even thinking of the cost. When she had recovered, no doubt she'd be parading up and down in her fine clothes, thinking she was accepted as one of them. She wasn't and she never would be and one day she'd get tired of it all and go back to where she came from, that bloody great mansion on Prince's Avenue.

Yet there were times when he couldn't get her out of his mind. She was a beauty, he admitted that. With that auburn hair, green eyes and pale skin, she wouldn't be out of place in Grafton Street or St Stephen's Green, or taking tea with the quality at the Imperial Hotel in Sackville Street. Her colouring was more Irish than English.

'Well, are you going to stand there looking like a waxwork dummy all day or what?' Pat rudely interrupted his thoughts about Leah Cavendish.

'No, I was thinking that before we start trying to fathom out how those infernal things work, those that Joe has in his hands, we'll go for a quick jar. Someone in the pub may know how they work, for sure to God I don't.'

Ethna – still smarting with hurt pride at being slapped, and filled with even more hostility towards her husband – Nora and Eileen Molloy were hanging curtains and pictures and unpacking china cups and plates and porcelain figurines.

'Do yer think it's wise puttin' all this stuff out?' Eileen rubbed a marble and gold clock on her apron. 'Yer know what Dan Fogarty would give yer on things like this. He'd easily sell them when yer pledge day was up. Once word gets around, the place will be cleaned out if she's out for longer than an hour.'

The same thing had been worrying Nora. 'Well, the front is safe enough. Good locks on the door and people would hear and see anyone trying to get in.'

'But would they care? What with the strikes and lock-outs and poverty, will a feller think twice about pinching this clock and pawning it to feed the kids and pay the rent, just because it's Leah Cavendish's clock?'

Nora bit her lip. What Eileen Molloy was saying couldn't be dismissed. She changed the subject. 'She said she's going to put plants and flowers in tubs in the yard and have it whitewashed and put a bit of a bench out there.'

'Oh, that'll look nice with the clothes hanging on the

line and the dolly tub and mangle,' Ethna said, a touch of envy and sarcasm in her voice. She couldn't for the life of her see why Leah Cavendish would want to live here.

'There won't be a washing line. All the linen, including underwear, will go to the laundry and the rest will be done by Lizzie Madden. The ironing too.'

'Why didn't she say something to me? I'd have done it.' Eileen was aggrieved.

'We thought we'd give Mrs Madden the turn, Mrs Molloy. You've got enough to do with Da and that lot.' Nora smiled at her. The woman wasn't as bad as she'd always thought. She was lonely, that was all, and she enjoyed cooking and cleaning. It was only her constant chatter that got on Da's nerves.

'And how is she now?' Eileen asked. The street had been up in arms over the attack, although there were some who said what else did she expect. A lady like her coming to live in a slum. She was fair game for every lout and thief in the neighbourhood. She'd had no money on her and the gold cross and chain she wore round her neck had not been snatched off. He must have been a madman, they concluded, and there were plenty of them around, Florrie Burrows declared, she was married to one.

'She's better but it will take time.' Nora balanced on a chair to put up a lampshade. 'The bruising is starting to fade but her ribs will take longer.' Dr MacDougal had bound them up and told her to move as little as possible. She had to sleep almost sitting up as it was so painful to lie down.

She'd told the doctor that she didn't know her attacker but she realised she'd been lured out of the house. It had all been planned. Surely Ernest Armstrong wouldn't go to such lengths, it was too preposterous. She wondered if she should mention it to Sean.

Sean Maguire was a regular visitor now to Vandries Street, although he and Leah often argued. He'd taunt her, saying she had a choice. She had chosen to come and live here but no one else had a choice and anyway she'd turned the house into a small replica of the home she'd left.

Leah always got annoyed and asked him what he wanted her to do. It wasn't her fault she'd been born into a wealthy family.

'It's all wrong, the system, I mean. The few at the top with money to burn, like you, while thousands live in houses like the rest of Oil Street and worse, in cellars and courts.'

'Well, it's up to the City Council to do something to help them!'

'That lot! And would you just listen to yourself. What you're saying is, It's someone else's fault, don't come looking to us to part with our money.'

'I'm not! What I'm saying is there has to be people successful in trade and business to give work to others. If there weren't, the whole country, except the real aristocracy, would be in a terrible state. If there were no docks, no ships, no cargoes, there would be no dockers, stevedores or carters.'

'And that's another thing. It's shameful the way they exploit us. Men fighting on the stands to be picked out for half a day's work. Men with families to feed and clothe. Every man is entitled to his bit of dignity, Leah. The bosses have taken that away. They're grateful for even a half day's work. That's what the union is all about. Dignity and a fair wage for the working man.'

'Well, there's not much dignity in going out on strike. All they do is lock you out.'

'Striking is the only weapon we have, you eejit!'

Nora would put an end to it by saying that if he was going to upset Leah then he had best stay away.

'I'm not after upsetting her and she knows it,' he'd laugh.

'I sometimes wonder, Sean Maguire, I really do,' Nora would answer.

Leah discussed the attack with Sean, though she was reluctant to admit all her suspicions.

'Sean, I've been going over and over it in my mind and I'm sure it was all planned. It had to be. That man knew all about the house, the floor, even Mr Romford's name. How could he have known all that if he hadn't been told. I'm sure he wasn't one of the labourers. I'd never seen him before.'

'I think you're right. It was a set-up.'

'One of the neighbours? Spite or jealousy?'

'No, it's not their way. The women would say it to your face and there's not a man around here who would beat a young girl.' His mouth twisted. 'Unless it was an errant daughter or his wife. Some men seem to think that marriage gives them the right to clatter their wives whenever the mood takes them.'

'Then who was behind it?'

'Who have you upset lately?'

'No one. Well, Mr Romford a few times over the house.'

'The night I carried you home Neely looked very pale and sheepish and was off like a scared rabbit when Joe told him to get Ethna home. He's a man I've never liked. Silent and secretive.'

'It couldn't be him, not Ethna's husband! Ouch!' She grimaced as she lifted the kettle to make him tea.

'Who does he work for, Leah?'

'My brother-in-law and . . .'

'And what?' he urged.

141

'He made an advance, he kissed me.' She shuddered at the recollection. 'I called him all kinds of names and threatened to tell everyone but—'

'He's your man then. Sure, he probably threatened Neely too.'

She gazed at him, stricken with horror. 'Oh God! Rhian! My poor sister!'

'You can prove nothing and he won't ill treat her.'

'But I'll get even with him one day, Sean, I swear to God I will!'

Pat and Nora decided to get married on the day King George V was to be crowned, Friday, 23 June.

'Well, why not? Everyone will be celebrating. There'll be street parties and processions, it's a good day,' Nora replied after Ethna had wondered at the wisdom of it. 'At least it's better than getting wed on the day of a state funeral.' She held little Alexander Joseph in the crook of her arm and tickled him under his chin.

'Don't remind me. Sometimes I think Ma Brennan was right.'

'Why?' Nora looked with concern at her sister.

'Oh, nothing. I've got used to him not speaking much.'

'Was it the way he slapped you? You were hysterical, you know; you weren't making things better.'

'No, it's not that. Oh, I can't explain. At least I have my baby and he's got his heir, which is more than can be said for the almighty Mr Armstrong who he bows and scrapes to.'

Leah, true to her promise, had gone to see Aunt Poppy every week and had been there the day Rhian had had her baby. She'd been livid when she'd returned home. Ernest had taken one look at his tiny daughter and walked out of the room. He hadn't held her or shown any interest in her at all. She'd had a very grand christening, of course, during which he'd acted the proud father. The baby had been baptised Penelope Edwina Lucy.

Ethna thought that Ma Brennan's words could also be applied to Rhian Armstrong.

'So, have you got it all arranged then, this wedding? I suppose Pat will move in with you?' Ethna was openly envious of the life Nora led. Her sister was at Barker and Dobson's sweet factory now. It was clean work and the pay was reasonable and she wouldn't even have to put up with a man's unpleasant and disgusting attentions to achieve it.

'How can he? There's only one bedroom. Leah and I share. No, we're going to look for a place of our own.'

Leah's bathroom had caused weeks of speculation and gossip. Those who had seen it – Eileen Molloy, Lizzie Madden and Florrie Burrows – went into transports of delight and envy when describing it to all and sundry. In the end Leah had decided to have what she termed an 'open bathroom' day to which she invited every woman from Oil Street, Vandries Street and even Vulcan Street, and she provided them with a cup of tea and a biscuit.

'Are you having a long dress and veil?'

'Yes, but nothing too fancy.'

'And I suppose Leah's going to be bridesmaid?'

'No, she can't be. She's not a Catholic, she's Anglican.'

'Oh, aye, I forgot she's one of *them*.'

'She's not one of *them*. Anglican's are High Church of England. They have a service like the Mass, the priests wear vestments, they have candles, flowers, Confession and nuns even. They're not like that lot from Netherfield Road. I want you to be my matron of honour and to hell with what your husband says. He can stay home and mind the baby if he gets a cob on over it.'

'And is Sean Maguire being best man?'

'Of course. It's all arranged. We've been to see Father Hegarty. Sean came too.'

'They'd get on well then, those two. Father Hegarty is always going on about Home Rule and Sean Maguire is always going on about the rights of the common people. A pair of troublemakers, if you ask me. So, its Coronation Day then?'

Nora nodded. It was only four weeks away.

That very evening when Pat called, Leah broached the subject of where they were going to live.

'Da says we can live there. Declan will share with him, but we want somewhere a bit more, well, private. Somewhere where people don't know us.' Nora felt embarrassed.

'As a wedding present will you let me give you the money for a decent house?'

Nora's eyes widened. 'Buy one?'

Leah nodded. 'That way you'll always have a roof over your head, even if there's no work.'

Pat shook his head. 'It's very good of you, Leah, it's more than good, but no, thank you. We'll find somewhere to rent.'

'Then let me pay the rent,' she pleaded. It was such a small amount. Their expectations of life were so small too. Everyone helped each other in this neighbourhood, that was one thing she'd learned. If someone was ill, everyone took over a chore of some kind. Curtains and precious tablecloths were lent to people who were having a wedding party in the house, clothes as well for such occasions. It was such a different world, a different community. They had nothing in material terms yet they gave what they did have readily – time, patience, comfort and advice.

Again Pat shook his head. 'Don't think I'm ungrateful, Leah, please, but I have my pride. How do you think I'd feel when it got around, and it would, that you were keeping us?'

'But I won't be! It's just the rent. Eight or ten shillings a week for decent conditions in a good neighbourhood.'

Nora reached out and took her hand. 'We may only get a room, but it will be ours, Leah. You've done more than enough for all of us. You gave up a life, a very comfortable life, to come and live around here because of me. You've turned that house into a real home with every comfort for Da and Declan and I know you put five pounds regularly under the teapot on the mantle, so don't deny it. Our Declan's got a gob on him like a parish oven. It means Da doesn't have to work, that he has good food and clothes and is warm and has all the time in the world now to take pleasure in reading. They were all the things I wanted to give him and I'm very, very grateful, but we want something . . . different.'

Leah nodded slowly. They did have their pride and she had no right to undermine it, as Sean so often told her she did without meaning to. Patronising, he called it.

She'd be lonely when Nora went. Oh, there were plenty of people only too willing to come in for a cup of tea and a gossip and envy everything she had. In fact lately she'd begun to feel so guilty and unhappy and confused. Should she go back? Rhian and Aunt Poppy and the staff would welcome her. What difference would Ernest's presence make to her? But no, she wouldn't live under the same roof as a man who had gone so far as to have her beaten, maybe even killed if Sean hadn't appeared.

It came to her then that she hated Ernest Armstrong. Really hated him to a degree she hadn't thought possible before.

Leah at last smiled. 'I can't be your bridesmaid, you won't let me help you with a house, what can I do for you?'

145

Now it was Nora who felt ashamed and guilty. 'Leah, we didn't mean . . . I didn't want things to be like this.'

'I know and there are many times when I feel I should have kept my nose out of your affairs. Aunt Poppy is right, I'm a meddler.'

'But you do it because you're kind and generous and you've got principles,' Pat said.

Leah's smile was a little woeful. 'That's not how Sean describes me.'

'Oh, take no notice of him. It's your class he's getting at, not you. He likes you. I mean it.'

Leah's heart gave a little leap. Sometimes she had doubted it and yet once or twice she had turned unexpectedly and seen the look in his eyes. The look that she now longed to see more often and to tell him that she felt the same way, because she was sure she was falling in love with him. But she didn't have the words and she thought the class divide between them was too great.

'Then let me buy your wedding dress and veil, Nora, please?'

Nora couldn't refuse. 'As long as it's nothing too fancy or too expensive. We're not going to Bold Street.'

'No, but it will be handmade just the same.'

On the evening before the coronation of King George V and amidst all the preparations for both it and Nora's wedding, Percy appeared on the doorstep of number four Vandries Street.

Even the meanest areas were being decked out in red, white and blue bunting. Pianos had been borrowed and dragged into the streets, tables and chairs were being put down the lengths of them and women and young girls scraped together every single farthing they could to put on some kind of a spread.

Oil Street and Vandries Street were doing it in style.

Leah had ordered cakes and jellies, ham, beef, chicken and soft white bread and real butter for the sandwiches and pork pies and trotters.

'None of yer Maggie Ann for us termorrer,' Lizzie Madden said smugly to a woman she knew who lived in Dublin Street.

Madeira wine and port and lemonade had been bought for the women and girls, ginger pop and lemonade for the kids and beer for the men.

'For God's sake, queen, don't give them any of the hard stuff or there'll be murder before the night's out,' Florrie Burrows advised. 'We'll have the scuffers down here by the 'undred with the battle wagons. I don't know what gets inter them when they've 'ad whisky or rum.'

Nora opened the door to Percy. Her hair was in curling papers and she was wearing an old dress. She was helping with the sandwich and jelly making. Declan had been chased off home after Nora had found him poking his finger in the jellies to see if they had set.

'What's the matter?'

'It's Miss Leah I've come for.'

Nora glanced over her shoulder. 'Why?'

'It's Miss Poppy, she's sick.'

'Get in then.'

As soon as Leah saw the lad, she knew something was wrong. 'Is it Rhian? Aunt Poppy?'

'Miss Poppy. Mrs Armstrong said I was to tell you to come soon, she's not well at all.'

'Has the doctor been?'

'Twice today.'

'Oh, God.' Leah began to untie her apron.

'Percy, go and find a cab, quick. I'll get Miss Leah's things,' Nora instructed, all thoughts of both the coronation and her wedding forgotten as she ran upstairs for a wide-brimmed straw hat and a silk jacket for Leah.

147

Percy came back panting, with a hackney not far behind him. Leah was already on the step waiting.

'Get in Percy. Oh, Leah, I hope she's going to get well again, I really do. Go on.' Nora hugged her friend and pushed her into the cab and shouted, 'Prince's Avenue as fast as you can!'

It seemed to take an age to get across town and when the cab stopped outside the house, Leah thrust a pound note into the driver's hand and ran up the drive, leaving the cabbie stunned at his good fortune.

The front door was ajar, the warm evening air heavy with the perfume of shrub blossoms and flowers. Miss Winthrop was waiting in the hall.

'Oh, Miss Winthrop, how is she? Why did no one tell me she was ill? Where's Rhian? Where's Mr Armstrong?'

'*He's* in the study, your sister is up with Miss Poppy. The doctor has just left. She didn't seem too bad, the mistress didn't want to alarm you.'

Discarding her hat and hitching up her skirt, Leah took the stairs two at a time and ran along the landing. She burst into Poppy's room. It was warm and stuffy. The curtains were drawn to keep out the evening sunlight. Rhian sat by the bed looking pale and worried.

'What's the matter? Rhian, what's the matter?'

Rhian shook her head, tears in her eyes. 'He said a mild heart attack and that . . . that there could be more, and at her age . . .' Rhian shook her head, unable to go on.

Leah crossed to the bed and knelt beside it. Aunt Poppy looked so small, so shrivelled, her skin like tissue paper. She looked like a little doll, but an old, wizened one.

'Aunt Poppy,' she whispered. The old lady's eyes were closed. She repeated it and Poppy's eyes opened slowly. She smiled, although Leah thought it looked more like a grimace. 'Aunt Poppy, what's wrong? What did the doctor say?'

148

Poppy made an effort to sit up. Instantly both girls rearranged the pillows and drew her up gently. It was like lifting a child, Leah thought.

Poppy's voice was weak but there was still a note of imperiousness in it. 'He's a fool, that man. I don't want to see him again. He wanted me to go to hospital. What's the point of that? I'm dying and I'm going to die in my own bed.'

'No!' Leah's cry was full of anguish. 'No, you're not dying, Aunt Poppy, you can't.'

'I've lived too long already, far too long. I'm weary of the world.' Her breathing was laboured.

Leah cast about in the turmoil of her mind for something to say to give her aunt a purpose, a reason to go on. 'But you can't die! You can't miss the coronation!'

Poppy smiled. 'I'd have liked to have seen it. He's a good man and she's . . . sensible. There'll be no decadence. No Lily Langtrys or Alice Kepples with this one. He's strict and that's good.' She sighed deeply. 'But my generation is dying out and the world is changing. Such poverty, such unrest won't be suffered for much longer and there is such greed for money and power that it will all end badly.' She clutched Leah's hand.

'Don't talk, save your breath. Don't get over-excited,' Leah begged, tears sliding down her cheeks.

Again the grim smile. 'Rhian, all the family jewellery is to go to you and then to little Penny. At least I have had the joy of seeing her, unlike your poor mother.'

Rhian was sobbing quietly.

'Leah, child, Mr Rankin has my will. You are well provided for, you'll have the . . . means . . . to . . . out . . .' The voice faded away into silence.

'I'll get Ernest.' Rhian rose, trying to pull herself together.

'No!' Leah's voice was harsh and determined. 'She

never liked him, Rhian, and I'm sorry but neither do I. I won't have him in here. It's not his place to be here.'

Rhian nodded slowly and returned to her seat beside the bed. They each held one of Poppy's hands while the sun sank, the moon rose and the hours passed.

It was midnight. The new day was being heralded by the slightly tinny chimes of the small marble clock on the mantelpiece. It was Coronation Day and Miss Penelope Cavendish died peacefully in her sleep.

Chapter Eleven

The church was packed for Nora's wedding. Father Finnegan, resplendent in his white and gold vestments, commenced with prayers of thanksgiving for the new King and Queen, followed by the national anthem. After that he devoted his full attention to the Nuptial Mass, preceded by the hymn 'Faith of Our Fathers'.

Joe had had tears in his eyes as he'd led Nora up the aisle. There was no more contented man in the church, he thought, and he thanked God for it. It had all come about because of Nora. Nora who looked radiant in white satin, the tulle of her veil covering her face and floating out behind her like a cloud of thistledown.

Leah, looking pale and tired and wearing a cornflower blue linen suit and matching hat, stood in the pews on the right, the bride's side. Her eyes were bright with tears of emotion as she sang the national anthem. Oh, Aunt Poppy would have loved this. If only she could have kept going. If only her spirit had been stronger. But what use now was 'if only'?

She fell silent for the hymn which she didn't know and had never even heard of. She looked over at Sean with affection and longing tinged with sadness. He was singing with the congregation.

> Faith of our Fathers living still
> In spite of dungeon fire and sword,

Oh how our hearts beat high with joy
When e'er we hear that glorious word,
Faith of our Father's Holy Faith
We will be true to thee till death
We will be true to thee till death.

She felt so isolated. She shouldn't be here. She no longer
felt part of this service and she should anyway be wearing
the black of deep mourning, but she also knew that Aunt
Poppy would want her to be here for Nora's happiest day.
Poppy had been fond of Nora.

Ethna, wearing a peach crêpe de chine dress, paid
for by Nora, and a wide-brimmed hat decorated with
deeper peach satin roses looked very well, Leah thought.
The colour suited her, it gave her complexion a slight
glow that was enhanced by excitement. She hadn't been
dressed up like this since the day she herself had been
married, she'd said when they'd had a dress rehearsal the
previous week.

'You look so elegant, Ethna, and the colour really does
suit you,' Leah had complimented her.

'And this outfit you'll keep, never mind what *he* says.
I paid for it, not him,' Nora added.

'But I'll never wear it again.' Ethna had sounded
wistful.

'So what? You can take it out every now and then and
put it on and do a bit of a twirl around and you never
know, something might come up when you'll need it.'
Nora had looked directly at Leah who had laughed and
told her to stop matchmaking.

Throughout the service Declan glared malevolently at
Jimmy Murphy who was one of the altar boys. Jimmy
had smirked when he'd seen his mate all done up in
a new suit with a brand new and therefore stiff and
uncomfortable shirt, collar and tie. One remark out of

him later at the street party and he'd belt him good and proper, Coronation Day or not.

In London hundreds of thousands of people turned out to see the procession to Westminster Abbey, and all over the country in cities, towns, villages and hamlets there were celebrations. Nora and Pat were toasted by everyone in Oil Street with glasses of Madeira wine or ale or ginger pop.

Nora refused to take off her wedding dress. The white satin was cut very plainly, with a high neckline (dictated by modesty and the Church) and long sleeves ending in a point. What made it so special that people in church had gasped as she'd passed by was the huge bow at the back. It was covered with silver bugle beads and the four-foot train which swept behind her was also heavily edged with beading. It had been handmade and was expensive. She'd had a fit when she'd found out how much Leah had paid for it. Nora did, however, take off her headdress and long veil for, as Ethna had said, it would be ruined if she kept it on. She looped the train over her arm.

As the afternoon wore on and eventually turned into purple summer dusk, the tables were taken back inside but the chairs were arranged on the pavements outside their respective owners' homes. Oscar – known to all as Ozzie – Daly sat down at the piano and the singsong began.

'Nora, gerrup an 'ave the first dance with yer 'usband!' Eileen Molloy shouted, and her sentiments were noisily supported by others until they began to waltz on the cobbled roadway, to a rousing cheer.

Nora looked up at her new husband, her face radiant with happiness.

'Oh, Pat, it's been the best day of my entire life.'

He looked down at her and a surge of love washed over him. She was his, his alone now. She was Mrs Patrick Ryan and for the rest of their lives he'd take care of her.

They'd share everything, the good times and the bad, for there would be hard times ahead. But they'd have children, they'd be a family.

'I love you, Nora Ryan, and I'll love you until the day I die.' He whirled her round and the white satin billowed around her as though it was a cloud as other couples got up to join them.

Leah was sitting on a kitchen chair and Sean was on the top step of the house, a glass of beer in his hand. Leah had had one glass of port and lemonade, a drink that had been urged on her by Maggie Cullen. It was an odd mixture, she'd thought, but obviously a popular one around here so she'd drunk it and had been surprised. It had tasted so nice.

''Ave another one, luv,' Maggie urged.

'Thank you, Mrs Cullen, I will.'

'It's Maggie ter you, luv. I'm 'avin none of this "Mrs Cullen".'

'Now you watch those things,' Sean warned Leah. 'You think they taste nice and sweet and they're as harmless as lemonade, but they'll give you a desperate head in the morning.'

'I don't want to think about tomorrow.'

'I don't blame you. I suppose the almighty Mr Armstrong is doing all the arranging?'

Leah nodded. 'And she'd hate it. She had no time for him. None at all.'

'Wasn't she a wise woman then.'

'She was. She was far cleverer and sharper than many people realised. Ernest thought she was just a batty old lady, an eccentric, and that it was best to humour her or leave her alone, but she never missed a thing that went on in that house.' She sighed and finally took off her hat. Everyone else had done so much earlier.

'When do you think the funeral will be?'

She shrugged. 'Early next week, I suppose. Will you come?'

He nodded. 'But just for the service and if Father Finnegan finds out, I'll be for it, attending a Protestant service. I'll be on my knees for months saying prayers for my sins and wouldn't your lot above in Prince's Avenue show me the door if I went back with you,' he laughed.

Leah didn't laugh with him. 'I shouldn't have been at Our Lady's today, but no one seemed to mind. It was only the hymns I didn't know, especially the first one. The service is very similar to ours. Did you know your priest and Reverend Hunter are friends?'

Sean nodded but smiled wrily. 'I do and I think it's a grand thing, especially in this city where they half kill each other twice a year in the name of religion. But "Faith of Our Father's" right after the national anthem was Father Finnegan's way of reminding us all of our allegiance not just to the King and Queen and Empire but to our faith and a greater King.' He laughed. 'If Father Hegarty had got his way, there would have been no national anthem, just "Wrap the Green Flag Round Me, Boys" or "The Croppy Boy". He has dreams. He's always looking at the past but I don't think his dreams will ever come true. Anyway, most people are too busy trying to keep body and soul together to worry about long dead Fenians. Ah, let's stop all this serious talk or we'll finish the night cryin' into our drinks. Will you have this dance with me, Miss Leah Cavendish?' He got up and made an exaggerated bow and she laughed.

'Thank you, Mr Maguire. I'll be delighted to.'

The narrow roadway was packed and it was a bit of a crush so he had to hold her closely. He tried to push the thoughts from his mind and the emotions from his body. He loved her but it could never be. It would be like reaching for the stars or the moon. He could offer her nothing and he wouldn't be kept by her money. Religion came second; he wasn't a fervent Catholic.

'Nora and Pat have a place. I haven't seen it yet, it's just one room, Nora said, but it's theirs.' Leah wondered whether Pat had said anything to Sean about her offers.

'You don't want to see it, either. It's number ten Blackstock Street, isn't it?'

She nodded. 'What's wrong with it?'

'With the room itself, not a lot. Sure, the house itself is a dump, like all these houses around here are, but it's the rest of them.'

She looked puzzled. 'What rest of them?'

'There are fifteen people living in that house already, ten of them kids. And by God, never will I understand why Pat agreed to take it. I mean, all over this city families have to live in one room, but to share the same house as Seamus and Annie Macardle, he must be off his head, so he must.'

Leah was stunned. By bribing with drink a few hard cases Sean had found out who had attacked her and why, and just as Macardle was recovering from the first beating, Sean and Pat had punched him senseless. They had also paid Neely a visit, when Ethna was at her Da's, and had told him what they'd done to Macardle and that he would be next, family or no family, if anyone laid a finger on Leah again.

Unfortunately they had encountered Leah on the way home and, seeing the blood on their clothes, she had virtually forced them to tell her of the entire episode, saying it was her right to know, she was the one who had been beaten. But Leah had promised not to tell Nora. She hadn't wanted to worry or upset her friend.

'Nora doesn't know him,' Leah said, gathering her wits. 'Pat can't have said anything or she'd have told me.'

'And I never should have told you his name either. I've the brains of an eejit at times.'

'I'm glad I do know Sean, but let's forget it all.'

'The other family, the Ahearns are decent enough and old Dai Morgan is one of the nicest fellows you'd wish to meet in a month of Sundays. He's a Welshman, spent most of his life down the pit until the dust got to his chest and he was no more use to the bosses. He moved here, earns what he can with his barrel organ and monkey and he'll get this new pension. But that lot. Holy Mother of God. Pat's mad.'

'Maybe he's told Macardle if he goes near Nora he'll kill him.' Leah was very concerned.

'If he hasn't, then I bloody well will!'

She sighed heavily and pushed the thought from her mind, there were only a few hours left of this day of celebration, tomorrow the humdrum chores of everyday life would resume and the sorrow would claim her entirely.

'You've a face like a wet week,' Sean said, trying to keep his longing for her from his voice.

'I'm sorry. I was just thinking that . . .'

'What?' He looked down into the green eyes that were so clear and lovely they'd tear the heart out of you.

'Tomorrow I'll have to go into mourning and I'm not looking forward to being on my own, with Nora gone. And I'm not going back up there.'

'Wouldn't it be wise if you did go back, Leah? You don't belong in this world, with this class of person.'

'I've made friends.'

'You've made acquaintances and neighbours, Leah. That's different altogether.'

Before she could reply, Ethna, carrying her baby and her hat, and Edward Neely appeared beside them.

'I'm sorry to break up the party, but we're going home

157

now. Little Alex is tired and so am I.' She made no reference to her husband.

Sean held Neely's gaze steadily until Ethna's husband was forced to drop his eyes before the hard, contemptuous stare.

'Have you enjoyed yourself, Ethna?' Leah asked.

'I have. I expect you'll miss our Nora.'

'I will.'

'Why don't you come up and visit me? Any afternoon. Alex has a sleep then so we'd not be disturbed.'

'And I'd be gone long before you have to prepare the tea for your lord and master,' Leah laughed. It had sounded flippant but it wasn't and Neely knew it. 'Well, I'll see you soon, Ethna. Good night.'

'One more dance and then I'm going to walk you home, Leah.'

'It's only round the corner, Sean,' she laughed.

'I know, but you know what happened last time you said those words to Pat.'

She became serious as she remembered that night. Then she wondered how Rhian and her husband had celebrated the coronation. Inevitably it would have been a sombre day for Rhian with Aunt Poppy lying upstairs in state, clad not in a decent shroud but in the old-fashioned pale blue crinoline, her bundle of letters and the sepia photo of her handsome confederate officer lying beside her in the casket. It had been a request, a promise she'd extracted from Rhian just a month ago.

Outside number four Vandries Street, Leah took her keys from her pocket and looked up at Sean.

'Thank you, it's been a . . . memorable day and I couldn't have got through it all without you, Sean. I mean that.'

'Oh, Leah. Leah Cavendish. What's going to become of you?'

She was puzzled. 'What do you mean?'

He couldn't help himself. He gave in. He gathered her to him and kissed her, a long, slow kiss. He felt her lips part beneath his and her mouth opened like a flower and she clung to him.

She didn't care about money, status or even religion. All she cared about was her love for Sean Maguire. She'd follow him to the ends of the earth if he asked her.

Reluctantly he drew away. 'I'm sorry, Leah.'

'What for, Sean? I love you.' Her shining eyes bore witness to the fact.

His heart leapt but he had to shake his head. 'No, you only think you do.'

'I don't *think*, Sean, and I know you love me.' She reached for him again but with a tremendous effort he drew back.

'Good night, Leah. Let me know when your aunt's funeral will be.'

He hurried away and Leah turned and let herself into her silent, empty house.

Nora had had a perfect day. The entire street had waved her off – those that were still able to stand – as Pat had swung her off her feet. She'd laughed and waved her veil and headdress and had given her bouquet to Eileen Molloy for all her help.

'Eh, Pat, yer not going to carry 'er all the way 'ome, are yer?' Jack Murphy shouted after them.

'No, I'm not!' Pat had shouted back.

They walked along Vauxhall Road and up on to Scotland Road, mingling with the crowds, thanking perfect strangers for their good wishes. Some were half drunk. They ignored the crude advice and remarks that made Nora's cheeks burn and Pat's forehead crease into a frown.

Everything had been done for their arrival. Lizzie Madden, Florrie Burrows, Eileen Molloy and Agnes Murphy had been up and scrubbed every inch of the floor, walls and ceiling and Jack Murphy had whitewashed the walls and ceiling.

'Put plenty of lime in that bucket, Jack. It'll 'elp kill the bugs,' his wife had advised.

New white cotton nets and chintz draw curtains hung at the window.

On the new lino was a large second-hand rug that had been thrown over Eileen's washing line and beaten until she'd worn herself out and then Florrie had scrubbed it. They had no money to spare for wedding gifts, but they gladly gave their time and effort to make the place clean for Nora. After all, her mam had been a friend of theirs.

The room was a bit crowded. As well as a brass bed with a new patchwork quilt, there was a chest of drawers and a small wardrobe, presents from her da; two new and comfortable easy chairs set each side of the blackleaded range, and a small, drop-leaf table and two dining chairs, all gifts from Leah. In one alcove shelves held crockery and pans. On the high mantelshelf over the range a red chenille cloth with a bobbled fringe held an assortment of small gifts: little china spill holder, two pretty china candlesticks, a second-hand but good clock, and from Ethna, in pride of place, a statue of Our Lady of Lourdes.

Nora looked around with shining eyes and flushed cheeks. 'Oh, Pat, isn't it great!'

'It's not as posh as Leah's place, but it's ours, Nora. Yours and mine, we can shut out the world.'

'I don't think we can do that entirely,' she laughed. 'They'll all be in and out just to see what I've got. "Can I trouble yer for a loan of a bit of sugar, Mrs Ryan,"' she mimicked Florrie's wheedling voice.

Pat's smile died and his eyes became hard.

'I'm not having anyone taking advantage of you, Nora, you're such a soft touch, I should have told you before . . .'

'Told me what? Pat, what's the matter?'

'You know that Bernie and Brigid Ahearn and their six kids live in the back downstairs room.'

'I know, I'll have to traipse through there to the scullery to get water.'

'Old Dai Morgan lives upstairs in the back room.'

'He keeps his barrel organ and monkey up there, I know that.'

'But what I didn't tell you was who lives in the other room upstairs.'

'Well, who does and why didn't you tell me?'

'I didn't tell you because if you remember you heard this room was going free and dashed up, looked around and said we'd have it. And you were so thrilled . . . Well, anyway, the feller's a head case and he drinks like a fish so there's bound to be fights and the scuffers will be called.'

'Oh, my God! Pat, why didn't you say something?'

'I have. Sean and I have been up to see him. He told him if he so much as knocks on this door he'll get a hiding. So don't be letting her or any of the kids in here.'

Nora looked perturbed. 'But Pat, I can't refuse her if she comes to beg a little tea or sugar. You know that we all help each other.'

'Whatever she borrows will be for him, not herself or her ten unfortunate kids. And never, never give her money, no matter how much of a sob story she tells you. He'll have that, too. You'll have to be persistently firm with them until they get it into their thick heads that no means no.'

'But what about when I'm out at work?' They had

161

decided that she should work until they started a family, to save a bit of emergency money. 'What if he tries to break in?'

'Then Mrs Ahearn across the hall has instructions to fetch the bobbies at once.'

The news had taken a bit of the shine off the day but it was partly her own fault, she had been the one to say they'd take it. She sighed and slid her arms round him. The day wasn't over. The best part was yet to come.

Chapter Twelve

Miss Penelope Cavendish was being buried with almost the same amount of pomp as the late King Edward, Leah thought as she sat with her cousin Richard and his father in the second carriage. Rhian and Ernest had, of course, gone in the first carriage.

The obituaries in the local papers took up many columns and there were numerous floral tributes, including ones from all Poppy's brothers and their families. This had been arranged by Charles Cavendish, Richard's father, who had happened to arrive on home leave from the diplomatic service on Coronation Day. He'd been astounded to learn that Leah no longer lived in Prince's Avenue but even after what he called a 'good talking to' he'd been unable to get anything further out of Leah herself or his son who didn't appear to care where his cousin lived. Charles had every intention of taking Richard back to Rhodesia with him. The lad was becoming an idle wastrel who drank far too much.

Leah and Rhian clung together at the graveside, fighting back the tears. It was her sister that Rhian turned to for comfort, not her husband. Ernest had organised the funeral, sparing no expense, but Rhian knew he wasn't sorry Poppy was dead. In fact there had been a definite air of triumph in his manner these last few days.

Leah was remembering her aunt on the day of Rhian's wedding, over a year ago. Standing erect, her head held proudly, no sign on her face of the pain of the arthritis. Conforming to propriety in her grey and black dress. She hadn't approved of King Edward and she'd hated his mother, yet she clung to tradition. Her life this last year had not been peaceful, what with the worry about herself and her dislike of Ernest. The only joy Poppy had had was seeing her namesake born.

Sean managed to slip away from work for an hour and sat in the back pews. He looked incongruous in his working clothes. He'd never been inside a Protestant church of any kind in his life and he was amazed. Leah had been right, there was very little difference between Catholic and High Anglican. There was no tabernacle on the altar and therefore no red sanctuary lamp burning, but the altar was highly decorated with carved wooden panels inlaid with gold and ivory. The altar slab itself was covered with a white and gold cloth and the candlesticks and cross that stood between them were magnificent. There were beautiful stained-glass windows through which the sun streamed, throwing beams of light of every colour on to the heads of the mourners. He noted a confessional box and there was even a Lady Chapel. No statue of the Virgin Mary, of course, but a beautifully made hanging depicting the Virgin and child in silks and satins and gold and silver thread.

But there *was* a divide. It was evident in the prayers and procedures that were missing, and the two hymns, the 23rd Psalm and 'Abide With Me', were unknown to him.

The slow, sonorous yet dignified notes of Handel's *Largo* filled the church as Miss Poppy's coffin was taken to the hearse. Sean couldn't see Leah's face properly as it was covered with heavy black veiling that reached almost to her waist. Both she and Rhian were in full mourning. But she acknowledged him as she drew abreast by the slight raising of her right hand clad in black lace gloves.

He went back to work more thoughtful. She was on her own now and she had still five months to go until she was twenty-one. Armstrong could do a lot of damage in five months and he had shown himself an utterly ruthless man.

The will was to be read by Mr Rankin at the house on Prince's Avenue at the beginning of July and each day Rhian thought that Ernest became more and more imperious, more domineering. Since she'd had the baby, Ernest had grown away from her. She'd always thought that babies drew couples together, but Ernest had made his displeasure clear and she remembered Aunt Poppy's words that she hoped he would have only daughters so that the business would not be called Armstrong's. It seemed like a curse now. For months she'd been trying to conceive, praying that if she did, it would be the son and heir Ernest wanted so badly. She was young and healthy and she longed for another baby, for a brother for Penny, for the return of Ernest's love and attention.

She was often miserable, missing the company of both her sister and her aunt. She knew she could go and visit Leah, she'd be welcomed with open arms, but Ernest would find out and there would be hell to pay. Life looked bleak. Her only ray of sunshine was Penny and the hope and belief that in time she would have more children.

They assembled in the study. Mr Rankin sat in John Cavendish's chair, his clerk beside him on a high stool brought from the kitchen and covered with a clean cloth. A trio of straight-backed chairs for Leah, Rhian and Ernest had been arranged facing the desk. Crystal decanters of whisky and sherry, with the appropriate glasses, stood on a silver tray on top of the bureau.

'Do you think our jobs will be safe?' Cook had asked Miss Winthrop after the solicitor had been ushered into the study.

'Why shouldn't they? Miss Rhian won't start getting new staff. I imagine everything will all be split down the middle between Miss Leah and Miss Rhian – Mrs Armstrong,' she corrected herself.

'Do you think she'll have made any small special bequests?' Cook asked.

'Like what?'

Cook shrugged. 'To us.'

Miss Winthrop raised her eyes to the ceiling. She certainly hoped they would get some form of reward for their service and loyalty. They had when the master and mistress had died.

Mr Rankin cleared his throat and arranged his features in a serious expression. He wasn't a dour man by nature and it often amused him to see the expressions on the faces of some of the relatives when they did not get what they expected, or got more, but he was an expert at hiding it all behind a sober and somewhat mournful expression and tone of voice.

'As you are all aware, Miss Penelope Cavendish was the sole executor of the wills of both Mr John and Mrs Edwina Cavendish, a duty she carried out most meticulously.' He turned some papers over. 'So I shall begin by reading again the wills of the late Mr and Mrs Cavendish.'

They all listened in silence. They'd heard it before – at least Leah and Rhian had, although at the time they were so shocked that most of it hadn't registered in their minds until later. Half the business, the house, the properties, the shares were to go to Rhian and Leah when they reached twenty-one or married, whichever occurred first.

Mr Rankin paused and set aside the papers and picked

up two sheets of vellum. He looked at the faces of the three people in front of him. The two girls looked tired and near to tears. Ernest Armstrong's expression was false, he'd seen it so often before. That serious, mournful expression that hid the avarice.

'I shall now read the terms and conditions of the will of Miss Penelope Cavendish, the estate having been left to her by her father Robert Cavendish, founder of the business.'

Ernest felt the excitement building in him. A few more minutes, just a few more minutes now and he'd have control of everything.

The solicitor cleared his throat again. '"The family jewels, with the exception of an emerald and diamond ring, are to go to Mrs Rhian Armstrong. The ring is to go to Miss Leah Cavendish as a token of remembrance and because the emerald matches her eyes. Also to Miss Leah Cavendish I leave my entire estate which comprises ten thousand pounds and two thousand shares in Cavendish's Haulage and Porterage which should yield an income of three thousand pounds per annum, all to be held in trust by Mr J. Rankin as executor until Miss Leah Cavendish becomes of age or marries, whichever is the sooner. To Miss Winthrop and Mrs Knowles I leave a sum of four hundred pounds each. To Joseph Blackett two hundred. To Percival Reading fifty pounds and to Nora O'Brian, my former maid, a sum of one hundred and twenty-five pounds." And that concludes the business in hand.'

Ernest sat stunned, a numbness creeping over him. The bitch! She'd been no slightly dotty old lady but a sly, conniving old bitch! Leah now had two thousand shares over and above those her father had left her. She held the controlling interest in the business! He shook his head slowly in disbelief. By God, he wasn't going to stand for this! He found his voice.

'I . . . my wife and I will contest this, Mr Rankin.'

The solicitor feigned surprise, he'd known what Miss Poppy Cavendish had done and why. 'I see nothing to contest, Mr Armstrong. It's all very straightforward and perfectly within the letter of the law.'

Ernest had got to his feet, his temper rising. He thumped the desk. 'It's far from straightforward! She's left the controlling interest in the business in the hands of this chit of a girl who chooses to live in the slums! She was out of her senses. Insane. She should have been certified!'

Rhian had risen. Ernest's accusations were too much to bear. She had loved her aunt. 'She was perfectly sane and I shall call Dr Ashworth to validate it.'

'And so shall I!' Leah, too, was on her feet. God bless Aunt Poppy. Oh, God bless her. She didn't care about the money, but Poppy had made certain Ernest Armstrong would never control the business and she'd left money for Nora too.

'I'd have expected some loyalty from you, Rhian, at least! You are my wife and it is not fair that all your aunt's money and shares go to your sister.'

'I have enough, Ernest. I have the jewellery, my home, a comfortable income. I don't care about shares or the business.'

Leah thought she'd never seen Rhian so determined.

Ernest stormed out, slamming the door behind him.

Rhian's face was scarlet. It wasn't often she took a stand against her husband. 'I'm sorry for . . . for my husband's behaviour, Mr Rankin.'

'Oh, don't let that worry you, Mrs Armstrong, I've had to suffer more than that in my career.' He smiled, a genuine smile of satisfaction. That would teach the pompous Mr Armstrong to dismiss old ladies as utter fools. 'Before I leave, I will explain to you both about the property that belonged to your father. We administer it through an agent who collects the rents which are then banked in separate accounts under both your names. Any repairs are noted by the agent and passed on to us and we see that they are carried out.'

Rhian nodded. 'That seems fair.'

'Could I ask, Mr Rankin, just what the property consists of and where it is?' Leah was curious. Was it shops, houses, warehouses?

He withdrew a sheet of paper from a folder on the desk. 'Certainly. The property consists of houses. Three entire streets, in fact, in the Trafalgar Dock area. Oil Street, Vandries Street and Vulcan Street.'

Leah went very pale and clutched her sister's arm as though she was about to faint.

Mr Rankin was alarmed. 'Miss Leah? Miss Leah, are you all right?'

Leah was shaking her head. No! It couldn't be true! It was some horrible twist of fate. Her father had been content to let people live in such terrible conditions and now *she* owned those dreadful slum dwellings! She thought of the first night she'd slept in Oil Street and the state of the house. She thought of her own home in Vandries Street. Of Lizzie Madden and Florrie Burrows and Eileen Molloy. Oh God, no! The room began to tilt and she clung to Rhian.

Mr Rankin poured a small amount of whisky and held the glass to her lips but she drew away.

'How could he? How could he, Rhian? How could Father have ever let people live . . . exist . . . in places like that?'

Rhian was also shocked although she'd only heard Nora and Leah's descriptions of the conditions.

'Leah, he probably didn't even know what kind of a state they were in. You heard Mr Rankin say it was all done through an agent.'

169

Leah couldn't be pacified. The hardship, the hunger, the deaths from disease all seemed to be laid now at her feet. And Sean. How was she to tell him? How could she go on living there? And yet she wouldn't come back here.

Before either of them could stop her, she ran from the room, across the hall and out and down the steps. She got a hackney halfway down the avenue and automatically gave her destination as number four Vandries Street.

She didn't know how long she sat in her kitchen; it may have been an hour, it may have been four. The fact that she was a very wealthy woman and held the controlling shares in the company meant nothing to her now. A loud knock on the front door brought her to her senses.

Joe O'Brian was standing on the step with a book under his arm, one she'd lent him.

'I brought the book back. Leah! Leah, what's the matter, girl? You look terrible.'

He followed her into the house, leaving the book on the small table in the hall.

'What's wrong, luv? Was it something in that will?'

At his words the floodgates burst open and Leah began to sob, the tears coursing down her cheeks.

Joe put his arm round her. It must have been something awful. Maybe the old lady had cut her out altogether for living here or for some imagined slight. It happened.

Between sobs and gasps for air Leah told him.

'You mean it was yer da who owned all these streets and now . . . now . . .'

'It's me and Rhian!' She clawed frantically at his supporting arm. 'Oh, God, Mr O'Brian, I can't believe it! I've been sitting here for hours thinking of my life and my home, while for all those years hundreds of people like you and Nora have suffered. You lost your wife because of me and mine! Babies have died because of the dirt and

170

disease, and young children too. I've got all that to live with now. How am I going to do it, Mr O'Brian? For God's sake, how?'

He was too dumbfounded and bitter to reply. She spoke the truth. Every single minute of misery, every illness and death could be laid in one respect or another at the feet of John Cavendish and his family. When this got out, her life would be as miserable as everyone else's had been. She'd instantly lose the friendship and respect she'd gained. She'd be hounded out of the neighbourhood and he would understand people's anger. She'd known nothing about it and she was generous and kind, but that would count for nothing.

'How am I to tell Sean? And Pat and Nora?' she pleaded.

He'd been thinking hard, pushing the bitterness to the back of his mind. 'I'll help you, luv. You didn't know, how could you? It's not your fault.'

'It *is*! I should have asked. I should have found out!'

She collapsed into sobs again and Joe rocked her in his arms like a child until Declan came looking for him. Joe sent him down to the Langden Dock to tell Sean to come as soon as he could. Leah was in such a terrible state.

Joe stayed with her until at last, at half past six, Sean knocked on the front door.

'Joe, in the name of all that's holy, what the hell's going on?' Sean was still wearing his working clothes so he left his jacket and boots in the hall by the door.

'It's the will. The old lady's will.'

'What about it?'

'Look, Sean, none of it's her fault. I've had all afternoon to think about it, aye, and I've held her while she's cried her heart out the way I did when I lost our Nell. She didn't know about any of it until today and she

171

would have gone on not knowing but she asked the solicitor bloke.'

Sean was mystified. 'Has she been cut off? Has she been disinherited because she lives here or because of me? She knows I don't give a damn for her money.'

'No, it's nothing like that. It's just the opposite. She's in a terrible state so remember what I said, Sean. It's *not* her fault, she knew *nothing* about it.'

Sean went into the kitchen where Leah sat at the table, her head in her hands, sobbing quietly. He went to her and, bending down, he gently pulled her hands away. Her eyes were red and swollen with crying and her face was drained of all colour. She looked so tragic and broken.

'I didn't know, Sean! I swear to God, I didn't know!'

'Know what, Leah? What's the huge disaster that has you in such a state? Is there no money? No part in the business or the house? You know I don't care if you haven't a farthing.'

'It's nothing like that, Sean. Oh, I wish to God it was just that, that I'd been cut off, but I have half of my father's estate plus all Poppy's money and all her shares. Ernest is furious because she outwitted him and I have the controlling interest in the business, but . . .' Her eyes filled up again and she shook her head.

'Holy Mother of God, Leah, will you tell me what it is?' he pleaded, hating to see her in this state.

'My father . . . and now . . . Rhian and . . . I own the property . . .' She struggled for breath and for words.

'So?'

'Oh, God, Sean! It's all these streets! Oil, Vandries and Vulcan Streets!'

He couldn't speak, he was so stunned.

She clung to his hands. 'All these people and those that have died . . . The dirt, the damp, the rotten woodwork, the poor sanitation. Oh, Sean! Sean! Everyone will hate and detest me and I can't blame them. I can't believe that Father could be so . . . so . . . callous.'

She laid her head on his shoulder, her body racked again with sobs and automatically he placed his arms round her but his face looked as though it had been carved from granite. Her father. Her bloody father had owned all these houses. No, not houses, squalid, filthy hovels with never a penny spent on repairs, nor thought given to the people who were his tenants. Her father and mother and she and her sister had lived in luxury while people had starved and gone without food and fire, boots and clothes to pay for the leaking roof over their heads! Men had stood outside the gates of Cavendish's and begged for work. Pat had been sacked for simply walking out with Nora, a girl he loved and had married. What kind of a reason was that to send a man packing? That was the kind of power men like John Cavendish and Ernest Armstrong wielded. They held men's lives in the palms of their hands and they crushed them without a qualm of conscience.

Leah raised her face, blotched and tear-stained, her eyes filled with grief and guilt. 'What should I do, Sean? How can I live with it all?'

He was becoming calmer now, remembering what Joe had said. 'Leah, it wasn't your fault. You didn't know.'

'But Aunt Poppy must have known. Why didn't she tell me?'

He shrugged. 'Old people are forgetful.'

'No, you couldn't forget a thing like this. She knew! I even described what life was like. She can't have cared. She knew *I* was all right and yet she never appeared selfish or hard-hearted. What can I do, Sean? What can I do?'

He gathered her into his arms although he felt the gulf between them now had widened even further because of

173

the wealth she had inherited. Riches beyond the wildest dreams of anyone who lived in these hellholes for which she was now jointly responsible. At least she cared. Armstrong didn't.

Gradually her sobs diminished and his thoughts became clearer. Her generosity and gentleness would be quickly forgotten and he wouldn't blame those who would revile her. But she didn't deserve to be blamed, to have to endure the hatred that would replace the friendships she'd built.

'Leah, there's no need for anyone else to know. Joe won't go telling everyone.'

'No. I want people to know, Sean.' She was emphatic.

'What for, Leah? Is it some sort of public confession you want? A sort of wearing of sackcloth and ashes for the sins of your father? No, that's not the way to go at all, not if you want to keep acceptance and respect. Get the repairs done. Make the bug-ridden kips habitable, comfortable, more sanitary.'

She nodded slowly.

'They really need demolishing and rebuilding but where would people go?' There was a bitter note in his voice. 'We could say a new landlord has bought them and has got rid of the bloody agents and lawyers. Then, in time, let it be known that *you* bought them. That *you* paid for them with the money your father left you.' He hated the ruling classes, the employers and the fat city councillors but neither Leah nor himself could fight the system alone.

She was growing calmer. 'I'll have every house done out, the way this one is, including lino for the floors of all rooms. I'll have a hot water system put in, the privies in the yards demolished and new ones built. One for each family, the closet, flushing type. The yards will all be repaved, the yard walls whitewashed and a small wash house built too. I can at least try to make amends, Sean.'

He nodded his approval. 'They'll have to be told that

174

there will be no increase in rent, otherwise they'll just up and find a place in another slum area. Do you know how much all that will cost, Leah? You'll have to have the council workmen down to do the drainage. To connect pipes and drains to the sewers. There could be a lot of opposition from the council itself and Armstrong has friends on the council.'

'I don't care, Sean. I'll fight him and his cronies every step of the way and through every court in the land if I have to. I don't care how much it all costs.'

He could only make a rough guess himself so he opted for the most outrageously high figure.

'The best part of three thousand pounds.'

'Sean, she left me ten thousand pounds and two thousand shares. Added to those I'll have half of the profit from the business. I'll have sixteen thousand pounds and a yearly income of three thousand when I'm twenty-one. It's obscene. It's all wrong for me to have so much in a city that has so many slums. When families have to live in cellars and courts and houses like these. What's three thousand out of all that? Just twelve months' income to me. I can't come to terms with that, Sean. I'll furnish the houses as well.'

The amount staggered him. He was speechless. Eventually he managed a smile. 'They'll pawn it.'

'They won't need to. I'll make sure everyone knows they won't be evicted if they get behind with the rent and it will be a peppercorn rent. Sixpence or ninepence and I'll open a savings fund for the children with it.'

'Ah, now that's open to abuse.'

'I don't care. There's no other way I can atone for the years and years of poverty and misery my family have subjected them to.'

Suddenly an idea hurtled into his mind and was blurted out before he had time to think about it properly.

'Will you come to Dublin with me, Leah? I'm going over to hear Jim Larkin speak. You might get some comfort from seeing how much worse conditions are there than here and he's a powerful speaker. And it'll give you time to think over all your plans, away from the place.'

Even as he spoke he knew the gap was growing wider. He wanted none of her money, not a single penny. He'd have no man say it was her fortune he was after, that he was just a smart Mick on the make. Yet to stop any such talk he would have to stop seeing her, stop loving her, and he knew he could never do that. It was a love that was doomed. He would have to learn to accept that and yet remain near enough to her to be of assistance or defence. As he had been on the night Armstrong's thug Macardle had beaten her. There were five more months yet before she would actually have access to her inheritance. He knew she had an allowance. He also knew how generous she was with it. No one was ever turned away from her door who came for the 'borrow of a shillin', till me da gets paid' or 'Leah, queen, could yer spare a bit of tea?' and often he'd seen young lads staggering home with a battered bucket full of coal.

He smiled. 'I might even take you to meet my sisters and herself, the Mammy.'

She, too, smiled. 'I'll go with you to Dublin, Sean. I'd like to meet your family.'

She didn't see the flash of pain in his eyes. He'd raised her hopes and he knew those hopes could only be dashed.

Chapter Thirteen

It was still warm and the air was laden with the mingled odours of the river, the dockside and the factories as Leah and Sean walked towards the tram stop the following evening.

She'd lain awake for a long time through the dark, sticky hours of the night. In her mind she had gone over and over the events of the day. The problems, the decisions, the solutions, the guilt and finally the anger all passed through her mind. She supposed she must be suffering from some sort of aftermath of shock for there were times when she'd grown cold and had shivered uncontrollably, drawing the bedclothes tightly round her, only to toss them aside when the warmth returned to her body. But when she'd finally fallen into a deep, dreamless sleep she'd made a decision. A decision that could have serious consequences for so many people.

She was determined to confront Ernest with the conditions of the houses Rhian owned but which Ernest treated as his by right. Sean, however, had refused to let her go alone when he'd called on his way home from work and she'd told him of her intentions.

'He can't beat me in a houseful of people, someone would call the police. He can only throw me out,' she'd protested.

'He can do that and then pay someone to hurt you again.' Reluctantly, she'd agreed. Nor had she made any protest when he said they'd get a tram and not a hackney.

When they alighted and walked up Prince's Avenue, Sean looked around at the huge houses with their gleaming paintwork, shining windows and neatly kept gardens. There were areas of Dublin like this, too. Fitzwilliam Square, Merrion Square, Morehampton Road and the houses that faced St Stephen's Green. He looked down at Leah who walked beside him. She would have lived in places like that had she been born in Dublin. His heart sank further. That was the class of people she came from and that was what divided them most, more even than religion.

A fresh-faced girl with freckles and red hair opened the door to them and as Leah informed the girl who she was and the reason for her visit, she wondered how long this replacement of Nora's would last. She seemed pleasant enough anyway.

'Will I take your jacket, miss?'

'No, thank you. It won't be a long visit,' Leah answered with a smile.

The girl looked inquiringly at Sean.

He shook his head and straightened his shoulders, gripping his cap tightly in his hands. Even the air inside the house smelled different. Outside it was heavy and the odours of the city prevailed over those of the flowers in the gardens. Here it was cleaner, purer, lightly perfumed with the smell of beeswax mixed with roses. Two huge vases of them stood on marble pedestals either side of the foot of the staircase.

Rhian came down the staircase, her step light and quick, her eyes shining with happiness to see her sister. As she caught sight of Sean, her expression changed to mild curiosity as she tried to place where she'd seen him before.

Leah kissed her and hugged her, then she turned to Sean.

'Rhian, this is Sean Maguire, a friend. He came to Aunt Poppy's funeral service.'

Rhian remembered and hesitated for a second before extending her hand to Sean. It was a hesitation he didn't fail to notice.

'Sean, this is my sister, Rhian Armstrong.'

They shook hands and Sean smiled politely and uttered the correct response to which Rhian inclined her head.

'Is Ernest home, Rhian? I've come to see about the property we now own.'

All the pleasure died in her sister's eyes. She looked apprehensively from Leah to Sean.

'Yes. He's in his study. Shall I go and get him?'

'We'll see him in there.'

There was a brittle edge to Leah's voice that Rhian knew from experience meant trouble. She said nothing but crossed the hall and knocked on the door then opened it.

Ernest had not had a good day. Tom Mann had formed a strike committee to represent all the unions and trade councils. He wished the bloody man would go to the other end of the earth or better still disappear from it altogether. Hundreds were now flocking to join the National Union of Dock Labourers. The seamen were still threatening strike action. The coalheavers, who had their own union, had joined the NUDL which didn't augur well for him. They were all looking for more money and fewer hours and the strength of the unions was growing every day. Some of the carters, but none of his own men as yet, were muttering threats too.

The blistering heat of the day had given him a headache which hadn't been improved by having to listen all through dinner while Rhian complained of the heat and

179

how cross it made little Penny and how fatigued she herself was.

'What do you want now?' he demanded rudely of his wife.

Rhian bit her lip and her cheeks flushed but she didn't answer.

'Is that any way to speak to a wife whose money you use to achieve your own selfish ambitions?'

Ernest Armstrong's eyes narrowed and he rose as he caught sight of Sean standing behind his wife and her sister.

Leah was just as blunt as she walked into the study, taking Rhian's arm and drawing her into the room. 'I've come to see just what you intend to do about improving the houses in the three streets Rhian and I now jointly own.'

'What improvements?' Ernest eyed Sean with mistrust. She'd obviously dragged him along as some sort of protector.

'You know damn well what conditions are like in those houses! The carriage horses stabled in the mews are better housed.'

'They've gone. I got rid of them and the carriages too. It's nineteen eleven, the days of the horse and carriage are over. I only kept them because *she* insisted on driving in the park like a bloody queen.' He folded his arms across his chest. 'And I don't have the slightest intention of throwing Rhian's good money after bad in patching up those hovels which, incidentally, bring in an income for yourself as well as us. And I know my wife supports me. I presume this is your "caring landlady" image?' he sneered.

Leah's temper began to rise. Her eyes glittered dangerously, signs Rhian knew well but which Ernest didn't recognise.

'We charge three and six a week for those hovels. Three and six out of a wage of only a few pounds, if that. Are you such a money grubber that you need half of eighteen pounds a week in rents?' She laughed derisively. 'How stupid of me. I forgot. That's just what you are, Ernest Armstrong. A money-grubbing clerk who has got too big for his boots. You control her money but you don't fool me or control *my* finances. So, you don't intend to do anything?' Rhian was white and shaking and Ernest was quivering with rage.

'No, we'll not spend a penny, on principle. What is the total sum? One hundred and eight pounds a year? Rhian spends more than that on hats. I've other matters on my mind, more important issues. Use your money. Put your hand in *your* pocket as you seem hell bent on living down there with the dregs of society.'

The colour began to rise in Leah's cheeks and she felt Sean's restraining hand on her arm.

He had remained silent, watching Ernest Armstrong closely, his hatred for the man growing by the minute, his admiration for Leah growing apace. She could more than hold her own and she had a tongue sharp enough to rival the market women in Moore Street and Henry Street at home.

Rhian clenched Leah's arms, tears falling down her cheeks.

'Oh Leah, please, haven't there been enough arguments? We're drifting apart and I don't want that, you're my sister,' Rhian pleaded.

Leah squeezed Rhian's hand, she did love her sister but wished she'd stand up to Ernest. 'Rhian, this will be the final argument, I promise, but you won't like the outcome unless you change your minds. I was sickened, utterly sickened when I found out that Father owned those houses and that Aunt Poppy knew it. She knew

181

what they were like, too. No one cared, Rhian. He still doesn't!' she blazed.

Rhian broke down: Ernest had had enough. 'Now that you've said your piece, you can leave. Do what the hell you like with your money, when you get it. Waste it all on people like the O'Brians and the other trash you live among. Now get out. I've work to do.'

Leah's eyes narrowed and she squared her slim shoulders. 'So, you'll do nothing?'

Ernest lost his temper entirely. 'Are you bloody stupid or deaf or both? Not a single halfpenny of our – Rhian's – money goes on those hovels!'

Rhian covered her mouth with her hand to stifle the cry that rose and her eyes were wide with fear. Leah had spoken too quietly. She was too calm.

'Then in four months' time, Ernest Armstrong, on the twenty-fifth of November, the day after my birthday, I'll close Cavendish's down or sell it. I have the power to do either and believe me I will. You, on behalf of Rhian of course, could try to buy me out but to do that you'd have to sell this house – half of which belongs to me – and everything in it, your precious car and all Rhian's jewellery!' Her voice was like ice and even Sean was shocked. He hadn't expected a solution like this. As Ernest's face went from deathly pale to puce he stepped closer to Leah and placed a protective hand on her shoulder.

'Harm one hair of her head, Armstrong, or that of Nora, Ethna or anyone else she loves and this grand house you have here and the fine things that fill it will be burned to the ground, I can guarantee it. Maybe even with yourself in it.' He turned to Rhian who was clutching Leah's arm tightly for support.

'Don't be alarmed now, Mrs Armstrong. We don't beat helpless women or children, unlike himself here,

182

although he hadn't the guts to do his own dirty work. He paid a criminal named Macardle to clatter Leah the last time and your one had half killed her before I laid him out, but you wouldn't be knowing anything like that, now would you? Just a little something that he neglected to tell you.'

Ernest was speechless and fighting for breath.

Leah gently disentangled herself and kissed her weeping sister on the cheek. 'Oh, Rhian, I'm so sorry. All Sean said is true. I was beaten. I'm so, so sorry for you, tied for ever to him, but you know I won't see you and Penny turned out on the street, that much I promise.'

When they were outside in the scented dusk, Sean turned to her. 'Holy God, Leah, I never thought you'd anything like that in mind.'

She looked up at him. The pupils of her green eyes still held pinpricks of fire in their depths. They were like those of a tiger, he thought, and a shiver ran through him; he'd never dreamed she could be so ruthless when she cared deeply about something.

'I meant it. I'll shut him down or sell. He'd have to beg, steal and borrow to buy me out, and that would kill his pride.' The fire in her eyes was fading. 'Did you mean what you said to him?'

He took her hand and drew it through his arm. 'I did so. You've humiliated him and backed him into a corner, Leah, and a cornered rat is dangerous. It goes for the throat.'

She was alarmed. 'He won't harm Rhian, will he?'

'No. As you told me, there are too many people in that house, someone would call the police, but he may try to get at Nora or Ethna or the rest of the family. I'll warn Pat. Well, what shall we do with the rest of this fine summer evening, Miss Leah Cavendish?' He was

183

smiling now, determined to shake off this impending catastrophe.

She smiled back, her tension lessening. 'Shall we go and see Nora and Pat? I haven't told her the good news yet, about her legacy.'

Sean threw back his head and laughed. 'God Almighty, haven't you got two sides to your nature and don't you change them like quicksilver. This I've got to see. Mrs Patrick Ryan being told she's an heiress!'

'It's not all that much.'

'Oh, it is, Leah. To people like me and them, it is an awful lot.'

To the woman he loved one hundred and twenty-five pounds was a paltry sum. He knew it was more than many men earned in a year.

When Leah had first seen the house in Blackstock Street she had been appalled, although it was no different in many ways to those in Oil Street. The paint was peeling, the woodwork rotten, the steps sagging, broken and chipped. The lobby floor was of bare wood so ingrained with dirt it looked as black as coal. The stench of seventeen people living under the one roof had been so powerful in the cloying summer air it was nauseating. But she'd said nothing to Nora, glad that she'd got the furniture, curtains and bedding as wedding gifts. She couldn't for the life of her understand why Nora wanted to live there. She'd wished fervently that Pat's pride hadn't stood in the way of letting her provide them with a better home.

'Now won't this be a surprise.' Sean grinned as he knocked loudly on the door of the front downstairs room. The sash window had been pushed right up to catch any breeze but they'd crept quickly past it.

'Leah! Sean!' Nora cried in delight.

'We thought we'd take a stroll, it being the fine evening it is.'

'And as we were in the neighbourhood,' Leah added, laughing.

'Oh, come in, the pair of you, and sit down. It's that hot I've got the window right up but can you stand me boiling the kettle on the gas ring?'

Leah sat in the easy chair that Pat indicated, while Sean pulled out a dining chair and placed it next to her chair.

'I'll go up to the Eagle Vaults and get a jug of stout,' Pat offered.

Nora was indignant. 'You don't expect us to drink flaming stout, do you?'

'I'll get a bottle of Sarsaparilla for you two.'

'What's that?' Leah inquired.

'It's sort of like lemonade, only it's not,' Nora explained.

'Mrs Ryan, that's a fine description and if you don't mind, I'm the one who's Irish.'

Nora laughed.

'It's a soft drink, nonalcoholic.' Pat was at the door.

'Will you just hold your horses a minute, Pat,' Sean said. 'Leah's got something important she wants to tell you.'

Pat looked quizzically at him but read nothing in his expression. Nora's eyes brightened hopefully. She knew Leah loved Sean. Oh, wouldn't it be great if they were going to get married.

'We've just come from Prince's Avenue, but let's not worry about that yet. We'll tell you all about that later.' Leah paused, her eyes dancing with delight. 'In Aunt Poppy's will she made a bequest to you, Nora.'

Nora was dumbfounded. 'Me? You mean she left me something? But I was only the maid and I wasn't there long either.'

'She liked you. She liked you a lot, Nora. She's left

185

you one hundred and twenty-five pounds. If you present yourself to Mr Rankin at his office in Dale Street, he'll give it to you.'

Sean leaned over and laid his hand on Leah's shoulder as Nora gaped at her friend, then at him, then at her husband and back to Leah.

'You mean she left me . . . all that?'

'Jaysus! Nora, don't you just look like a cod on a fishmonger's slab!' Sean laughed.

Nora couldn't believe it. She pressed her hands to her cheeks. It was a fortune! An absolute fortune and all she'd ever done was to be pleasant and sympathetic to the old lady.

'Holy Mother of God,' Pat managed at last to get out. 'Well, do you think now we can all have a drink for the day that's in it? The good stuff, mind. They don't sell Jameson's at the Eagle but they'll have Powers.'

'What will you do with it?' Leah asked eagerly. 'Will you move? Get a nice house and put some away for emergencies?'.

'With *that* much money there'll never be emergencies!'

Pat slammed the window shut. 'We're all going out.'

'Where to?' Nora demanded. 'It's late, I'll have to get changed. I look as though I've been dragged through a hedge backwards.'

'To the Eagle, it's the nearest.'

Although still stunned, Nora was outraged. 'Are you mad, Pat Ryan? You can't take Leah in that place!'

'Why not?' Leah demanded. 'They have parlours or snugs or separate rooms for women, don't they?'

'Yes, but you get the likes of Agnes Murphy in one of her bouts of depression in the snugs and the Eagle hasn't got a parlour.'

Leah stood up. 'If it's good enough for Agnes Murphy,

Nora, it's good enough for me. Besides, it will broaden my experiences.'

'Oh, it'll do that all right,' Sean commented, wondering about the wisdom of it all.

They were all just a little merry and had sung most of the way home.

'You see what happens when I let you mingle with the lower elements,' Sean rebuked Leah laughingly as he straightened her hat, but there was no laughter in his heart. She'd been so totally out of place. Every head in the room had turned when they went in. There had been a gradual hush and the landlord had immediately directed them to the back snug. Conversations had begun again but in low voices and censorious looks were directed at Pat and Sean.

Things had lightened after Leah had insisted on standing the entire clientele of the Eagle a drink, via Sean, who informed them that she'd come up on a horse, which had sent Nora into fits of laughter because Leah didn't know a single thing about horse racing. The level of noise increased again and there was the usual coarse laughter and banter in the bar, most of which Pat wished Leah couldn't hear or understand.

Nora and Pat discussed their good fortune through the long hours of the sticky night. They would move, possibly to Kirkdale. Nora liked the idea of being near Ethna. They'd only rent, of course, but they'd have every room furnished and the bulk of the money would be put by. Leah had told Nora to ask Mr Rankin's advice and they'd both been stunned to learn that you could actually accumulate more money by just *having* money. Interest, Leah had called it. Their future was secure. Any children they had would never want for food or warmth or clothes.

Nora went to see Father Finnegan to ask if it was possible to have a Mass said for a deceased person not of the Catholic faith. He thought hard about it but when she said the person was of the High Anglican persuasion, he said it was possible. He'd heard from his friend, the Reverend James Hunter, of Miss Cavendish's death. Nora must have been included in her will. So the following morning she walked down to her old parish for seven o'clock Mass for the repose of the soul of Miss Penelope Cavendish. It was the least she could do, she thought.

Then she took the tram up to see her sister, to ask Ethna whether she knew of a house up for rent.

'I thought you said you couldn't afford a house. You turned Leah's offers down, although you must have been flaming mad.' Ethna was flustered. Alex was teething and had cried most of the night and the weather hadn't helped. She'd prayed for a storm to clear the air, but her prayers remained unanswered. Edward had been grim-faced and snappy, things at work were worrying him. Nothing she should concern herself about, he replied bluntly when she'd asked. She was still clearing breakfast dishes off the table.

'Anyway, why aren't you at work? What time is this to be paying social calls?'

Nora plumped herself down on the sofa. 'I'm not going to work today, I'm having a day off.'

'You'll get the sack with that kind of attitude.'

'God, Ethna, who wound you up? You're so ratty.'

'And so would you be if you'd had a night like I've had, what with the baby and this heat and . . . everything.' She stopped short of saying anything about Edward. For some months now she'd begun to think that she'd made a terrible mistake. She had known full well he was a dour, dull man and she hadn't loved him, but she had thought

188

it would be better than this, and each day that thought depressed her more.

Nora got up. 'Oh, I'm sorry. Look, sit down. We'll have a cup of tea and then I'll clear up for you and we'll take Alex in the pram to the Rec.' Its full name was the Kirkdale Recreation Ground but everyone called it the Rec.

Ethna sat down wearily, pushing untidy wisps of hair from her already damp forehead as Nora put the kettle on. Nora also gathered up all the remaining dishes and took them into the scullery where she left them to steep in the brown stone sink.

'Leah and Sean came round last night. They'd been up to her old house and there'd been a terrible row with that Armstrong feller. Sean was telling Pat. Leah wanted to know if he was going to spend any money on improving all the houses, because she is.'

'Why? What houses?' Ethna asked.

Nora sighed, she'd forgotten Ethna didn't know. 'In the will she found out that her father owned them and those in Vulcan and Vandries Streets. She was in a terrible state over it. She broke her heart crying to Da and Sean.'

'You mean. *Leah* owns three whole streets?'

Nora nodded. 'Anyway, he said he wouldn't spend a single penny and told her to get out.'

Ethna was still trying to digest the fact that Leah Cavendish was now her da's landlady. 'What did she say to that?'

'She said if he didn't help, then the day after her birthday in November she'll either close Cavendish's down or sell it. She's got more money and more shares or something. I don't really understand all the ins and outs of these shares. But she *can* do it. That solicitor feller said so.'

Ethna's hand went to her throat. 'Oh, God, Nora,

189

she won't will she? What about all the jobs?' She was thinking of Edward's in particular.

'You know Leah, she's as stubborn as a mule and Sean told Pat he'd never seen her more determined. She didn't yell or scream at him. She was dead cold and calm and that seemed to be worse than bawling at him.'

Ethna crossed herself. 'He'll have to help her with the improvements, Nora. He'll just *have* to.'

'Sean said if anything happened to Leah or you or me or anyone else, he'd make sure that that house up there would be burned to the ground and with Armstrong inside it! I didn't know that bit until we got back from the Eagle.'

'You took *Leah* to the Eagle Vaults?'

'We were in the snug and she enjoyed it. Anyway, what she came to tell me and why we were all up there celebrating was that Miss Poppy has left me something in her will. A legacy, like.'

'What kind of legacy?' Ethna looked closely at her sister, thinking it might be jewellery. What a day it had been so far and it was only nine o'clock.

'Money.' Nora couldn't contain herself any longer. 'One hundred and twenty-five pounds! I still can't believe it! Me, with all that money. It's a fortune!'

'Jesus, Mary and Joseph! Are you sure, Nora?'

'Of course I'm flaming well sure. And there's all kinds of things we can do with it to make it into more money. But we want to rent a nice house, like this one, around here.'

'You can get something much better than this with that kind of money.' There was a note of bitterness in Ethna's voice.

'No, something like this will be great. We'll furnish it, and save the rest. We'll know we'll have a secure future and isn't that a great blessing? I had a Mass said for

Miss Poppy this morning. So, will you ask around about a house?'

Ethna nodded.

'It'll be great, Ethna. We can go shopping together, call around for a jangle and a cup of tea.'

'So you're not going to work then?'

'Pat says it's up to me and I probably will. I'll try and get something in a shop, part-time maybe. It's not fair to carry on full-time at the factory. There's others have more need of the work. But thank God Pat won't ever have to worry himself sick trailing around from one dock to another for half a day's work like Da did.'

'Well, there's enough work to do in a house, you should know that by now,' Ethna sniffed.

'Not when it's a decent house with good things around you.'

'What about Da, have you told him yet? Will you take him and Declan to live with you?'

'I'd not thought of that. I'll have to ask Pat and see what he says, but we'll get somewhere with room for them too.'

Ethna sipped her tea. Nora hadn't sat still while she'd been talking. The tea had been made and poured, the tablecloth shaken and folded neatly.

'He mightn't want to move, Nora. He's settled, and as for our Declan, all he'll do is moan like hell about missing his mates, flaming hooligans though they are. I had enough of our Declan when he was here with me!' Ethna raised her eyes to the ceiling.

'Right, let's get a move on then, we're wasting the day. You get yourself and Alex ready while I do those dishes, then we'll stroll down to the Rec.'

They spent a pleasant morning, although Leah thought her sister seemed quieter and more preoccupied than usual and she wondered whether she had upset Ethna

191

with her news. She decided that when she got her money she'd buy Ethna something personal. A nice brooch or necklace maybe.

She bought a quarter of ham and a quarter of tongue in Costain's on Scotland Road, remembering the way Edward Neely had denied them the leftover meat from the wedding breakfast. Well, it would be one in the eye for him, the miserable old get, she thought with satisfaction. She bought some firm tomatoes, the crumbly white cheese Da liked and a loaf of white bread then went down to see him.

Joe listened in silence to her excited plans and chatter while she prepared the meal, but when she'd finished he shook his head slowly.

'No, Nora, luv. It's good of yer and I'm made up that you've got the money. That feller had no right to sack you like he did, but I'm happy here. I've got me comforts, me mates, good neighbours. Even Eileen and me get on better these days now she understands there'll be nothing more than friendship on offer. She's a good woman but no one can replace yer mam, Nora. I told her that and she agreed with me. Anyway, I don't want to be under yer feet.'

'But, Da, you won't be. We'll find a house with plenty of room and Pat can keep his eye on our Declan. Where is he, by the way?'

'Most likely swimming in the canal with his mates. God knows what he'll catch in that mucky water. I won't be sorry when school starts again.'

'You should make him get some kind of work, even if it's only helping out somewhere for a few hours. You see, he's a worry to you now and the older he gets the worse it'll be.'

'Nora, luv. Yer mam and I moved in this house the day we were wed — well, in the front room to start with — and we managed to rear you and Ethna together, like, until she died, God rest her. I've got me memories, luv. I don't want to leave them. Can yer understand that?' He hadn't been feeling too well lately but he blamed it on the weather and a life of poor food, backbreaking work and worry.

She sighed and gave in. 'All right, but if you change your mind, tell me. Anyway, Leah is going to have all these houses improved when she gets her money in November.'

'She's a sympathetic, thoughtful girl with strong morals, is Leah, an' that's unusual in her class. The rest of them don't care. They pretend they do, when it suits them, but when it comes down to it they don't give a damn. God bless the day she came to us.'

'She went up to see Armstrong. Sean went with her.'

Joe had seen them together and knew that they loved each other, it was obvious in so many ways, yet he also knew that Sean Maguire was strong-minded, proud and had a chip on his shoulder. He had high principles and hopes and was dedicated to the aims and efforts of Tom Mann and Jim Larkin.

'She's going to make Ernest Armstrong pay half.'

'He won't be very happy about that.'

'He wasn't. There was murder over it, Pat said. But he'll pay up eventually. He'll have to because she'll get control of the business in November and she told him she'd sell it or close it down if he doesn't cough up, and you know Leah, Da.'

Joe smiled. 'Aye, I do, and I know they broke the mould after they made her.'

Chapter Fourteen

Ethna had all afternoon to think about Nora's legacy, as she'd begun to think of it. She'd never been jealous of her sister in her life before, but now it looked as if Nora, who had married the man she loved, was going to have everything. All the bad times, all the sacrifices she might have had to make wouldn't come about now. Not even if Pat wasn't jobbed for months like Da had been that summer long ago.

It hadn't been Nora who had had to cope with Da's grief and bring Declan and herself up after Mam had died. Oh, those years had been hard, very hard. She'd only been a bit of a kid herself and she, too, had grieved and missed her mam. She'd lost count of all the nights she'd cried herself to sleep. Then later she'd gone out to work and run the home. The very reason why she had married Edward was to escape from all that. Now she felt it had all been in vain. She was trapped in a loveless marriage. He was mean, churlish, selfish and often rough and brutal in their lovemaking. She thanked God that these days his demands on her were less frequent. She had Alex, though. The only good thing in her life.

She managed to get him fed, bathed and asleep by the time her husband got home. He was just as hot, tired and bad-tempered as when he'd left the house that morning. He slammed the front door after him and the baby began to cry.

'I've only just got him off to sleep. I was up with him all last night. Why can't you close the door quietly like other people or come in the back way?' Ethna snapped at him.

'I'll do what I bloody well like in my own house and I won't come in the back way. Is that any way for a decent man to enter his home? There's no dirt on my boots or clothes to make the place a midden like some.' He flung his jacket and bowler hat on the sofa and sat down at the table.

Ethna seethed at the implied slur on her da. In silence she put a plate of cold meat, mashed potato and peas in front of him and then got her own meal. Alex had stopped crying, at least. She watched her husband while he ate, wondering what in God's name she had ever thought remotely attractive about him, except his secure job which may not now be secure at all.

'Our Nora came this morning. We went to the Rec,' she said to break the hostile silence. She'd been worried all day about what her sister had told her, so why shouldn't he worry too? 'Miss Cavendish left her one hundred and twenty-five pounds in her will.'

He looked up in amazement. 'You mean that daft old bat left your Nora money?'

'She did. They're going to rent a house around here and save the rest. At least their future's all settled, which is more than can be said for yours or mine.'

'What do you mean by that, Ethna?'

Ethna pushed aside her plate, folded her arms and leaned on them. 'Our Nora said Leah Cavendish and Sean Maguire went to see Mr Armstrong and there was a row. Leah told him he had to pay half of the cost of improving all the houses in the three streets they apparently own. The street where I came from, the one Leah now lives in and Vulcan Street.'

196

'She *owns* those streets?'

Ethna nodded. 'Her da did, now they belong to her and him. Needless to say, Mr Armstrong refused.'

'I don't blame him. She's as flaming daft as her aunt was. Running off to live in a slum. Playing Lady Bountiful and thinking she's doing them all favours. People like that don't deserve favours. They won't be "improved" even if their houses are.'

It was on the tip of Ethna's tongue to point out that her da and Nora and herself were 'people like that' but she bit back the reminder. Oh, now she would really enjoy seeing his reaction to her next piece of news.

'She said if he didn't, in November when she's twenty-one, she'll get control of everything and that she'll close down Cavendish's or sell it, and she meant it. Our Nora said she can do it, too, and she'll own half of that big house and her "daft old bat" of an aunt left her thousands and thousands of pounds. Sean Maguire threatened him too. He said that if anything happened to Leah or Nora, me or Da he'd burn the house down around Armstrong's ears.'

Edward Neely pushed his plate away, his face ashen with shock. God Almighty! If she closed the place down, where would he be? Out of a job in a strike-torn city. His complexion paled even further as a worse thought struck him. Suppose she decided to take over Cavendish's herself and put that damned Irishman in charge as manager? Then he'd have to take his orders from a bloody upstart follower of Mann and Larkin from a Dublin slum.

He got up so quickly that the chair crashed backwards but Ethna didn't move.

'Where are you going? You've not finished your tea and soon we may not be able to even afford meat.'

He picked up his jacket. 'You and your bloody sister! I should never have got involved with you. She goes and gets bloody stupid ideas about going into service instead of staying as she was, a factory hand. Then she drags that bloody stupid bitch to live in Vandries Street.'

'Leah Cavendish came of her own free will, our Nora didn't "drag" her. Anyway, if Mr high and mighty Armstrong hadn't sacked our Nora for seeing Pat Ryan, none of it would have happened.' It was the first time she'd ever argued with him but she didn't care. She was too full of bitterness.

'Don't you speak to me like that, woman!' he yelled at her.

She didn't flinch. 'I asked you where you were going.' Her tone was frosty.

'To the pub. Maybe after a few pints I can forget that in four months I'll either have no job or have to work for a bloody Irish slummy.'

The door slammed again and Ethna dropped her head in her hands. In one respect he'd been right. It was partly Nora's fault but it wouldn't be Nora who would suffer, it would be herself. As her baby began to cry fretfully she, too, let the tears roll down her cheeks.

The following evening Nora and Leah had tea in Leah's tiny back yard. Rose bushes and multicoloured godetia grew in tubs and the cuttings of ivy, their roots in the small holes at the foot of the wall, had begun to stretch dark green fingers upwards over the whitewashed bricks. You would think you were in a proper garden if it hadn't been for the soot-blackened walls of the warehouse that towered over one side of it, Nora had told Pat.

At Leah's latest piece of news, Nora's eyes widened with incredulity.

'You can't go to Dublin with him on your own, Leah. What will people say?'

198

'I don't care what people think,' Leah answered forcefully.

'I didn't say "think". Around here they only do that after they've given you the height of abuse. Leah, it's just not proper, especially for you – you're a lady.'

'I thought we'd got all that out of our systems. At least I thought you had.' Leah was thinking of Sean. 'I still don't care. They all think I'm mad anyway.'

Nora grinned. 'Mad but harmless and generous. I'll tell you something, Leah Cavendish. The day you're twenty-one there'll be the biggest do we've had around here for years, even better than the coronation.'

'Why? Because I threatened to close down the business, put men out of work?'

'No, you'd never do that. You'd sell it first and the roof over Ernest Armstrong's head too.'

'So why will there be a celebration?'

'Because everyone thinks you're so great and so generous. They'll be all too happy to join in a knees-up for your birthday.'

Leah sighed and Nora refilled their cups as a slight breeze, against all the odds, managed to penetrate from the river and stir the edges of the white cloth that covered the small round table the tea tray was set upon.

'Do you think we might have something else to celebrate?'

'Like what?' Leah asked. The last rays of the setting sun coming over the yard wall caught her hair, turning it into a mass of fiery curls.

'Well, when my mam and yours, God rest them, were young, if a girl went away from home for three days with a young man and without a sister or aunt or some other respectable woman, they'd have to get married.' She waited for Leah's answer, studying her friend's face.

Leah looked intently into her teacup. 'I do love him,

Nora, and I know he loves me, but he holds back all the time. It's my money, my class, my religion.'

'You can have too much pride and you can make your life a misery because of it, and he will. That makes him a fool, in my book. You've rejected your class, you'll give all your money away, if I know you. You don't really care about it but that's because you've never been without it. You were brought up with money. Anyway, you'll go and spend it all on other people and he knows that. That only leaves religion and from yours to ours isn't such a big step.'

Leah stared hard at her. 'You mean change?'

'Convert.'

'Can I?'

'I think they'd welcome you with open arms, especially as you'd be the only one in the entire parish with a small fortune. There's mould starting to grow at the bottom of the wall behind the statue of the Sacred Heart. I heard Father Hegarty telling Da. Even the church is starting to need repairs and it's no use them asking anyone for money, there isn't any.'

'How would I go about it, if I was to convert?' Leah asked. It was something she would have to give a lot of thought to.

'I'd take you myself to Father Finnegan. Isn't he a friend of your vicar?'

'Priest,' Leah amended.

'See, you even call him a priest,' Nora cried triumphantly.

'I'll think about it. But I don't want you to tell anyone, Nora.'

'I won't, on Mam's life I swear it. But I'll work on Pat.'

'You just said—'

'No. I mean I'll say how thick Sean Maguire is because

200

he loves you but won't marry you because you're rich. I'll say he's a fool because you've given that lot on Prince's Avenue the cold shoulder and you'll be spending your money on other people anyway. Eventually it might get through to that thicko that it's only his stupid flaming pride that's stopping him. He might take notice of Pat.'

Leah sighed. 'I wish he would. Anyway, it doesn't matter now what anyone thinks or says, I've been down and bought the tickets. Sean insisted I book a cabin for myself but that he'll go like the rest, steerage, and he'll pay his own fare.' Suddenly she lost her temper. 'Oh, God! I wish I'd been born as poor as a church mouse.'

'No you don't,' Nora said flatly. 'I was and I know what it's like. But he's right. You'll be best off in a cabin. I've never been over myself but they don't call them the cattle boats for nothing. They pack the steerage passengers in like sardines. People sleep where they can, on the floor, on seats, sitting up, in the alley-ways. Half the fellers are blind drunk when they get there and if it's rough it takes longer and everyone's sick.'

Leah shuddered.

'Where will you stay when you get there?'

'The Imperial Hotel.'

'It sounds posh.'

'It is. He insisted. At first he said I should book into the Shelbourne that faces St Stephen's Green which is a big park. Apparently all the quality stay at the Shelbourne so I said there was no way I'd go there. The Imperial isn't quite so grand but it's on the best street in the city. Sackville Street, soon to be called O'Connell Street, so he says. When I asked him who O'Connell was, he said I was the biggest ignoramus he knew and hadn't I been taught history.' Leah laughed.

'Were you?'

'Of course I was but I hated it. Everyone was dead and I couldn't see anything interesting in dead people. Can you?'

Nora shook her head. 'What will you do there?'

'Go to Liberty Hall to hear this man, Jim Larkin, speak. Apparently he's a very radical person. All for the working-class people and their rights.'

'An Irish Tom Mann?'

Leah nodded. 'Sean said he'd take me to see his mother and sisters, but I don't know if he meant it.' She paused and looked wistful. 'Sometimes I think he's sort of laughing at me.'

'He wouldn't do that, Leah. It's not in his nature. He does love you and maybe if he takes you to see them . . . well, who knows?'

Leah shook her head. 'No, it will be more to see the conditions there. The home, the background he came from.'

'Well, just don't go telling anyone, that's all. Say you're having a bit of a holiday, after the funeral, like,' Nora advised.

'Nora, do you think I should take them something, just in case I do meet them?'

Nora puzzled over it and eventually shook her head. 'No. It would only make things worse.'

Miserably Leah nodded her agreement.

Rhian had been terribly upset ever since Leah had come with that young Irishman. She had to admit he was handsome but he was also rather terrifying. After they'd gone, she had walked out of Ernest's study in a daze and had gone straight upstairs. She'd rung for Maisie to bring her some strong tea.

She couldn't believe what that young man had said about Ernest. It *must* be all lies. It just *had* to be. Ernest

202

would never, never do anything like that. But Leah had said it was true.

Rhian was shocked and confused. As she sipped her tea, she tried to put it all out of her mind. She just couldn't cope with it all. Leah had changed so much since she'd left home. Ernest said she'd let her standards and morals slip, that she'd been indoctrinated by the scum she lived among, but they couldn't all be scum. Nora hadn't been.

She'd been shocked by the descriptions of conditions in the slum areas, but there had always been slums in Liverpool. The city was too small for the thousands of people who flocked here from all over Europe and Ireland. Most of them went on to America but a lot stayed. There were always poor people and always would be.

The whole affair hadn't been mentioned again by Ernest and he'd been so considerate and generous since that night that she now doubted Leah's word. She had nightmares about the terrible threat her sister had made. What had prompted her to demand that Ernest spend a fortune on improving those houses? Probably the people who lived in them. Oh, if only Father were alive, none of this would have happened. All she could do now was to try to mend the broken bridges between her sister and husband. She didn't realise that there had never been any bridges between them in the first place.

The same idea had occurred to Ernest, but he'd resolutely dismissed it. He'd never go cap in hand to that little bitch. Instead he explored other avenues. He sought legal advice from a top London barrister, through Mr Rankin, about his position and back had come the answer. If Leah Cavendish held two-thirds of the shares in the company, she could do what she liked with it. Also, if she was so inclined, she could demand her part share of the house in cash or kind.

There was just no way out. He cursed both Leah and Poppy but he cursed that upstart Irishman Maguire even more. He was just the sort to know the very type of people who would lock him inside this house and then burn it down around him. Maguire had meant what he said. It was no idle threat.

He was trapped. Every door was closed against him. When Rhian tried to suggest some kind of reconciliation, with herself as mediator, he quickly put her straight. It was not her place to interfere, although he didn't quite put it like that. He had to tread carefully with her for the time being. He was thankful that she didn't seem to believe what Maguire had said.

He couldn't even have Maguire beaten up because Leah would go straight to the police and, if pushed, Rhian would back her up. Rhian was weak and woolly-minded and easily confused but she loved her sister. Nor could he contrive to have the man sacked and blacklisted. He was a stevedore, young for the job, but it was a respected position and he was a union man. If he did manage to get him sacked, the consequences didn't bear thinking about. His associates in the various businesses connected with the river, its docks and industries would blame him for adding unnecessary fuel to an already smouldering fire.

The only thing he could do was promise to help finance the improvements but drag out for as long as he could the actual payment of any money. He'd blame Rankin; everyone knew how long solicitors took to get things done. It was the only way he could keep his position, the business he looked on as entirely his own, his fine home and his money . . .

It was a beautiful calm, clear night. The dark water of the Mersey was like a mirror reflecting the light of the sickle moon and the brilliance of the stars. The *Munster* cast off and moved away from the landing stage and slowly out into the river. The ferry was one of the few ships not laid up and that was because of a special agreement between the seamen and the British and Irish Steam Packet Company, for it was the only method of transporting not only people but more importantly the Royal Mail to Ireland.

Its black and green funnel, banded with a thin white stripe, was illuminated and men, women and children crowded the open deck, loath to go down to the public saloon where it was stuffy and smelled faintly of coal and oil. They would go eventually, at least many would, when the bar opened, although it was warm enough to sleep on deck.

Leah stood next to Sean on the starboard side beneath the bridge, the green navigation light throwing an eerie glow on the people below. Leah had been startled by the three long blasts of the steam whistle, the *Munster*'s farewell to Liverpool, until she returned tomorrow.

They watched the buildings of the waterfront fade into the distance as the ferry picked up speed and the vibration of its screws could be felt. Along the coastline were dotted clusters of lights – the outlying suburbs of the city, villages and small towns. They passed Litherland, Crosby, Formby, Southport, and then they were out past the bar lightship and into the dark waters of Liverpool Bay and the Irish Sea.

It was much fresher now, there was a breeze as the ship increased her rate of knots.

Leah sighed. 'How long does it take?' she asked. It was a magical night with the soft wind on her cheeks, the faint silver pathway that stretched over the sea made by the light of the moon, the foaming white crest of the *Munster*'s bow wave as the ferry cut through the dark green water. Surely he could feel the magic too.

'Eight hours and on a bad trip it can seem like eternity. You managed to book us on the ferry not to Dublin but Kingstown but I didn't want to upset you. We'll be in Kingstown harbour by seven. You'll like Kingstown, or to give it its Irish name, Dunlaoghaire. It's a wealthy class of a place.'

She looked up at him, her eyes full of sadness. He'd broken the spell.

'Sean, why do you always say such things? You know they hurt me. I'm doing the best I can to help people, to put things right.'

He was instantly ashamed of himself, he didn't know exactly why he did it. It was as if a small devil inside him prodded such words of bitter resentment out of him.

'Ah, I'm sorry, Leah, I am. Will you forgive me?' He placed his arm round her shoulder and drew her closer to him.

She smiled and reaching up gently touched his cheek. 'You know I will. I love you.'

He bent and kissed her softly on the lips, glad there were still people on deck, for he didn't trust himself.

They stood facing into the night breeze. It bore the strong tang of the sea which he thought was somehow better, more appropriate than any other scent.

Chapter Fifteen

They stood together on deck again early next morning. It had been a calm crossing but there were many people who looked pale and tired, Leah thought. Mist shrouded the peaks of the mountains of County Dublin and Wicklow, which formed a magnificent backdrop to the wide sweep of the bay, and sunlight sparkled on the green water. Two long piers stretched out towards them, enclosing the harbour, and the air was fresh and pleasantly warm. Later it would grow uncomfortably hot as the July sun rose in the sky.

They were near enough now to see the fine Victorian villas, hotels and shops that faced the strand and rose gradually into suburbs. It looked clean and neat and colourful.

'You were right. It is a wealthy class of a place.' She looked up at him with mischievous laughter in her eyes.

'Don't be making a mock and a jeer out of me, Leah Cavendish,' he replied, his eyes also full of laughter. He was nearly home and his heart was lighter, his cares lessening by the minute. He hadn't been home for over two years and it had been hard to go among strangers at first, but he knew that no matter how long or how far away he was, this green and misty island would always be home.

He placed his arm round her shoulder as they went

to her cabin to collect her luggage. There seemed an excessive amount of it for so short a trip.

'What have you in here? Is it a month you're thinking of staying?' He himself had one small, battered case.

'Well, it was you who insisted I stay at the Imperial. Besides, girls need more . . . things than men.'

'Well, we'd better get this lot up and join the queue to disembark although it should have more or less cleared by now. There's always a desperate stampede to get off.'

Leah could sense the change in his mood, hear the note of pleasure in his voice. He must miss his home and his family.

'Is it far, Sean, into Dublin?'

'You'll be in the hotel in an hour. We'll get a tram, you get a good view from the top deck. Unless of course you want to arrive in style. There's always plenty of jarveys waiting for the mail boats to arrive.'

'No, we'll get the tram. I want to see things.'

'Ah, well, there's some things you might not want to see.' He was still unsure of the wisdom of taking her to see the place where he grew up, where his mam and sisters still lived.

She didn't reply but concentrated on lifting her skirts clear of the wooden planking of the gangway. Sean's heart filled with longing. She looked so beautiful. It wouldn't take much for him to lose the run of himself and take her in his arms and kiss her.

She wore a sprigged muslin dress and a wide-brimmed light straw hat which was held safe from any breeze by a pale blue scarf of some flimsy material. Her white gloves were spotless and just visible beneath the hem of her dress were white buttoned boots with a high heel. In the crystal clear light of the summer morning she looked so fresh and dainty, and just exactly what she was – a lady. Those white kid boots would become covered in dust and dirt, those gloves would get grubby, the dress creased and crumpled very quickly on the way to the decaying, ramshackle terraced house that was his family's home in one of the roads that ran between Bull Alley and Patrick Street. It had once been the fine Georgian house of a wealthy Georgian Englishman. How in God's name could he contemplate taking her there? He'd show her the sights of Dublin, they'd go to Liberty Hall to hear Larkin speak and then he'd take her back to her hotel.

It was pleasant on the open top deck of the tram. Sometimes the trolley hissed and crackled and sparked as it crossed the junctions of the wires above. He pointed out things of interest as they passed through Booterstown, Sandymount and into Ballsbridge along Merrion Road, crossing the Grand Canal at McKenny Bridge.

'What's that?' she asked as they trundled down Mount Street.

'Merrion Park. It's smaller than Herbert Park but bigger than the one in Fitzwilliam Square. This is where the quality live. All the houses that surround Fitzwilliam Square have their own keys to it so no one else is allowed to use it. That's the quality's way of going on.'

'It's the same in Liverpool, Sean. In Abercromby Square and Faulkner Square.'

They were coming into the city proper now as the tram went down Clare Street, Nassau Street and slewed slightly to the right as it passed the imposing entrance to Trinity College, Dublin's university, from which all Catholics were barred no matter what their background or finances. The road narrowed as it passed the iron railings, on the other side of which were the statues of Goldsmith and Burke.

'That on the other side of the road is the Irish Parliament building, but there's been no Irish Parliament

209

since Grattan and the other eejits voted themselves out of existence nearly a hundred and thirty years ago.'

Leah looked closely at the semi-circular building with its Corinthian pillars. It was a beautiful building, as was Trinity College, but something was puzzling her. Finally she realised what it was.

'It's got no windows.'

Sean laughed. 'It was built that way to stop the members having their attention distracted by gawping out of windows at what was going on in the world outside and to shield them from any gapers outside who had the brass neck to peer in at them. They needn't have bothered. They weren't in residence long enough for it to have mattered.'

The tram stopped at the top of Westmoreland Street and before her Leah could see the waters of the Liffey flowing between the arches of O'Connell Bridge. The bridge was as wide as it was long.

'It's not far now. Once we're over the bridge, two more stops and that's it. We're there.'

Leah was twisting from side to side. 'You never said anything about it being so beautiful.'

He shrugged. Seen through a stranger's eyes, he supposed it was. At least the city centre and the suburbs south of it were. To the right the great dome of the Customs House stood out against a cloudless sky, and to the left, down beyond Batchelor's Walk and the Ormond Quay, was the classical building that housed the law courts.

'We have a castle too, although it being Dublin it doesn't look like one at all.'

The tram slowed down and he helped her to her feet and descended the stairway ahead of her in case she tripped and fell.

The conductor, seeing a pair of dainty white boots and the hem of the pale skirt descending, was all attendance.

'Aren't we here now. Give me your hand, miss, it's not tripping up I'll have you doing offen my tram.'

Leah smiled at the man who raised his peaked uniform cap to her when she was safely on the pavement outside the General Post Office. Sean was collecting the luggage.

The conductor beamed. 'That's a fine collection of baggage you have there but haven't you missed the Royal Horse Show week entirely.'

Leah laughed but Sean glared at the man.

He guided her through the traffic of the wide thoroughfare, at the bottom of which was the O'Connell Monument. Beside them, Nelson's Column, known as the 'big yoke', soared upwards, Lord Nelson atop surveying through his one stone eye the city and countryside beyond.

The doorman of the Imperial in his green and gold uniform relieved Sean of his burden, looking askance at the unusual couple. He summoned a porter to take in the cases.

'When will I see you?' Leah asked.

Sean looked thoughtful. He wanted some time to absorb the sights, the sounds and the smells. He wanted to lean on the parapet of the metal span of the Ha'penny Bridge or the walls of the quays and pass the time and maybe have a conversation with one of his fellow Dublinmen. And most of all he wanted to talk to his mother. He knew Treasa and Shelagh would be at work. Treasa worked in the kitchens at Bewley's in Grafton Street and Shelagh in a factory that made ladies' hat boxes.

'Would you be upset if I came to call for you after the Angelus this evening?' Seeing her puzzled expression he went on, 'The church bells ring twice a day, at noon and at six, and people stop to say a bit of a prayer to Our Lady.'

211

It was a simplified version but he wasn't going into the full explanation here on the hotel doorstep. 'You'll be on your own for most of the day but . . .'

She smiled up at him. 'Sean, you've not seen your mother for two years, nor your sisters or friends. You owe them at least a day. I'll be fine. I'll have a rest and get changed, then maybe take a stroll and look at the shops.'

'Then I'll come by to collect you just after six.'

'I'll be ready and waiting.' She reached up and kissed him quickly on the cheek as the doorman, his eyebrows raised, held open the heavy double glass doors for her. He was thinking that the English had some very queer and bold ways of going on. She obviously had money, but there was no chaperone with her and the lad was a working-class Dub by his accent and dress.

Leah was shown to her room by a porter who answered all her questions on where the best shops were located, what time lunch, afternoon tea and dinner were served in the dining room and inquired if everything in her room was satisfactory. She gave him half a crown for his help and pleasant manner and in return he wished the blessings of God and all His Holy Saints on her for her generosity.

She smiled as he closed the door and she took off her gloves and hat and went over to the open window. She was two floors above the street and had an excellent view both up and down it. She could look down and see the balcony of the dining room on the first floor. It was a very comfortable and well-furnished room and she was sure it was every bit as 'grand' as the Shelbourne. She'd have a bath and get changed and then she'd take a stroll, but she'd think of him when the church bells rang for the noon Angelus.

Sean walked back across O'Connell Bridge and turned

along the Aston Quay, stopping now and then to lean on the wall and look down at the Liffey. He remembered it well in all seasons and weathers. Now, in summer, calm and sparkling; in autumn, choppy and often mist-shrouded; in winter, dark and crested with sleet, snow or driving rain; and in spring sometimes calm, sometimes windswept and foam-flecked but always smelling the same.

He strode on down Wood Quay and turned off and walked up Winetavern Street. Ahead of him was Christ Church Cathedral, he was back in the Liberties where he'd been born. Once into Nicholas Street, the spire of St Patrick's Cathedral was in plain view. He smiled wrily. Two cathedrals in a predominantly Catholic city and both of them Anglican. Maybe Leah would go to the service at Christ Church on Sunday and he'd go to St Audoen's to Mass.

Even without the sight of the building in whose shadow he'd grown up, he knew he was back by the change in the uneven surface of the road, the packed tenement houses with the wooden poles stuck out of every window, to which was attached a tattered assortment of washing, and the stink from O'Keefe's, the knackers yard, that hung over the place in a pall and pervaded every nook and cranny.

Nothing had changed, he thought, as he turned into Vincent Street. Children with bare feet, cut down ragged clothes and dirty faces sat on the equally dirty, broken and sagging steps. Doors stood wide open, the once beautiful, ornate fanlights above them now dilapidated, the glass broken and fly-blown. Through warped sash windows, now pushed up to catch any breath of air, came the sound of voices. Mainly women's and children's but in the house to his left a man and woman were fighting, their bitter abuse and accusations clearly audible. The

213

sound seemed to echo from one side of the street to the other.

The door of number seven was open and he walked straight in.

'Hello, Mam. How are you in yourself today?'

Peggy Maguire turned round, her faded blue eyes wide with utter astonishment. 'Jaysus! You put the heart across me! Is it yourself, Sean? Is it really you?'

He crossed the room and threw his arms round her. 'It is so, Mam. In the flesh, and I'm sorry I gave you a start.' He looked down at her with affection. Her hair, once as dark as his own, was prematurely grey. Her face showed the harshness of the life she'd lived, the suffering she'd borne stoically, sustained by an unshakable belief that at the end of her time on earth, there was a better life waiting and a reunion with her Gerrard, dead from an accident on the North Wall docks twelve years since.

'Why didn't you write? Why didn't you let me know at all?'

'Wasn't it a quick decision I made. There wasn't the time. How are Shelagh and Treasa?'

She smiled. 'Well, aren't you here now. Wait while I put on the kettle and wet the tea. I was just going to do it and take up a cup to Mrs Brophy who has the two-pair back, she's badly, poor soul. And is it any wonder with himself out of work and that great amadan of a son coming in last night and breaking all before him after being out on a tear.'

Sean took off his jacket and sat down on a battered chair by the equally battered table and looked around the room. With both the girls now working and with the bit he always managed to send each month, things were better. There was furniture, albeit worn, instead of boxes and packing cases. There were curtains at the window, a rug on the floor and a crucifix over the huge fireplace with its marble surround that looked so incongruous, a leftover from grander days. On the wall by the door was a small holy water font.

In the other room he knew there would be an iron-framed double bed with a flock mattress and a few blankets, once occupied by his parents but now by his sisters, and a single bed for Mam. All five of them had slept in there at one time, himself and the girls on straw-stuffed mattresses on the floor with a collection of old overcoats to cover them. His joy at being back in his own city with his family was dimmed by thoughts of Leah. How could he bring her here? Oh, he knew she'd stayed with Nora in Oil Street, but it hadn't been for very long and poor as the O'Brians were, they had more than his mam did.

'Wouldn't it be a poor thing to come home to no tea?' she said fondly, her voice full of a mother's love and happiness. 'And what is it that made you come to this "quick decision"?' she asked as she poured out the tea into a cracked mug.

'I heard that Big Jim is to speak tomorrow night at Liberty Hall.'

She was incredulous. 'And you wasted money on the fare just for that?'

'Mam, don't be giving out to me and me hardly in the door. It won't be wasted.' He was quietly emphatic. 'Times will change.'

'Ah, that's right enough, but not for the better. Not for the likes of us.'

'There's great changes in Liverpool. All the unions are supporting each other. Deals with the bosses have been made for better wages and conditions.'

'And you're thinking things will change like that here too, is that the way of it? Aren't the carters and dockers and foundrymen in and out on strike by the minute and nothing gained.'

215

'It *is*, Mam. Larkin speaks for us all and when he does speak, hasn't he the ear of the bosses? Hasn't he already put a stop to the stevedores paying the dockers in the pubs? Hasn't that put paid to the greed of some of them? And hasn't he arranged a set overtime rate for the carters?'

'And aren't you a stevedore yourself?'

He could see she was proud of him. His da had never reached such eminence. He'd only ever been a docker.

'I worked hard, learned fast and was in the right place at the right time. I've no favourites amongst the men and I'll not take bribes in the way of a drink or money.'

'Would there were more like you. It's proud I am of your honesty and your da would have been too.'

'I know, Mam.'

'Our Treasa is walking out with Maurice O'Shea from the top end of Kevin Street.'

'And does that suit you?'

'It does. He's a good fellow. He's in the Young Men's Confraternity and wasn't it Father O'Neill who got him a place at Bolland's Mill. Steady work, Sean, and thanks be to God for it.'

'So, will they get married, do you think?' He was wondering how she would manage without his sister's wages.

'They will and she says they'll live here to start with. We'll move things around a bit, sure we'll manage right enough. We always have.'

He looked down into the weak tea. He'd grown up on tea and bread with maybe fish or a bit of meat when Da had had a full week in, which wasn't very often.

'I brought someone with me.'

She scrutinised his face closely. 'And would this someone be a girl, by any chance?'

He nodded. 'It would.'

216

'Well, where is she then?'

'I didn't want to be bringing her in on top of you right away. She's at the Imperial Hotel.'

'Holy Mother of God! What class of a girl is she?'

'Will you give us a drop more tea and take poor Mrs Brophy her cup, then I'll tell you about Leah.'

Peggy got up and refilled the mug then she took the other one and left. She had never even heard a name like that before and the girl must have a rake of money to be in the Imperial, for she knew her son hadn't the price of a room there. She sensed that he was miserable about the situation and she herself had her doubts, though she'd not go bringing the girl down before she'd met her.

As the sun rose higher and the midday Angelus sounded, Sean told her all about Leah Cavendish, and Peggy Maguire's heart grew heavier by the minute. A Protestant, middle-class English girl and her son? It could never be, even though the girl sounded, in her way, to be a decent, caring person.

'And she came with you to hear Larkin? To see with the eyes in her head that there are worse slums here than in Liverpool? Worse houses than the ones she owns? Did you intend to bring her here at all, Sean?'

He got up and walked to the window, his back to her. 'I don't know, Mam, and that's the truth of it. One minute I want her to meet you and I know she wants to come, and the next I think . . .'

'That she's not your class.'

He nodded.

'And she's a Protestant. You can never marry a Protestant, Sean, you know that. I'd be heart-scalded if I even thought . . . and what would I be telling Father O'Neill? Wouldn't we all be excommunicated? And what about the neighbours? Sure to God, we haven't our own cathedral. They won't let us into Trinity, even if we had the means

217

an' all, and you know there's places of work where we're not allowed in the door.'

'I know all that. Jaysus, Mam, haven't I been over it all again and again in my mind?'

'Don't be taking His name in vain in this house!'

He was instantly contrite. There were degrees of blasphemy and he'd overstepped the mark. 'I'm sorry, but I love her, Mam, and she loves me.'

Peggy sighed heavily. 'Son, aren't there tribes of good Catholic girls of your own class over there? Can't you find one?'

'I could but I don't want to. And anyway, even if Leah was a Catholic, what could I offer her, Mam?'

It was her turn to nod her agreement.

'Would you mind if I went out for an hour? Just to get the feel of the place again? Just to wander around and think?'

'Ah, get off out with you. Have you the price of a pint of porter?'

'I have but I don't want a drink, just a walk. I'll be back later.'

'I'll have something ready for you. I've to have a meal on the go for the girls.'

'I'll take mine early. I said I'd meet Leah just after the Angelus, but I'll be back in time to see those two rossies.' He managed a grin. 'And will the prospective brother-in-law be here later, when I get in?'

'He will. Now get off out with youse, I've things to do,' she chided, her hand reaching into her apron pocket for her rosary. If he had his mind set on this girl, she'd have to storm the gates of Heaven with her prayers for a change of heart. They all would.

As she watched him walk down the street, stopping to have a few words with the children on the way, she made up her mind that she wanted to meet this Leah Cavendish.

What she would say to her she didn't know, but she just wanted to see with her own eyes the girl her son loved but could never marry.

Leah was ready and was standing chatting amiably to the doorman when he arrived. The heat of the day was abating and she had changed. Her pale green blouse was of some soft silky material, the slightly darker green skirt was braided round the hem. She had swapped the wide-brimmed hat for a plain straw boater trimmed with a green ribbon.

'Leah, have I kept you waiting long?'

Her face lit up as she caught sight of him. 'No, I've been having a chat to Mr Nolan here, he's been telling me all about the castle and Leinster House and Phoenix Park. He was in the army. He served out in the wilds of India, on the North West Frontier.'

'Aye, most of us have to take the King's shilling or the emigrant ship,' Sean replied but not bitterly as he exchanged a respectful glance with the older man.

Sean took Leah's arm and they began to walk down the street.

'I thought I'd treat you to a tour of Dublin by carriage. We'll walk to the top of Grafton Street and get one there but we'll have a hard time keeping the jarvey quiet, they're full of the chat. They have it all off pat.'

'A carriage? It must be expensive. Can't we walk?' As soon as the words were out, she regretted them.

'I can afford a bit of entertainment. Wasn't it me who asked you to come to Dublin in the first place?'

She nodded and hastily changed the subject. 'Was your mother surprised and glad to see you?'

'Indeed she was, after she told me off for putting the heart across her, walking in off the street like that.'

'Is she well?'

'Oh, in fine fettle.'

'And your sisters?'

'At work. I'll see them later, but I think there may well be a wedding in the family soon. Our Treasa. I'll be meeting the prospective brother-in-law later tonight.'

Leah remained silent, waiting for him to speak, but he, too, was silent as they walked past Trinity, up Westmoreland Street and into Grafton Street.

'I walked up here this afternoon. I bought a few things in Switzer's,' she said to break the mood.

'I knew a lad who worked in the parcels department there once.'

'What happened to him?' She wasn't really interested but it was conversation of a sort and better than silence.

'He went out to his brother in America.'

She sighed deeply. 'On the emigrant ship. Does no one ever stay in Ireland, Sean?'

'Some. They work the land and make tweed cloth or linen in the north. There's more work in Belfast and Derry – for some. Families are big, there's not enough work to go around. There never has been.'

'Your family isn't big.'

'Only because my da died so young.'

They'd come to the junction of Grafton Street and St Stephen's Green where a line of open carriages were waiting. The horses stood patiently, occasionally shaking their heads and flicking their tails to dislodge the flies that annoyed them. Their drivers stood in a group, smoking and talking.

'Here we are.'

Leah looked at the stretch of verdant greenery across the road.

'Can we walk through the park first? It looks very lovely and I was just too tired and hot this afternoon.'

Her mind went back to the many, many walks and drives through Prince's Park she'd taken in the past.

'If you like.'

It really was lovely, she thought, the winding paths between shrubs and trees, the banks of flowers, the lake where ducks and swans glided on the glass-like surface. The little pavilions, the quaint stone bridge on which they stood, the breeze rustling in the canopy of leaves formed by the branches of the surrounding trees. The vista of more open green grass, paths and trees.

'You would think you were in the middle of the countryside and it's so cool.'

'I heard someone say it's the biggest park in the middle of any city, although others say Central Park in New York is bigger.'

'But not as beautiful, I'm sure.'

There were plenty of other people taking advantage of the coolness, the peace and quiet of the pathways and the benches set beside the lake or in secluded stone bowers where ivy and wild cyclamen grew in profusion. They were oblivious of them all. The summer evening air, filled with the perfumes of the park, bewitched them both. Sean took her in his arms and kissed her and she clung to him, returning his kisses until he managed to control his emotions and pull away from her.

She looked up at him, her green eyes full of love and longing, her pale skin translucent, her lips moist.

'I love you, Sean,' she said simply.

'I know, Leah, and I'll love you until the day I die, that I'll promise you.'

'Then will you take me to meet your mother, please?'

He couldn't resist her. 'I will. Tomorrow. Tomorrow afternoon.'

Chapter Sixteen

They'd taken the carriage ride but their minds were not on the beautiful buildings, the elegant houses, and the jarvey rattled off his accumulated store of knowledge of his city without interruption.

Leah was to go to the service at Christ Church the following morning. She would then return to the Imperial for lunch and Sean would collect her at three o'clock. Later, in the evening, they would cross Butt Bridge to Beresford Place and Liberty Hall to hear the words of the man who was trusted and honoured by every working man and woman in the city.

He'd dropped her off at the hotel and it had been a formal parting. There could be no embraces, no kisses in full view of the street. Mr Nolan came forward as Sean helped her down, ready to escort her the few steps across the pavement. She clung to Sean's hand tightly.

'I'll see you at three, tomorrow.'

He had nodded, acknowledged the doorman, got back into the carriage and told the driver to drop him off on the other side of the bridge. He'd walk the rest of the way. He needed time to find the words to tell his mam she was having a visitor tomorrow.

In the event he had no opportunity to tell her until much later, after Maurice O'Shea, a pleasant enough fellow, had departed and the two girls had gone into the bedroom.

'You've something on your mind,' Peggy stated, sinking back down into the armchair.

'I have.'

'Well, tell me.'

'I'm going to bring Leah here tomorrow afternoon, Mam, if that's all right. She asked me and I said yes. She's going to Christ Church in the morning. I said I'd collect her after she'd had her dinner, or lunch as she calls it.'

Peggy looked up at her son with pride. He was a fine young man she'd reared, despite everything. He was tall and handsome, his skin tanned from working outdoors. There was no droop to his shoulders, no air of despondency about him. She uttered a prayer that he wouldn't be broken by something that could never be.

'She'll be made welcome. I'll not have it said that I closed my door in her face.'

Sean bent and kissed her on the cheek, his heart full of gratitude. 'Thanks, Mam. Now go to your bed, we've to be up in the morning for Mass.'

She touched his cheek before leaving him. 'God bless you, son.'

'Mam, before you go, don't go chasing around the neighbourhood borrowing the best cups and plates the neighbours can lay their hands on.'

She knew he was teasing her. 'Ah, get yourself settled on that couch and don't be making a mock and a jeer of an ould woman!'

Again she was talking with Mr Nolan when he arrived and again she looked fresh and lovely, although he noticed that the dress was very plain. There were no frills or flounces or braiding. There was no fancy hat either, she wore the simple straw boater again. Her gloves and boots were cream, not the delicate, pristine white. She would easily fit in with the crowds of girls and women who were strolling up and down the street.

The doorman drew Sean aside. 'Herself tells me you're taking her to hear Larkin speak tonight.'

'I am.'

'Then if you're set on it, for the love of God take care of her. The DMP are in a very edgy mood these days.'

'When were they ever anything but?'

'I mean it, lad. A few wrong words, an imagined slight or just a look and you'll get belted to bits.'

Sean nodded and thanked him, then took Leah's arm to walk along the quays.

'I came this way this morning,' she informed him.

'Did you walk or get a cab?'

'I got a cab for part of the way.'

'And is it a beautiful church then?'

'It is. Have you never been inside? Never even taken a quick look through the doors?'

He laughed. 'It's easy to see you've never been to Ireland before. Wouldn't Father O'Neill skin us alive if we so much as went up the steps, never mind a quick look inside.'

She blushed.

'I wasn't getting at you again, Leah, truly. It's the way things are.'

She smiled up at him, her apprehension partly relieved.

Despite Sean's joke, Peggy had sent both Shelagh and Treasa around the neighbours and had managed to borrow a clean white cloth with which she covered the scratched and marked table top, six cups and saucers, although they didn't match, and four assorted side plates. She'd made some soda bread but there was no butter or margarine to spread on it.

'It won't matter, Mammy. Sure, she won't have tasted

225

it before. She'll not know that it's better with a bit of butter or jam on it,' Shelagh said disdainfully.

'Don't have us disliking the girl before she even sets a foot in the door,' Treasa chided. Maurice was coming over too. Sean's 'lady from Liverpool', as she'd described Leah to him after Mass, and all her Mam's unprecedented preparations were not to be missed.

As they entered the Liberties, Leah looked about her. It was depressingly familiar. It was like Oil Street, Vandries Street, Vulcan Street and the whole of the Scotland Road area.

'You're seeing it on a good day,' Sean informed her, still doubting the wisdom of his decision. 'They've all got their best stuff out of hock. It'll all be back for the week in the morning.'

'The way they take it to Mr Fogarty's at home?'

He nodded. He was thankful that O'Keefe's closed down on Sundays and they were all spared the additional assault on their nostrils of the stench of boiling bones and hides to make glue.

The houses were bigger, she thought, much bigger. In fact at one time they must have been like the beautiful houses in Rodney Street, Parliament Street and Gambia Terrace in Liverpool.

He opened the door and she took a deep breath not knowing what kind of reception awaited her.

She was introduced to them all and given the best chair. The room was shabby but clean and no worse than Nora's home in Oil Street had been, she thought. She knew the two young girls, both with the same dark hair and blue eyes as Sean, were taking in every inch of her outfit and Treasa's young man seemed unable to utter a word, totally stunned by her accent, or so she assumed.

There was no hostility or coldness from Sean's mother and that surprised her. The woman regarded her as a

226

guest and was treating her as such; she could see that Mrs Maguire had gone to a lot of trouble to provide a bit of afternoon tea. But Leah had the impression that there was no question of her being there 'on approval' as a prospective member of the family, as Maurice O'Shea was. Mrs Maguire treated him with far more ease.

'Himself there tells me it's off to Liberty Hall tonight to hear Big Jim speechifying.'

'That's right.' Leah took the piece of soda bread from the plate that Shelagh offered.

'Treasa, what's the name of your one who's a keen supporter of Mr Larkin? Hasn't she some grand title?'

'Countess Markiewicz.'

'The very one.' Peggy smiled at Leah. 'You see, you'll not be on your own.'

Leah smiled back.

'Leah. I've never heard such a name before.'

'Mammy!' Shelagh hissed loudly, blushing furiously.

'It's Jewish, from the Bible. My mother liked it. My sister's name is Rhian, which is a Welsh name.'

Peggy nodded sagely. 'I knew there was Celtic blood in you somewhere. What with that hair and those eyes.' Again Leah smiled. She and Peggy Maguire seemed to be the only ones in the room who were relaxed enough to hold a normal conversation, but she knew that was only because Sean's mother saw her as no threat to her son or his religion.

Peggy was watching Leah closely but couldn't fault her. She looked as though she'd spent her life drinking tea from borrowed cups in shabby rooms in a slum, and it was to her credit. The girl was at ease, which was more than could be said for the rest of them. She'd taken note of her clothes too. The dress was plain, obviously so, but well cut. The hat was like hundreds of others worn by the better off working-class girls on Sundays in summer. Only the gloves and the boots gave her away. Working-class girls never wore such an impractical colour.

When the tea was over, the dishes were removed to the top of the dresser to be washed and returned to their respective owners later. Peggy looked round at her family.

'Sean, why don't you and Shelagh go and get some air and have a chat, you've not seen each other for two years. And Maurice, why don't you take our Treasa out too. It's a grand afternoon and don't you both work inside for the rest of the week?' Sean looked as if he was about to refuse but Leah nodded her head at him briefly.

When they'd all gone, Sean casting an anxious backward glance at Leah, Peggy settled herself in the chair opposite. Now was the time to really talk to the girl.

'I've taken a liking to you, Miss Leah Cavendish, but is it all true, what himself has told me about you? That's what I'm asking myself. Why would a girl like yourself, reared in the lap of luxury, up and follow a domestic?'

'It's all true, Mrs Maguire, and I went because Nora was my friend and I can't abide my brother-in-law or his practices.'

'Sean told me his way of going on. God help your sister.'

Leah nodded slowly. 'Rhian is weak and sometimes I think she's afraid of him.'

'And I can see with my own two eyes that you're afraid of no one.'

'Nor am I hard or devious or calculating.'

'Then you must be one of the few of your class who isn't.'

'That's why I'm here, to see and listen to Mr Larkin.'

'Amongst other things, Miss Cavendish,' Peggy added.

'Will you call me Leah, please?'

Peggy looked at her steadily. She *did* like the girl and

she was sure all this wasn't an act of some sort, but it was useless to go any further down this road.

'I know you love him and I know he loves you,' she said, 'but there's no future in it all, child. It's not your class. I'd be content with that if Sean could come down off his high horse and accept that you've money. Pride is a sin and besides it doesn't fill the empty bellies of the children. No, it's not money or class.'

'Mrs Maguire,' Leah interrupted. 'This morning I was supposed to go to Christ Church but I didn't. I went to Saint Catherine's instead.'

'Holy Mother, you never did?'

Leah nodded firmly. 'Nora told me there wasn't much difference between "yours and mine", as she put it, and I wanted to see for myself. She's right, there isn't. I've been thinking about it, even before I came to Dublin, and I've decided I want to change, convert,' she corrected herself, 'to Catholicism.'

Peggy was stunned. This was something she had never expected. 'Does Sean know?' she eventually asked.

'No, and I don't want you to tell him. When I've taken instruction and been accepted, then I'll tell him.'

Peggy shook her head. She'd never met anyone like this girl before, but love and determination filled her eyes and her pale skin seemed to glow with some inner force. Maybe her prayers had been answered but certainly not in the way she'd expected. If so, who was she to go against such a force?

'I know I'll still have to convince him that because I was born into a wealthy family it doesn't matter, but if I have your approval, it will help.' Leah's gaze and tone were pleading.

Still stunned, Peggy shook her head to try to clear her mind. 'There are some things that even I couldn't make him change his mind about, child.'

'I'm not asking you to try, just to approve.'

'If you mean what you say, and I think you do, then you'll have all the approval from me that you'll need.'

'Did you get the full inquisition?' Sean asked that evening as they sat on the tram en route to Beresford Place.

When he'd returned to Vincent Street, Leah and his mother had been chatting amiably but he didn't know for sure if it was all an act put on for his benefit. Leah certainly hadn't looked upset in any way and there had been no sign of censure or annoyance in his mother's manner. In fact, she'd looked quite pleased with herself. Rather like a cat that had got the cream. His probings had led nowhere.

'Why wouldn't I like the girl?' she'd said after he'd escorted Leah back to her hotel. 'She's very civil and loyal and, as you'd expect from the quality, polite and respectful.' And that was all he'd managed to get out of her. Now he was determined to get some straight answers from Leah

'Leah?' he prompted when she didn't immediately reply.

'She asked me why I'd followed Nora and I told her. I told her about Ernest and I told her I loved you, but she already knew that. She said you had more sense than to go wasting the ferry money just to see Big Jim, as she called him. She knew there was something more on your mind and that you hadn't come alone.' She looked sideways at him from beneath her lashes. 'She also said that pride is a sin.'

'That bit was meant for me.'

'It was. She said apart from being a sin it didn't fill the empty bellies of children.'

He was puzzled. If she'd been going on about his pride and children, what was in her mind?

230

'Did she say anything else?'

'Yes, she said she didn't hold my class or my money against me.'

'Holy God, did you bewitch her?'

Leah laughed. 'Don't be ridiculous.'

'Did she not mention religion then?'

'Oh, yes, but that's the confidential part of our discussion and there's nothing you can say or do, Sean Maguire, that will prise it out of me.'

'Well, I'll get nothing out of her, that's for sure and for certain. Did you say you'd see her again before we leave?'

'No, but I said I'd write. Not frequently, just a letter now and then to keep her informed with the news about the houses and such like.'

'That's just as well, she hasn't the reading nor much of the writing either.' There was a note of shame in his voice. It wasn't her fault. Half of Dublin was illiterate but he wished Leah had left literacy out of the conversation.

'I know that too, Sean. She'll get Father O'Neill to read them to her and he'll write her replies. Occasionally.'

'Jaysus! Leah, am I hearing this right?'

'You are and less of the blasphemy, it's Sunday.'

'Holy Mother of God, you even sound like her.'

She laughed and changed the subject. 'There are an awful lot of people ahead, are we nearly there?'

Sean dragged his attention from Leah's astounding revelations and stood up to get a better view.

'That we are. I think we'd be better off if we walked from here. It looks as though half the city is out on the streets tonight.'

After they alighted, he held her firmly round the waist as he pushed forward with the crowds streaming across Butt Bridge towards the shabby building that was once the Northumberland Commercial and Family Hotel but

231

was now the headquarters of the unions, the rallying place for the new order that was emerging, albeit slowly and painfully.

'Hold on tightly to me. If we get separated I'll never find you again in this lot.'

She clung firmly to his jacket lapel, thankful she hadn't worn anything with frills or braid that would be a hindrance and could be caught and ripped in the crush. The crowd around them was packed so tightly that it was beginning to be claustrophobic and hard to breathe but Sean pushed ruthlessly on until they were only fifty yards from the front of the crowd. The heat of the evening and the tightly pressed bodies made the air stifling but she didn't feel faint.

They had seen no police presence, but others in the crowd around them reported increased numbers of both the Dublin Metropolitan Police and the Royal Irish Constabulary along the quays on both sides of the river.

A ripple of anticipation ran through the huge crowd and grew to a deafening cheer. To Leah it seemed to shake the very ground they stood on. A big man with dark hair, strong features and a bushy handlebar moustache, unwaxed at the ends, appeared on the platform in front of the building. So this was the legendary man, Leah thought. She was not disappointed in his appearance in any way. He was a big man, in both stature and confidence.

The crowd fell silent as he raised his arms. So silent and still that if someone had dropped a penny it would have been heard. As she glanced around, still clinging to Sean's jacket, she saw many women and girls in the crowd, some dressed like herself, some without hats, some with old faded shawls over their shoulders but with their hair pinned up neatly. Then flinging his arms wide as though to embrace them all, Larkin began to speak.

Leah was entranced. Never in her entire life had she heard such a powerful voice or such vigorous, spellbinding oratory. She was sure his words could be heard clearly even by those at the back of the crowd. There was a fire, a vital energy in the voice that seemed to engulf everyone, including herself, and as she looked at Sean's face she knew that he was feeling the same force.

The voice thundered on, the accent familiar, for it was part Liverpudlian, part Irish. He was offering them no easy life. No guarantees of more money, fewer hours, better conditions. In fact it was just the opposite but for the first time she realised why they loved and respected him. He cared. He cared for them all, something no one had ever done before. They were the poor, the ignorant and the illiterate, the lower orders who were looked down on or ignored entirely.

No one on either side of the sea that separated the two islands cared a damn for the people who couldn't help themselves, who were dependent on the employers and councillors for their living, for life itself. In Leah's opinion, no one should wield such power. Only men like James Larkin and Thomas Mann would fight and battle on their behalf. No wonder the employers were so afraid of them. Well, she was an employer too. Half of Cavendish's belonged to her and when she was twenty-one, there would be some changes, that she promised herself silently as Larkin's voice echoed in front of Liberty Hall. The flaming tarred torches held by people on the platform and others on the perimeter of the crowd caught the expressive gesticulations that were Larkin's trademark and made them appear bigger and all-embracing.

She was so deeply moved by the man that when he'd left the platform and the crowd began gradually to disperse, she was silent, absorbed in his words on the unfairness, the injustice and the cruelty heaped on the heads of the unfortunate masses. She was so absorbed that at first she didn't see the disturbance until she felt Sean stiffen. She looked across the road and saw a young man and a girl being manhandled by three policemen.

The crowd around them was thinning and Sean was remembering Nolan's words of warning and his exhortation to look after Leah and keep her safe. But before he could stop her, she'd broken free and was pushing quickly and purposefully towards the group.

'Jesus, Mary and Joseph, they'll clatter her,' he muttered, beginning to run after her.

As she reached the group, Leah could see that there was blood coming from the corner of the man's mouth and that the girl had lost her hat, her dark hair had fallen around her shoulders and there was sheer terror in her eyes.

'Take your hands off that man and apologise to the young woman for your brutality.'

The cold authority of her tone, the clipped and unfamiliar English upper-class accent made all three turn towards her.

One recovered more quickly than the others. 'And who do you think you're talking to? This feller here is a known troublemaker.'

'What offence has he committed? What offence has she committed?' Leah snapped, but before he could answer she went on, 'It is for the courts to decide whether your accusations are true or false, not you. You have neither the position nor the intelligence. You are paid to uphold the law, to keep the King's peace, and what are you doing? Beating and terrifying defenceless men and girls.'

The sergeant, his face twisted, his eyes bulging with rage at her slur, moved towards her.

'One step more, Sergeant, and your career will be over. You'll be unemployed, like most people here. I have noted all your collar numbers and I have friends in high places. Very high places. Higher than the castle even.' She was burning with anger inside but not a trace of it showed on her face. Her words were like shards of ice and their effect was stunning even though they were untrue. She knew they wouldn't risk calling her bluff.

They backed away. One of them picked up the girl's hat and handed it to her. Then casting a look of pure venom at her, the sergeant bawled at his underlings to turn and march.

Sean let out a long, slow breath of relief. He'd known she was lying but her accent, her cold confidence had defeated them every bit as much as her threats.

'In the name of God, Leah, you could have had us all arrested.'

A small crowd had gathered, the girl was wiping the young man's mouth with a handkerchief. Her hat, so like Leah's own, was ruined.

'But I didn't. If I can use what I have, my nationality, my class, my accent to stop anyone being hurt then I will. I stood there and listened to Larkin and I realised that it is *my* class of person, as you say, who has caused so much misery and it's time someone did something about it. Was I expected to look the other way, Sean? To leave these two unfortunates to their fate? Those three were brutal cowards. Without the uniform they'd be nothing!'

The girl touched her arm. 'Miss, may God give you a long and happy life, for it's a saint you are.'

There was a murmur of approval.

Leah shook her head. 'No, I'm no saint, but I wasn't going to stand by and let them beat you. How did it start?'

'Didn't one of them stick out his foot and have me trip over it and then say I was drunk. I haven't had a sup all day.'

235

Sean took Leah's arm. 'I'm taking you back to the hotel and for God's sake don't go doing anything like that again. You put the heart across me. We could have been arrested for obstructing the police in the course of their duty.'

She was still shaking but she smiled up at him. 'I'm tired, but it was worth it. All of it. They should put a statue up to Mr Larkin.'

'Haven't we enough bloody statues in this city as it is and the day they put one up to him will be the day that a man will walk on the moon! You, miss, are having an early night and I'll be instructing your man on the door that you've not to set a foot out of it until tomorrow morning.'

She was calm now and was content to sit on the tram and lean her head on his shoulder. Her anger, as usual, had died as quickly as it had flared.

She lay awake for a long time, listening to the sounds of the city outside her open window gradually diminish. It had been a day of such great importance in her life, of such huge decisions. She hadn't really set out to go to St Catherine's, but an urge, a strong urge had made her walk onward.

She'd been amazed at the accuracy of Nora's words. There were differences, but as she'd knelt in one of the back pews, with the heady perfume of incense, the quiet, reverent Latin responses of the congregation and the sweet clear voices of the choirboys filling the air, she'd felt at peace. The terrible guilt she felt over the conditions of the houses and the working practices at Cavendish's could be overcome. The paths were different but they led to the same God. When she got home she'd ask Nora to take her to see Father Finnegan and then she'd write to Mrs Maguire.

After her birthday things *would* change at Cavendish's and she *would* overcome Sean's pride in the end for she had the full approval now of his mother.

Chapter Seventeen

You could feel the tension in the hot sultry air. It was almost tangible, Leah thought as they disembarked. She'd stood on deck and watched as they'd come up river. Ships were lying idle in all the docks. The dockside cranes were still, looking like huge metal arms reaching skywards as if in supplication to the heavens. The pierhead and the streets they passed through on the way home lacked their usual clatter and clamour. The trams were running and the hackneys, there were a few motorcars, but there was an obvious and significant reduction in the horses and carts.

Sean was quiet and preoccupied on the tram and Leah sat thinking over the events of the weekend. He saw her to her front door and then went in search of Pat. No sooner had Leah taken off her hat and gloves than Nora arrived.

'You must have just passed Sean, he's gone looking for Pat.'

'Maybe he went up the jigger, it's quicker.' Nora's eyes were sparkling. 'We got the money, Leah. He was very nice about it, that Mr Rankin. He and Pat had a good chat. I didn't understand most of it, but we're going to find a house to rent, put some into a bank account and the rest in investments. He was using all kinds of words I didn't understand, securities and bonds, I came out with a headache. Imagine *us* with a bank account!'

Leah smiled. 'Don't worry, I don't understand much

either, but I'll learn. We can both learn if we have to, you're as bright as a button, Nora Ryan. What's been going on here? The city looks deserted.'

Nora sighed. 'The railway men started it – again. They want more money and less hours. The strike committee said that all transport workers would support them, so Pat told me. The shipping bosses lost their rag and told everyone if they didn't go back to work by the fourteenth, everyone would be locked out. Thank God for your Aunt Poppy. Pat's only got to worry about Sean and his mates. We won't go without.'

'If you know anyone who needs help, Nora, let me know.'

'I will. You're too generous, you know, Leah.'

Leah shrugged. 'What's that thing Florrie Burrows always says? "It's made round to go round."'

Nora decided to change the subject. 'How did the weekend go then?'

'Well, he took me on a sightseeing tour in an open carriage.'

'Oh, get you!'

Leah laughed. 'It wasn't like the carriage we had, or the horses either. It's a beautiful city, but like Liverpool it's got fine buildings and terrible slums. Beautiful old Georgian houses four storeys high and with cellars, half falling down for want of maintaining and with a family in every room. Sean says there are twenty thousand rooms in Dublin and a family in each.'

'Like round here, only with more rooms in each house. Did he take you to see his mam in the end?'

Leah nodded. 'Yes. I liked her and his sisters and Treasa's fiancé. He has a steady job but he didn't seem to be able to string two words together.'

'Well, that's certainly something new in an Irishman. But did *she* like *you*? His mam, I mean.'

'She was suspicious at first but in the end she approved of me, after I told her I was going to change my religion. I went into a Catholic church on Sunday, just to see, and after that I made up my mind.'

'You really are going to convert? Does he know?'

'Yes to the first question and no to the second, and I don't want him to know either, Nora, not yet. I'll tell him when the time's right.'

Nora nodded solemnly. 'I'll go and see Father Finnegan and explain and make some arrangements.'

'I'd be glad if you would.'

Nora still looked perplexed and Leah felt there was something troubling her.

'What's the matter, really the matter? I know you and there's something bothering you.'

Nora sighed and frowned. 'It's me da. He's not well but he won't admit it. He's got no colour in his face, he's tired and he's in pain. When he thinks I'm not looking I've seen his face screwed up as though he was in agony.'

'Do you think he needs to see a doctor?'

'Yes, but how the hell will I get him to go?'

'Bring the doctor to him but don't tell him.'

'But which doctor?'

'Dr MacDougal.'

Nora nodded. 'I'm worried about our Ethna too. I know she's as miserable as sin and I can't say I blame her, stuck with old misery guts. Still, I'm going to buy her a nice gold locket. Pat agrees with me that she deserves something out of my "inheritance" as he's always calling it.'

Leah looked sadly at Nora. Poor Ethna, it must be so awful for her. 'I think that's lovely, Nora. She can keep a photo of little Alex in it.'

Nora picked up her hat, a straw boater much like the one Leah had worn in Dublin. 'I'll go now and see

Father Finnegan and then I'll come back and tell you what he says.'

Leah unpacked and began to think about Joe. He wasn't old. He was only in his fifties, yet he looked seventy. The harshness and deprivations of life had aged him so much. She was very fond of him. He'd cared enough to put his own bitterness aside and comfort her on that awful, awful day.

That led her mind back to Rhian and Ernest. He certainly wouldn't be happy, not with his men on strike, and he'd take it out on her poor sister. If only Rhian would stand up to him, but she just didn't have the temperament. Maybe one day she would, if she was really goaded. Even a worm will turn, Leah thought. Percy had said that once to Cook and had had his ears boxed for his pains.

Leah decided to go round and see Joe for herself. She'd tell him all about Jim Larkin. Joe would appreciate every detail of that.

Declan and his mates were playing cricket with a long flat piece of wood for a bat and a proper ball that they'd found somewhere. The wickets were chalked on the base of the lamppost, which definitely gave the batsmen a huge advantage, Leah thought with amusement as she waved to him.

She'd only got one foot on the first step of the doorway when the sound of breaking glass stopped her. She turned round and looked up the street. The cricketers had all scattered, Declan was pounding down the street towards her while a furious Lizzie Madden stood on her doorstep, hands on hips, and called them every name she could think of, finishing with the threat to 'take the lot of youse down the police station'.

'Here, go and give that to Mrs Madden and apologise.'

Leah thrust a two shilling piece in Declan's grubby hand, thinking of how annoyed Joe would be.

'I can't do that!' Declan protested. 'She'll murder me! She'll kill me stone dead, she's gorra terrible temper.'

'I don't wonder with cricket balls flying into her front room showering broken glass everywhere, never mind the expense of replacing it. Now go and apologise.' Leah gave the lad a shove and watched as he slowly and cautiously approached Lizzie Madden's house, then she turned and walked up the hall.

'It's only me, Mr O'Brian. Back from across the sea to Ireland.' She smiled at the borrowed phrase from the song 'Galway Bay', but when she walked into the kitchen the smile turned to shock. Joe was lying on the floor, his head just a few inches from the sharp corner of the new brass fender.

She dropped to her knees beside him. 'Mr O'Brian! Joe! Joe!' She shook him gently and turned his face towards her. He was unconscious but breathing. She moved him until his head lay in her lap.

Declan burst in the door but stopped dead as he saw Leah and his da.

'Go and get Nora, she's at the church, then go and get Dr MacDougal and tell him it's urgent. I'll stay with him.'

'Is he . . .'

'No, he's not, but he needs help, so move!'

Declan needed no further telling.

Nora arrived first, perspiring and panting, her cheeks red.

'Oh, Leah!'

'I've sent for the doctor but he looks as if he's coming round.'

Nora knelt beside Leah and took her father's hand.

'Da. Da, can you hear me? It's Nora.'

243

Joe's eyes, clouded with pain, opened slowly.

'You passed out but you didn't hit your head, thank God. I'm sorry I bought that flaming fender. Dr Mac is on his way.'

Joe struggled to rise.

'Stay still, Da. Rolling around isn't going to help.'

An agonised groan escaped Joe's lips and the two girls exchanged glances.

'I told you so,' Nora mouthed to Leah, who nodded her understanding.

Dr MacDougal arrived in his car with Declan beside him. The ride in the car had temporarily lessened Declan's shock.

Between them they got Joe into a chair and the doctor asked the girls to leave while he examined his patient.

They waited in the tiny, sparsely furnished front room. Declan was sent out to find his mates. He was better out of the way.

'But for God's sake keep out of flaming trouble!' Nora hissed at him as he left.

Joe answered all the doctor's questions evasively. Dr Mac was not a man to be easily fooled or fobbed off and abruptly told his patient that if he didn't give more definite and truthful answers, he was leaving. He wasn't wasting his time.

Joe reluctantly agreed to be more forthcoming and explicit.

The examination was thorough and painful and when it was over, Dr Mac sat down in the chair opposite Joe.

'I can see by the look on your face that it's serious, Doctor.'

'It is.'

'What's wrong with me then? Seeing as you wanted honest answers, can I have them too? You can tell me the worst.'

244

Dr MacDougal looked steadily at Joe. He did have a strong, resilient nature, forged most likely from the hard life that had been his lot.

'It is the worst, Mr O'Brian. It's a growth and probably there's more than one. From what you've told me, I'm as certain as anyone can be that they're malignant. It's called cancer.'

Joe's gaze was steady. 'Will it kill me?'

Dr Mac nodded. 'I'm afraid it will, Joe.'

There was a heavy silence in the room. It was at times like this that Angus MacDougal hated his job. He felt so useless. His purpose, his knowledge and experience were supposed to save life.

'How long?' Joe asked at last. Now he knew, it didn't seem so bad. It had been the not knowing that had been worst.

'Six months at the longest. I can give you something for the pain now but in the later stages it won't help much.'

Joe nodded. Death in all its forms haunted these dirty, verminous streets. Nell's had been peaceful in the end but obviously God had different plans for him. He'd have to suffer before St Peter would tick off his name and he could join her.

'Don't tell Nora or our Ethna either, please, Doctor.'

'They'll have to know sometime.'

'Not yet. Give me a bit more time and some dignity.'

Dr Mac nodded and took from his case a small brown bottle. 'Take a few drops of this when the pain gets unbearable. I'll call and see you next week.' He rose slowly and reached for his hat.

'I don't want to be rude, but what for?' Joe asked. 'Can't I just send someone for more medicine? If the girls see you coming here every week they'll soon twig on there's something really wrong and once our Nora starts, she's like a dog with a bone. She'll keep worrying and nagging until she gets the truth.'

'If you're sure.'

'I'm sure.'

Dr Mac took Joe's hand and gripped it tightly as he shook it. 'You're a brave man, Joe O'Brian, and I respect you for that.'

Joe managed a smile. 'I was always a fighter. You can let the female contingent in now while I tell them a pack of lies.'

'You mean we'll both tell them a pack of lies. A little known disease that sometimes affects men who have worked on docks in all weathers all their lives. But treatable with medicine. Will that do?'

'Aye, that'll do.'

After the doctor had gone and both Nora and Leah seemed pacified by the explanation, Joe asked Nora to send Pat round later. He felt like a pint and a bit of a walk.

She grinned and agreed. 'Well, that medicine must work wonders if you're already feeling fit enough to go out and have a bevvy.'

Once outside, Nora turned to Leah. 'You're to go down to the presbytery this afternoon at four.'

Leah nodded. 'I'll say a prayer of thanks, too, that your father's not seriously ill.'

'So will I, on me way home. If he wants to go to the pub, well, I'm dead relieved and yet . . .'

'What?'

'He's not gone into a pub for years. He's not all that keen on drink.'

'Can't the man change his mind? Stop worrying and thinking up dire reasons for his every move.'

'You're right. Well, I'd best get back. I've shopping to do.'

*   *   *

246

At a quarter to four Leah closed her front door behind her and walked up towards the church. The afternoon was so hot that she felt beads of perspiration spring out on her brow and she knew the starch in her blouse would wilt.

She was shown into a parlour decently but plainly furnished, by an elderly woman who informed her that His Reverence would be with her shortly. Leah looked around. She'd seen statues in Ethna, Nora and Joe's homes. There were pictures on the wall here too. She recognised the Crucifixion and the Madonna and Child but the others, mainly nuns and monks, one surrounded by animals, she didn't. The door opened and the parish priest entered.

'Ah, Miss Cavendish.'

Leah extended her hand. 'Thank you for seeing me so quickly, Father.'

'Not at all. Sit down, will you?'

Leah sat in the chair he indicated. He stood with his back to the empty firegrate.

'Young Mrs Ryan tells me you want to become a Catholic?'

'I do, Father.'

'And might I ask why?'

Leah thought for a moment. 'I . . . I've fallen in love with Sean Maguire and I know he will never marry me because of his faith, among other things. I've just returned from Dublin and last Sunday, instead of going to Christ Church I went to Mass, just to see for myself. Nora had told me there wasn't a lot of difference and I think she's right.'

He nodded. This was the usual reason. Few and far between were those struck like St Paul on the road to Damascus.

'Ah, well now, there *are* differences, child. Substantial ones.'

'I know.'

'And will you be prepared to accept them? Wait now until I've finished. The main ones of course are the infallibility of the Pope as head of Christ's Church, the successor of St Peter himself. But that doesn't mean he's right about everything all the time. Ah, no. Only in matters of faith and dogma. The other is transubstantiation. We believe that during the sacrifice of the Mass, the bread and wine actually become the body and blood of Jesus Christ. Your church believes it is just a symbol. There are other things too.'

'Father, as I knelt in St Catherine's, I *knew* what I wanted,' Leah said quietly but firmly.

'Then you are welcomed with open arms, child, and we'll begin immediately.'

'It's not like you to fancy a pint, Joe,' Pat said with a hint of amusement in his voice as they strolled up towards the Victoria pub on the corner of Vandries Street and Great Howard Street.

'No, it's not, and I don't feel like one at all but I've got to talk to you, lad.'

Pat was instantly serious. 'About what?'

'Not now.'

Pat nodded his understanding and wondered what on earth it was. He knew Nora had been worried about him, but Nora worried about everything.

Pat ordered two pints of bitter from Ted Young the barman.

'It's a bloody miracle the roof 'asn't fell in,' Ted grinned. 'First time I've seen Joe O'Brian in 'ere for years.'

'Well, a feller can change his mind, can't he?'

'Don't get airyated with me, la, I'm not complaining, it's all business. Cash in me pocket.'

Pat carried the drinks over to a table in an alcove by the window. Its top was scratched and scarred and none too clean. The chairs were pretty much the same and the sawdust on the floor needed changing.

'So, what's the secret?'

Joe took a sip of his drink and puckered his lips at the unfamiliar sour taste. 'I want you to promise me, Pat, that you'll look after our Nora, Declan and, if needs be, our Ethna too.'

Pat was alarmed. 'Joe, what the hell's the matter?'

'I'm bad off, Pat. I'm dying. Dr Mac says six months or less. It's something called cancer and I've been in pain for a while back but this morning I collapsed and Leah found me and sent for him.'

Pat stared at his father-in-law, stunned. 'I . . . I . . . Isn't there . . .'

'A cure? No, lad. No cure. Just some drug to help with the pain. Opium, morphine, something like that, it is.'

'Do they know?'

'No, and I don't want them to know. Any of them, not yet anyway. I'm sorry, lad, to lumber you with them, especially our Declan. I worry about that kid. I don't want him ending up in Walton.'

'Nora will kill me for not telling her, Joe, you know she will.'

Joe smiled. 'Aye, she's got a tongue that would cut a garden hedge, has that one. She's like her mam, God rest her.' He looked down into the clear amber depths of his drink. 'That's the only thing that'll keep me going, Pat. The fact that it won't be long now before I see Nell again.'

Pat couldn't trust himself to speak; he just shook his head.

'Nor do I want either of you spending a fortune on a fancy funeral. You'll need that money.'

'What about Leah?' Pat managed to get out.

'You can tell her the same but she'll not listen. Leah will do whatever she likes with her money. She's the first of her class I've ever met who has a heart of gold. She's a treasure that was sent to us, Pat. A pearl that was cast from Prince's Avenue among swine like us, to use a bit of the old saying. So, will you look after them for me, Pat?'

'I will, Joe, I promise. Especially that young horror. He's not bad, you know. There's no wickedness in him, just devilment. He'll not end up in Walton.'

Joe nodded. 'Well, I suppose I'd better drink this stuff seeing as it's been paid for. This is one place I certainly won't miss,' he finished grimly.

Pat ducked his head, afraid Joe would see the incipient tears. Why now? Why now after the man had slaved and struggled all his life? Just when he had no money worries and was enjoying his retirement. Why the hell was it all going to be snatched away? Sometimes it was hard to keep faith. But as Joe had said, he'd soon be with Nell and he must have missed her badly all these years, just as he himself would be heartbroken if anything happened to Nora.

'What's the situation at work?' Joe asked suddenly, trying to lift the mood.

'Pretty bloody desperate. If we don't go back a week on Monday, the fourteenth, they'll lock us out for as long as it takes to break us. There's a meeting on Saint George's Plateau next Sunday. Tom Mann is going to speak. Thousands will be going because something's got to be done, we can't go on like this for ever. Sean's going and he said there's nothing on earth that will stop Leah either. When they went to hear Larkin speak, the police were rough and Sean said she was bloody marvellous. She tore into them, threatened to have them kicked out of the

250

force. She told them she had friends in very high places, and they weren't to know she hasn't. She brought it off with that posh accent she has. They backed down.'

'She shouldn't go to meetings like that.'

'Just try and stop her, Joe. If she ups and follows our Nora, leaving all that comfort behind, well, she'll not stay at home.'

'Then I'm coming too.'

'You're not well enough, Joe, and Nora will raise the roof. She's not going and I might try and get her to change Leah's mind.'

'Thank God she's got sense, but you're not going to talk me out of it, lad. There's nothing much left I can do, but I'd like to show support to the men I've worked with.'

Reluctantly Pat nodded. Joe had always been a strong supporter of workers' rights and now he was prepared to stand with them, faithful to his mates and his beliefs to the end.

The following Sunday morning Sean came with Pat and Joe to call for Leah. All week Nora had tried to persuade her against going but she was adamant.

'I'm not going to chain myself to a statue and then get dragged off to the police station, and I won't be the only female there. I wasn't in Dublin, and besides, it's just a meeting,' had been the final and determined answer.

As they approached the bottom of London Road, the crowd was getting thicker and Leah saw that she'd been right. There were women and girls among the men. As they waited, the crowd grew and grew until it covered the entire plateau, spilled down the steps, across the pavement and road, right to the doors of the Empire theatre. Men and boys climbed on to the bases of the statues of the mounted Queen Victoria and Prince Albert. They swarmed over

the huge crouching lions and around the Steble fountain
and the column that was Liverpool's monument to the
heroic deeds of Wellington. From its summit, the Iron
Duke's stone eyes looked unseeingly upon the multi-
tude far below. Two trams, advertising 'Crawford's
Cream Crackers', were at a standstill, marooned in a
sea of people. Brightly coloured union banners waved
in the light breeze. All were represented, dockers,
seamen, carters and coalheavers, railwaymen and tram
drivers.

'We'll never get near enough to hear what is being
said,' Leah complained.

'God, I'd never imagined it would be like this,' Pat
said to Sean.

'It's a good turnout, all right. They won't be able to
ignore this.'

'Stay on the edge if you can, push over towards Lime
Street Station,' Joe advised.

With great difficulty they did so and Pat laughed
suddenly and pointed.

'What's so amusing?' Sean asked.

'See over there, on the corner of Skelhorne Street? It's
Dai Morgan and his barrel organ and monkey. He lives
upstairs to us.'

'This is no place for a bloody barrel organ. It's not a
picnic,' Joe said sharply as pain began to gnaw at his
abdomen. He'd taken a few drops of his medicine early
on, but they were wearing off. He'd just have to put up
with it. It would be his last, personal stand for a decent
wage and a better life for those who would follow him.

'Ah, leave the poor old feller alone, Joe. Sure, he's
only trying to earn a few coppers to keep body and
soul together. Didn't the pit finish him as a worker?
And did anyone care about that? Divil a bit, they did,'
Sean chided.

252

As the sun rose higher, the heat was almost unbearable but at last the speakers appeared. A hush fell over the enormous crowd.

'I can't hear a word even with those megaphones. Why didn't they have Jim Larkin? You'd have heard him with or without one of those things,' Leah protested.

'Hush,' Pat admonished.

Leah stood on tiptoe but she couldn't see the speaker.

Sean turned round in annoyance. Somewhere over to his right at the bottom of Lord Nelson Street, the narrow lane that ran up beside the Empire and joined St Vincent Street at the top, there seemed to be some sort of scuffle going on. Then his eyes widened as he realised what it was. The police were hidden up the smaller roads that led off Lime Street, Skelhorne Street and Copperas Hill. They'd been out of sight, but not for much longer.

'Jaysus, Pat! We've got to get Leah and Joe out of here quick.'

'Why?'

'The police. Look over there, they're about to charge in with bloody batons.'

Suddenly mayhem erupted around them as the police charged en masse, batons flailing indiscriminately. The air was filled with yells, shouts, curses and the screams of terrified women.

'Pat, get a good grip of Joe,' Sean instructed. 'Leah hang on to me like you did in Beresford Place. If we—' He staggered and Leah's piercing scream was added to the rest.

Pat turned but as he did so Joe was bludgeoned hard on the head and began to fall forward. Pat grabbed him to keep him upright. If any of them fell, they stood no chance at all. Sean would have to look after Leah. Dragging Joe with him, he pushed and fought and ran when he could. As he got to the corner of Skelhorne

Street, he stumbled over something. It was old Dai Morgan lying face down on the cobbles. His arm, now bloody and twisted, was over the little monkey who had shared his solitary existence and whom he'd tried to protect. Now it was just a crumpled little ball of fur. The barrel organ was smashed to matchwood.

There was no time to think of anything else except getting Joe to safety and it was only when he reached Ranelagh Street and Central Station that Pat stopped. He was exhausted for he'd half carried, half dragged Joe all the way. With his handkerchief he tried to staunch the blood that was turning his father-in-law's grey hair scarlet.

The police baton had caught Sean on the shoulder and his left arm hung limply at his side. Leah clung to him like a limpet but her temper was rising. Blows were still raining down on the fleeing figures around her and there seemed no way out. As a truncheon flashed past within an inch of her nose, she instantly shot out her hand, caught it and dragged on it with a strength fuelled by sheer fury. To her surprise the cord that held it round its owner's wrist snapped. She lashed out, catching the policeman a glancing blow across the top of his arm.

'How dare you!' she yelled at the startled constable. 'How dare you batter these people as though they were cattle! Who's responsible for this?'

Again, her accent, her furious demand and her confidence had its effect.

'The . . . the Head Constable,' the unfortunate young man replied.

'Then he will pay for all this! This was a peaceful demonstration until the Head Constable assumed otherwise!' The words 'Head Constable' were spat out with stinging sarcasm.

A red-faced sergeant pushed the constable aside and

made a grab for the truncheon Leah still held, but she was too quick for him.

'Don't you lay a finger on me!'

'I'm arresting you for assaulting a police officer in the course of his duty!' He attempted to catch her shoulder but she brought the truncheon down hard across his knuckles. His face went white with pain and fury and she knew she'd broken his hand. Well, now he'd know how it felt.

'I am Miss Leah Cavendish! Joint owner of Cavendish's Haulage!'

'I don't care if you own the bloody museum, I'm arresting you.'

For an instant she faltered but then plunged on. 'Is that so? I really wouldn't advise it. My godfather is the Earl of Sefton and Lord Lieutenant of the County Palatine and unless you clear a path and do not molest me or this man you've already injured, I'll have you, your Head Constable and most of your senior officers dismissed out of hand for this whole fiasco and their pensions will be forfeited!'

She wondered if she had gone too far this time. She could see him wavering. She certainly couldn't look much like the goddaughter of the Earl of Sefton. Her hat had long gone, the lace on her blouse was torn, one sleeve spattered with blood – whose she didn't know – but at least her hair had stayed tidily in place.

'Well, do I have to beat a path through myself with this weapon you all use so indiscriminately?' she demanded imperiously.

He was in excruciating pain but couldn't take the chance. She certainly wasn't afraid of him. She was furious and even though she looked untidy, the breeding in her features and bearing and in her speech were clear. The consequences, if she was who she claimed to be, didn't bear thinking about. Clutching his hand, he instructed the young constable to clear a way through. He would have liked to see her get the hiding she deserved but he couldn't take the chance.

Behind her the police repeatedly charged the defenceless crowds. Injured men and women sat or lay on the ground while others with blood streaming from wounds fled in all directions.

At last they reached the comparative safety of Lewis's department store and she turned and handed the constable back his truncheon.

'I'll not forget either of you. I have your collar numbers,' she snapped, glaring at their retreating backs.

'Holy God, Leah! How the hell do you get away with it?'

'Because they're imbeciles, that's why! Can you walk? Is your arm broken? Shall we go to the hospital?'

'I'm not going to a hospital. There'll be more deserving cases than me for them to deal with. I can walk. I think it's my shoulder. Did you see Pat and Joe?'

'No.'

'Then the best plan is to go to Oil Street. There's no use searching for them here.'

She nodded and they headed down Ranelagh Street towards Church Street to catch a tram. She prayed that Pat and Joe had managed to get home in safety. She was still shaking with shock, fear and the force of her anger.

Chapter Eighteen

Declan, white-faced and with eyes wide with fear, opened the door to them. The lad's eyes went to Sean's pale, pain-filled face.

'Is 'e hurt as well, Leah?'

'Yes. Are Pat and your dad here? Did they get home safely?'

Declan burst into tears. 'Me da's bleedin'. Pat brung him home. Me da's going ter die, his head's all bashed in.'

Leah caught the boy to her and held him close as he sobbed.

'No, he's not going to die, Declan.'

Sean was making his way slowly towards the kitchen.

Joe was lying on the sofa, his face totally without colour, even his lips were bloodless. His shirt and jacket were soaked with blood, as was the towel Nora had wrapped round his head. Pat looked ghastly, his face was scratched, one eye was already turning black and his lip was cut and swollen. There was dried blood all over his shirt. Ethna was holding Alex in her arms and sobbing.

'You took a bit of a clattering, Pat, but what happened to Joe?' Sean winced as he perched on the edge of the table.

'He got a truncheon blow, full force on the back of his head. It split it open. I did what I could. And you?'

257

'A clout on the shoulder. Leah got us out.'

At that moment Leah came in, still holding Declan against her. She looked at them all in utter horror. Ethna let out another tragic sob.

Suddenly Nora's overwrought nerves snapped. 'Ethna, for God's sake shut up or go home!'

Leah took charge. 'Declan, wipe your eyes and go out and find a hackney, tell him to come at once. Then run down for Dr Mac and tell him what's happened. Come on, pull yourself together, you're a grown lad now.' How ludicrous that sounded, she thought. Telling him to pull himself together when she was near to hysteria herself.

'Ethna, give Alex to me and make a pot of strong tea. Then when the hackney arrives, take him home, this is no place for babies. Nora will let you know how your father is.'

Rocking Alex in her arms, Leah went to Nora's side while Ethna, calmer now, lit the gas ring and filled the kettle.

'How is he?'

'I can't stop the bleeding. He must have lost pints. Look at the state of him and Pat.'

'Dr Mac may recommend he goes to hospital, although they'll be overcrowded.'

'Holy Mother of God, what happened, Leah? Was there a riot?'

'No. The police just charged the crowd, for no reason at all. Look, I can hold the towel in place with my free hand, you see what you can do for Pat.'

Nora left her father in Leah's care and got water and a clean towel and began to bathe Pat's injuries. She was thankful they weren't serious. 'You're going to look a right mess for a while,' she said, her voice a little shaky.

'I got off light, luv.'

'I know and . . . and thanks for getting Da home.'

He tried to smile but grimaced in pain. Then he remembered Dai Morgan. 'I think poor Dai Morgan is dead. I saw him stretched out flat, poor old sod. The little monkey had been trampled and his barrel organ was in bits.'

This more than anything else brought the tears cascading down Nora's cheeks. She'd been fond of the quiet old Welshman who was always pleasant to her. 'What was he doing down there in the first place, Pat?'

'Trying to earn a few coppers, that's all.'

Nora shook her head, blinded by tears, and Pat drew her into the circle of his arms.

Ethna had just poured out the tea when Declan arrived back.

'Ethna, get your things and here's Alex and,' Leah delved into her purse and drew out some coins, 'the fare.'

'The doctor's 'ere too,' Declan announced, looking at the circle of pale, worried faces. Dr MacDougal had managed to calm him down a bit, saying even small cuts on the head often bled a lot.

'Thank God,' Nora said, drawing away from Pat.

'I'm staying,' Ethna announced calmly.

Nora looked pleadingly at Leah.

'Declan, can you take Alex back home so Edward can look after him? Tell him, as slowly as you can, what's happened and then come back home in the cab.' Leah passed over more coins and with reluctance on the part of both Ethna and Declan, the baby was handed over just as Dr Mac entered the room.

He was informed briefly and succinctly by Leah what had happened. He went first to Pat.

'Doctor, it's my da who's the worst,' Nora cried.

'It's all right, Mrs Ryan, this will only take a few minutes.' He nodded curtly at Pat. 'Nothing to worry about there. Now, let's have a look at you.' He turned to Sean who hadn't said a word but had watched Leah with admiration, despite his pain.

Leah, too, was startled. 'Doctor, please, Mr O'Brian is . . .' From the corner of her eye she saw Pat slowly shake his head and she fell silent. There was something ominous now in the atmosphere.

'I'd say a cracked collar bone. I'll put a sling on and all you can do is rest it, which, the way things are going in this city, is all anyone will be doing. There'll be few fit or able to work after this episode.' He was a dour man who had spent all his working life in the slums and he had little time or patience for the employers, the City Council and the police. He'd seen too many women die in childbirth, too many babies and children die of starvation and disease.

Finally he turned to Joe. Slowly and gently he removed the blood-soaked towel and looked at the wound. It was deep and he could see the exposed and crushed skull, fragments of which were twined in Joe's hair. He took the fresh towel Nora passed him and then bandaged over it. He knew it would do no good but it would help pacify the poor frightened lassies. He took Joe's wrist; he could only just feel the slow pulse.

Joe opened his eyes. The faces around and above him receded and then merged together. 'Is that you, doctor?'

'Aye, it is. Why the hell did you go?'

Joe was having trouble with his speech. 'Had to. No good for anything else. Better . . . like this . . .'

Dr Mac looked up at the six faces. 'He's a brave man.'

'Isn't there anything you . . .' Nora couldn't finish her question.

'No. I'm very sorry, lassie. Miss Cavendish, will you go for the priest?'

Ethna stuffed her hand in her mouth to stifle her cry as Leah turned and flew down the hall.

Dr Mac shook his head and looked at them all. 'He was already dying and he knew it. He had six months to live at the most and he would have been in terrible agony. It's a death without dignity. Whoever hit him did him a favour. It's better this way.'

Pat drew Nora to him and Sean held out his good hand to Ethna. She seized it as though it was a lifeline.

'That's what he wanted to tell me last week when we went out to the pub,' Pat said quietly, thinking dazedly, was it really only a week ago?

Nora raised eyes full of confusion to his face. 'You knew?'

'I swore I wouldn't tell you, any of you. He said he'd tell you when the time came. I . . . I promised to look after all of you, especially Declan.'

'Do you want me to stay?' Dr Mac asked.

'Will it be worth it, doctor?' Sean spoke for the first time. He'd admired and respected Joe O'Brian so much and now, in the light of what had been said, that esteem grew and he understood why Joe had made the decision to go today.

'Not really. Not in any professional sense, but I'll wait for the priest and for the youngster to come back.'

Nora could only nod her thanks.

Joe O'Brian died at half past six surrounded by his family, with the exception of his son-in-law and grandson. Leah, too, was there. By that time the police, acting on the orders of a panicking City Council, had cleared Lime Street in the only way they knew how – by brute force. A contingent of the Warwickshire Regiment was

261

posted along the whole of the street with bayonets fixed. The Riot Act was read but as the sun finally set and darkness enveloped the city, angry men and women took to the streets, this time armed with missiles and staves. Battles raged and there was wholesale looting. The Riot Act was again read but it had little effect and, to add to the violence, the age-old sectarianism between Catholics and Protestants flared up.

Little of this was known in the house in Oil Street where only shock and grief prevailed. Ma Dudley laid Joe out in the front room and shocked and saddened neighbours called to express their condolences and pray by his side. They brought with them news of what was going on in the city, but no one really seemed to care.

Ethna had been persuaded by Nora and Leah to go home. Alex would need her, even if Edward Neely didn't.

'What will you do, Nora?' Leah asked.

'I'm staying here, with him. I won't leave him on his own. Pat, will you take Declan to our place?'

'If you're sure that's what you want, luv.'

She nodded and dabbed her swollen eyes again.

'I'll stay with you,' Leah said in a voice full of determination. They'd been through so much together, she wouldn't leave Nora now. Besides, she'd come to love Joe as she'd once loved her father. She turned to Sean. 'Take my keys. Stay at my house tonight. You're worn out and hurt and there's no comfort or peace in that place in Lightbody Street.'

'People will talk.'

'Oh, to hell with what people will say. After that bloody massacre this afternoon, I don't care what anyone says. By the sound of things, there won't be many people in to see anything anyway. They'll all be out fighting and looting, and good luck to them, I say. I hope they strip the damned shops bare. Let the poor have the upper hand for once in their lives.'

Pat, Dr Mac and Father Finnegan had been astounded when Sean had told them how she'd probably broken every finger of a police sergeant's hand and then made him carry out her orders to clear a way through for them.

'You'd best be careful, Sean. I wouldn't like to get on the wrong side of that one,' Pat had said quite seriously.

Father Finnegan had sighed heavily, wishing he could tell Sean of Leah's conversion. Instead he said, 'She's a brave girl and the man who gets her will get something more precious than all the wealth she has.'

But Sean couldn't condone what she was saying now. 'Leah, stop talking like that! People are angry and they've a right to be, but it's not just the big stores that will suffer, it will be all the small shopkeepers as well, people like Dan Fogarty. Your nerves have been stretched to breaking point today!'

Only then did Leah let the tears of grief slip down her cheeks freely. Sean drew her to him and she buried her head against his uninjured shoulder.

A few minutes later Pat led a sobbing Declan out of the house and Sean followed.

Together the two girls sat beside Joe, the four candles giving a mellow but shadowy light. They held each other's hands tightly and prayed.

The rioting and looting continued for days. Trams and carts were guarded by escorts of police brought in from Leeds and Birmingham and by detachments of the mounted 18th Hussars and Scots Greys. The battle cruiser HMS *Antrim* lay out in the river, ready if needed. And Joe O'Brian was buried beside his wife in Ford Cemetery.

263

To Pat's statement that Joe wanted nothing fancy, Leah turned a deaf ear. There were to be six carriages for family, friends and neighbours. Official mourners would walk before the horse-drawn hearse and she herself would provide the refreshments in her own home for as many as wished to call.

'There'll be no wake. There's enough fighting going on already. We don't want the army coming down on us,' Pat had stated firmly and had asked the parish priest to inform the congregation of the fact.

At the end of a very long, exhausting and fraught day, Leah at last closed her front door. Just the family and Sean remained.

Ethna put the kettle on.

'We've decided to move back. To live in Joe's house,' Pat informed Ethna, Edward, Sean and Leah.

'Our Declan is too upset to have to change schools and leave all his mates,' Nora added.

Edward Neely inwardly breathed a sigh of relief. He'd not wanted to have to take the lad, nor had he wanted Nora and Pat to move anywhere near his home.

'That would be best for him,' he said, nodding wisely. 'Particularly with the city in the state it's in. It's time these people learned they can't just do as they please, fight and loot and go out on strike if it suits them.'

Sean's blue eyes were cold with hatred. Only because he was Ethna's husband was Neely tolerated here. 'It's the police and the military that have destroyed the city,' he said coldly, 'and the bosses too. All this can be laid at their doors, so it can.'

'I suppose you could do better at running a business,' Edward Neely sneered.

'I'd make a better bloody fist of it than the likes of Armstrong!'

'That's enough!' Leah's voice was full of the cold

264

authority that had subjugated members of both the DMP and the LCP. 'This is neither the time nor the place for arguments. It might be best, Mr Neely, if you took your wife and baby home, they're exhausted.'

Edward Neely's eyes narrowed and the flush of anger tinged his cheeks. 'We'll not stay where we're not welcome. Get your things, Ethna.' He turned towards the door.

'No, *you* are not welcome. But for Nora and Ethna's sake, I wouldn't have had you over my doorstep today. You'd be wise to think about your future, too, Mr Neely, for I've not forgotten in whose pay a certain Mr Macardle was.'

Edward slammed the front door behind them and all the way home Ethna's hatred for him burned more deeply, adding to her grief and humiliation.

Leah sank down at the table and dropped her head in her hands. 'Oh, I didn't mean to say that, not in front of Ethna. She has enough on her plate as it is.'

'I'm the one who should be sorry, Leah. I should never have risen to his baiting.' Sean laid his hand on her shoulder and she looked up at him with longing. Oh, why couldn't he see how much she loved and needed him? Why couldn't he just ignore her money and upbringing? It had its advantages. Twice it had helped her to browbeat and threaten the police into submission even if she had used a pack of lies to do it.

'Everyone's had a rotten day, I'm not blaming you,' she said wearily.

'God, will it never end?' Nora's voice was taut with grief.

'It will have to end sometime. They can't go on escorting everything that moves,' Pat replied.

'Are you staying in Oil Street tonight?' Leah asked.

'Yes. Tomorrow Eileen Molloy, Florrie Burrows and Lizzie Madden are going to give Nora a hand to sort the whole place out. Then I'll have our stuff brought down from Blackstock Street and I'll get new carpets and curtains and maybe do Declan's bedroom out. We'll buy him a Hornby clockwork train set, and a proper football, just to try and help him get over it all a bit. We'd better go and collect him from Agnes Murphy's house soon too. It's not fair to shove him on to her. She's enough to do with that tribe of her own.'

'She won't mind,' Nora said tiredly.

Immediately after he'd had something to eat and drink, Declan had been sent over to the Murphys to be with his mates. Before the funeral Pat had bought him a box of lead soldiers to provide some diversion. Sean had remarked that it was a bit insensitive in the light of current affairs, but the lads hadn't thought so. They played with them for hours, so Agnes had told them.

Leah and Sean watched Nora and Pat walk slowly down the road and round the corner. 'Why do some people seem to have so much tragedy in their lives?' Leah sighed, leaning against Sean. It was a question she was going to ask Father Finnegan tomorrow afternoon.

'Only God knows why he inflicts more on some than on others. Haven't you had enough of it yourself? Your mam and dad, Aunt Poppy, Joe, and in a way you've lost your sister too.'

'I can stand it, Sean. At least most of the time I can, with help. I only lash out, fight back, when I'm really angry and my tantrums don't last long. I feel just like Nora and Ethna, upset, hurt and vulnerable.'

'From the way you altogether demolished certain members of the constabulary both here and in Dublin, I'd say you don't need much help. Sure, you do all right on your own.'

She knew it was meant as a compliment but his words pierced her heart like splinters of ice.

Chapter Nineteen

On 25 August the dockers went back to work after negotiations. They were followed by the carters, seamen, the railwaymen and tram workers. The transport strike that had crippled the city and had come close to causing a revolution was over but as the heat of August gave way to the cooler days and chillier nights of September, Edward Neely grew more and more concerned about his job.

There were only two months to Leah's birthday. Would she sack him? Or would she put that bloody Irish upstart in as a manager over himself and the other three foremen? That's what he lived in fear of and it was beginning to take its toll. He was short-tempered, moody and sullen.

He'd never been one to waste money on drink, in fact he rarely went into a pub. He took his social standing seriously. It demeaned a foreman to be seen knocking back pints in the pub every night, slurring his words and staggering home. Men would mock and sneer among themselves, and openly too. Lately, however, he'd begun to temper those views. Frequently he found it relaxing to have a couple of pints on his way home from work. Only a couple but this was something Ethna definitely didn't approve of, though as yet she'd said nothing. She just wore a tight-lipped, sour expression on a face that was becoming increasingly plain and was also ageing. Then she slammed down his meal on the table.

To make matters worse, over the last weeks his sleep

had been interrupted night after night by his son's fretful crying, which always seemed to start as soon as he arrived home. It grated on his nerves. The novelty of being a father, the pride of having an heir was fading. A man was entitled to a bit of peace and quiet after a day's work, not to be greeted by a whining brat and a sour-faced wife.

Ethna was tired out. She could cope when she had an unbroken six or seven hours' sleep, but Alex's teething pains and the uncomfortable hot summer nights had allowed little chance of that. The poor little mite was in such discomfort and there was little she could do, except nurse him. At least it was cooler now. They would all have got a decent night's sleep had it not been for Alex's teeth. She'd tried all the remedies given by her mam's old friends. She'd rubbed whisky on his gums, then oil of cloves. She'd given him a tiny amount of crushed-up aspirin in his bottle, she'd bought teething rings, but everything had been to no avail.

'Aren't teeth the most unmerciful and contrary things, from birth to death,' Agnes Murphy had commiserated. 'You'd have thought God could have come up with something better when he created Adam, wouldn't yer, queen? Never mind, once it's broken the gum it gets better. Be thankful, our Jimmy cut every one of 'is with the bronchials.' It wasn't much in the way of consolation, and Edward was no help at all.

Ethna was sick to death of the sight of him and now he'd taken to drinking. She'd lost count of the number of ruined meals. Well, tonight there'd be nothing cooked until he came in and if he complained she'd just tell him. Somehow, since the death of her da, she'd found more confidence, or maybe it was just the fact that she didn't care a fig for Edward Neely now. She knew that even if Leah sacked him, she and Nora would never see herself and Alex go short.

As was his habit, Edward meticulously hung his jacket on a coat hanger then hooked that on the stand in the tiny hall. He brushed the bowler hat and hung it on one of the pegs and then rolled up his sleeves. Already the fretful crying had started. The table was set, as usual, but there was no sign of his wife.

'Ethna! Ethna! Where the hell are you and where's my dinner?'

He heard her step on the stairs and hoped she wasn't bringing Alex down with her. If she was, she could just damn well take him back up. He was late tonight. He'd had a bad day. Mr Armstrong had been in an even more vicious mood than usual and Jim Billington was off with a bad back and no sign of him returning this week. So he'd had three pints and two small whiskies, but he wasn't drunk, just tired, he told himself. Nor had he staggered on the corner, it was the broken, uneven paving stones. He had some dignity, he thought grimly. He was relieved to see that Ethna didn't have Alex with her.

He sat down at the table. 'I've had a bloody awful day, so where's my dinner?'

'I've had a bloody awful day too and I'm so fed up with you coming home late and seeing good food ruined that I haven't started it yet.'

'What do you mean you haven't started it yet?' He felt his temper rising at the tone of voice she had used. Offensive and bad-tempered.

'Exactly that. I'll start to cook it now. I haven't had mine either.'

His face grew redder. 'When I get home I expect a meal ready and waiting.'

Ethna turned on him. She had a pounding headache, a pile of unironed shirts over the maiden that she'd have to do tonight, and Alex was crying upstairs.

'*When* you get home. That's exactly it. *When*! When

271

you start to come home on time and not stay in the pub until all hours, then your meal will be ready when you come in!'

He kicked the chair back and lunged at her, catching her a blow across the mouth with the back of his hand. 'I'm not having you speak like that to me, you bitch!' he roared.

Suddenly all the bitterness, frustration and hatred that had been building in Ethna, fuelled by tiredness, broke loose.

'I'll speak to you the way I want to. I must have been flaming mad to have married you. You mean, miserable and disgusting pig! My da was ten times the man you are even though he wasn't a foreman!'

A red mist of anger was blurring Edward Neely's vision as he hit out again. He heard her cry then groan with pain. The sounds only increased his anger. He caught her by her hair and slammed her head hard against the wall.

Ethna felt sick, lights danced before her eyes, the pain in her stomach was terrible but it hadn't entirely diminished her fury.

'I hope Leah puts Sean Maguire in over you! In fact I'll ask her to. Then you'll have to bow and scrape to him otherwise he'll kick you out or maybe Leah will. Either way I'll laugh! Do you hear me? I'll bloody well laugh!' she screamed at him.

He roared like a wounded lion and rained blows on her until she slid to the floor. Then the high-pitched crying coming from upstairs penetrated his mind. That bloody kid! Forever bawling and keeping him awake and the way she fussed over it! Well, he was finished with the pair of them. They could get out now. He took the stairs at a run, snatched the baby from his cot and came back down. Alex's cries became louder and louder at the rough handling.

272

Ethna looked up, she was hurting so badly she knew he'd broken bones, but at the sight of him with Alex, a flame of fury shot through her and she dragged herself to her feet.

'Leave him alone! In the name of God, leave my baby alone!' she screamed.

He shook the infant hard and then threw him into the pram that was kept by the kitchen door. He bent down to pick up a cot sheet that had fallen on the floor, intending to throw it into the pram.

Again Ethna screamed and this time she snatched up the heavy scouse pan. The fury that consumed her deadened all pain as she lifted it and brought it down on the back of his head. He was going to hurt Alex! He had tried to kill her and now he was going to kill her baby!

Blow after blow rained down on Edward Neely's skull until he fell to his knees but in her demented rage Ethna carried on striking him.

When she stopped, he was lying on the floor and there was blood everywhere. The back of his head had been crushed like an eggshell and she screamed as she looked at the pan and then her hands. All were covered with blood.

She dropped the pan and sank to the floor. The pain was searing and she felt faint. 'Oh, God! Oh, God! I've killed him! I've killed him!' she sobbed hysterically. Slowly she dragged herself over to the pram and using the wall and the handle pulled herself up. She reached out to pick the baby up but she couldn't, the pain was too intense, she felt dizziness wash over her. She managed to pacify him with his dummy and soothing sounds that came from swollen lips.

At last he stopped crying, utterly exhausted, and she slid again to the floor, rational thoughts now beginning to creep slowly into her mind. She'd killed him. She'd murdered him and . . . and the police would come and she'd hang. No jury would fail to find her guilty. What kind of a life would Alex have then? His father dead and his mother a murderess, hanged as the law demanded, in Walton Jail. He'd bear that stigma all his life. No! No! He had to have a chance. She tried to clear her mind. She wouldn't let that happen. She wouldn't. She dragged herself over to where her husband lay and managed to roll him on his side. She didn't look at his face, she couldn't. She fumbled in his waistcoat pocket and found what she was looking for. A small notepad and a pencil. Slowly and laboriously she scrawled five words.

'Nora. Take care of Alex.'

She reached up and caught the edge of the tablecloth and with a great effort pulled at it. Cutlery, crockery and condiments fell around her, as did the bread board and knife. She was sobbing quietly as she drew the knife across both her wrists. The pain was no greater than all the other pains that were racking her. Alex was still asleep. Soon it would all be over. Nora would take him. He'd have a good life. She'd love, care and protect him.

It was Mrs Pitt from the adjoining house who found her. She'd commented earlier to her husband that there seemed to be a hell of a row going on next door. He'd told her to mind her own business. It was no concern of theirs. Then it had become quiet and she'd felt that Ernie had been right. Later still she'd heard the baby crying, but as he'd been crying a lot lately, at first she took no notice. When it didn't stop or even lessen but instead grew louder, she got seriously worried.

'Ethna never lets him cry like that. I'm going to see if they're all right.'

Her husband sighed and put down his newspaper. 'I'll

come with you and if he orders you out, it will be your own fault.'

The sight that greeted them was one they would see over and over in their dreams and would never forget.

'I'll go for the police,' Ernie Pitt said faintly.

'No! Go for her sister first. We don't want them coming in here mob-handed then going down to Oil Street and putting their size-twelve boots in it. Go and get Nora first.'

He nodded and left.

Mrs Pitt took Alex from his pram and began to try to quieten him.

Leah was with Nora who was testing her on the catechism and Pat was trying to tidy the yard when Ernie Pitt arrived and, without giving any details, told them there had been a terrible tragedy in Kirkdale Road. Declan was up in his room with his mates, playing with the train set. Pat immediately went up and told Jimmy Murphy to go for his mam to come and watch them.

'What for?' Declan asked.

'Because we've got to go to Ethna's for a bit. We won't be long but I know you, meladdo.' Pat managed a grin to ease Declan's mind.

When they reached the house on Kirkdale Road, Pat and Ernie went in first. When Pat came out again, his face was drained of colour.

'Nora, luv, I . . . I don't think you should go in.'

'I've got to, Pat. I've got to,' she cried.

'She . . . she's dead, Nora, and so is he. It looks as though he beat her up and she went for him with the scouse pan.' He held out a small piece of paper. The writing was untidy, on one corner was a dried bloodstain.

Nora took it, her hands shaking. 'Oh, Holy Mother of God!' It was a prayer of entreaty. 'The baby?'

275

'Mrs Pitt has him next door.'

'I want to see her, Pat!' Nora's eyes were round with shock.

'Nora, luv . . .'

'Nora, wait, please,' Leah urged, holding Nora tightly in her arms. 'How . . . ?' Leah's green eyes were fixed on Pat's face.

'She . . . she cut her wrists.'

A cry like that of an animal in pain came from Nora's throat and Leah's grip tightened.

'Nora, you won't want to go in. You can see her . . . later.'

Nora raised a grey, tear-streaked face. 'Leah, she is . . . was . . . my sister.'

'I know, but please, not yet. Pat, can you get some things for Alex? Nora, we'll have to go and see to Alex.'

Pat nodded in agreement at Leah's ploy and returned to the room where both Edward and Ethna lay among broken furniture and crockery and where almost everywhere you looked there was blood.

While Nora sat with Mrs Pitt, nursing her nephew, unable to take in the terrible events, Ernie accompanied Pat to the police station. Leah stayed at the house until the police arrived. She didn't go into the kitchen.

'I'm Leah Cavendish. A friend of the family,' she introduced herself when the police arrived, her voice a little shaky.

'Of Cavendish's Haulage?' the tall, burly sergeant asked.

She nodded.

The sergeant took a quick look round the kitchen where the bodies lay. It didn't need more to know what had happened.

'What will happen now?' Leah asked when he re-emerged.

276

'There will have to be an inquest, Miss Cavendish.'

'When?'

'As soon as we can possibly arrange it.'

'Will there be any need for all . . . this to be made public? The family are only recently getting over their father being . . .' Adroitly she changed tack; she couldn't say 'killed'. '. . . their father dying.'

'The coroner and the police won't advertise the fact, miss, but the court is open to the public and the neighbours will know something is wrong, seeing us here and the ambulance when it arrives to remove the bodies.'

'It will come out sooner or later, Leah. People will wonder why we've got Alex, where Ethna is,' Pat stated.

Leah nodded slowly. 'I'll take Nora and Alex home now, Pat.'

'Aye, do that, Leah, please. Seeing to Alex might take her mind off things.'

'Sean is due to call. Shall I send him up?'

Pat nodded. God knows how Nora would cope with this so soon after losing Joe.

The inquest was opened quickly and proceeded swiftly. On Edward Neely the verdict was unlawful killing. On Ethna it was suicide. Nearly all the neighbours' sympathy was with Ethna. No one had liked Edward Neely.

'Look at the state she was in, God 'elp 'er,' Eileen Molloy said, summing up all their feelings. 'Half out of 'er mind. That bloody feller had 'alf killed her. Who's ter say 'e wouldn't 'ave gone for the little lad an' all. He's no bloody loss. Poor Joe hated 'is guts.'

Nora was coping better than Leah had expected. Pat had been right, having Alex to care for was helping. Leah took Pat to one side and told him she'd booked them all into a small hotel in Rhyl on the North Wales

277

coast for a few days after the funerals were over. 'It will get you all away from here. I can see the strain in your face, Pat. Declan's too quiet and a change of air will benefit both Nora and the baby. Will you be able to take the time off?'

He nodded. He was only casual, there was money in the bank and his absence would give a few others the chance of some much needed work.

'What would we do without you, Leah?'

'You'd manage, Pat, because you've all had to manage all your lives.'

'Nora's real cut up about Ethna's funeral.'

'I know. I'm going to see Father Finnegan about that,' she replied.

'Leah, I'm glad you came,' Father Finnegan said. 'I was after thinking that because of all the terrible tragedy you wouldn't feel up to instruction at the moment.'

'I came to see you, Father, mainly because Nora's in a terrible state over the funeral. Please, isn't there some way Ethna can be buried in consecrated ground and have a Mass or some form of service, no matter how brief? Mr Neely is entitled to that, but in my mind it was he who was in the wrong. He'd beaten her very badly. The pathologist said there was a possibility she could have died from her injuries. You knew Ethna all her life, Father. You knew she would never do a thing like that unless she was driven out of her mind.'

Father Finnegan shook his head. 'Suicide is a crime in the eyes of the law, Leah. And it is a heinous sin in the eyes of God even without the black stain of murder already on her soul. Our lives belong to God, we have no right to snuff them out ourselves. She died in mortal sin.'

'She might have prayed for forgiveness for everything before she died.' Leah was clutching at any straw.

'She might, but we've no way of knowing. I'm sorry, child, but she can have no Catholic burial.'

Leah bowed her head. It wasn't right. It just wasn't *right*. Ethna had been driven beyond the edge of endurance and sanity. Leah was certain she'd thought only of her baby. She would have known that she would have been tried and hanged for murder.

'This is your first and biggest test of faith, Leah,' Father Finnegan said gently.

She nodded. She had to conform, to obey without question the laws of the Church, but she knew it wasn't just this faith; Reverend Hunter would have given her the same answer and who was she to question God?

'It . . . it hurts me for Nora's sake, Father, but . . . I know that the law is right, that God is right.'

The priest placed one hand on her head, and with the other he made the sign of blessing.

'*In nomine Patris, et Filii, et Spiritus Sancti.*'

'Amen,' Leah replied softly.

'Go now, Leah. It's not the time for teaching and learning. I'll pray for Nora and the rest of the family and I know you will too.'

She put her hat on, intending to go into the church, but she saw Sean turn into the narrow pathway that separated the church and the presbytery.

'Leah?'

'I . . . I . . . came to see if I could get Father Finnegan to change his mind.'

He smiled down at her sadly. 'Then we thought alike. Was there ever a chance of it?'

'None at all. I don't think Ethna was in her right mind but it's still a sin and a crime. It doesn't seem very fair.'

'What's that?' Sean asked, staring at the small book in her hand.

279

She'd forgotten about it. Forgotten to put it in her bag. A great weariness came over her. She hadn't the energy to lie to him. 'It's the catechism. I've been coming to see Father Finnegan for instruction. I wasn't going to tell you yet, but now . . .'

He didn't speak for a few moments, then he took her in his arms, trying to find the words to express the humility and love he felt.

'Oh, Leah, do you love me so much?'

She closed her eyes. 'Yes. It was Nora who helped me. Oh, poor, poor Nora and Ethna!'

'It's a crime and a sin, so the Church says, but I don't believe God is so hard or unforgiving. She didn't plan to kill Neely, she must have been demented with pain and terror. I don't believe she'll be punished for eternity for what she did.'

Leah felt comforted. She wasn't alone in her belief. 'Shall we go and tell Nora we tried?'

'Pat will tell her. He asked me to go back to him after I said I was coming to see what I could do here. He said one thing Nora's determined to do is to see that Neely has a pauper's burial. There'll be not a single penny spent on him, nor a single person present.'

Sean's voice had a bitter edge but Leah understood. It was the worst insult possible. Even people who had virtually nothing managed to put a penny a week away for a decent burial. And no matter what the Church preached about forgiveness, in her heart she could find none for Edward Neely. Ethna would be buried in a small plot of land on the other side of the cemetery wall with no ceremony at all, but no one could stop them from attending her burial or taking flowers or saying prayers and she clung to Sean in what she deemed the darkest moment of her life.

Chapter Twenty

The November gales swept up the Mersey estuary from
the sea and whipped the grey waters into waves that broke
against the dock walls in a cascade of white spray. The
trees in the parks were bare now, their branches black
against the grey skies that from time to time released a
deluge of rain that the wind drove almost horizontally
across streets, squares and gardens alike.

At the end of September Nora and her family had
returned from their holiday, much better, much brighter.
Alex was a chubby, placid ten-month-old now, Leah
thought as she gazed out of her bedroom window, catching glimpses of the grey and angry river between the bleak
warehouses.

She had continued her instruction and would be ready
for acceptance by Christmas or just after, so Father
Finnegan promised. Downstairs there were boxes of
food. The yard was filled with crates and barrels of
ale, for in two short days she would be twenty-one and
then things would really begin to happen in this street and
the other two, and at Cavendish's, for Ernest had shown
no sign of doing anything. She'd not had a single word
from him or from Mr Rankin on his behalf.

The light in her eyes dimmed as she thought of Sean.
They went to Mass together now on Sundays with Nora,
Pat, Declan and Alex, but she knew her birthday would do
nothing to change his attitude. She often saw the torment

in his eyes. He loved her, more so now, he said, but there was still his pride. His damned pride. Even after she'd shown him the letter that Father O'Neill had written for his mother, asking how much more did he expect of her and that his pride was becoming an obsession and that both were sins, he'd said nothing. Nothing at all.

She heard Nora calling her from the kitchen.

Nora had changed, she thought as she went downstairs, but who wouldn't have? All traces of girlishness and youth had gone now. She was a woman. A wife and surrogate mother to both Alex and Declan, even though she was only twenty-one.

'We'll have to get the lads to move some of this stuff, Leah,' Nora said, indicating the boxes of food, 'or we'll spend all our time tripping over it.'

'I know. Mr Murphy and Mr Madden will come after work. Eileen, Florrie, Lizzie and Agnes have offered to help with the sandwiches and cakes and jellies.'

'I somehow thought they'd all be falling over each other to help. They'll feel important, be able to give themselves airs and graces over all the other women.'

Leah laughed. 'Everyone will be able to give themselves airs and graces by the time I've finished with these three streets.'

'We'll have people on day trips coming down to see them. We'll have the whole of the Scotland Road down here to gawp and go back green with envy.'

'That's *not* my intention, Nora.'

'I know. I was only teasing, like. But everyone is looking forward to the do. Do you think everyone will fit into the parish hall? It's not that big.'

'It's bigger than anyone's house and you know that if I'd hired Blair Hall or some other place like that they'd have all felt out of place and wouldn't enjoy themselves.'

282

'That's true. They'll all be wearing their Sunday best even though it'll be Friday. Navy serge suits for the men, white blouses, grey or black skirts for the women, and their best black shawls. It's like a uniform.'

'Did they send all the crêpe paper I ordered? I thought Declan, Jimmy, Jackie and some of the other lads could cut it into strips and make chains to hang around the walls.'

'That should keep them out of mischief and it will brighten the place up. It's a bit dark and gloomy in that hall, you've got to admit.'

The hall at the back of the presbytery was used only for meetings of the Men's Confraternity, the Knight's of St Columbus or the Union of Catholic Mothers, but it did have the advantage that the piano from the presbytery could be easily moved into it. Its position would also ensure that the celebrations didn't get too rowdy, which all the women agreed was a very big bonus. There would be no blind drunk husbands to get home. The fact that the men would have to go to work on Saturday morning would also help to keep them sober. Everyone was going to the party and everyone would enjoy themselves, but not to the point of overdoing it.

'Did you get your dress?' Nora asked, searching among the boxes for the crêpe paper.

'Yes. It's the fanciest dress I've had in a long time.'

'Well, for God's sake, Leah, it is your party, you ought to be the belle of the ball. They're all expecting it. Go and put it on. Let's see it.'

'No, I'm saving it as a surprise. What have you got?'

Nora tutted with false annoyance at being denied a glimpse of Leah's dress. 'A nice fine wool crêpe. It will be serviceable afterwards.'

'What colour?' Leah, too, had started to rummage through the boxes.

'A sort of dark lavender, trimmed with black braid.'

Leah understood. Nora was still in mourning for her sister and father.

'Pat's got a new suit. I insisted. I had to drag him down to the fifty-shilling tailors. All I could get out of him was, "I've already got a suit." He's had it years and it's all shiny on the sleeves and seat of the trousers.' Nora gave up looking for the paper as a bad job. 'What about Sean?'

Leah shrugged. 'I can't very well drag him anywhere. Not to the fifty-shilling tailors and certainly not down the aisle.' She ducked her head so Nora wouldn't see the colour rush to her cheeks.

'He's a flaming idiot. Is it still the money and the business?'

Leah nodded.

Nora didn't know what to say. Pat, at her persistent urging, had tried and tried to talk some sense into Sean but it hadn't worked. He wouldn't budge. He loved Leah and always would, but it was more than just pride. It was dignity.

'Dignity be damned!' Nora had scoffed.

She decided to change the subject. 'Have you heard anything from your brother-in-law?'

'Not a single word. He probably thinks I didn't mean it, that I was just bluffing, but I'm not and that's something he'll find out very soon – maybe even tomorrow morning.'

'I'd love to see his face, Leah, I really would.' Nora clasped a cooked ham shank to her, completely forgetting she wore no pinafore over her dress.

The previous week Sean had called a meeting, on Leah's behalf, to inform everyone that it was Leah's intention to completely renovate to the standard of her own home, all the properties in Oil, Vandries and Vulcan Streets, and that furniture and fittings were to be included.

He'd had to call loudly for 'order' over the din that followed the few seconds of silence after his announcement.

'Leah and her sister own all the houses. She didn't know until the old lady died and ever since she's been desperate to change conditions but the law wouldn't allow her to. Not until she's twenty-one.'

'Trust the bloody law!' someone had cried.

Now Leah waited, thinking some word might arrive from Ernest or Mr Rankin, while everyone plunged into the frenetic activities of cooking, slicing, baking, getting the hall decorated, taking the drink and all the glasses up as well. That's when they weren't talking about their miraculous good fortune. The food would be taken up on Friday afternoon and set out by the women. They had obtained a special Dispensation from the Archbishop himself, to put aside the Friday abstinence. Father Finnegan had gone personally to explain Leah's conversion, her generosity to the Parish and the fortune she would inherit on that very day.

Everyone then went home to change into their best clothes. The kids would be scrubbed until they glowed, only the thoughts of jelly, custard, ice cream and cake alleviating a process they all hated.

By Friday afternoon you could feel the excitement in the air.

'Dear God in heaven, Lizzie, we won't know ourselves when she's finished with these middens of 'ouses. Virtually rebuilt! Everything new and furniture and carpets thrown in!' Agnes Murphy was standing while Lizzie Madden did up the top few buttons at the neck of her blouse, those that were always so fiddly being so small and awkward to reach.

'I know. I can't believe it. Me dream's out! An' a wash

285

house. What'll we do all day, Ag? There won't 'ardly be anything ter clean?'

'There will in our 'ouse with that tribe of flaming savages I've got. But I've already told them. "No one goes in me parlour except me, Jack and the priests." Mind, I don't relish 'avin ter move in with Mary Dodd down the street.'

'Well, it won't be for long an it's worth waiting for.'

'Aye, yer right,' Agnes replied.

Leah had sought the advice of an architect and a surveyor and their recommendation was that six houses on each side of the road should be done at a time. That was the safest way, under the circumstances. Their occupants would move in with relatives or neighbours lower down the street. Leah would be employing a large number of men and two master builders as overseers. The surveyor would also keep his eye on things.

'Come next summer we'll all be livin' like flaming kings an' queens. Yer know, I pray for that girl every night, on me knees, an' if anyone says a wrong word about 'er I'd murder them with me own two 'ands.'

'Lizzie, shurrup about murder, for God's sake!'

'Oh, aye, I forgot.'

'Are yer right then? 'Ow do I look?'

'Like one of Lewis's dummies, Ag. Now, let's gerrup there and see that all our flaming kids don't start stuffin' themselves an' showin' us up.'

Nora had arranged things so that Leah would be the last to arrive. Normally, as it was her party, Leah should have been first to arrive to greet her guests, but Nora had secretly arranged for everyone to get there fifteen minutes earlier and to go in twos or threes and up the back jiggers and not to stop and jangle under the street lamps.

Sean was in on the plan and called to escort Leah. When she came down the stairs in the dress that had been made

286

in Bold Street, he was stunned. She had never looked more beautiful, he thought. Her hair was swept up like a halo of burnished copper and held with pins decorated with tiny clusters of pearls and diamanté droplets. Her dress was of pale apple green chiffon over taffeta and was cut low across the front and back. Small bunches of white silk roses looped up and held the loose swathe of chiffon that was draped across the neckline and over the top of her arms. There was a larger spray of them attached to the right side of the narrow waist and smaller clusters swept across the skirt to where the short train began.

It was a ballgown, the like of which would be worn at a big state function, he thought. She wore long white evening gloves that came up over her elbows, and from her ears, round her neck and wrists sparkled diamonds and emeralds that usually resided in a bank.

'Ah, Leah, you look . . .' he just shook his head in wonder and took her hands.

'Do I look beautiful, Sean?'

'Leah, you know you do.'

'Do you love me?'

Her eyes were pleading with him and he knew what she wanted to hear, especially now, on the night of her birthday, but he couldn't. He couldn't say the words or ask the question. It would be like betraying his class, betraying Joe and all the other men who stood on the stands each day, waiting for work. That hadn't changed after the strikes and he wouldn't join the ranks of the bosses. He wouldn't be a kept man.

'You know I do, Leah, and . . .'

'And what, Sean?' The pleading note in her voice tore at his heart.

'And everyone at the party tonight loves you too, Leah. Pat suggested they should officially make you "Lady Liverpool".'

Her smile held sadness and her eyes were dewy with tears of disappointment which she was trying hard to hold back. 'No. No, I wouldn't want that. I've left all that behind me.' Her tone had changed. It was abrupt. 'We'd better get a move on or we'll be arriving at the same time as the guests!'

Sean draped the black velvet evening cape round her and then carefully covered her head with its wide hood lined in white satin. Then he placed an arm round her shoulder. He felt no pleasure now, he had ruined the evening for himself and probably for her. He would have to try and turn it into something good. He knew everyone would be waiting to greet her.

As they approached the presbytery, Leah frowned. 'I asked Pat to go up early and make sure all the lights were lit,' she said, annoyance in her voice as she viewed the squat building which was in darkness.

'We're obviously the first to arrive.' Sean opened the door to the hall for her. 'You take off your cape and I'll get stuck into getting the place lit up.'

She untied the black velvet ribbon that held the cape fastened and peered around in the gloom for something to put it on. She thought she saw a chair and reached out for it but her fingers brushed against warm flesh and she uttered a startled cry. Then one by one the gas jets were lit and she looked around in amazement at the delighted faces of all her friends and neighbours.

She turned to Sean. 'You knew! You knew!'

He grinned as the room reverberated with laughter and then Lizzie Madden began, in a raucous voice, to sing 'Happy Birthday' and everyone joined in. Sean took her hands in his and kissed her on the forehead.

'Happy Birthday, Leah Cavendish!'

The tears sparkled on her lashes, tears of joy. The best

288

decision she'd ever made in her life was to follow Nora to Oil Street.

The singing finished and suddenly she was swamped by women who wanted to hug her and admire her dress and jewels. And then Ozzie Whittle thumped out a loud chord on the piano and the party began.

Everyone wanted to dance with her and Sean looked on thankfully. She had no time to be thinking of him. She was absorbed and enjoying herself. He thought back to the day when she'd told him just how much money and power would be hers when she was twenty-one, and now that day had arrived. The jewels that sparkled so brightly were probably worth a small fortune too and yet here she was, an heiress, a girl who now owned two-thirds of one of Liverpool's biggest businesses, dancing, chatting and laughing easily with men who could barely read or write, who worked for a pittance, lived in squalor and had no manners on them at all, although tonight they were all trying hard. She was a total mystery to him and always would be.

'God, what's up with your face?' Pat handed him a glass of beer.

'Nothing. I was watching her, can't I do that now?'

'You're bloody mad, you know that. Look at her. Got up like that she looks like a princess and she could have her pick of the highest in the land. But no, she goes and chooses a bloody eejit like you to love!'

'Jaysus, Pat, don't start again, not now. Haven't we been over it all a million times already? I'd be selling you all out, acting like a scab, becoming one of *them*. I can't do it! God knows I love her, but I just can't . . .' The rest of his words were drowned out by an explosion that deafened them and shook the entire room. The gas lights flickered and went out and above the cries and yells of panic could be heard the roaring and crackling of flames.

Pat was first out of the door, followed by Sean and the other men.

'Jesus, Mary and Joseph! It's Bibby's! It's gone up like a bloody rocket!' Sean stared in horror at the flames that were leaping from where the factory roof had been. The explosion had blown it off. Iron doors had been flung across the street and the sound of falling masonry and wood was clear. Everyone ran from the hall, the women grabbing their children, making sure they were all accounted for.

Factory buildings surrounded them and Sean feared that they, too, might catch. Quickly he told the men to get their families away from here, to get them home. The alarm had already been raised, the clanging bells of the fire engines could just be heard.

Leah was beside him. 'Leah, for God's sake get home as quickly as you can. The fire bobbies are on the way but they'll need more than just the city's engines to fight that.'

'I'm not leaving without you,' she said determinedly.

He grabbed her hand, she hitched up her skirts and they ran but her high-heeled shoes and the train of her dress hampered her. When they reached the bottom of the road another sound came to them.

'What's that?' she cried breathlessly.

'God knows.'

As they rounded the corner they both stopped dead and watched in horror as slowly, like a pack of cards, the houses at the top end of Oil Street began to lean and collapse.

'No!' she screamed. 'No!'

Figures were huddling together in the middle of the road, clutching a few possessions. It looked like a scene straight from Hell, Sean thought, as the sky above turned

290

red and the smoke and dust swirled around. When he turned to speak to Leah, she wasn't there. She was running up the road. She'd kicked off her shoes and was tearing at the chiffon of the train of her dress.

'Leah! Leah!' he yelled and started to follow her. With his long strides he soon caught her up.

The light from the inferno that was Bibby's Animal Feed Mill was reflected in the depths of her eyes. He'd only ever seen her look like this once before – the day she'd given Ernest Armstrong the ultimatum.

'Thank God everyone's out,' she said grimly. 'I'm going up there to see that . . . that selfish bastard!' She was yelling now, to make herself heard over the din.

'You can't get through all this and the Dock Road will be blocked by fire engines.'

'I don't bloody care!'

'Then I'm coming with you!'

'No! People need help, they're terrified. This is *my* fight and this time I'm going to finish him!'

He watched her as she again hitched up her skirts and began to run. She was right. It was her battle.

She managed to get a cab on the corner of Formby Street and the Dock Road. She gasped out the address to the driver and then leaned back, trying to regain her breath but seething with fury.

When they arrived, she realised she had no money. She dragged off a bracelet and thrust it into the driver's hand.

'The stones are real and it's gold. Take it. I forgot my purse.'

He gaped at her but she was up the drive and the steps in a flash and was hammering fiercely on the front door.

Blackett opened it. 'Miss Leah!'

She stormed into the hall. 'Where is he, Blackett? Where is he?'

'The dining room. Miss Leah, what's happened?' She was dressed for a ball but the gown was torn and dirty and she wore no shoes.

She ignored him but flung open the door of the dining room so hard it crashed back against the wall.

Rhian screamed and Ernest jumped to his feet.

'What the hell do you think—'

'*SHUT UP!*' she screamed at him.

Her sister sank back into her chair, numb with shock.

'You can't hear the noise of the fire engines or the flames from here but you must have heard the explosion!'

'What explosion?' Ernest barked.

'Bibby's. The roof was blown off, it's an inferno, but that's not why I'm here. Today is my birthday, in case you'd forgotten. I was at a party with my friends.'

'I can see that.' Ernest tried to sneer, taking in her appearance, but he was very uneasy. The letter he'd written to her promising assistance lay on the hall table. Blackett was to have taken it to her later tonight.

'When I left, at least five houses in Oil Street had collapsed. God knows how many more have gone by now and *you're* responsible! I don't blame Rhian. You controlled the money, made the decisions. You. *I* could do nothing until today, but *you* could. You're finished, Ernest Armstrong. Sacked, just as you sacked Pat Ryan. You could have started the renovations but you didn't! You're no longer part of Cavendish's. Now that I control the majority of the shares I'll sell it. You will never set foot in that office again and what's more I'll see that your part in all this is on the front page of every newspaper in the entire bloody land!'

Ernest sat down, his face ashen, his hands trembling. He'd gambled and lost. Lost everything. He was ruined. He'd be vilified by all those he called friends.

Rhian had got to her feet. There were two pink spots on her cheeks as anger stirred. How dare Leah come in and scream at them like this. How dare she accuse and sack Ernest.

'Get out of this house, Leah!'

Leah was taken aback for a second. Rhian had never shown a hint of courage before. 'Half of this house is mine, Rhian, or had you forgotten that as well?'

'You really have become one of *them*, haven't you, despite your evening dress and jewels. A dirty Liverpool-Irish slummy, that's what you are. That's what Ernest calls you!'

'You missed something out, both of you. Catholic. I'm one of those too, or will be, and you can call me all the names you like but I know I'm a better person and they are better people than either of you will ever be. Go to hell, Rhian! In fact the pair of you can get out of this house now. I'll buy your half. A few thousand should cover it. Ernest is finished and by morning all the neighbours will know. Is that what you want, Rhian? To stay and be shunned or pointed at?'

Rhian's temper had deserted her, her lip trembled and she began to cry. 'Where will we go?'

'I won't see you without a roof over your head even if you are prepared to sit here safe and sound while other people's houses are crashing down around them. There's the hunting lodge at Brecon, Grandfather Lloyd-Thomas's lodge, you can go there. And don't worry, you'll get your share of profit from the sale of the business, you won't starve, but I never want to see either of you again and I want you out of here by tomorrow, otherwise your names will be on the lips of everyone in this city and they'll curse you.'

She stormed from the room, slamming the door behind her. In the hall, Blackett, Cook, Miss Winthrop, Percy and a maid she'd never seen before stood huddled together in a group.

'Percy, go and find me a cab, like a good lad. There's no need to worry, you're jobs are safe, but Mr and Mrs Armstrong will be leaving tomorrow – for ever. You probably heard every word so I don't need to explain. Miss Winthrop, could you find something from Mrs Armstrong's wardrobe that's more suitable than this, please?' Her dress was ruined but that was the least of her worries, she needed something plain and sensible to go back home in.

Miss Winthrop went swiftly upstairs and Leah followed. When she came back down, she was wearing a grey and white check dress which was plain except for a bit of braid at the neck. The torn and dirty apple-green chiffon, which had cost fifteen guineas, lay in a discarded heap on Rhian's bedroom floor along with her gloves. She'd stuffed her jewels into a handbag of Rhian's. Percy was still in the hall but Blackett was missing. The dining-room door remained firmly closed.

'Where's Blackett?' Leah demanded.

'He's bringing the car round, Miss Leah, he'll take you back.'

She turned to Cook. 'I'll be back tomorrow. I may have to bring some people to stay, I don't know yet.'

Cook nodded but fervently hoped it wouldn't be necessary. She remembered hearing from Nora how dirty they were.

Blackett helped her into the car. 'Let me know if there's anything I can do to help, Miss Leah.'

'There will be plenty for you to do, Blackett, and thank you for offering.'

She leaned back against the leather upholstery, still shaking. Her birthday had been a momentous one, but for all the wrong reasons.

Chapter Twenty-One

The City Council launched an inquiry into the explosion and fire that had half demolished Bibby's and caused six houses in Oil Street to collapse but no blame could be apportioned. The cause of the conflagration remained unknown but arson was ruled out. Spontaneous combustion seemed the most likely explanation. Only one person had been injured, Bibby's nightwatchman. 'Thank God everyone from Oil Street was out and none of those that had run home were near the damaged houses,' one of the fireman had commented to Pat and Sean after a head count had been made of all the occupants of the houses.

Leah's architect and the surveyor told her that the collapse of the six houses was something of a blessing in disguise since the explosion had confirmed what they had already suspected, that the buildings' structural defects were beyond repair.

As usual in times of emergency, people helped each other. Those families who had lost everything moved in with relations and neighbours. Agnes Murphy, her husband and ten kids had been hard to find accommodation for and so Leah had taken them up to the house on Prince's Avenue. Ernest and Rhian had been in the process of packing.

When Agnes saw the place, she shook her head firmly. 'Ah, God, queen, I couldn't live 'ere. It's like a palace an' this tribe of hooligans will 'ave everything broke and wrecked in ten minutes an' 'e'll get blind drunk on whatever's in them cut-glass bottles. No, it's not right an' it's not fair on the servants, 'aving ter wait on the likes of us. I wouldn't be surprised iffen they didn't up an' leave.'

'But Agnes, where can you go?'

'I'd sooner camp in the street, luv. I'd be mithered to death all the time here and I'd be frightened to open me mouth, especially as yer sister an' 'im are still 'ere.'

'They won't be here for much longer,' Leah had replied, but in the end they'd slept at the presbytery. Leah rented a house for them in Eccles Street and promised that theirs would be the first one to be rebuilt after the rubble had been cleared.

She had a meeting with the three remaining foremen at Cavendish's and she told them that no matter what happened, their jobs and all the jobs of the employees were safe. In the meantime, she put them in joint charge of the yard and the checkers. Mr Spencer, the senior clerk, would supervise the clerical section and anything that needed discussion and a decision was to be referred to her and she'd take advice on it.

In the first week of December work started and Leah and Nora watched the first layer of bricks being laid.

'It's not going to be much of a Christmas for most of us, is it?' Leah commented to Nora, who she thought wasn't looking well at all. She put it down to the terrible events of the last few months.

'I don't suppose it will, but at least next year will be better – it certainly couldn't be worse,' Nora replied. 'I'll be glad to see the flaming back of this year.'

In the event it proved to be better than either of them expected. At Midnight Mass on Christmas Eve, Leah was accepted into the Church of Rome and made her first Communion. Sean was beside her at the altar rail, with Nora on her other side. And Nora was pregnant.

On New Year's Eve, Nora, Pat, Sean, Declan and Alex gathered in Leah's house for supper and then two minutes before midnight everyone went out into the narrow street. It was crowded with their neighbours and people from Oil Street and Vulcan Street too. Agnes and her family had also come down from Eccles Street.

'Well, I wasn't stayin' up there with that lot. I wanted to be with me own,' she informed Lizzie Madden.

Hundreds of voices began to chant the countdown until they reached zero and a cacophony of noise exploded around them. Every church bell in the city pealed out, every ship in the river and the six miles of docks blew their steam whistles, and everyone joined hands and sang 'Auld Lang Syne'.

Leah hugged Nora and Pat, and then Sean took her in his arms.

'Happy New Year, Leah Cavendish.'

'Happy New Year, Sean Maguire, and I know it is going to be a good one for everyone. Just look around at people's faces. This time next year their homes and lives will have been transformed. Nora and Pat will have a son or a daughter, a playmate for Alex, and I'll have your . . . love.'

There was just the slightest hesitation but he noticed it.

'Leah, I do love you. You've given up your class, you've changed your religion, all for me, and . . . and I *want* to marry you, but—'

The rest of his words were silenced as she placed a hand over his mouth. 'Don't say it, Sean. Not tonight, please. Don't let's start the New Year like this.'

He didn't have time to reply for she was swept away by Jack Murphy who told him not to be so flaming selfish, other people wanted to kiss her and wish her Happy New Year.

The following morning, which was a normal working day, Leah went to see Mr Rankin.

'Miss Cavendish, may I offer you my best wishes for the coming year.'

'Thank you, but I do wish you'd call me Leah, we've known each other long enough. In fact, you've known me all my life, you came to my christening.'

'That's very kind of you but I could never do that, I'm afraid. Maybe Miss Leah?' He was a very formal man and adhered rigidly to a code of behaviour that had its roots deep in the strict Victorian home he'd been brought up in. His profession had fostered that code and familiarities formed no part of it.

'I want to withdraw a large proportion of the money my father and aunt left me.'

'That's entirely your affair now.'

'But I'm afraid that the manager of the bank will be horrified and will think me absolutely mad, so would you write a letter of confirmation or approval or something for me?'

'Are you sure you'll really need it? Mr Henshaw knows you well. Your father banked with him.'

Leah smiled. 'Mr Rankin, I want two banker's drafts of five thousand pounds each. One to be made payable to Father Finbar Conor Finnegan, the other to Mr James Larkin.'

For the first time in many years Richard Rankin allowed surprise and a degree of shock to show on his face but he quickly hid his emotions and nodded gravely. 'I see what you mean. I will write a letter for you now.'

She watched him as he wrote, dipping the pen fastidiously into the silver inkwell. After the bank, her next visit

300

would be to the offices of the British and Irish Steamship Company, then she would go to see her parish priest.

When Mr Henshaw read Mr Rankin's letter, he went quite pale and asked her whether she was absolutely certain about this. It was a very large amount to lend, he pointed out.

'Oh, I'm not lending it, Mr Henshaw, I'm giving it. I think if you read Mr Rankin's letter again it will state that quite clearly. That was the point of the letter. To show you I *am* certain and quite determined. There is still seven thousand left and business is booming.'

'That is something else you ought to consider, Miss Cavendish. You can't have clerks and foremen running a business like Cavendish's.'

She smiled. 'I know. It's just a temporary measure. I have plans to resolve the situation there before spring.'

She thanked him, assured him of her continued patronage, and left, tucking the drafts into her handbag.

She had concluded her business with the British and Irish Steamship Company and was halfway along Great Howard Street when she met Nora, pushing Alex in the pram. It was a cold day but a fine one. The sky above the dockside buildings was pale silvery blue and was reflected in the river.

'Do you really think you should be pushing that pram in your condition?'

'Oh, don't you start as well, Leah. Pat is driving me mad. You'd think I was a china doll. I've told him I'm fine and that I've a home to run and that Dr Mac said fresh air and exercise will do me good. Will do us both good.'

'Well . . .'

'I know. The air around here isn't fresh at all, even the sparrows have coughs, but if it's fine at the weekend we might go over on the ferry to New Brighton. Where've you been?'

301

'To see Mr Rankin, then the bank manager, then down to the B and I shipping office and now . . .'

Nora stopped and gazed at her with curiosity. 'Where are you going and just what are you up to, Leah?'

Leah smiled a little sadly, then her mouth became set with determination. 'I'm going to force Sean to marry me. At least I'm going to have a damned good try. He said last night he wanted to, but . . .'

'It's a big "but", so how?'

They began to walk again and Leah rested her hand on the pram handle.

'All we're left with in the way of obstacles to his damned pride are money and the business. Well, by tomorrow I'll only have enough left for all the building and renovations. I'm on my way now to see Father Finnegan to give him five thousand pounds for repairs to the church and for the poor of the parish. Then tonight I'm going to Dublin and first thing tomorrow I'll go to Liberty Hall and leave another cheque for five thousand there, made out to Jim Larkin. Then I'm going to see Mrs Maguire to enlist her help.'

'Holy God, Leah, you mean you're giving *ten thousand* pounds away?'

'I am. Five thousand pounds won't go far in a parish like this and I've enough to live on, Nora. The business is profitable but that's the last obstacle. Somehow I've got to persuade him to manage it for me. I can't do it on my own.'

'You could run the flaming country on your own,' Nora interrupted.

'And I don't want to run any business,' Leah continued, ignoring Nora's remark. 'But that will be the hardest part of all because he thinks he'll be turning his back on everything he's fought for. That he'll be betraying all the men he's been out on strike with and locked out with

302

and that they'll think him a hypocrite. But they won't, Nora, because he'll see that every man at Cavendish's is treated fairly. He said so himself. And he'll show all the other employers that running businesses and making profits *can* be done by a working-class man who has a good brain, common sense and integrity.'

Nora nodded. She knew Leah loved him to distraction and she knew her friend was very, very determined, but to give away nearly every penny of such a vast fortune was utterly bewildering. The amount in itself was so staggering that she found it hard to take in.

'Nora, if he comes looking for me tonight, I don't want you to tell him anything. Anything at all.'

'So what am I to say when he asks where you are? Gone off to a health spa for your nerves?'

Leah laughed. 'Tell him . . . Oh, use your imagination. Make something up.'

'I'm not such a good liar as you, Leah. I haven't got the right accent.' Nora grinned impishly and for a second Leah saw the young, carefree girl Nora had been before tragedy had touched her.

'Oh, you'll think of something. Tell him I've taken Declan and his friends to see a moving picture show, as a treat.'

'He might wait outside for you and our Declan can't keep a secret to save his life. Don't you remember what Da used to call him? Mighty Mouth.'

'Oh, honestly, Nora, will you help me or won't you?'

'You know I will.'

They had reached the corner and Nora turned into Oil Street. 'Will you come round before you go and tell me what Father Finnegan says?'

'No, in case Sean comes home from work with Pat. I'll tell you when I get back, tomorrow evening.'

*　　　*　　　*

Again she watched the buildings of the waterfront grow smaller and smaller, but she didn't stay on deck long. It was cold and windy and once out into the bay, without the protection of any point of land, she knew it would be rough and prayed she wouldn't be sick. She pitied all the poor people forced to sleep wherever they could, but she had a feeling that a lot of them would be on deck, hanging over the side, for most of the trip.

To her relief she wasn't sick but the ferry was an hour and a half behind schedule because of the weather. She'd certainly felt queasy as the ship had rolled and pitched in the heavy seas. Joe had once told her that the best place to be in rough weather was on the lowest deck, midships. There was far less movement there. Fortunately her cabin was in just such a position. She'd found it easier to sleep on the cabin floor, after she'd been thrown out of the bunk and had banged her arm as she'd hit the deck.

This time she'd made sure she would arrive in Dublin at the North Wall and there could have been no greater contrast between its huge, dingy embarkation sheds this bleak January morning and the flowers and fine houses of Dunlaoghaire that warm summer morning she'd arrived with Sean. She hadn't booked a room anywhere and she carried just one small bag. She hoped Sean's mother would let her have a wash and get changed before she caught the late evening boat home.

Dawn was finally beginning to break and shed its light over a city which looked changed. Dublin was still locked in the grip of labour unrest. She walked along the quay past Gandon's magnificent Custom House. On her left the waters of the Liffey were dark and choppy. The wind was raw. The spires and towers of the churches and Nelson's pillar all seemed to merge and blend with the grey drabness of the sky. The trees in St Stephen's Green would be bare now, the park empty of strolling people.

As she entered Liberty Hall, the bare, scuffed boards creaked beneath her feet. There were a few men in rough working clothes gathered round a small table, talking. As they caught sight of her they stopped their conversation and looked at her with suspicion. She understood. She took out an envelope from her bag and handed it to the nearest man.

'Could you please see that Mr Larkin receives this.'

'And who might you be and what might your business with Big Jim be?'

The man rubbed the envelope between his fingers to gauge its quality and weight.

'It's nothing sinister, I promise. It's a . . . gift from a well-wisher, to help cope with the lock-outs and strike pay, that's all.'

Leah turned and walked out on to Eden Quay where the biting wind now hurled rain across the cobbles and the cries of the gulls wheeling overhead were borne away towards the sea. She'd cross Butt Bridge and get a hackney to Vincent Street, otherwise she'd be soaked to the skin in minutes, for in her haste she'd forgotten an umbrella.

Sean had moved back to the rooming house in Lightbody Street after Ethna had died and Nora, Pat and Alex had gone to live with Declan in Joe's house. There had been arguments at the time. Nora had said they would all manage, but he'd firmly refused.

Tonight he'd been back to his lodgings to wash and change and then he had something to eat in Lilly's Cannie on the Dock Road. After that he made his way to Leah's. When he received no response to his knock on the door, he went round to Pat's.

Nora opened the door to him.

'Is Leah here?'

'No, she's not, but come in just the same. I want to talk to you.' Nora had made up her mind that afternoon that there was nothing she could tell him that he'd believe, and anyway it was about time Leah stopped this secrecy. She hadn't wanted him to know about her conversion either.

Pat was reading the newspaper. He wanted no part in all this. He'd more than done his bit, he'd told his wife.

'Sit down.'

'God, is she always like this, Pat? Is it an inquisition I'm after getting?'

'Never mind talking to him. We've agreed that he should stay out of this.'

Sean looked worried. 'Out of what, may I ask? Leah's all right, isn't she?'

'Oh, she's fine, except for the fact that she worships the ground you walk on and you won't marry her. Yes, yes, I'd say she's just great.' Nora's tone was heavy with sarcasm.

Pat slid down in his chair and retreated even further behind the newspaper.

'She's lived here for two years, she's become a Catholic and now she's about to give all her money away. She gave Father Finnegan five thousand pounds this afternoon, for the repairs to the church and the poor of the parish, which means nearly everyone. I believe Father Hegarty had to give him a large whisky, he was that shocked, and Mary Brannigan, the housekeeper, says the pair of them have been on their knees in front of the high altar in church all afternoon and may even still be there, for all I know.'

'She's done *what*?' Sean couldn't believe his ears but Nora carried on.

'Now she's on her way to Dublin to give another five thousand to Jim Larkin for union funds and the poor, of which there are bound to be as many, if not more, as there are in Liverpool.'

Sean was on his feet.

Nora looked up at him, undaunted. 'So, after all the building work and furnishings have been paid for, that will be it. Her entire fortune distributed, and I'll bet her da is turning in his grave. Now, what have you got to say for yourself, you flaming idiot?'

'I'm going after her.' Sean's face was full of anger and regret. 'She's mad!'

'It's too late, the ferry's gone and you're the one who's mad! If she had any sense she'd have told you to go to hell long ago. I would. All the single fellers in the neighbourhood, no, in the city, would give their right arm to marry her and you . . .'

He sat down again, his head in his hands. How could he deny her any longer? He had never dreamed she loved him so much or that love could be so deep and all-consuming. It was time to forget his pride. Nora was right, he was a flaming idiot.

'I'll get the next boat.'

'By then it will be too late, she'll be on her way back, she wasn't stopping. She was going to see your mam.'

'Nora, I'll *have* to see her.'

Nora was delighted, she could see by his face that at last he had capitulated.

Pat decided it was time for him to come out of the depths of his chair, abandon his paper and intervene.

'Send a telegram telling her to stay put, that you'll be over on the next boat.'

'I'll go down to Victoria Street now. Do they close for telegrams?'

'Of course they don't. They don't close for any of the mail, they work shifts.'

'Do you have the money?' Pat asked.

Sean nodded. 'Just, but I'll have to borrow the fare from you, there's no pay until Friday.'

'You'll have to get the train to Holyhead and go over with the livestock, there's no boat out now until tomorrow night and, knowing Leah, telegram or no telegram, she won't wait that long. She'll telegraph back saying she's coming home on the evening ferry.'

Sean nodded. It was a terrible, circuitous journey. The actual crossing time was shorter but you had to put up with the racket out of the animals and a long train journey. He'd have to start out well before dawn.

The house looked far worse in winter, Leah thought as the hackney deposited her in Vincent Street.

Peggy opened the door to her. 'Leah! Holy Mother, you put the heart across me! Why didn't you write and let me know? Come in quickly, it's like the North Pole in this hall, so it is.'

The front room looked exactly the same but it felt cold and damp despite a small fire burning in the hearth, much too small to heat the high-ceilinged room. Newspaper had been jammed all round the edges of the window to try to keep out the draughts.

'Sit down while I put on the kettle. A drop of tea will warm you up, you look frozen, child.'

Leah sat at the table under the window. Even with the makeshift draught excluders she could still feel the cold air of the street seeping through.

Peggy, she noticed, was wearing at least two old woollen jumpers and her shawl.

'I still have the letter you sent me at Christmas,' Peggy said while she prepared the tea. 'I'd have loved to have been there at the Mass to see you at the altar rail with himself beside you and your friend too.' She stopped to wipe a tear from her eye on a piece of torn cloth that was obviously used as a tea towel. 'And has everyone got over that explosion and their houses coming down around them? Wasn't that a desperate thing altogether? Wasn't it the mercy of God that no one was killed and didn't I say that to Father O'Neill when he read it out to me. And now, will you tell me why you've come across the pond by yourself and with the waves as big as mountains in this weather, and where's that fine bucko of mine?'

'He doesn't know I've come.'

'Would he have come with you, do you think, or would he have tried to stop you altogether?'

Leah shrugged. 'I don't know.'

'And he's still playin' the eejit, I suppose. My knees are wore out from me never being off them, with the novenas and the Thirty Days Prayer.'

Leah nodded. 'Yes, that's why I've come. I've given away all my inheritance. To the parish at home and to Jim Larkin for the union and the poor here. I've just come from Liberty Hall.'

Peggy dropped the kettle. 'Holy Mother of God! Does Sean know that's what you had in mind?'

'No, although I suppose in time he'll know from Father Finnegan. I swore Nora to secrecy. I didn't want him to know I was coming here and I'm going back this evening. I'm going to try and force his hand, Mrs Maguire, even if it means I have to sell Cavendish's. What I really want is for Sean to take it over. He's clever enough, he could do it. My brother-in-law could and he was a fool, so it should be easy for Sean. At least he'll have the men behind him.'

'You're well rid of that Armstrong feller. Criminal, that's what it was, doing nothing about those houses. But I still think you've a fight on your hands. Jaysus, if I had him here I'd knock some sense into his thick head, so I would! There's our Treasa and Maurice grabbing every farthing so they can afford to get married, while *that* one has the world on a plate shoved under his nose and refuses it! He has me heart scalded, Leah.'

'I know. He has my "heart scalded" too. Do you think I could have a wash and get changed later on?'

'This house is your house, child, not that there's a rake of things in it in the way of comfort and I'll have to go down to O'Malley's for a bit of something, you must be starved.'

'There's something else I wanted to ask you.'

Peggy, having retrieved the kettle with not too much of its contents lost, had returned it to the fire and was selecting the best of her mugs. There wasn't much to choose between any of them, they were all cracked. She looked up. 'What?'

'Will you accept this? For yourself and Shelagh and Treasa and Maurice? Please, please, don't refuse me, I couldn't stand another rejection.' She passed over a cheque to Peggy who put down the mugs and sat down opposite Leah.

'And what might it be?'

'It's a cheque. You take it to the bank and they exchange it for money. I'll come with you, if you like. We could go now, they should be open soon.'

'Am I seeing this right or are they just dots jumping up at me from the paper?'

'They're not just dots,' Leah answered quietly.

Peggy counted them again, moving her index finger, the nail broken and dirty, slowly over the figures. Then her chapped red hands began to shake. 'You're not after giving me all this? Sure, himself who owns the tramways has money like this, not the likes of Peggy Maguire from the Liberties.'

'Well, you do now, and you're every bit as good as Mr William Martin Murphy and his like.'

310

Peggy laid the cheque flat on the table and stared at it, then crossed herself as understanding dawned. It meant a grand house with good furniture and heat and food and decent clothes for all of them for the rest of their lives. It was for two thousand pounds.

She reached out and took Leah's hand in her own. 'I'll go up to O'Malley's just the same and Brady's Choice Wines and Purveyors of Superior Spirits and we'll all have a drink for the day that's in it before you go back. And if that eejit doesn't marry you now, I'll come over there and belt him to bits, so I will!'

Leah laughed and then drank her tea. It would be the last time Sean's mother would have cracked and chipped mugs. From now on it would be the best of everything. They'd go to the bank first and she'd make some arrangements to open an account that Peggy could draw on immediately.

Before they could set off for Sackville Street, there was a knock on the door and a lad stood there with a telegram in his hand.

'Are yez Mrs Maguire?'

'I am so.'

'Then this here isn't for youse. It's for herself there. The young wan. Miss Cavendish. Only it's got care of Mrs Maguire, seven Vincent Street writ on it.' He handed it to Leah.

Peggy was incensed. 'Get out of me sight before I clatter yez. It's shockin' the young bowsies the Post Office employs these days.'

Leah ripped open the envelope. 'It's from Sean.'

'Well, so much for your one back there swearin' absolute secrecy.'

'He's on his way over. He says I've to stay put. I'll kill Nora, I will!'

'Ah, leave it, Leah. It may be for the best after all.

Sure, won't I be able to see him an' all and give him the cut of me tongue. Well, seeing as we'll be in Sackville Street, hadn't you better go into the Imperial and book a room for tonight? I can't have yourself sleeping here, it's not fit, but you can rely on me, his mammy, to talk sense at him.'

Chapter Twenty-Two

Before Leah went to spend the night in the warmth, comfort and cleanliness of the Imperial Hotel, there was a family conference. In Peggy's eyes Leah was now definitely part of the family.

Shelagh, Treasa and Maurice O'Shea listened to the news in stunned and total silence.

'Well, haven't yez any manners? Is it struck dumb yez are altogether?'

'Will I be able to give up me job?' Shelagh asked.

'You will not, for the divil finds work for idle hands, but we'll be moving. We're as good as the quality now.'

'Moving where to?' Shelagh asked.

'Rathmines or Sandymount maybe,' Peggy replied firmly. 'Away from the stink and muck of the Liberties. And you'll have a nice little cottage, Treasa, and a decent wedding an' all. Maurice's job at Bolands is secure.'

Maurice finally found his tongue. 'Will I be able to get something better, do you think?'

Peggy looked sceptically at him. He was not the brightest but he was biddable and that was a great thing altogether in a man. 'What will you want to do that for? Isn't the one you've got great and didn't His Reverence put in the word for you? Sure, it would be flyin' in the face of the clergy to go getting ideas. This money has to last us all our lives and no doubt I'll have grandchildren to see to, in time.'

Leah listened in silent amusement. Peggy was certainly going to keep a firm hand on the purse strings. She'd been amazed at Peggy's quick grasp of the rudiments of banking and she had even asked about investments, although she hadn't used the actual word. 'Where will it be best to put all the rest of it, would you say, for the future?' was how she'd phrased it. Leah could see where Sean got his agile brain from. Though she could barely read or write, Peggy Maguire's illiteracy was due to circumstances, not a lack of intelligence.

Leah wondered what Sean's reaction would be when he arrived to find a solid wall of family approval behind her. She prayed he wouldn't be so angry that he'd upset them all. She didn't want him to think she was bribing herself into their affections.

Next day Leah went to nine o'clock Mass at St Catherine's, the church where the tortuous path to become Mrs Sean Maguire had started. Then she went shopping, just for small gifts, and after she'd had lunch at the Hibernian she went back to Peggy's.

'I was thinking that perhaps I should have gone to the North Wall.'

'It's not trailing down there you'll be going. No, let meladdo come here,' Peggy said firmly and they settled down to wait, Peggy giving her the life history of every person in the house and then asking Leah for every detail of her life before she left Prince's Avenue.

Shelagh and Treasa had taken the day off work to shop for clothes. They were coming home laden with parcels when they saw Sean ahead of them, at the corner into Bull Alley.

314

'Will I shout him and tell him we've a fortune now?' Shelagh asked.

'No, you will not! We'd be killed. She'd belt us to bits, you know she would,' her sister muttered in reply. Sean had caught a faint snatch of the familiar voice and turned and waited, eyeing the parcels. Leah had been busy again.

'You look full of misery,' Treasa said to him.

'Well, isn't that a lovely way to greet me? And you'd be full of misery too if you'd been flung from pillar to post all the damned way and with the noise and stink of seasick animals too.'

'Ah, Sean, she didn't mean it like that. Go on in now. Leah will have come down from the Imperial.'

Shelagh glared at her sister. 'Aren't you the tactful one,' she said grimly.

Sean kissed his mother and then took Leah's hand. 'I've come through one of the worst storms ever and on the boat from Holyhead with the livestock to see you, Leah Cavendish.'

'And isn't that the way it should be too,' Peggy said, putting on the kettle. 'You'll feel better after some tea and a plate of rashers and cabbage, then you can go out, the pair of you, and get all this sorted out. It's a fine, soft day.'

'Mam, it's January. It's cold, windy and it's starting to drizzle. It's far from a fine, soft day.'

Peggy glared at him but said nothing.

While Peggy cooked Sean's meal, Shelagh and Treasa tried on the new finery in the bedroom with Leah, whose opinion was sought on every item. Then Peggy came in and told Leah to get her coat and hat on.

'Where will we go?' she asked as they left the house. It was cold and damp.

'Somewhere we can talk in peace and privacy.'

315

'We'll get a hackney to St Stephen's Green. I know it won't look anything like it did last summer, but it will be quiet.'

He was too tired to argue. She'd told him she'd stayed at the Imperial but, judging by the meal his Mam had put before him and the parcels and the giggling coming from the bedroom, he knew she had been giving more money away.

They walked through the almost deserted park and took shelter in one of the small pavilions, sitting down on the narrow seat.

'Leah, why did you do it? Why give it all away?'

'I felt I *had* to, Sean. That was the last of it. It's all gone now and everyone I love is financially secure.' She paused, wondering how he would react to the next piece of news but if she didn't tell him, Peggy would.

'I . . . I gave Peggy enough to buy a nice place in a decent area and to see her comfortable. I *had* to, Sean. She's your mother. Do you understand?' she begged, her eyes downcast, her hands clasped tightly together in her lap. Oh, please God, don't let us fight over this, she prayed.

Sean was silent and immobile for what seemed like an age. Then he reached out and took both her hands in his.

'Sure to God, Leah Cavendish, I've never met a woman like you.'

'You're not . . . angry?'

'Angry is it? Why should I be angry? She's my mother and to see her living just above the line of poverty has had me heart scalded all these years. And then you come along and she . . . she'll never want for anything again. Is that a reason for anger?'

Leah breathed deeply with relief.

'I didn't want the money. It was just something else

316

that stood between us and I wasn't foolish with it. It will help God knows how many people.'

'Including the mammy back there and those two rossies.'

She nodded. 'She's had too harsh a life already and so have they. And it wasn't a fortune.'

'So, that leaves the business,' he said, standing up and thrusting his hands into his coat pocket.

She, too, got to her feet. 'I'll sell it if I have to, Sean.'

He turned towards her and took her in his arms. 'No, Leah. It's all you have now. Oh, God! I don't deserve your love.'

'Well, you've got it, all of it. *You* can make the business pay, Sean. Keep it successful. You told Edward Neely you'd be a better boss than my fool of a Brother-in-Law. Think of all the jobs. You'll deal fairly with the men, I know you will. You can show all the others that it can thrive and grow without grinding every ounce of labour and sweat from the men for as little reward as possible. The men will have dignity and pride in what they do because they know their labour is valued, they'll be loyal.'

'I won't be very popular with the other bosses though.'

Her heart was hammering against her ribs. All the joy and happiness she longed for was now really within her reach.

'So what? Do you really care about them? I don't. I never did.'

He stroked her cheek gently. 'No, you never did. If you had you would never have followed Nora.'

'And I would never have met you, Sean.'

He drew her to him and kissed her for a long time. He believed her now and it would be a challenge. He'd need help but he'd make it a success.

317

When he at last drew away, she was looking up at him with a mist of tears in her green eyes.

'Where would you like to go for a honeymoon, do you think?'

She smiled through tears of pure joy. 'I think Dunlaoghaire is a nice class of a place, don't you?'

On Saturday, 3 February 1912, the Church of Our Lady was packed. It had never looked so beautiful, Father Finnegan thought, his eyes going over the huge floral decorations that banked the altar and the small Lady Chapel. Around each of the stations of the Cross was a floral garland. The whole church was filled with white lilies, yellow and peach roses, and carnations that stood out against dark green foliage.

She had so many friends. People who truly loved her for her generosity which had been given freely and without any hint of patronage or sanctimonious speeches or posturing. There were many men in the congregation who now had jobs for life and a pension to look forward to when they retired.

At Cavendish's the working hours and conditions had been improved but instead of the expected plunge in profits that the members of the Shipping and Employers Federations looked forward with malice to seeing, the men worked harder and business increased. In time many would look at Cavendish's closely and with envy.

Father Finnegan reflected on all this as he stood in his new white and gold vestments waiting for the bride, while the organ softly played the Air from Handel's Water Music, a piece he'd always liked but could never remember the name of. Pat was best man and Nora was matron of honour. You would hardly know she was carrying her first child. He thought of all the tragedy the poor girl had suffered in her young life and of her poor

318

sister. Ah, would that Ethna O'Brian had never married Edward Neely.

There had been some difficulty over who was to give Leah away. She wanted none of her blood relations, she'd said emphatically, even had they condescended to come from the various corners of the Empire they resided in. They'd been through all the men who were her neighbours and friends and who would have considered it a great honour to lead her up the aisle, but Leah had been loath to single out one for fear it would cause ill feeling. She wished Joe O'Brian was alive, she said sadly.

In the end Father Finnegan had taken the issue to his Archbishop and between them they'd found a solution. It was unusual but perfectly in order with canon law. Leah was a convert and so the Church itself, in the form of Father Hegarty, would give her in marriage to Sean Maguire.

The first thundering chords of the Prince of Denmark's March brought Father Finnegan out of his reverie and he went down the altar steps to greet the bride.

Every head in the church turned towards her and every woman and girl gasped.

She walked alone, which seemed to add grandeur to the occasion, for Leah would always remain what she'd been born – a gentlewoman, in the true sense of the word. Father Hegarty waited at the foot of the altar steps, as did Sean who felt so moved by the sight of her that tears blurred his vision. For she was just that. A vision.

Her dress was of white organza over duchess satin. The tight bodice and leg-o'-mutton sleeves were finely pintucked, as was the high collar. The edge of the collar and the deep cuffs were decorated with tiny seed pearls and the train, which seemed to stretch for yards and yards behind her, was edged with seed pearls. The cloud of silk tulle that billowed behind her was as long as the train and was held in place by a diamond and emerald tiara. It had been made from the necklace and earrings she'd worn for her birthday party and it had been Nora who had persuaded her to have it made. It would be sold after today; she would have no use for it. She carried an armful of white Madonna lilies tied simply with a white satin bow.

Nora walked behind her, her dress very plainly cut but in a rich scarlet velvet that both looked and felt warm. A band of cream and scarlet silk flowers encircled her head and she, too, carried lilies.

Florrie Burrows and Eileen Molloy sniffed audibly.

'Ah, God, Florrie, doesn't she deserve 'er happiness?'

'She's . . . she's an angel and she looks just like one terday an' all.'

'I sometimes think 'e doesn't deserve 'er. All that contrariness. She's given everything up for 'im an' 'e's made 'er wait all this time, an' the business is doin' well.'

Behind them Agnes, Lizzie and Maggie Cullen were in tears. They had all just been installed in their brand new homes, to which every woman in the three streets had been invited for a viewing.

In the pew behind her son and his best man sat Peggy Maguire, resplendent in a dark blue costume edged with black velvet and a large hat in a matching shade but overdecorated with flowers, ribbons and even a stuffed bird. Treasa had said it looked desperate and she hoped she wasn't going to wear it for *her* wedding, which had started a huge argument.

Peggy had overheard Florrie's comments. She turned round, narrowly missing poking Florrie's eye out with the tail feather of the bird. 'I couldn't agree with yez more, missus, an 'e's me own flesh an' blood. Contrary is the word all right an' I could add a few more to describe him, iffen I wasn't in the House of God.'

Treasa tugged at her mother's sleeve, sensing that a loudly whispered conversation was about to begin. 'Mammy, will you mind where we are and not have your man above on the altar glaring at us as though we were tinkers.'

'An' I'll remind you, Treasa Mary Maguire, not to call His Reverence "your man",' Peggy hissed back.

Shelagh and Treasa raised their eyes to the vaulted ceiling, then turned them with unconcealed envy on the vision that was about to become their sister-in-law.

Those who were still capable, after the celebrations, went down to see the bride and groom off on the ferry *Connaught*, bound for Dunlaoghaire. It was a mild night for February, and they stayed on, shouting and waving and throwing coloured paper streamers until the boat pulled away from the landing stage.

Sean and Leah stood on deck. Their luggage had been taken down to their cabin and Pat had joked that it was a pity to have to spend your wedding night in bunk beds. Nora had poked him sharply in the ribs and glared at him, but she wasn't really annoyed. The tears had been tripping her as she'd followed Leah down the aisle. Leah deserved her happiness so much and she herself was overjoyed that she was pregnant.

Remembering Pat's remark, Leah laughed.

'What's so funny now?' he asked. He held her tightly against him, shielding her from the freshening wind.

'The bunk beds.'

Sean laughed with her and then became serious.

'What will we do with the house on Prince's Avenue? Could we not turn it into some kind of home for girls and women like poor Ethna?'

They had both agreed they didn't want to live in it and

321

all the staff had been given a generous pay-off and found other employment.

'It's a good idea but it wouldn't be allowed, Sean. It would be seen as encouraging women to break their marriage vows and leave their husbands, even if their husbands are no good and beat them. Everyone would be up in arms over it. The churches, the council, the government even. To say nothing of the neighbours.'

'I don't think the Suffragettes will be up in arms. They want the vote for women.'

'We'll get that when you get Home Rule – never. Things like that don't change.'

'They will, Leah. The world will change. Look how it's changed over the last couple of years. I know things will change as sure as I know that the Mersey will always flow to the sea.'

The ferry was in the estuary now, the coastal lights were fading.

'In fifty years' time, if we could stand here, Sean, where the Mersey flows, what would we see?'

'Two old people in a world so changed that maybe it would frighten the divil out of us. But we're young, Leah Maguire, and we've a life ahead of us and together we'll make some kind of a fist of it, I promise. We're alike. We're both rebels.'

She raised her face and he bent to kiss her. Suddenly she thought of her Aunt Poppy and the young 'rebel' she'd let go. She would never let Sean Maguire go, she'd fought too hard for him ever to do that.

The Liverpool Matchgirl

by

Lyn Andrews

Liverpool, 1901. The Tempest family is all but destitute, barely able to put food on the table. When Florrie falls ill with pneumonia and Arthur is imprisoned after a drunken fight, their thirteen-year-old daughter Lizzie finds herself parentless, desperate and alone.

Despite her young age, Lizzie has spirit and determination. In a stroke of luck, she gets a job in the match factory, and foreman George Rutherford takes her under his wing. A new home with the Rutherfords promises a safe haven, but the years ahead will be far from trouble-free. And when Lizzie gives her heart, how can she be sure she has chosen a better man than her own father?

Available now from

HEADLINE

Liverpool Sisters

by

Lyn Andrews

It is 1907 in bustling Liverpool. Thanks to their father's success, sisters Livvie and Amy Goodwin are moving to leafy Everton. But tragedy strikes when their adored mother Edith dies in childbirth. The girls are still missing Edith every day when Thomas introduces their new stepmother-to-be – a woman just a few years older than Livvie.

Thomas is an old-fashioned man, who expects to make the important decisions in his daughters' lives. He plans for Livvie to marry a wealthy neighbour's son – not Frank Hadley, the kind and handsome factory manager Livvie is attracted to. Livvie's relationship with Frank is a dangerous enough secret, but her interest in the Suffragettes could drive Thomas to the edge.

For the Goodwin girls, the happy future they once took for granted is far from certain . . .

Available now from

HEADLINE

Heart and Home

by

Lyn Andrews

Cathie Kinrade is all too used to hardship. Growing up on the Isle of Man in the 1930s, she sees her da set sail daily on dangerous seas while her mam struggles to put food on the table. Cathie has little hope for her own future, until a chance encounter changes her fortunes for ever.

Fiercely determined, Cathie leaves for Liverpool, a bustling modern city full of possibility. With a lively job as a shop girl in a grand department store, and a firm friend in kind-hearted Julia, Cathie has found her niche.

But the discovery of an explosive secret could put everything at risk. And when love comes calling, Cathie's new friends fear that she may be set to trust the wrong man with her heart . . .

Available now from

HEADLINE